A
GREATER
WORLD

CLARE FLYNN

Dedication

For Kathleen Flynn who often had to travel where she
didn't want to go, but always made the best of it.

And over the Blue Mountains
We found a greater world.

From The Blue Mountains (A Song of Australia)
Alfred Noyes (1880 -1958

With permission from The Society of Authors as the
literary representative of the estate of Alfred Noyes

CHAPTER ONE

THE ENGAGEMENT

Hunter's Down, Weardale, England 1920

Someone had made a bit of a mess of tying the coloured bunting between the trees. It was fluttering loose at one end, so the breeze lifted it and swept it up against the grey stone of the chapel wall and down again. The man smiled, thinking the pastor would not be happy as the string of brightly coloured triangles looked as though they belonged to the chapel, instead of marking the coming Miners' Gala. Bunting and Methodism didn't really sit well together.

He sat down on the wooden bench opposite the chapel, elbows on knees, fists tucked under his chin, and waited for Minnie. He saw her hurrying towards him from the row of cottages that fringed the other side of the green.

She flung her arms around his neck and he grabbed her by the waist and swung her around. Her long hair smelled of soap and he couldn't resist running his hands through it.

'You've just washed your hair?'

'So?'

'Was that for seeing me?'

Minnie smiled and pulled him down beside her on the

bench. 'Who says everything has to be for a fellow? Can't I please myself?

What was so important that you wanted to see me out here instead of coming round our house, Michael Winterbourne?'

Michael hesitated and wondered whether to broach the idea of their leaving Hunter's Down, before or after his proposal of marriage. He plunged in, the words spilling out of his mouth so fast he was almost tripping over them.

'You know what I'm going to ask you, Min. And you know I'd have asked it long ago if it weren't for the war and showing some respect for your Da and your brother and then there's been your mother and the bairns to think of. I know she's been relying on you to help out and I couldn't rightly expect you not to be there for her, but now they're a bit older...'

'Yes. The answer's yes. I'll have you, Michael. There's no need for a long speech.' She leaned back against the wood of the bench and smiled at him.

'You're a one,' Michael said.

'Aren't you going to kiss me then?'

When they finally pulled apart, he wondered whether it was even worth him putting the other part of his proposal. He knew inside what the answer would be, but he decided to have a go anyway.

'There's something else to sort out. You know how I feel about working in the mine?' He looked towards her for some encouragement, but she was staring fixedly at her lap, where her hands were folded.

'I hate it, Min. Everything about it. Sleeping all winter in bunks in a cramped barrack room that stinks of unwashed feet and stale cabbage. Seeing man after man going down with the black spit. Breaking me back doing work I hate. And much as I hate it, living with the even bigger fear that it all might stop tomorrow. The Crag's still employing but

2

we don't rightly know how much longer. You know as well as I do. It's time for a change, Min. You and me together. A new life while we've got the choice, rather than waiting till the Company shuts us down and I'm one of many on the scrap heap trying to find work.'

She interrupted him. 'I said I'll marry you, but not if it means leaving here.'

'Look, I know you love it here. I do too, but the world's changing. I've changed. The war did that. I want to make me own decisions, not have some mine boss down in London make them for me.'

'Our Bill said just last night the Company will keep the Crag open until there's no lead left in the ground.'

'Mebbe they will, but we don't know when that'll be. Might be sooner than you think.'

'Nah! How many men's working there? Go on – tell me.'

'There's forty of us underground and another twenty up top.'

'That's sixty jobs if me sums are right. And you're a good worker, Michael – they'll not be losing you in a hurry. If there's layoffs there's others they'll cut afore you.'

'It's not just about jobs. I don't want to be hanging on and hoping and putting me life in the hands of others. I had enough of that in the war. I want to decide for meself.'

'What about me?' A frown and a down-turned mouth replaced her smile.

He reached for her hands and held them between his. 'Don't you see – now's our chance - while we're still young and there's just the two of us. It'll be much harder when we have bairns.'

She laughed. 'Aren't you getting a bit ahead of yerself, Michael Winterbourne? Who said anything about bairns?'

Her laughter encouraged him to press on. 'You've no idea what's outside the dale. The world's out there waiting for us. Great big cities, fancy buildings with electricity in every room, moving pictures, motor cars, so much to see and do.'

She cut in. 'There's a whole world right here and it's our world. It's been good enough for our families and it's good enough for me. Why are you so restless? Can't you just get on with life like the rest of us? You can worry about finding another job if you lose this one. But right now you've got a job and you earn a decent crust, so stop your yammering. Please!'

'But Min…'

Then she began to sob, first quietly then big jerky gasps. She brushed aside his proffered handkerchief and taking his hand pulled him over to the newly built stone memorial in front of the chapel. She pointed to two of the dozen or so names engraved there - William Hawthorn, Ypres 1917 and George Hawthorn, Mons 1914 and turned back to look at him, tears now coursing down her cheeks.

'Mam needs me and I don't want to leave the place I've lived me whole life in. Me Da and our Georgie are gone now and this slab is all I've got left to remember them by, and every time I walk past it I think of them and say a little prayer for them. I'll marry you but only if we stay here. It's your choice.'

He wrapped his arms around her shoulders, feeling the rough wool of her shawl against his hands and the wet of her tears on his shirt.

'I'm sorry. Don't cry. I shouldn't've asked. We'll stay put. I'll not mention it again.'

'Promise?'

'Promise.'

She dried her eyes and smiled up at him, then they walked hand in hand towards the row of houses. 'Let's tell me Mam. She'll be made up. I'll race you!' She let go his hand, and ran off, with Michael running after her.

An hour later he emerged from the cottages, replete

with Mrs Hawthorn's buttered scones and a cup of strong tea. He was relieved the decision was made, even if it wasn't the one he wanted. After the long years of the war he'd do anything not to be apart from Minnie again. But he was disappointed that in this they hadn't seen eye to eye. He wondered whether she had guessed what he was going to say and had planned her response in advance. He looked back towards the war memorial. Before the war he would not have thought of leaving here, so was it surprising that Minnie should be so resistant?

She was going to marry him. The jaunty bunting could be for them, never mind the Miners' Gala. The sun burst through the clouds and lit up the green sward between the chapel and the hillside. As he set off for home he heard barking. His dog scampered down the hill to meet him.

'What're you doing, old thing? Worried you're not me favourite girl any more?' He ruffled the fur round the Collie's neck, bringing on more appreciative barking.

'You and Minnie know how to get on the right side of me don't you Stone! Come on let's get home. How about you and me taking our Dan out to find a few rabbits tomorrow.'

They headed off up the dale, the dog running back and forth, fetching the sticks he threw for her all the way home.

Michael shared the news of his engagement as soon as he got home.

'About time too' his mother said. 'I hope you're not going to waste time afore making me a granny!'

His father cracked open the bottle of Scotch whisky he'd won several years ago for pinning the tail on the donkey at the Gala. It had been gathering dust and he was glad at last to have the occasion to open it.

Their cottage was one of four conjoined in an L shape, huddled up against the side of the dale, as though sheltering from the elements. The adjoining cottages were also occupied by lead miners. That night the Winterbourne's tiny home was crowded with neighbours.

'You took yer time, lad – or were that lass leading you a dance then?' one of the lead smelters spoke.

'Hush, Walter – you know it weren't right to have a wedding celebration too soon after the poor lass lost her father and brother' said his wife.

'What happened to your plans to go looking for gold in California?' another miner asked. Laughter rang round the crowded room.

'Don't be daft. That girl'd not gan further than the end of Nantshead Dale. This place is in her blood' Mrs Winterbourne said. 'And glad of it I am too. She's talked some sense into my Michael's head. More than his father and I managed to do.'

'Under the thumb already are you?' The good-natured laughter erupted again.

Michael looked over at his brother, who was sitting on the floor leaning back against his mother's knees, and saw that Danny was grinning. It would have been hardest of all leaving him behind, so it was another reason to be glad not to have to do it. Their mother, as if thinking the same thing, tousled the younger boy's hair and smiled up at Michael. Margery Winterbourne had given up hope of carrying another child to term when Danny had arrived and disrupted the quiet of their lives with his puppy-like energy, laughter and chatter. The fourteen year old was her special gift, to be treasured and loved for being so unexpected.

Next morning, Danny rushed his breakfast, eager to take advantage of one of the first warm and sunny days of the spring. He had woken at dawn and tried to drag Michael from the bed they shared at weekends and holidays. During the working week in the winter months, Michael and their father slept over at the mine barracks, the trek over the dales being too long to be done comfortably before and after every shift, especially in bad weather. Now the day-light hours were lengthening and they could manage the walk there and back each day. But today was Sunday and Michael had a bit of a headache from his father's whisky and the home-brewed beer the neighbours brought in. He was determined not to get up before he was ready, so he feigned sleep, drowsing and thinking of Minnie.

They decided to walk south over the dales to a place they knew was a good spot for rabbits. It was rare to encounter another human being in this remote area. Winters were bleak up here and it was not unusual to be snowed in for weeks. But today the sunlight bathed the dale in a honey-coloured glow and the rough grass was brightened by swathes of white cow parsley. May trees heavy with white blossom lined the edges of the fields, like a collection of oversized bridal bouquets.

Around noon they stopped to eat their bait - chunks of bread and cheese their mother had pressed on them that morning. When they finished, they lay on their stomachs a few yards apart in the long grass, motionless as they watched the slope in front of them, ready for the serious business of the day to begin. The dog, Stone, lay between them, her ears twitching with anticipation. There were several warrens at the base of the slope and here, where the hill was topped by a small copse, was a favoured spot.

Danny Winterbourne frowned and flicked a fly away as it settled on his brow. As usual, he was fiddling with the small stone he carried with him everywhere. It was a large pebble with a hole in the middle and the boy loved to throw it in the air and catch it, rub its already smooth surface between his palms or sometimes thread string through the hole and swing it around his head. He even slept with his talisman under his pillow and it was this that had caused the family to name the dog Stone, as Danny was inseparable from her too. Now he was lying propped on his elbows, rubbing the stone between his palms.

'I don't get it Michael. We bagged half a dozen last time and we haven't seen a single one yet.'

'Be patient, Dan. If you keep blethering and fidgeting, you'll scare the blighters away. Stop messing about with that bit of rock or the rabbits'll sense you're there. Get yerself away over there, keep yer mouth shut and yer hands still.'

Danny was beginning to irritate him with his endless chatter. Michael knew he would never succeed in teaching his brother to shoot. He himself had learned as a small boy and it was second nature. Even the years serving in the Great War had not put him off. He had been away from the worst of the action on the front line, digging trenches and tunnels with the Engineering corps.

They lay in the rough grass with only a couple of lapwings for company. The black and white crested birds broke the silence of the dale with their distinctive peewit calls. It was hard to believe that under this open and empty landscape was what was once one of the biggest and most profitable lead seams in the world. In their father's youth there were mines everywhere, but most had long ago given up the last of their lead.

A large jackrabbit emerged from the trees and stopped at the top of the slope. Michael put his finger to his lips and nodded at Danny, then raised the gun and aimed, but as he did so a shaft of sunlight blinded him. He held the gun steady and squeezed the trigger. As the shot rang out he was aware of a sudden movement. Damn – he'd missed the bugger. He wiped the sweat from his brow and raised the gun again. Where had it gone? To the right of where it had been before he sensed movement and fired. He'd get the bastard after all.

He turned to Danny with a grin. The boy liked to race the dog to retrieve the prey. It was a silly game he always played – even though Stone had never lost a contest yet. But Danny wasn't racing up the hill. Michael looked back at the top of the slope as his heart pounded his ribcage. Stone was whining. He dropped the gun, shaded his eyes with both hands and looked into the blinding sunlight. His brother was in the long grass, arms stretched out in front of him as though trying to grab what was a very dead rabbit.

He screamed Danny's name and raced up the slope. God, let him be alive. Let him be alive.

Danny was on his stomach, a pool of blood seeping from under his body and a dark hole burnt through the back of his jacket.

Michael turned the boy over and lifted him up. The dog howled as he tried to make Danny stand up. Realising the futility of this, he sank to the ground, cradling his brother in his arms.

'No! God No! What've I done? I'm sorry. Please, please, wake up! Dan! Don't die.'

The boy's face had a puzzled expression: eyes still open wide.

There was no time for any last words, for Michael's plea for forgiveness to be acknowledged, or the chance to comfort the lad before he died: the bullet had gone straight through his heart. Michael's guttural cry seared the silence of the dale.

He kicked the carcass of the dead rabbit into the trees. The foxes or crows could have it. He lifted Danny and carried him over his shoulder, with Stone trailing behind, the dog's whimpering an eerie accompaniment.

As he walked towards the cottages, his shirt red with his brother's blood, his arms aching with the weight of the boy, neighbours came to their doorways and several walked out to meet him. He was blind to them.

'What's happened? Is he hurt bad?'

'Let's help you carry him.'

He ignored them all and staggered on in silence.

Michael knew he would never be able to forget the way his mother looked at her dead child. The boy's face had a look almost of pleasure and it was hard to believe that his spirit had fled the still-warm body. She began to keen, her voice rose like a banshee as Michael and his father laid the boy on the kitchen table.

'Danny, Danny! My baby. Me little, lovely lad.' She turned to Michael. 'What happened? What did you do?'

Michael looked down at his boots and shook his head. His mother rushed towards him and hammered her fists into his chest.

'You were supposed to look after him. He were just a wee bairn.'

'It were an accident Mam…the sun were in me eyes…I didn't see him move…' The words sounded lame as they came out of his mouth and he stopped trying to answer.

His father eased her towards the bed and made her lie down, then turned to Michael. 'Son, what the hell possessed you? For God's sake man! How did it happen? We trusted you to look out for him.'

He shoved his hand roughly into Michael's shoulder, but then collapsed back into a chair, his head in his hands and began to sob. Michael had never seen his father cry before.

He left them and walked up the hill behind the houses avoiding the scrutiny of the neighbours and their well-intended words of comfort.

No one in the cottage slept that night. Michael's mother sobbed, inconsolable, while his father kept a vigil by the body of the dead boy. Michael lay on the bed he had shared with Danny, thinking of the many times he had complained when Danny stole the bedcovers or kicked him during a bad dream. Now the narrow truckle bed felt large and empty.

He could not dispel the image of Danny's face, with its surprised half smile. Danny had been afraid of the dark and Michael hated the thought of him being shut up in a wooden box and left to rot away under the soil. He thought of all those other men and boys, blown to pieces and left to mingle with the mud in shell holes or their body parts anonymously buried in communal graves. He and Danny had been spared that fate, but right now he would gladly be lying in a grave on the Somme if it meant Danny would be alive.

His father was awake when he rose just before dawn, slumped in his chair, staring at the embers of the fire. On the floor beside him was a scattered collection of carrots and parsnips, still lying where he had swept them off the table to accommodate Danny's corpse.

The morning of the funeral was wet and blustery. The rain was almost horizontal, blowing water straight into the faces of the mourners. Michael, his father and two of their fellow miners carried the coffin, hair plastered to their faces in the driving rain. The Gala bunting that had bobbed about so brightly just a few days ago, trailed limply from the branches of the trees.

Michael left the chapel and found Minnie and her mother in a line of friends and neighbours, waiting to pay their respects. Mrs Hawthorn hugged him warmly, but Minnie lowered her eyes and stiffened when he embraced her.

She spoke quietly, barely a whisper. 'Sorry, Michael. Danny were a lovely lad. We'll all miss him.' Her voice broke and her eyes filled with tears, then she turned and walked away from him. He went after her, reached for her arm and said, 'We need to talk Min.'

She shrank from his touch and moved away slightly from the pressure of his hand on her arm, looking past him in the direction of her mother, as though hoping for rescue.

Her voice was soft: 'I have to go. Mam wants me to take care of our Billy and Jenny while she's at the wake'.

'Aren't you coming?'

'I'm sorry.' She shook her head and walked away across the green, moving slowly, head bowed, in contrast to the exuberant way she had run across the same grass just a few days before.

He decided not to go into the miners' hall to the wake. He pulled up the collar of his jacket and set off towards the dale. Alone under the dripping trees on the hillside, he made up his mind.

'Da, I'm going away for a while.'

'We need you here, son.'

'I can't stay. It's best if I'm not around. I don't want you and me Mam looking at me and thinking about what's happened. Blaming me and hating me.'

'Your Mam and me could never hate you.'

'Maybe not, but I can't bear to see your sadness and know I'm the cause of it. I can't face it.'

'Look, son, I'm sorry about what I said before. I were shocked. I didn't mean to blame you.' His voice broke and his words came out in a sob. 'He were such a good boy. I were angry with him the day he died for whittling sticks and leaving the bark in the hearth and playing about with that bloody lump of stone. I yelled at him. Oh God, why did I do that? My last words to him were angry ones.'

'You weren't angry. Danny knew that. It were water off a duck's back.'

Tom Winterbourne looked up at his son and put a hand on his sleeve. 'Please stay, Michael. Yer mam and me 'ave both said things we didn't really mean. You're all we've got now. You can't just go like that.'

'I've made me mind up Da. I'd been thinking of going away for a long time. If I'd not hung around so long, hoping I'd get Minnie to come with me, I could have been long gone and Dan would still be alive. But I put her first. I know now that were wrong.'

12

'Don't be daft lad. I'd've done the same for your mother.'

'Mam loves you, Da and that means you'll both get by. You'll help each other. You don't need me. I'd just make it harder for you. And now I know Min doesn't really care for me.'

'Course she does.'

'Today after funeral, it were like she were afraid of me – disgusted by me.'

'She doesn't mean it. She's as shocked as we all are – and specially for her after losing Georgie and her da in the war. And she were right fond of our Dan. She spent a lot of time with him when you were away fighting. She'll come round in the end son.'

'She won't. I know her like you don't, Da and I also know that Mam would never have looked at you the way Minnie looked at me today.'

Tom Winterbourne shook his head.

Michael said, 'I'll send money when I can. I won't forget about you just cause I'm out of sight.'

'There's no need for that. Where'll you go?'

Michael shrugged. 'Depends what ship's in. America? Or mebbe New Zealand or Australia - I met a few chaps from there during the War. They were good lads.'

His father grunted, 'It's t'other side of world! What'll you do for money?'

'I've enough put by to pay the passage. I were saving a long time to get wed. There's some I've left in a box under the bed. It's there in case Minnie should ever be short. There's no point in me offering her money now as she'd not take it. Use it to see her right if she or her mam need help. She'll not be on her own long I expect.'

'Aye she's a bonny lass. There's some'd say you're daft in the head to give her up.'

'I think she's given me up, Da. She's just afraid to tell me that. If I write her a letter will you give it her?'

13

He sat on his bed and tore a blank piece of paper out of the back of a hymn book and began to write. He had rarely had occasion to write since school and he did so slowly, forming the letters carefully.

Dear Minnie

We know each other that well we don't need words. I know you don't want to marry me any more. I don't blame you. I have to get away now I've lost you and Dan.

I wish you a long and happy life and always will think of you fondly. Please go to my Da if you ever need anything.

Your Michael

The next morning, as soon as it was light, he parted the curtain that partitioned his parents' bed from the living area and leaned in and kissed the forehead of his sleeping mother. He stroked her hair and whispered. 'Bye Mam. I'm sorry for what I've done.'

His father was standing in front of the fire, waiting for him.

'Do you have to go right now? Why not wait a bit? Yer Mam'll come round in the end. And the Hawthorn lassie will too.'

'I'll get by without Minnie. Better to find out now than later that she doesn't really care for me.'

'But yer mam?'

'There's more chance of her coming round if I'm not here. If I'm gone it'll mebbe get a bit easier for you both with time. And then one day I'll come back.'

As he said the words, he knew he never would.

The barn was pitch dark. Somewhere in the distance, a fox screamed. The dog stirred, then settled, tired after their long walk.

Stone had followed him for two days, refusing to go home. She had been a loyal friend and companion and until now, had shown unstinting obedience. In truth, he was glad of her presence. It was lonely on the road. They had walked all day, avoiding roads and villages, travelling cross-country and sheltering in barns or shepherds' huts at night. He was grateful for Stone's body heat and curled closer around the dog.

Liverpool was another day's walk - at most two. He would take whichever ship left port soonest. Ever since the Titanic went down, he'd not relished crossing the Atlantic. Australia or New Zealand took weeks, but there wouldn't be icebergs on the way.

Next morning, he knew he must send Stone back. At the top of a hill he knelt and put his arms around the dog's neck, breathing in her familiar smell. She seemed to read him and at once began a low whimper.

'We have to say goodbye, girl.. A ship's no place for a dog. Go on lass! Get yourself home! Go and watch out for Mam and Da. They need you. Go on Stone!'

He could not bear to look in the dog's eyes. He walked away, changing the tone of his voice, hardening it. 'Go home, Stone. Go! Now!' Then he pulled his cap down, stuffed his hands in his pockets and felt the smooth surface of his brother's other treasured stone. This one would go with him on the voyage. He set off down the other side of the hill, pretending that the cold wind was the reason for his wet eyes.

CHAPTER TWO

THE LETTERS

Northport, England 1920

The front door banged shut and a tennis racket clattered into the hall-stand. Elizabeth Morton stuck her head around the drawing room door and spoke to her sister, Sarah. 'I'd kill for a cup of tea. Shall I ask Cook to bring a pot? Smells like she's been making shortbread.'

'I had three cups while I was waiting for you to come home.'

'Waiting for me? What for? I always play tennis on Thursday. What's happened?' Without waiting for an answer, she continued. 'I got clobbered by Margaret Barry today. Jolly embarrassing, with half the club looking on. My backhand was appalling.'

'Hurry up and sort your tea out – we need to talk. We've had letters from Father.'

Elizabeth's face lit up. 'Why didn't you say! Where?'

'On the mantelpiece.'

An envelope was propped against the carriage clock, its stamp bearing a kangaroo on a map of Australia.

'How marvellous! It's been so long.' She ripped open

the envelope, almost tearing the letter in her excitement. A printed ticket fell out onto the floor and Elizabeth bent to pick it up.

'It's a ticket for a passage to Sydney on the White Star Line.' She frowned. 'In my name.'

She turned her attention to the letter. As she read, her brow furrowed, and she looked over at her sister from time to time. Sarah avoided eye contact, looking out of the window. Eventually, with a snort, Elizabeth stuffed the letter back into its envelope, crushed it into her the pocket of her cardigan and flung herself into an armchair.

'Father's lost his mind. Must have. Gone completely barmy. There's no other explanation. Do you know what it says? That he wants me to go out there and marry some chap called Jack Kidd. All he says is that he's a widower and is fifty-seven. Fifty-seven! It's some kind of joke.' She was shaking her head. 'Come on, Sarah, admit it. He's pulling my leg.'

'Don't be ridiculous, Elizabeth. Why do you have to be so dramatic?'

Elizabeth looked at her sister as though seeing her for the first time. There was a hardness about Sarah's eyes and her mouth turned downwards, making her appear petulant. Her light brown hair with its tight marcel waves was cut to follow the shorter fashion of the year, but did little to flatter her round face. Her velvet dress strained over her pregnant belly, while her small, delicate hands fluttered up and down, constantly smoothing out imagined wrinkles in the fabric.

'It is a sensible solution, Lizzie. Father clearly has your best interests at heart.'

'Good Lord, you don't take this nonsense seriously do you?'

Elizabeth jumped up and took up a position in front of the unlit fireplace, her elbows on the mantelpiece and her chin resting on her hands, while she tried to compose herself. Without turning round, she spoke again, slowly.

'You know as well as I do that Father's not been himself since Mother died. I'll write to him immediately and tell him his plan is impracticable. Don't worry – I'll resist the temptation to tell him it's bordering on insane.'

'For heaven's sake. It's not insane. You must write and tell him you agree to marry Mr Kidd.'

'You're as crazy as he is!'

Sarah became exasperated. There's no money left. Father has lost everything. Charles can't support you.'

Elizabeth pretended not to hear. 'Father must have been drinking when he wrote it.'

'That's not fair. How else are can you find a husband at twenty-seven, when you're penniless? You should jump at the chance of a wealthy husband, your own home and a new life in a new country. Laid out on a plate. Your stubbornness is breath-taking.'

'Stubbornness? It's not you who's being asked to marry a man you've never set eyes on. This is 1920 not 1820!'

'Father can't support you any more. He's only doing what any good father would do.'

She plumped up the cushion behind her and took another opportunity to stroke her bulging abdomen proprietorially. 'Really, Lizzie. Mother bent over backwards trying to find you a husband. I've lost count of the number of eligible men you poured scorn on.' She counted on her fingers. 'Not clever enough. Too pious. Too shallow. No interest in music. Too old. Too dull. No sense of humour. It's as though you want to be an old maid. I don't understand you.'

'That's obvious.'

'You can't keep carrying a torch for someone who's never coming back.'

'That's enough, Sarah!'

'I'm sorry Stephen was killed. We're all sorry. But you're not the only woman in that position. With so many men killed in the war, you can't afford to be picky. As for this Mr Kidd, being a widower I'm sure he believes other factors to be more important than love the second time around. And so should you.'

It's not picky to want to be in love with the person I marry. Maybe you don't understand that. After all you can't have been in love with...'

'Don't you dare speak of Charles and me that way. We're talking about you. Don't you want to be married?

'I'd rather be single than marry a man for whom I have no feelings. My fiancé was blown up in the middle of a muddy Belgian swamp. And yes I know that doesn't make me unusual. And no, I'm not complaining about my lot. But since Stephen died, I've not found another man whom I can love. It may be a sentimental approach to life, but it's how I feel. It should be possible for a woman to forge a life for herself if she so wishes, rather than be obliged to marry to survive.'

'You aren't forging a life for yourself – you're dependent on Charles and me. It's a situation that we can't sustain with our growing family.'

'I've always contributed more than my share to the household expenses. And I intend to continue doing so. You and Charles haven't had to pay a penny to the upkeep of the house until now. If Father's stops my allowance I'll take on more pupils.'

'More pupils!' There was contempt in Sarah's voice. 'Your pupils pay buttons. Besides, Charles is not prepared to put up with strangers trooping through the house and scratching and wailing away with those dreadful violins for hours on end.'

'Charles is at work when my pupils come.'

'That's beside the point. Charles says it's bad for the babies to be exposed to noise and all those people bringing germs into our home. He's had enough and so have I.'

'I'd like to remind you that this is my home too. Charles has no right to dictate what I can and cannot do here.'

'That's where you're wrong. Didn't Father explain?'

Sarah pulled another letter from the drawer of a small sewing table that stood beside her chair and thrust it at Elizabeth.

'Read what he wrote to me.'

Elizabeth opened the letter, and read with growing dismay. Her father had not been the same since her mother's death left a huge hole in the fabric of the family. After a few months of withdrawal from the world, when he stopped going to his office and shunned all social events, he had emerged from self-imposed purdah and found a new-found passion for gambling. What had once been a sizeable fortune, built from his small but successful coffee importing company, was decimated by a throw of the dice, a hand of cards or a bad choice in the four o'clock at Aintree or Chester. Out of the blue, he had announced that he would be leaving for Australia, where at first he had prospered. The remains of his fortune, and luck at cards on the voyage out, provided enough cash for a share in a small mining consortium. His letters home were filled with optimism and enthusiasm. He claimed to have stopped gambling and intended to buy land to build a house. Six months passed with no further word, but Elizabeth continued to receive her monthly allowance through the bank. One month ago the payment had not arrived.

His letters today explained that a drinking spree, celebrating a possible gold-strike, had turned into a binge when the gold failed to materialise. The alcohol brought on a loss of self-control and he turned to the card table like a plant towards light. In a few hours he lost everything that he had built.

The contents of Sarah's letter were similar to Elizabeth's until the last page.

With Elizabeth to be married, I must also think of you, Sarah.

It's no secret that your mother and I were opposed to your marriage, but in my present straitened circumstances I want to protect the family home from any possibility that I could one day put at risk my grandchildren's inheritance. My latest misfortune has demonstrated how I can lose all reason when I sit down at a card-table. I have instructed my solicitors to transfer the deeds of Trevelyan House into your husband's name.

I will remain in Sydney until Elizabeth arrives and is married, then I plan to make a new start – I have heard good things of the city of Melbourne.

With fondest love and respect, your father,
William M Morton.

A chill spread through Elizabeth's body as she realised the limited choices before her. Charles Dawson had tolerated her presence only because she had more right to be in the house than he did.

Elizabeth had never understood why Sarah had married him. He was dull, older than his years and sullen to the point of rudeness. He found laughter undignified and had no trouble avoiding it. Elizabeth thought him selfish, materialistic and short-tempered. He was cold to his children and showed no affection to Sarah.

When Sarah had announced her engagement her parents were dismayed, but in the face of her evident happiness, consented. While accepting the marriage, William Morton continued to keep the clerk at arm's length, making no attempt to include him in business decisions.

The day William Morton announced to the assembled family that he had sold Morton's Coffee, Dawson's hopes of being accepted by his father in law were dashed. His job was safe – he was to be transferred to the new owners along with the other company assets, as if he were a bushel of beans or a gross of sacks – but any possibility that he would inherit the family firm vanished with the sale.

Elizabeth avoided her brother-in-law. She often contrived to be elsewhere, maintaining a social life that included dining at the homes of close friends, concerts in Liverpool or Manchester and trips with friends to Northport's popular new picture house, where she could indulge her fascination with the films of Rudolph Valentino. Dawson shut himself away in the small back parlour, where he was usually to be found studying religious tracts. He spent little time with Sarah and his daughters, preferring to make regular visits to his elderly mother on the other side of Northport.

'So you mean to throw me out of my own home?' Elizabeth said to Sarah.

'Stop the drama, Lizzie.'

'That's what it amounts to – no matter how you phrase it. Father has handed the family home to your husband and you're saying he won't let me stay here.'

'Why should he be expected to share his home with his wife's spinster sister? You've had plenty of chance to marry. Mother used to despair of you.'

'Don't bring Mother into this.'

'She wanted you to be settled and happy.'

'I'm settled and happy here and Mother would be horrified to know that you're trying to throw me out of my home.'

'There's *no more money*! Charles's salary is pitifully inadequate. Handing over the house is the least Father could do after selling the firm out from under Charles and never giving him the status and salary he deserves. You'll be fine. You'll be close to Father. You'll have a rich husband and will want for nothing. I can't believe you're not the least bit excited about all this?'

Elizabeth curled her lip. 'Excited? Excited at being treated like a piece of baggage to be shipped across the world and handed, sight unseen, to an old man? What's wrong with you, Sarah?'

'There's nothing wrong with me. I have two children and another on the way and a house to run with no income other than the paltry sum my husband brings home. The servants will have to go too. Susan's been here since Mother and Father married and Betty since you were born. It's not just about you, you know.'

Elizabeth tried to be conciliatory. She knelt on the floor and took Sarah's hands in hers. 'We'll get through this together. We'll find a way. I'll look for a post in a school. The salary will be better than I'm getting now. I can work full time. I'm not afraid of that. I'll apply for a position at Harbour House. It's very exclusive. High fees. I can earn enough to make up what Father used to send us.'

'Charles would not be happy.'

'Why? If I pay my way? You can make him understand? He'll listen to you.'

Sarah picked up a glass paperweight and turned it over in her hands, then polished the glass on her velvet dress. She frowned then took a breath, replaced the paperweight and answered her sister. 'We need your bedroom.'

'But the girls are still tiny and ...'

'Charles has decided to move his mother in here. She's very frail and he wants her close by. He's going to tell her this evening and there isn't room for you both. It's Charles's house now and it's understandable that he should put his mother first.'

'You mean Charles already knows about Father's letters? The pair of you have got it all worked out!'

'Of course he knows. As soon as I read the letter I went over to the office to discuss it with him. It's a great relief to him to be able to care for his mother and to know that he has at last been accepted into this family.'

'Not by me he hasn't! Not when he's throwing me out of

my home! Wait till father hears about this... I'll send him a telegram. He'll put a stop to this nonsense.'

'He won't... He can't... The title deeds were transferred today. We can talk about this again tomorrow morning.' Her tone was less strident. 'Maybe when you've slept on it you'll see the merit in Father's plan. I've not been comfortable sharing a home with you, now that it's just me and Charles and the children. It was different when Mother and Father were still here. I don't feel it's appropriate having you here under the circumstances.'

'Under what circumstances? What do you mean? Why are you being so cryptic?'

Sarah rose from the chair and smoothed her dress down again. With her hand on the door she said, 'We'll talk about it tomorrow. I've a headache and I'm going to lie down. Ask Susan to bring me a tray. You'll be eating alone tonight as Charles is dining with Mrs Dawson. Goodnight.'

It had turned dark while they had been talking and Elizabeth drew the curtains and switched on the lights. The maid cleared away the tea tray and set a fire in the grate. Elizabeth asked to have her supper set up on a side table in the small parlour, rather than sit alone at the end of the long mahogany table in the dining room. After picking at the cold cuts and taking a couple of spoonfuls of rice pudding, she pushed the tray aside. She was too distressed to pick up a book and read, playing the gramophone was out of the question with the children and Sarah in bed, and her hands were shaking too much to sew. She paced up and down in front of the fireplace, angry. She opened the breakfront cabinet where her father kept the decanters and glasses, and poured a glass of sherry. The warmth of the liquor coursed through her body, helping to calm her frayed nerves.

She fell asleep and woke to find the fire had gone out and the room was chilly. She pulled on the cardigan she had cast off earlier in the warmth from the fire, and dragged the sleeves down over her hands, tucking her feet under her as she curled up in the big leather armchair that had once been her father's favourite. It was just after eleven. She was wide awake, but knew the maid would have gone to bed. Building another fire herself would only give Sarah the excuse to chide her for her profligate waste of coal. The sherry had left a cloying, over-sweet taste in her mouth, so she went downstairs and poured herself a glass of water. There was no point in going to bed yet. The earlier sherry-induced sleep had left her restless.

She was incredulous at the behaviour of her father. The relative modesty of her own requirements and the regularity of her father's cheques meant she had never seen any need to put money aside for a rainy day. She had a few war savings certificates, but that was the sum of it. When she had been engaged to Stephen, the eldest son of a cotton manufacturer, she had been assured of a future free of financial worries and more recently had presumed that her father would continue to provide for her. She had failed to anticipate just how quickly he could exhaust what had been a sizeable fortune.

She chided herself for her lack of foresight, and was filled with anger at her sister and her brother-in-law. Surely they must realise that what her father proposed was cruel and impractical? He had always loved her - rather more than her sister, she suspected - and yet he wanted to hand her over to an old man he had met in some sleazy, Australian gambling den. It was barbaric. This Mr Kidd had not even had the courtesy to write a letter to accompany that of her father's, to make himself known, to ask for her hand, to reveal something of himself. A sane and decent man would have had the grace to suggest that they meet first and a courtship proceed if appropriate, not to order her to be delivered to him like a delivery of groceries.

She looked at the ticket again, and then put it back in

the envelope with the crumpled letter and stuffed them into her cardigan pocket. She would speak to Charles and Sarah in the morning and find a way to make them see sense. There was plenty of room in the house: the box room would be fine for Mrs Dawson, or if Charles insisted, she could move in there herself. If he would not allow her pupils to come here, then she could go to their homes. She would also investigate whether she might find more lucrative employment at Harbour House School.

She smiled at her reflection in the over-mantel mirror, tucked a stray curl behind her ears and straightened her shoulders. All would be well in the morning. She had a plan. She had choices. Her mother had always said nothing was so bad if you still had choices.

When the clock struck midnight, she went up to bed. As she stepped onto the dark landing, she sensed movement behind her. She fumbled for the electric light switch. A hand covered her mouth and pushed her into her bedroom. She lost her footing and banged her shoulder against the doorframe. The hand across her mouth was clamped so hard that she could not move her jaw. Blood and adrenaline surged through her. She couldn't breathe. Her heart was hammering in terror as she was thrust into the room and the door closed behind them. She struggled to escape her assailant, who had a vice-like grip on her jaw with one hand, while pinioning her arms behind her with the other. She tried to twist around and break free but he pulled her arms back, jerking them upward behind her, making her cry out with pain. She could smell the whisky on his breath as she struggled to breathe.

'Keep still.'

Despite the slurring brought on by the whisky, the voice was unmistakeable. She stopped struggling and he lowered his hand from her mouth and pulled her back against his body, still keeping a tight grip on her arms.

'Let me go, Charles. You've been drinking! Go to bed. You'll wake the children.'

She was shocked. Charles had never been known to take a drop of alcohol and had often pontificated on the benefits of temperance at dinner while her father enjoyed a glass or two of fine wine, unmindful of his critical gaze.

'Don't tell me how to behave with my own children. They're two floors up so there's no chance of them stirring.'

The relief she felt on discovering it was Charles, rather than a burglar, was replaced by a sense of alarm. He rarely spoke to her. He had never so much as touched her hand, apart from a brief and obligatory handshake on the occasion of his wedding. Now here he was manhandling her, his hot whisky breath on her neck.

'Let me go! You've had too much to drink. Go to bed. We'll forget this happened.'

He shoved her onto the bed, throwing himself on top of her, crushing the breath out of her. 'You won't ever forget this happened. I'll make sure of that. I'm tired of you acting as if I don't exist or I'm filth under your feet. You're never going to forget me now.'

Winded, she was unable to fight. He dragged her arms back above her head. 'I know what you want,' he said. 'You're a whore like your sister. You tormented me for years, flaunting yourself at me. Now you're going to get what you've been asking for. Something to remember when you're in Australia.'

Elizabeth was trapped under his weight. Panic, fear and nausea filled her as she realised what he intended to do. The darkness of the room heightened her fear, but spared her from seeing his face or what he was doing. The rough fabric of his woollen dressing gown rubbed against her face as he used one hand to pin her arms back, while the other reached down to pull up her skirt. Summoning every ounce of strength left in her body, she tried to lift herself to push him off. It served to inflame him further and as she pushed up against him she realised he was naked under his open dressing gown and felt the hardness of his erection. Her panic mounted as his penis pressed against her stomach and his hand dragged at her underwear. The silk tore and he forced her legs apart. She tried to twist sideways but he was too heavy and her pinioned arms meant she could gain no purchase. With a grunt of triumph he entered her. She tried to make her mind a blank, while her body fought to be free of him. His sour breath made her gag. Realising her attempts to shake him off were futile and served to excite him more, she stopped struggling and lay as impassive as a corpse, while he pounded into her, arching his back and bearing down on her in triumph.

'Just like her upstairs. Filled with sin and lust. But the Lord knows you're a bad woman. He will punish you for your wantonness, just as he smote the inhabitants of Sodom and Gomorrah.'

His words came out in panting breaths, in rhythm with the ramming motions of his body. 'You take pleasure in tempting a man, in trying to lead him to damnation. You are a filthy whore and you will be punished by God for this.'

Elizabeth prayed that he would stop, or that she might pass out or die, but he continued with a relentless momentum, excited by his own words. He reached up to the neck of her blouse and forced his fingers between the buttons, tearing them open. She made herself play a piece of music in her head, working through a difficult violin exercise, trying to visualise the notes on the stave, desperate to transport herself away from what was happening. His mouth closed over her left breast and his teeth bit into her nipple. The semi-quavers vanished from her head and pain coursed through her. Tears overflowed from her eyes and ran across her cheeks into her ears. Then he was done and with a cry, slumped forward onto her chest. She felt his shrivelled penis still inside her and freed herself of it, wriggling her way out from underneath his now inert body.

Unwilling to turn the light on and see her attacker, she stumbled to the door and reached the safe haven of the bathroom, where she bolted the door, filled the basin and began to scrub her body clean. As well as semen, there was blood between her legs and across her breast where he had bitten her. She dabbed herself with a towel and tried to staunch the bleeding. She found a sanitary napkin in the medicine cabinet and cut it in half, pushing one piece inside her blouse and the other inside her panties. It was the best she could do with what was available in the bathroom. She filled up the basin again and splashed the cold water over her face then looked at her reflection in the mirror. Fighting back the tears she felt a cold rage. This was her home, her sanctuary, the place she had lived in all her life. Her bedroom had been hers since childhood. It was somewhere she had been safe, cared for, loved. Her father had stroked her hair as he bade her goodnight as a small child. Her mother had sat on the edge of the bed reading her a story, stroking her forehead and whispering her back to sleep after a nightmare. Now violated.

She had to wake her sister: Sarah had to know. It changed everything. She buttoned up what was left of her torn blouse and stepped back onto the landing. The landing light came on. Sarah was standing in the doorway of Elizabeth's bedroom. Behind her Dawson's snoring reached a stentorian crescendo.

Sarah moved quickly and before Elizabeth could speak she felt her sister's hands clutching at what was left of her torn blouse.

'You can't get a man for yourself so you decided to steal my husband! That's why you wanted to stay in this house.'

She launched herself at Elizabeth and shook her by the shoulders. 'How long has this been going on? Don't tell me

- I know. It explains why he's not been near me for months. You've been enjoying my husband under my nose. Get out and don't come back.'

She reached behind her into Elizabeth's room and dragged a large carpetbag through the doorway. She had evidently been busy while Elizabeth was in the bathroom. 'Take your things and get out of my house. I never want to see you again.'

'Sarah! He forced himself on me.'

'Get out!'

She was screaming now and from the floor above them Elizabeth heard one of the children start to cry.

'I'm trying to tell you he raped me!'

Sarah, white with rage, lunged and Elizabeth was forced to step aside or risk being hurled down the stairway. As Sarah grew more hysterical, Elizabeth decided to retreat, before the servants and children all woke up. She grabbed the carpetbag and went down the stairs, pausing in the hallway, then stepping into the drawing room.

'I'll wait in here until morning. I can change and pack properly once that man has left the house.'

'You'll leave now.' Sarah stood on the bottom step of the stairway.

'Sarah it's the middle of the night. I can't leave. I won't leave.'

'You should have thought of that before enticing my husband into your bedroom.'

'You're not being rational. You know I've never so much as looked at Charles. This is horrible. He's hurt me. He's blind drunk. He's been drinking whisky.'

'And who put him up to that? He never touched a drop before tonight. Before you got him to join you.' Sarah moved into the room.

'What are you talking about?'

'I'm talking about this.' Sarah pointed to the abandoned

sherry glass, sitting on the mantelpiece where Elizabeth had left it.

'I had a small sherry before I went to bed. I thought it would help me sleep. I didn't even hear him come in. I'd no idea he was in the house until he jumped on me.'

'You disgust me. If you don't leave now I'll throw your bag onto the street and you after it.'

Knowing it was hopeless, Elizabeth made one last plea to her sister. 'I'd like to say goodbye to the girls - or at least look at them one last time.'

'Get out! Get out! Get out now! I don't want you near my babies.' Sarah's voice was just short of a scream.

Pausing only to gather up her coat, a hat and her handbag containing the steamer ticket, money order and the letter from her father, from where she had left them on the hall-stand, Elizabeth stumbled outside. The door was slammed behind her and she stood for a few moments at the top of the wide flight of stone steps. She gulped lungfuls of the night air, then walked away from what had been her only home. She moved blindly, her eyes stinging with tears, her coat buttoned tight against the cold and to cover the torn blouse underneath.

After walking aimlessly for half an hour, Elizabeth found herself outside the home of her friend, Sylvia Gregory. She stood in front of the large Georgian house, but decided against knocking on the door. The prospect of a warm bed and some comfort from Sylvia and her mother, who had been a close friend of Elizabeth's own mother, was tempting, but she could not face telling them what had happened. She felt deeply ashamed. She knew she had done no wrong, but could not bring herself to tell anyone what Dawson had done to her and risk the look in her friends' eyes that might signal that they thought she had been complicit in the act. Rape was something that happened to other people, not to people she knew. Her friends would be horrified. They would be caring of her. But they would also pity her and quite possibly, while never vocalising it, blame her for somehow helping to make it happen.

Turning to Sylvia and her family would also mean telling them what her father had done. Elizabeth had always suspected that Mrs Gregory secretly harboured the belief that Maria Morton had married beneath her. Elizabeth did not want to vindicate this judgement.

There was no one else to turn to. The only relatives she was aware of were distant cousins of her mother who had sent a letter of condolence when she died, but did not feel sufficient kinship to make the effort to attend her funeral.

She walked through the silent town to the railway station. The first train to Liverpool was at five thirty. She checked her watch. It was just before two. The station waiting room was locked. It would be a long cold wait. She looked over the road at the Station Hotel, where there was a welcoming light coming from the lobby. Picking up her bag she hurried across the road. It would be money she could ill afford to spend, but a hot bath and the chance to change out of her torn clothes were too good to pass up.

CHAPTER THREE

SETTING SAIL

Michael pushed through the early morning crowds waiting
for trams to carry them to work throughout the city, and
made his way towards the Mersey waterfront. The night
before, in a public house, he'd heard there was a ship about
to sail for Africa and Australia. He hoped he'd be in time,
but if he wasn't, there were plenty of ships plying their way
across the Atlantic to America. During his years in the War
he had met men from all three continents and was drawn
most to the Australian 'diggers' for their sense of humour
and lack of pretension. He had also got the impression
that a Pom, as they called the likes of him, would fit in
easier there than in America. Australia had the advantage
of being further away from Britain, yet closer in terms of its
way of life and it was still part of the Empire. The clincher
was that they were offering men like him assisted passages.

He liked the feel of Liverpool. It was a place full of life
and full of people. The streets were packed with double
decker trams and smart new automobiles, as well as horses
and carts. Everyone appeared cheerful and despite the coal
smoke that had turned its handsome Victorian buildings
as black as the back of a grate, it felt an optimistic, bright

sort of place. The people rushing by were a real mixture – he could tell that from their hats: men in bowlers, cloth caps, naval uniform caps, boaters and fedoras, women in brimmed hats, cloches, the poorer ones in head scarves, and nuns under dark peaked veils. He pulled his own cap low on his brow and pushed his way through the crowds thronging the pavement to look at the display windows of Blacklers. He had never been in a department store before and for a moment was tempted to go in and look around. Then he remembered there was no point; he no longer had Minnie or his mother to treat to some colourful ribbon or a pair of gloves.

The smoke-blackened side walls of the buildings were covered from the roof line to the pavement with posters, advertising everything from the latest speaker at the Picton Hall to Veno's cough mixture, Reliance bicycles and the timetable for the Birkenhead ferry. It was so different from the dales. Part of him was tempted to linger longer in this city and see what it had to offer him. He began to wonder if a short trip here might open Minnie's eyes to new possibilities, but he pushed the thought from his mind. He had to forget the past and forget her. He needed to get himself somewhere far away where there was no chance of turning back.

He was in luck and got himself a berth on the SS Historic to Sydney via Tenerife and Cape Town. He stood on the dockside looking up at the vessel, patting his pocket with the ticket inside. A passing sailor addressed him.

'You sailing on the Historic, mate?'

He nodded.

'She's a good little ship. Only just back to doing passenger trips. Troop carrier during the war.' The pride in the sailor's voice was evident.

'It's hardly a little ship!' Michael felt dwarfed by it. It towered above him, making it hard to believe that it was a boat, not a building.

'Sailed before, mate?'

'To and from France. But the boat were tiny compared to this monster!'

The sailor pointed out the four masts and the central funnel 'Four sticks and a stack. Built in Belfast. Nearly nineteen thousand tons. She can carry 600 passengers. Not to mention tons of cargo. A real beauty.'

'I've not seen owt like it!'

'Wait till you get on board. There's a couple of salt-water swimming baths and a gymnasium. You're going on yer holidays, mate!'

Elizabeth leaned against the railing watching the seagulls swoop towards the water. They dived down to the surface in what was a fruitless search for fish, then soared upwards again in a continuous repetitive cycle. The sky was dull grey and the Mersey was murky. She did not want it otherwise. Sunshine would have been a mockery.

She had secured a berth in one of the last cabins available on a ship about to depart for Sydney via South Africa, in three days time. She found accommodation in a small travellers' boarding house, venturing forth only to deal with the paperwork she needed for her entry into Australia and to cash in her war bonds. She avoided the shops of Lord Street and Church Street, fearful of seeing anyone she might know and having to explain what she was doing. But Liverpool was full of people busy with their own business and it was easy to merge into the crowds.

She looked back at the Pier Head, where the Liver Building, the Cunard Building and the domed offices of the Mersey Docks and Harbour Board formed the impressive Liverpool skyline. She had seen them many times before from the New Brighton ferry but, from the vantage point of the upper decks of this enormous ocean-going steamer, they looked particularly imposing: symbols of the power of the British Empire and the reach of its trade and passenger ships. This morning, when she had waited on the landing stage looking up at the ship, she was overwhelmed by its towering size. It would be her first time on a ship, other than the ferries and her first trip overseas, unless you counted a brief holiday on the Isle of Man before the War. In other circumstances, Elizabeth would have been elated and excited about what lay ahead of her, but now she was wretched.

The edge of the wind cut into her face, and she clutched at her hat – she didn't want to lose it, as now it was her only one. She made her way, one hand anchoring the hat, across the deck and away from the crowds on the starboard side, to look across the Mersey to New Brighton. Stephen had taken her to the Tower Gardens, where they listened to the military band, then after an early dinner, danced in the Tower Ballroom. She remembered that she had read in the Echo that the New Brighton Tower was being dismantled. Like Stephen and so many young men, it was cut off in its prime by the War – closed for the duration, it had rusted and was now beyond economic repair. There was an air of decay and neglect about the whole country and she decided she was glad to be leaving. All she had left was her father and he was six weeks' worth of ocean away. She longed to see him again, despite his ill-thought plan to secure her future. He was the only person to whom she could confide what had happened with Charles Dawson. But as she looked across the dirty river, she decided not to tell him. It was too late to halt the transfer of the house – and she wanted her nieces to be secure. Telling him would cause him pain and anguish and would not make her situation any better.

She leaned into the wind, eager for the huge ship to pull away from the floating dock, down the river and out into the open sea. Every time she closed her eyes he was there. The smell of his whisky breath, the still sharp pain in her breast where his teeth had broken her skin, and the feeling of shame he had left her with.

Was her joie de vivre gone forever? She wanted to be hard, cold and closed, to reinvent herself; become a new person in a new world.

The foghorn sounded a farewell blast and the engines burst into life, drowning out the noise from the crowds on the wharf. The ship moved slowly away from the dock, its milky wash spreading behind as the tugs pulled it through the Mersey's bottleneck into Liverpool Bay and the open sea. The smell of coal smoke from the funnel was acrid and she tried to breathe in the cold air from the Irish Sea. A little jerk of fear went through her stomach. What lay ahead?

Marrying Mr Jack Kidd was out of the question, but there was no reason why she and her father could not build a new life together in Australia. She would steer him away from the gambling, try to establish some stability and security at the centre of his life, as her mother had once done. Given time, she would wean him from the compulsion to gamble. She could support them both by teaching the violin. It would not pay much - but enough to feed and clothe them. They might even scrape together enough money to buy some land, build a house and grow their own food. She wanted to shut herself away from everyone except her father; to bury herself away where no one would know what had happened to her and she could be left in peace.

As the ship sailed past the sand hills of Waterloo, Elizabeth thought of happier times. A few years earlier, her mother had been the beating heart of Trevelyan House, her father was dedicated to his work, Sarah an awkward, affectionate schoolgirl and she herself in love with Stephen. What had been the point of it all? What value now was her middle class morality? She was even angry with poor, dead Stephen. They had walked in the sand dunes at Birkdale early in September 1914, just weeks after the war was declared. She had offered herself to him but he demurred.

He had thought the war would be over before winter, but instead he was dead the next year. She was bitter at his misplaced gallantry. Why was he so keen to join up? Why had he been so reluctant to make love before they were married? She was torn. Loving him, yet angry that because of his wretched principles, her first sexual experience had been one of pain and violence, not love and tenderness.

'Damn you, Stephen and your bloody, high-minded sense of honour and your pig-headed desire to do the right thing.' Yet it was hard to be angry with someone who had been dead for five years; a man who had inhabited another world, a world long gone: an age of innocence – or blindness, before the war had sent young men in their masses to their unmarked foreign graves.

What if Stephen hadn't jumped to his feet and brushed the sand from his new uniform and stretched out a hand to pull her onto her feet beside him? If instead he had let her undo the brass buttons on his tunic and done the same with the small ivory buttons that ran down the back of her silk blouse? But he had believed he would be home from the Front within a couple of months, that the War would be over, that they would be married and have the luxury of making love for the first time in the comfort of a large bed in a first class London hotel, en route to a continental honeymoon. Instead he was sleeping forever in his continental grave. She knew he had wanted her as much as she had him, but 'Do the right thing' had been his motto, and sticking to it had cost him his life and cost Elizabeth what could have been a memory of a moment of happiness to offset some of her pain. Instead, every time she closed her eyes, her head was filled with the image of Dawson.

Michael stared at the featureless expanse of open sea, as the wind cut the back of his neck in the space between his collar and the back of his cap. His coat blew open as the strength of the gale increased. It was going to be rough.

The steward had warned him earlier that they were in for a bumpy passage across the Bay of Biscay. He looked around the deck. Deserted. The few passengers who had been taking the air when he first emerged, had retreated to the warmth below decks. Good. He preferred to be alone.

The ship that had seemed so huge and solid when he had gazed up at it from the Liverpool quayside, was bobbing about like a cork. The sea was swollen - it had happened so quickly, without warning, changing from millpond into pitching roller-coaster. He set his feet apart and leaned into the motion, giving himself up to the power of the waves and the razor-like slashes of spray on his cheeks. He would have some colour in them after this - unless he succumbed to seasickness. He doubted that would happen; it was too exhilarating, like a wild joy ride. Not rough enough to cause him unease - all those tons of steel looked protection enough against the harshest of seas - but then they'd said that about the Titanic and look what happened to that.

Someone tapped his elbow. It was the cabin steward. 'You should move below, sir. It's getting very rough. You'll be safer below. Nip into the saloon for a nice cuppa and warm yourself up.'

'Thanks, mate, but I want to stop here a while longer.'

The steward shrugged and stepped away, moving on down the deck, presumably to warn any other crazed thrill seekers. Michael turned his face back into the wind and spray, feeling the shafts of icy, cold, salt water sear his face. The wind was so strong that he had to gulp to take in air. He wanted to smoke a cigarette, but it would be futile trying to light it. Bracing, that was the word - no - abrasive was more like it. The salty spray scrubbed the surface off his skin; it was as harsh as the scrubbing his mother used to give his back on a Saturday, when she got the tin bath out and he, his father and Danny took turns to soak away the week's grime from the mines and the fields, ready for chapel the next morning.

Until now he had avoided the public spaces of the vast ship, eating his meals quickly in the anonymity of the enormous dining room, then returning to the cabin he shared with three brothers from Manchester or taking a solitary walk around the decks. But he knew the three lads were suffering from seasickness and he couldn't face the the smell of vomit and the groaning from their bunks. He was tempted by the prospect of the warming effects of the cup of tea the steward suggested and was about to head for one of the state rooms, when he realised he was not the only passenger still on deck braving the elements. A few feet away, a woman was gripping the guardrail, staring out to sea as though in a trance, oblivious to his presence and to the wind and spray battering her face. He paused for a moment, curious. She looked well-to-do, in a smart green coat with a fur collar, well-polished leather ankle boots and a hat that perfectly matched the coat. Her hair was light brown, slightly wavy and swept back into a loose knot at the back, where several undisciplined strands were escaping from under her hat. He could see her face only in profile, but it looked as though it carried all the cares of the world. Her brow was furrowed and her mouth set firm. He could not see her eyes, but sensed instinctively that they were as troubled as his own. He wanted to walk over and stretch out his hand to touch her, to offer some words of comfort for whatever was troubling her. As he fought this instinct, she pulled away from the railings and stepped off the deck and into the hatchway. She had not even registered his presence.

His thoughts returned to what had happened back at home. It was like watching the moving pictures. The images moved across his brain but, unlike the flicks, they were in vivid colour and flowed smoothly and relentlessly.

He thought about climbing onto the metal balustrade and diving into the cold wind-tossed waters below. He was a strong swimmer, so it might take him a while to die, although the cold of the water would overwhelm him soon enough, if he wasn't sucked down under the draught of the ship and crushed by the propellers. Pointless even speculating; he knew he couldn't do it, much as he wanted to. The impulse that drives some men to take their own lives was absent in his make-up.

His hair was plastered to his head, his cap so sodden he took it off and stuffed it in his pocket. As he did so his hand closed around the small stone with the hole in the middle that had been his brother's. He ran his hand across his face, wiping the water away and watched the violent sea and the darkening sky.

Elizabeth headed for the upper deck. Most of the passengers had retired to their cabins, so she thought there was a good chance she'd be undisturbed in the general room or the writing room. She was keen to avoid the woman with whom she was sharing a cabin. At least she had managed to secure a two berth rather than a four on this single class liner, although her cabin companion, Mrs Briars, talked enough for three people.

The general room was almost deserted and she settled herself into a cane settee beside one of the large brass-framed windows. She picked up a magazine and flicked through the pages without reading them, distracted and restless. The ship was rising and falling over the swollen sea and hoped she was not going to succumb to seasickness. The room smelled, as did the whole ship, of an odd mixture of linoleum polish, brass cleaner, wood varnish and coal smoke. Today it was accented with the tinge of damp wool. At the far end of the room, a man was playing dominoes with a small boy, the boy laughing loudly when the pieces fell off the table with the pitch of the ship. On an adjacent table two women were engrossed in a game of cards.

A shrill voice interrupted her solitude. 'There are you are Miss Morton. I've been looking for you everywhere! I was about to sound the alarm – I thought you'd been washed overboard!' Her laugh was like a snort.

Elizabeth tried not to show her irritation. 'No need to worry. I'm quite safe and sound and enjoying a moment of quiet.'

The woman didn't take the hint. 'I was going to suggest afternoon tea in the writing room, but you look well settled in here so I'll ask the steward for tea.' She signalled to a young man hovering in the distance. 'Pot of tea please, Reggie dear. And some of those nice cheese scones.'

'Mrs Briars, I'm about to go below.' Elizabeth said.

'Nonsense, my dear. You need to keep out of the cabin. If you lie down, you'll end up like the rest of them. They're dropping like flies! A good walk on deck would sort them all out. Lying down on a bunk makes it worse; very unsettling to the stomach with all this pitching and rolling about.'

'I'm not feeling ill at all. I was just thinking I might have a nap.'

'A nap!' The woman snorted. 'You're far too young for afternoon naps. A cup of strong tea, a nice game of cards and a brief promenade on deck, and you'll be ready for your supper!'

'I don't play cards. But it looks like there are a couple of ladies over there who do. I'm sure they'd welcome another player.'

Mrs Briars ignored the suggestion. 'I'll just have to teach you, my dear. Plenty of time to Cape Town. By the time I leave the ship you'll be a regular card sharp.'

The steward brought their tea and the card-playing ladies, the man and the boy left the room together. Elizabeth sipped her tea and tried not to think about how long there was between now and Cape Town, where Mrs Briars would be disembarking.

The older woman said, 'Tell me again, my dear - I'm so forgetful these days - how long has your father been living in Australia?'

'About eighteen months. He went soon after the war ended.'

'He finds it agreeable?'

'I believe so.'

'I do hope so, for both your sakes. But it's such a terrible distance. Mind you, so is Cape Town.'

'Have you visited Africa before?'

'No, no. When my late husband was alive he would never have entertained the idea of leaving England for the colonies. But now he's gone and my elder son taken from us in the War, Robert my younger son is keen for me to join him there.'

Elizabeth forced herself to feign interest. 'What does your son do?'

'He's a farmer. He's done very well for himself. He went out as an officer in the South African War, took a fancy to the place and never came home again.'

'Does he have a family?'

The woman snorted her laugh again. 'I do believe I may have piqued your interest, Miss Morton! And no he doesn't! One of my aims is to help him put that right by finding a nice young lady like yourself to be his help mate.'

Elizabeth blushed, more in annoyance than embarrassment. 'Really, Mrs Briars! I was certainly not fishing.'

'I'm teasing! But you would be perfect for dear Bertie. He's such a lovely boy, but much in need of a woman's steadying hand. I'm going to have to work hard over the coming days to prevail on you to break your journey in Cape Town. Who knows what might happen?' That terrible nasal laugh again.

Elizabeth forced a smile. 'There's no question of that. My father is as anxious to see me as I am sure you are to see your son.'

Their conversation was interrupted by the sound of the door banging, as a man who looked as though half the Atlantic Ocean had washed over him, entered the room. He pulled off his cap and made his way to a chair on the far side of the room, only for Mrs Briars to call to him.

'Young man! Over here! Come and join us! The whole ship is going down with seasickness, so those of us still on our feet need to rally round and stick together!' She snorted again in appreciation of her own words.

The man gave a small movement of his head that was somewhere between a nod of greeting and a shake of refusal.

'Come on, it's perfectly ridiculous for three people to be sitting on opposite sides of this enormous empty room. Do join us. I'll ask the steward for more tea – and it looks like you could do with a towel and a blanket. It's nice and warm over here by the stove. I won't take no for an answer!'

Elizabeth threw him an apologetic glance then pretended to look for something in her handbag, trying to distance herself from her cabin companion's behaviour.

Looking reluctant, he nodded in greeting to Mrs Briars and crossed the salon to join them.

'Pleased to meet you, Ma'am.'

'I am Mrs Briars. And this is Miss Morton.'

'Michael Winterbourne.'

'Do sit down and stop shuffling about like that, Mr Winterton. You're making me nervous. Now where was I? Oh yes I was telling Miss Morton about my son Bertie. He has a large farm on the Cape and is one of the most important growers of wheat in the Province, you know?'

Winterbourne and Elizabeth exchanged a glance then looked away quickly. Elizabeth raised her eyes again to take in the stranger. His thick hair was weighted down with seawater and rain and he kept brushing it back nervously. The steward arrived with a towel and the man jumped to his feet and moved away from them to dry his hair roughly, embarrassed at doing this in front of the two women. Elizabeth took advantage of the moment to look at him. He was tall, lean, but strongly built, as though accustomed to physical labour. His clothes were cheap cloth, poorly cut, but he had a natural elegance that needed no help from a tailor. Finished with the towel, he resumed his place beside them. There was an uncomfortable silence. Elizabeth was immediately self-conscious, feeling small and exposed next to the man, acutely aware of his physical presence, his proximity. She was tongue-tied, awkward, shy and looked away, annoyed with herself. She wished Mrs Briars had not invited him to join them.

Mrs Briars breezed on oblivious to the changed dynamic. She addressed Winterbourne, 'I've been trying to convince Miss Morton to take a break in her journey and come and stay with us on The Cape, but she's quite determined to head on to Australia. I'll just have to keep on trying, won't I? I can't bear to let the dear girl go! We have become firm friends, haven't we, dear? And where are you headed, Mr Winterton?'

'The name's Winterbourne. I'm going to Australia. To Sydney.'

'And do you have family there? Miss Morton is joining her father there.'

Michael looked at Elizabeth and then dropped his eyes. 'No. No family.'

'So you're off to seek your fortune in the great unknown! How thrilling! And what do you plan to do when you get there?'

'I fancy trying me hand at sheep farming – but I'll do whatever they'll pay us to do Ma'am. I'm not particular as long as it's honest work.'

'But what is your profession, Mr Winterbottom?'

He sighed, deciding that correcting her again was pointless. Exchanging another glance with Elizabeth, he replied,

'I don't suppose you'd call it a profession. Back home I were a lead miner, like me father and grandfather.'

Mrs Briars raised her eyebrows. 'A lead miner? How interesting. I had no idea I would meet such a broad spread of humanity on an ocean liner. Most educational.' Then she sniffed and, twisting in her chair, turned her back on him and addressed Elizabeth.

'Miss Morton, will you be attending the harp recital tonight? The chief steward assures me that the lady harpist is quite exceptional. She's performed before the Princess Royal. And I hear Mozart may be on the menu. Isn't that marvellous?'

Before Elizabeth could respond, Winterbourne was on his feet and with a hurried nod in their direction and a mumbled 'Excuse me', left the room.

'Really my dear, how rude! He's not even waited for his tea. What a common man. Breeding will out won't it? I won't waste time making conversation with him again. No manners at all. Imagine – a miner! What is The White Star Line coming to? My dear sister did warn me about taking a ship with just one class – the old fashioned way was the best. The likes of him would never have been allowed above decks in the old days. Steerage. That's where he should be.'

Michael went back out on deck, careless that he was now half dry and about to be soaked again. His cheeks burned with humiliation. He felt diminished and belittled by the woman's snobbishness. As he paced the decks, he realised it wasn't the words of the old lady that perturbed him, but that she had humiliated him in front of the young woman. Why the hell should he care? And yet he did. Perhaps it was the way she had stood there on deck in the swell, staring out across the bucking sea? Her quiet containment and her evident sadness intrigued him. She seemed to exude an inner strength and yet also a vulnerability. He cursed his own stupidity. Why was he thinking like this about a woman, when he'd just walked away from his fiancée; when he should be atoning for what he had done to his family? And who the hell did he think he was, to even suppose that a woman like her would so much as notice a man like him?

It was impossible to sleep. The three Mancunians were sitting on the cabin floor, their backs against the lower bunks, playing a noisy game of cards. Eventually Michael leaned over the side of the bunk and called down to them.

'Look lads, can't you play in the smoking room? I can't get any shut-eye with you lot yammering on like that.'

The eldest placed a card triumphantly on the discard pile and called his brothers. The other two groaned in protest. The victor looked up and said, 'Give us a break Mick! We're nearly done. Ten minutes? I told you, you should've joined us.'

Michael pulled the pillow over his head and rolled onto his stomach. He was thinking about the woman again. He'd seen her sometimes in the dining room or walking around the decks. He always retreated but took every opportunity to observe her from afar. There was something about her. He could not put his finger on what it was. She wasn't conventionally pretty like Minnie. She had a sorrowful air, but her eyes hinted at a suppressed sense of life and energy, as though the unhappiness was a veneer. He wanted to peel it back, to see her laughing. Her face was interesting, her features fine, her eyes bright, yet the sum of them stopped short of classical beauty. Striking. That was a better word. But in a quiet way. There was nothing ostentatious about her. He liked the way her hair seemed to have a mind of its own, stray curls breaking away from her attempts to drag them into submission in a chignon. He imagined she herself was like her hair, reined in, but wanting to break out. Then he pushed the thought away. She was from another class. Well educated. Refined. Probably wealthy, judging by the cut and fabric of her clothes. Everything he was not. And besides, what was he doing thinking about a woman anyway?

He turned onto his side, trying to conjure up a picture of what Australia might be like, but his imagination failed him. Counting kangaroos was no more effective than counting sheep. He had been sleeping badly since he came on board. He couldn't blame the lads from Manchester. Tonight's game was an exception: while they were boisterous and annoying in the mornings, with their mindless banter and corny jokes, most nights they stayed in the bar until late, then slept like the dead, not even snoring. When he did manage to sleep, he dreamt of the war, his sleep troubled by the rattle of gunfire, the pounding of shellfire and the smell of sulphur. And the corpses. Everywhere the corpses. Limbs torn off, faces obliterated, bodies crushed. And every dead body he saw on the battlefields of his dreams had the face of his brother. He woke in a sweat, fearful to sleep again. Before dawn, he climbed down from his bunk and pounded the decks in a pointless circuit then stripped off and swam up and down the salt-water pool in the dark.

As the voyage progressed down the west coast of Africa the sea calmed and the sun warmed the decks. The public rooms were lively and crowded again. When the ship eventually docked at Cape Town, Elizabeth stood on the upper deck, looking at Table Mountain. She felt the warmth of the sun on her cheeks. The pallor of Northport had given way to a healthy glow in her complexion from all the sea air.

The deck was crowded with people enjoying the view as they waited to disembark. She noticed the man she and Mrs Briars had met over tea. He was standing alone looking ashore. Since that afternoon, she had not seen him again.

She thought it strange, because as huge as the Historic was, it was hard not to keep seeing the same people on board. Perhaps he had been avoiding her? On impulse she decided to speak to him now.

'More impressive than the Pier Head isn't it?'

He started in surprise. 'Aye, it is that.'

'The mountain certainly lives up to its name.'

He looked at her with a mixture of interest, mistrust and shyness. 'Why? What's it called?'

'Table Mountain. And it does look like a big flat table, sitting there between the sea and the sky.'

'Aye it does that.' He looked away, as though ending the casual exchange but then, when she remained standing beside him, he nodded towards the crowd of people waiting on the lower deck. 'Not joining your friend then?'

'She's not my friend.'

He turned to look at her. 'Not your cup of tea, eh?'

She smiled. 'Is it that obvious? Three weeks of sharing a cabin with that insufferable woman would have tried the patience of a saint, let alone me.'

'Just have to hope her replacement will be an improvement.'

'There'll be no replacement. The purser's just told me I'll have the cabin to myself for the rest of the voyage.'

'Lap of luxury eh, Miss? I'm sorry I can't remember what yer name is? I were that keen on getting away from your cabin mate.'

Elizabeth stretched out her hand to him. 'Elizabeth Morton, Mr Winterbourne.'

He looked embarrassed. 'I feel really bad now, Miss Morton. You must think me quite rude not to have remembered yer name when you've done me the honour of remembering mine.'

'Not at all. I've a memory for names and in your place I'd have run a mile to escape from Mrs Briars – especially when she kept getting your name wrong. Unfortunately I was stuck with her! I was sorely tempted to sleep on deck under the stars to escape her! It took her at least week to stop calling me Miss Milton! And she was very rude to you. I'm sorry.'

'No need to apologise for 'er.'

'Are you travelling with Mrs Winterbourne?'

'There isn't one. No, I'm sharing a cabin with three brothers from Manchester. They're all right and leave me alone, which suits me. I'm not one for conversation.'

'I'm sorry. I didn't mean…'

'No, Miss Morton. I don't mean you.'

'So are you going ashore for a while?'

'Mebbe later, once the crowds 'ave gone. I were thinking to enjoy the peace and quiet on board for a bit. To be honest I'm a bit bothered that when I stand on dry land again I might fall over after being so long on board.' He adopted the gait of a sailor and started to rock slightly from foot to foot.

Elizabeth laughed and realised it was the first time she had felt light hearted since leaving Trevelyan House. She said, 'I was keen to disembark and have a look around, until I realised that if I did, Mrs Briars intended to wrap me in the bosom of her family and I might never have escaped!'

'I can see why that wouldn't appeal much.'

She was about to speak again, but was overcome with shyness. It took her by surprise. It wasn't that she didn't know what to say, just that she was terribly self-conscious saying it. Her words seemed too big for her mouth and she was acutely aware of the sound of her own voice. She didn't want to look at him, turning towards the crowds pouring down the gangplank. What was wrong with her? She was like a tongue-tied schoolgirl.

Michael interpreted her turning away as a wish to be left alone. He raised his cap, mumbled a quick good morning and walked off down the deck.

She looked at his retreating back view. His rough tweed jacket was patched at the elbows and his cloth cap was threadbare and grubby at the front where his hand had grabbed at it over the years. He was wearing heavy boots that looked as though they had seen neither polish nor the attention of a cobbler in a long time. He was from another world and yet she liked him and wanted to get to know him better. She willed him to turn around and walk back to re-join her, but he disappeared into the queue waiting to disembark.

CHAPTER FOUR

AFTER CAPE TOWN

The day after they left Cape Town she saw him again. To avoid the other passengers, she had developed the habit of slipping up to the boat deck. It was out of bounds to everyone but the crew, but she discovered a spot behind one of the huge ventilator fans, where she would be out of sight. It was shaded from the sun by the adjacent lifeboats and she could lean back against the fan housing and watch the sea slipping by below.

The sound of the passengers was distant and muted as they played deck quoits, swam in the pool or promenaded round the deck below her. She was engrossed in a book when a shadow fell across the page. She looked up.

'Good morning, Miss Morton.'

'Mr Winterbourne. You've found me out! Trespassing in the crew-only zone.'

'Well if you're trespassing then so am I.'

'The crew can see you if they look this way from the Bridge. You need to sit down here out of the sight lines.'

'You've got it all worked out, Miss Morton.'

'I suppose that makes me a hardened criminal?'

'Aye, you could say that. But it makes me an accessory to yer crime.'

She smiled up at him, blinking in the sunlight and gestured to the deck beside her. Hesitating a moment, he sat down beside her.

There was an awkward silence until Elizabeth spoke. 'I love it up here. Away from the crowds and noise.'

Michael looked around them but said nothing. She wished she hadn't asked him to join her. 'Tell me something about yourself, Mr Winterbourne. Why are you going to Australia?'

'There's not much to tell. There wasn't much of a future for me back home and I heard Australia's a good place to start a new life, so I thought I'd try me luck. The government pays most of the fare as they need labour out there.'

'You said you have no family?' She hesitated, 'No wife?'

'No wife.'

'And parents?'

'Not any more.' His voice was harsh and the tone of his voice made it clear that he did not want to explain further. She decided not to push him. They lapsed into silence again, then he gestured towards the book that lay open on her lap.

'What're you reading?'

'*Wuthering Heights*.'

'What do you think to Emily Bronte?'

She looked at him in surprise.

'Aye. I've read it.' His voice was cold and Elizabeth realised he must be think her no better than Mrs Briars: a snob who assumed a miner must be uneducated and ill mannered. The words stumbled out of her mouth as she hurried to speak and to cover any unintended offence.

'I first read it years ago when I was at school. I've just finished re-reading *Jane Eyre*. But I thought she was a bit of a prig.'

'Catherine Earnshaw more to yer taste?'

'No. Stupid girl. I can't imagine what possessed her to marry Edgar Linton when she was so in love with Heathcliff.'

'You like Heathcliff then?'

'Gosh no. He's positively evil. Yet when I was a girl I thought him the most romantic character.'

'A bit too rough and ready for you, eh, Miss Morton?'

'Not at all. He's a cruel man. Not my idea of a romantic hero at all.'

'I dare say you're right. But then I doubt I've read as many books as you.'

He looked away, appearing distracted, bored even. Elizabeth was keen not to end the conversation so abruptly this time.

'You like books?'

'Aye. Though I expect yer friend from Cape Town thought I couldn't even read.'

'Mrs Briars may think she has a superior education, but she's an ignorant old… Sorry. I shouldn't speak that way.' She smiled. 'She caught me reading *Sons and Lovers* and told me reading it would corrupt me.'

'And have ye been corrupted?' he smiled.

She laughed. 'Actually I was moved. I've never read anything like it before. Brutally honest. Painful. What do you like to read?'

'Anything as comes my way. I suppose it were being deprived of books for so long. They taught us well enough at the local school. The mining company saw to that. Believed in good works and education. God knows why, when it were no use to most of us as went underground. We had no books at home apart from the Bible. I got into reading in the War. My commanding officer had been studying Classics at Oxford University when the war started. Read all the time. Shells going off all around and he kept his head buried in his book.'

'When he was supposed to be fighting?'

He smiled and rolled a cigarette. 'We didn't do much fighting. Not where we were. None at all really. We sat around until it were time to go and dig a big hole in the ground, then we'd sit around again waiting to be told where and when to dig another big hole. We talked and smoked, wrote letters back to Blighty and read the ones we were lucky enough to get.'

He looked thoughtful and she could see he was mentally back there. He carried on speaking, drawing on his cigarette. 'He were called Rockhill - Greville Rockhill. He weren't like the rest of us. All he ever wanted to do was study. Some of his books was in Latin and Greek, but he loved novels too. Dickens, Trollope, Henry James. Used to get a few books sent every week. I don't know how he pulled it off – must have 'ad a mate or a relative in the War Office. When he were done, he'd pass the books on to the rest of us and I always got first crack.' He drew on his cigarette again, watching the smoke curl in the air. 'He didn't make it.'

'He died?'

'Aye. Day after he were killed another parcel of books came. They kept us going till the War were over – it were only five or six weeks more, though we didn't know that then. I took some of his books back to Blighty. Read 'em again and again. Trouble with books is they put ideas in yer head and make it hard to put up with what you've got.'

'What do you mean?'

'When I got back to the dale, I wanted more. I wanted to see something of the world.'

'So what do you want, Mr Winterbourne? What are you looking for?' She leaned forward as she spoke and he moved away slightly and looked out to sea, frowning.

'I'm not sure as I know any more, Miss. The world doesn't seem quite so enticing once you're out in it.'

'Feeling homesick? Do you want to go back?' She raised an eyebrow.

'I'll never go back. What's done is done.'

'You make it sound as though you've done something terrible! Are you running away, Mr Winterbourne?'

He frowned and his eyes darkened. 'Mebbe I am.'

She folded her hands in her lap and looked up at him earnestly. 'Maybe we all are. The whole ship! I can't imagine what else would possess so many people to give up everything, pack their bags and sail across the oceans into the unknown. Not if they didn't have to.'

'They? Or you?'

'Me too, I suppose. I certainly never planned to do this. I didn't lie awake dreaming of seeing the world or going to Australia. I'd have been happy to see my days out in Northport.'

'So why are you here?'

There was a tremor in her voice when she spoke. 'My father needs me. My mother's dead and he misses her. There's nothing for me at home. Not any more.'

'What'll you do in Australia?'

'Try and make the best of things I suppose. I play the violin and hope to make a living teaching it and I'll keep house for my father of course. Who knows? Maybe one day we'll have saved enough to return to England?'

'To go back?'

'Yes. Why not?'

'It's never right to go backwards. You have to keep moving forward in this life. To keep going. To move on.'

She smiled at him. 'Quite the philosopher, Mr Winterbourne?'

'I'm just a survivor is all.'

They fell into an awkward silence and then Elizabeth picked up the threads of their conversation again. 'So, what book are you reading now?'

'*The War of the Worlds*. You'd think I'd have had enough of wars wouldn't you? But it were on the shelf in the general room so I thought I'd give it a go.'

'Any good?'

'Aye. It's keeping me gripped enough. And defeating a

bunch of alien beings is a change from taking on the Kaiser.'

'I don't know how I'd exist without books.'

'Me neither.'

'Was the War very hard for you?'

He looked thoughtful. 'I had an easy war compared to most. Never went over the top. Had plenty of mates that did. Being a miner, they reckoned to keep me digging underground and that kept me out of the worst of it.'

'I'm sure it was still terrible for you. I can't imagine what it must have been like over there. Did you lose many friends, apart from the officer you told me about?'

'We lost nine men from our little village. That left a big hole. One of 'em was me cousin, Joe. He were me best pal.' Before she could reply he added, 'What about you? Any of your family?'

'My father was involved in planning troop movements. All done from a desk in Liverpool. I have no brothers. But I did lose someone close to me.'

'I'm sorry to hear that.'

'We were engaged to be married but he never came home.'

'Where did he die?'

'In the Ypres Salient. On the Menin Road. His name was Stephen. And do you know I can't even remember what he looked like any more. Isn't that terrible?'

'Mebbe it's how we get over things. How we're able to carry on when summat like that hits us.' As he spoke the words he wished them to be true in his own case but feared they were not.

She carried on. 'I feel guilty. You know. That I don't think about him all the time. Some days I don't even think of him at all. The time we spent together seems unreal, as if I dreamt it rather than lived it. It was another world we lived in before the war, wasn't it? It's all different now and I find it hard to be the person I was before or even to understand the person I was before. Stephen is now just a name carved on a war memorial.' She hesitated, then stretched her hands out in front of her as though appraising them. 'I stopped wearing his ring. It didn't feel right. I gave it back to his mother. It had belonged to his grandmother and I thought his mother should have it back. I don't know why I'm telling you all this. It's like I'm betraying him and yet… I don't really know who he was any more. Am I making any sense?'

He sighed. 'You are and I know exactly what you mean. The chaps I grew up with who died over there are like ghosts, like shadows. Hard to believe they existed. Even me cousin Joe. We were in the same company - signed up together. He caught it early on. Shrapnel. I didn't know it were him at first when I carried him on a stretcher, he were that cut up. But he knew it were me. He must have recognised me voice because he grabbed me hand and said me name as we was lifting him into the ambulance. Died before we got him to the hospital tent. At least I were there with him I suppose. Even though I couldn't do a bloody thing about it.' He banged his fist on his knee. 'I'm sorry. I didn't mean to swear in front of you.'

'When I think about Stephen dying, I like to think that if it wasn't instant then someone like you or some kind nurse held his hand as he died. I don't suppose that's what happened, but it makes me feel better to imagine it.'

'I know what you mean about the war changing everything.' He was gazing out at the water in front of them. 'I were engaged to be married too. We were that close afore the war. Did everything together. We'd known each other since we were bairns. But when I came back after Armistice it were different. We still got on and all. But different things were important to us. She wanted it all to be the same and I knew it couldn't be. She wanted to stay put and I wanted to see the world.' He laughed drily. 'Sounds stupid I know. Now that I'm on me way to t'other side of the world I'm not so sure I want to be.'

'What happened to her?'

He paused for a moment, weighing his words then said, 'She decided she didn't want to be married to me after all.'

'I'm sorry.'

'Don't be. We'd grown apart. She probably saw that afore I did. You women are much quicker at seeing that sort of thing. And anyway I wanted to get out of the mine and the dale and she'd never have gone along with that.'

'And Australia?'

'Not sure it's about Australia so much as about just getting away. I'd as easily 'ave gone to America. There's so much more in the world than I'd ever get to see in our little village. I don't know what I'm looking for. Just reckon there has to be more. How about you?'

'The last thing I wanted was to leave Northport. My life was calm - every day the same and I liked that. But now everything's changed. I feel a bit lost. I don't know. Perhaps I'm like your fiancée – wanting to keep things the way they've always been.'

'Aye but they're not the way they've always been. They can never be like that again. Not since the war.'

'I know. But that doesn't mean I'm happy about it.'

They were silent for a few moments as he lit another cigarette.

'How did your friend Greville die? If you weren't in the fighting?'

'He took a stray bullet. From a sniper. It were quiet. No gunfire. He just fell down in front of me. One minute walking along and the next lying there dead. Got it straight through the heart. It were a bit of a fluke.'

'How dreadful.' But as she spoke, she saw he was already withdrawing from her. His face was pale and pained and he scrambled to his feet, throwing his cigarette into the ocean.

'Have to go now. Good morning Miss.' And he disappeared behind the bulkhead.

She tried to carry on reading but her heart wasn't in it. When she pictured Mr Heathcliff, his features were those of Michael Winterbourne: the dark, heavy hair, the intense brown eyes, the ill-concealed unhappiness. Pull yourself together, Elizabeth she told herself, but there was something about the man that aroused her curiosity and drew her in. His manner was sometimes abrupt and distant and yet she felt a kind of intimacy between them that went beyond the words they exchanged.

The next day, he appeared again, standing in front of her as she leaned back against the ventilation fan on the boat deck.

'I told you, Mr Winterbourne, you'll give me away if you stand there like that and I shall be banished below by the captain. Or thrown to the fishes! Come and sit down out of sight!'

He took his place next to her, his long legs in their brown corduroy trousers, stretched out in front of him. He fished in his pocket for his tobacco tin and she watched fascinated as he rolled a cigarette. He said 'You want one? I'm afraid they're just hand rolled.'

She didn't know any women who smoked but on a whim she said, 'Yes please! I've never tried before. I've always secretly wanted to.'

'I'm not sure that would be such a good idea if you've not tried before. This is strong baccie. You'd be better off with a ready rolled one – and mebbe one of those long fancy cigarette holders.'

'Not at all!'

'First time I tried smoking I were sick as a dog. Nine years old. Our Joe dared me I couldn't smoke two in a row. I coughed and spluttered and then I were sick. Me Mam gave me a right good hiding when she found out.' He grinned at her and she fancied she could see the mischievous nine year old in his eyes.

'It's a wonder you ever took it up then.'

'Hard not to. Everyone smokes in the mines. First thing you do when you come up from below is light up. Then in the trenches all the men smoked. Passed the time. Calmed the jitters.'

At that moment calming the jitters seemed an appealing prospect to Elizabeth. Why did his proximity make her nervous? But in a good way, like opening a present when she was a child.

'Go on. Let me try,' she said.

He moved closer and handed her the unlit cigarette he had just rolled and she placed it between her lips. She could feel his leg against hers as he leaned towards her, cupping his hands over the match. She bent to take the light, steadying his hand with hers as she guided it to the end of the cigarette. His skin was warm and she wanted to keep her hand there, but the moment was destroyed as her throat filled with smoke and she began to cough and splutter.

'Don't say I didn't warn you!' He was laughing at her as she handed the cigarette back. His face changed when he laughed – the little worried lines that were usually etched around his eyes and mouth relaxed and his face was open and happy. She expected him to throw the cigarette overboard but he put it to his own mouth and inhaled. She blushed at the thought of the thin paper moistened from her own lips now resting between his. It seemed a curiously intimate thing for him to do.

They sat in silence, as her breathing gradually returned to normal and he puffed away contentedly on his roll-up.

'Still with Cathy on the Yorkshire Moors then?' He nodded towards the book on her lap.

'No. I finished it. But I wish I were. I mean I wish I were there really, instead of here amidst all this endless ocean. I long to feel grass under my feet again. Solid ground.'

'Aye me too. The best part of the sea is the bit that's next to the land. All this empty space gives me the willies. It's as though we're at the end of the earth and over the horizon there we might just sail off the edge and fall into space.'

'So you're a flat earther are you, Mr Winterbourne?'

He smiled. 'If I am, I reckon this voyage'll cure that!'

'If you don't like the open sea, what do you like?'

He didn't hesitate. 'The fresh air on me face and the smell of cut grass in summer. The sound of a curlew flying over the dale. Burning leaves on an autumn afternoon. Catching a trout in a stream as clear as glass, me bare feet in the cold water and smooth stones under them. Me mam's lamb hotpot when times are good and her vegetable soups when they're not. And me old dog. I s'pose I sound right daft don't I? But I do miss the dale. Like I never thought I would.'

'You lived there all your life. It's understandable.'

'What about you? What do you like?'

'Let me think… the sound of the conductor tapping his baton to ready the orchestra and that little tremor of silent excitement and anticipation that ripples up inside you as you wait for the first chord to sound and the concert to begin.'

'You like music then?'

'Don't you?'

'I don't know anything about that kind of music. I grew up with just hymns in chapel. I've never been to a concert or heard an orchestra. Only the music hall. That were alright – but there's no conductor tapping his baton and no one waits in silence for it to start. More like as they're all yelling for the performers to get on with it. I like the idea of a classical concert though. A proper one.'

'Then you must go! When you get to Sydney.'

'That kind of music isn't for the likes of me.'

'It's for everyone. For anyone.'

'I'd be uncomfortable.'

'Then come with me!' As the words spilled out of her mouth she felt embarrassed but excited, fearful she had overstepped the mark, but already anticipating the pleasure of sitting in a darkened auditorium beside him. 'I mean, only if you'd like to... I could explain what the music was about. Just to get you over the first time. Then you'd be relaxed enough to go on your own.'

'In that case, I'll have to do the same for you.'

'What do you mean?'

'Take you to a music hall or take you fishing.'

'I'd love that!' Her face lit up.

Then Michael's face clouded over. She sensed him withdraw from her. She was confused by him: one moment enthusiastic, open and warm, making her feel privileged as his confidante, and the next closed down and silent, brooding. She supposed it was the War. So many men were like that these days.

The next day, when she went into the dining room for lunch, he was sitting alone.

'Mr Winterbourne, may I join you?'

The man got to his feet and nodded at the seat opposite him.

'I hate eating alone, don't you?' she said.

He shrugged and she wished she'd sat elsewhere. Her words were not even true. She preferred eating alone to making small talk with other passengers. The fact was she wanted to be with him. Just as she was debating whether to apologise and excuse herself with a forgotten item in her cabin, he looked up at her with a shy grin.

'Truth is, Miss Morton, I find eating in 'ere a bit of an ordeal. I were used to eating at home with me family or out of a mess tin in the army and at the pit. I find all this a bit much. Having to mind me Ps and Qs.' He gestured around the room. 'S'pose you're used to it?'

'Not really. I'd never dined in a vast room like this one.' She looked around them at the long lines of wooden tables with the ranks of swivelling polished wooden chairs, each fixed to the floor. 'Not since school. We had long tables there, but I thought I'd left all that behind me!'

He studied her face for a moment. 'Posh school was it?'

She blushed. 'I wouldn't say that exactly. But it was a private school. My father was quite wealthy.' She looked down at her lap. 'Not any more though.'

'It were the village school for me. And then just till I were 11. Then I went to work washing the ore. No time for schooling after that.'

'Gosh, that's awfully young to be working.'

'That were the way. We all did it.'

'Did you mind?'

'Didn't think about it. Me Da were in the mines too and his father afore him. It were the same for the whole village. And there's worse work.'

He told her about his life in the mine and his childhood in the dale. She could not imagine a life more different from her own. As he spoke, his face relaxed and he became less laconic. It was as though the dale was in front of his eyes and he was watching the men trundling into the mine.

'Was it very beautiful up there? When you spoke about it yesterday you seemed to miss it very much? It must have been hard to leave?'

'Not so hard. Not leaving the mine. But yes the dale is beautiful. Quiet. You could walk all day and never see another soul. It's wild and when you're there, you know it's been the same for centuries.'

'But not the mining?'

'That too. They've been digging the lead out of those hills for hundreds of years. Even the Romans mined there.'

He talked on and she listened, transfixed by words and his face. But she felt he was holding back, slightly guarded, almost suspicious. Yet when their eyes met it was as if she could see right inside him. She liked his face: the still boyish features and the bright eyes and the way his hair was always rumpled as though he'd just got out of bed. She wanted to run her hands through it. She surprised herself with the way she sought out his company: she had never been so forward with any man and had certainly never met or spoken to a working man like him. But it felt right being there with him.

Lying in her cabin that night she thought of him again. What was she doing? Where was this leading? So much for the promise she had made to herself to close herself off from other people? And what future was there in this? But then she told herself that they would soon be in Sydney and she would never see him again, so what harm was there in spending time with him while they were stuck on the ship? Avoiding him in this confined space was futile. Once they landed, they could say their farewells and go their separate ways.

The next morning she woke from a nightmare about Dawson. The sheets were drenched with sweat and she ran into the bathroom and threw up. She decided, rather than facing the world, to stay in her cabin and have her meals brought to her by the steward. But it was worse. Stuck in the small space she felt cornered and trapped and every time she closed her eyes Dawson's face was looking down at her. She went up on deck to get some air.

Returning to her cabin, as she rounded a corner, she saw Winterbourne ahead of her in the corridor, engaged in conversation with a woman. She stopped in her tracks and slid into the recess of the door to the empty smoke room. Leaning out cautiously, she saw him place a hand on the woman's shoulder – Betty, one of the stewardesses. Elizabeth watched him pull the woman towards him and hold her for a moment in his arms, her head on his shoulder as his hand stroked her hair. Then the pair pulled apart and after a few words that Elizabeth couldn't make out, the stewardess went off up the passageway. Elizabeth stood motionless in the doorway, trying to take in what she had seen and the effect it had had on her.

Back in her cabin, she tried to sort out the thoughts that were racing through her head. Why should she be surprised? Betty was an attractive woman and Winterbourne was a free agent. But she felt a sense of loss as the emotion welled up inside her. She had thought him an ally and believed he was becoming a friend: the only person on the ship with whom she had willingly spent time. Betrayed. Not just that. Jealous too. She wished it was on her shoulder that he had placed his hand and that it was she who had been folded into his arms. She thought about how it would feel to have those arms around her, to bury her head in the warmth of his chest; to feel his hands upon her hair. Sitting there on the bunk, she clenched her firsts and smashed them down into the mattress, a little cry escaping from her lips. All those intentions to be strong, to be hard, to be brave, had abandoned her. She was alone, lonely and felt rejected.

He had made no advances, had made no promises, had behaved impeccably. She could not blame him for seeking the company of an attractive woman. No doubt he felt more at home with a woman nearer his own social class. She cursed her naivety and stupidity and swore to avoid him for the rest of the voyage. She got up and looked at her reflection in the mirror. You silly goose. Fancy falling for a fellow like that! You've no business to fall for anybody. Not any more. Not after what's happened to you. Stop thinking about him. Focus on the future. On Father. On your new life together.

She abandoned her daily expedition to the boat deck, preferring to go to the ladies' saloon or stay in her cabin. At mealtimes, she waited until the dining room was almost empty and he had already finished. Whenever she reminded herself of her stupid suggestion that she take him to an orchestral concert she cringed and wondered what must he think of her?

As the Historic sailed into Sydney Harbour she couldn't help but feel uplifted. The panorama in front of her was so beautiful: the clear blue sky mirrored in the crystal water, the myriad inlets and outcrops of the natural harbour, the rich green vegetation and the impressive growing development of the city spreading inland from the water's edge. As the ship docked at the quayside, she searched in vain for her father's face among the crowds, then remembered he would have had no idea she would be on this particular ship or arriving so soon after his letter.

She felt a hand on her sleeve and jumped in surprise.

'Miss Morton, have you been ill? I've not seen you in a while. I hope it weren't the ciggie I gave you the other day?'

She tried to adopt an aloof expression and her coolest tone of voice. 'I've been quite well, thank you.'

He looked crushed but doffed his cap and stretched out his hand to her. 'All the best for the future, Miss Morton. It were a pleasure to meet you.'

She prayed she wasn't blushing and tried to repress the little leap her heart gave. But she knew he was courting the stewardess. There was a bitter taste in her mouth as she forced herself to reply, ignoring his outstretched hand by pretending not to see it.

'You too, Mr Winterbourne. May you find what you're looking for in Australia.'

He hesitated, as though about to say something else, but Elizabeth had already turned away and started to walk towards the gangway. He looked after her, a frown creasing his brow.

'Fancied your chances with the posh lady did you, Mick?' One of the Mancunians slapped him on the back and laughed loudly. His brothers joined them.

'You daft lad! A bit of class like her 'd 'ave nowt to do with the likes of you, mate!'

'Eee! - you're soft on 'er aren't you?' the first one punched his arm playfully.

The oldest brother pulled the peak of Michael's cap down over his eyes. 'Come on don't deny it! We've seen you, Mick. All doe-eyed whenever she's in view. Can't say as I blame you though, She's a bit of alright. But out of your class, mate!'

'Alright, lads. You've had yer fun. Now I'm getting off this heap of steel and getting me mug round a pint of Australia's finest. And I'll not be sad to see the back of you lot!' And with that Michael knocked the cap off the first of the brothers and made his way through the departing throng, trying to force a smile through the hurt that he was feeling.

CHAPTER FIVE

BAD NEWS

The Rocks, Sydney

The houses were gathered close together in rows as if retreating from the advance of the ships in the harbour opposite. The buildings were at least a hundred years old and looked rather the worse for the passage of time, their shabby paintwork highlighted in the Sydney sunshine. A girl sat on the steps of the first house, nursing a scraggy ginger kitten in her lap. Ignoring Elizabeth's approach, she stroked the matted fur and whispered words of affection into the creature's ear.

'He looks a friendly little cat. Does he have a name?' said Elizabeth.

The girl looked up, her eyes blinking into the sun, weighing up this uninvited intruder into her feline communion.

'Not yet. I haven't decided. I might call him Fluff. Or maybe Pickles.'

'Pickles is a good name.'

'Yes we had one before called Pickles, belonging to my brother, but he died.'

Elizabeth hoped she was referring to the cat and not the brother.

'That's sad - cats don't live as long as people. Even though they're meant to have nine lives.' She set her case down on the pavement and looked past the little girl at the façade of the house. The front door was open but the interior was dark and she could not see past a small entrance lobby. There were a few scruffy daisies in a pot on one of the window-ledges, a half-hearted attempt at beautification. A rug hung from one of the upstairs windows, presumably after a good beating. These small signs of domesticity and the clean, if plain, attire of the girl lent an air of respectability to what otherwise was a very run-down street. Elizabeth noticed all the other houses had their curtains closed despite the late hour of the morning.

'Is this Mrs Little's boarding house?'

'Are you looking for a room?' the little girl replied.

A portly woman materialised on the doorstep, arms akimbo. 'That's enough, Molly. Go and fetch the bread like I told you and stop fussing over that cat.' Then nodding at Elizabeth, 'Are you looking for a room?' She eyed her up and down in an unapologetic appraisal.

'I believe my father is staying here? Mr William Morton.'

The woman smoothed her hands over her apron and frowned. She stepped back towards the doorway and said, 'Best come inside, Miss Morton.'

Elizabeth picked up her case and followed her inside, squinting to see in the sudden gloom. The woman led the way to the rear of the building and into a small, sparsely furnished parlour.

'We didn't expect you so soon, Miss Morton - please sit down. You must be tired after your voyage. Can I bring you some tea?'

'That would be very kind. But is my father here now? May I see him?'

The woman frowned again and hesitated, then grasped the edge of her apron and began to squeeze it through her hands, as if it were a cloth she were wringing out.

'There's no easy way to say this and sure enough no easy way to hear it. It's bad news I'm afraid.'

Elizabeth cried out. 'What's happened? Is Father ill? Has he been hurt? Where is he? Let me see him.' She moved towards the woman who stepped backwards towards the doorway, still clutching at her apron.

'Miss, I'm truly sorry. He's dead.... It was just a week ago it happened.' She moved towards Elizabeth and took her by the arm and eased her into a chair.

Elizabeth could not take the words in. The room spun in front of her and her heart began to pound a rhythm in her chest. She took several large gulps of air.

'That can't be true. He wrote and asked me to join him. The ship only got in this morning. He can't be dead.'

'I'm sorry. He was such a nice gentleman. Better class than we're used to here. They tend to be sailors or travellers or folk from the outback in town for a few days. He was a nice man. A bit down on his luck you might say, but a gentleman all the same. Very polite.'

Elizabeth started to sob.

'You have a good cry, Miss. Let it all out. When Molly gets back I'll have her make up a bed for you and you can get some sleep.'

'What happened? He was in good health and not an old man - he was only fifty-five. Was it an accident?'

'Seems that way. He went out one evening and didn't come back. He told us he was going for a couple of drinks and would be back around midnight. There's a place he went to near here that's not that particular about the licensing laws. The front door's never locked. I wait up, if I know my guests won't be too late, and make them a hot drink. That night he told me not to wait up. So it wasn't till the next morning that I realised he hadn't come home at all. Don't get me wrong, Miss, but I think he may have had a few jars too many. Liked the drink he did Mr Morton - but always took

71

it very well. There was never a peep of trouble from him. He was having some hard times lately - not having much luck and he sometimes had a few too many - to console himself I suppose. He was walking back in the early hours and must have lost his footing and fell into the Harbour. His body was found just two days ago. I'm sorry Miss.'

'What am I to do? I've nowhere to go and no one else here. Oh, Father, what have you done?' She started to sob again, her body shaking in shock. Then she looked up at her hostess and said, 'You say he was found just two days ago? Where is he? Has he been buried yet?'

'Funeral's tomorrow. His friend Mr Kidd has arranged it. My husband and I will be going of course. Now you just wait there while I get you a nice cup of tea and that's Molly I hear now - so we'll have that bed ready in no time.'

The woman left the room. Elizabeth leaned back, rubbing her eyes with her sodden handkerchief. Never for a moment had she entertained the thought that her father would not be here, that she would never see him again, that she would be alone on the far side of the world.

She tried to recall his voice, always gentle, but resonant and deep. The harder she struggled to recreate it in her head, the fainter it grew. What had their last conversation been, goodbyes apart? What had they ever talked about? There had been a strong bond between them and a teasing affection, but now that she had lost him forever, she couldn't remember any specific conversation: the words he used; the things he teased her about. It was just a blur, fading in the force of the unbearable truth that she was never going to see him again.

Mrs Little returned with a tray of tea. 'Get this down you. It won't make you feel better but it might calm you a little - I've put plenty of sugar in — and a drop of the hard stuff - it's supposed to be good for a shock, Miss Morton.'

'Please call me Elizabeth, Mrs Little.' There was no one else now who could address her by her given name.

'Then you must call me Peggy - everyone does. We don't stand on ceremony in Australia. I'm sorry it's such a rotten start for you. This is a wonderful country, even though you may not believe me right now and I wouldn't blame you. I've been here twenty years and never regret coming. We came out just after we married. He was a coal-miner so we had ten years in the coalfields over at Lithgow - but we wanted to live in Sydney. I've seven children - Molly's the youngest and the only girl - and we thought the city would be a better place for them. We didn't want our boys going down the pits. But it didn't make any difference. My eldest two, Bobby and Matt, they went to work in South Australia in the opal mines. I haven't seen them in two years, but I'm hoping they'll be back once they've made a few quid. Listen to me – once I get started I find it hard to stop.'

'I like you talking. It stops me thinking.'

'Ah, bless you, my lovely.' The woman flung her arms about Elizabeth, crushing her to her ample bosom. 'Excuse me, dearie, but you looked like you need a good hug.'

'Thank you. I've just realised I don't even have a photograph of Father. I can't even remember what he looked like.'

'You will remember. You're still in shock.'

'And his voice. I can't remember how it sounded. Or anything he ever said to me. We used to talk about music and books. But I can't remember anything personal.'

'That's grief. It will all come back to you soon and you'll have some very happy memories. I promise you.'

'But I'm angry with him, Peggy.' She looked up at her hostess. 'Does that shock you? I'm bloody angry. I've come all this way and I needed him to be here for me. He's abandoned me. What am I going to do? He didn't even have the grace to wait till I got here, before going and dying.'

Peggy rubbed her shoulder gently, but said nothing.

'You think I'm selfish don't you? But if you knew the half of it! You'd understand why I'm mad. Why I feel justified in being angry, when I've travelled across the planet and he couldn't even hang on until I got here. He's let me down.'

'He talked about you often, Elizabeth. He showed me your photograph. Right proud of you he was. Told me you played the violin like an angel from heaven.'

'Did he?'

'He loved you very much, my dear. Now let's get you upstairs so you can rest up. Try and get a little sleep.'

The bedroom was small and sparsely furnished, but spotlessly clean, with painted wooden floorboards and a colourful quilt on the bed. Elizabeth lay down and closed her eyes, trying to submit to much-needed sleep.

After a couple of hours she admitted defeat. She washed her tear-stained face with the pitcher of cool water on the washstand and decided to take a walk. She thought more clearly when moving about, frequently taking long walks on the hills above Northport, when she wanted to work through a problem or coax out an idea.

The house was quiet and she met no one as she left through the wide-open front door. The street was bathed in sunlight. Although the day was cool, she felt the sun on her head and shoulders. She would need to buy herself a wide-brimmed hat or she would end up looking like a field worker. This reminded her of her situation. She had so little money. Finding work must be a priority but how much demand was there for music teachers?

She walked through the city, along the grid of streets with their large stores and solemn looking buildings. The roads sounded so English, named for faraway English towns, politicians and royalty. It made her desperately homesick. She walked past the Circular Quay, with a tide of humanity pouring on and off the ferryboats to cross the Harbour. The blue of the sky and the sea was so different from grey and cloudy Liverpool, but she would have given anything to be back there.

Eventually she reached a rocky promontory and stopped to look out at the panorama before her. A small island with some kind of fortified building interrupted the channel in front of the green sweep of gardens surrounding the Governor General's residence. The beauty of the scene made her feel even more isolated. If only she were sharing this with her father; instead tomorrow she must bury him. That would mean meeting Mr Jack Kidd and working out how she would repay him the cost of the funeral.

Never in her life had she felt so utterly lonely. Unable to help herself, she leaned against the stone parapet overlooking the Harbour and gave in to the tears. They were silent but flowed like a river, blinding her to the view.

She didn't know how long Michael Winterbourne had been standing there. She just became aware of his presence beside her, leaning against the wall, looking at her. Embarrassed and irritated that her privacy had been invaded, she searched in her pockets for her handkerchief. He anticipated the need and pressed a clean white handkerchief into her hand. She mumbled her thanks and dabbed at her face, gratefully.

'I'm sorry. I didn't realise there was anyone there. I'm feeling much better now. I'm sorry to have ruined your handkerchief.'

'That's what it's for, Miss Morton.' He smiled, but his eyes remained unchanged. They stayed fixed on her, lit by concern, but wary.

Then he turned his head to look out towards the island. She was glad to see him again. Her hurt and embarrassment about misconstruing his intentions towards her seemed insignificant when weighed against the fact that he was here now, handkerchief at the ready.

'I didn't expect to see you again. I didn't think to see anyone here. I thought I would be undisturbed.'

'I suppose that's a way of telling me what I should be

doing now.' He pushed himself off the wall and started to move away. He was so prickly, so quick to take offence.

She tried to smile. 'No. Please. I didn't mean that. Don't go. And I still have your handkerchief.'

He looked at her for a moment then said 'Would you like to walk for a while? I find me troubles usually feel better when I walk them off. I sometimes walk for miles. It's good medicine.'

'Yes. That was what I was trying to do. To walk through my problems - but this time it doesn't seem to be working. The problem is just too big.'

'Then you could try sharing it.'

She thought of Betty. Surely he'd be wanting to spend time with the stewardess before the Historic sailed again. 'I'm sure you've better things to do than that?'

For a moment she thought he looked hurt, then told herself it was her overactive imagination again, misconstruing things.

'I haven't and I'd like to walk with you. Unless you don't want me to?'

'Thank you. You're very kind. Let's walk.'

And so they walked beside the wattle trees and she told him about the death of her father. He listened with concentration and she felt again as she had when they sat on the boat deck, that there was a special bond between them. She allowed herself to forget the stewardess and accept his presence gratefully as a sympathetic ear. There was something about the way he listened that made her feel as though she was the only person in the world when she spoke to him. But then some men had that ability. A kind of charm. It didn't mean anything.

Then she told him she couldn't bear to think of life now with neither parent. She skated over her estrangement from her sister, but spilled out how desolate her father's death made her. The telling came easy, and he listened intently but without comment or question, walking slowly in step beside her. She said nothing of Charles Dawson and the event that had precipitated her departure, nor of the arrangement William Morton had made with Jack Kidd and how she had to extricate herself from it as well as find the means to repay him for the funeral.

They rounded the curve of a cove and reached some sandstone rocks at the end of the garden where the path ended. There were stairs and a bench built into the rock and without indicating their intent to do so, they sat down, side by side.

'I'm sorry to burden you with my troubles. You must think me awful. Telling you all this when I barely know you.' Again, was she imagining a look of hurt in his eyes?

'You're not burdening me and I don't think you're awful. And right now it looks like I'm one of the few people you know in Australia and you're the only person I've spoken to since we docked this morning. So we might as well be friends. What do you think? You could start by calling me Michael.' He smiled and this time the smile lit up his eyes as well, even if it failed to dispel their underlying sadness.

'Then call me Elizabeth. I'd be honoured and happy to be your friend, Michael.' She held out her hand. His grip was firm. His skin felt warm and she smiled at him, then looked away embarrassed, as she felt the intensity of his gaze.

Breathing slowly, she turned back to him, hoping that he would by now have dropped his eyes. But he hadn't. Again she looked away, uncomfortable, embarrassed. This must be what it felt like to be one of the fictitious women who fell under the spell of Rudy Valentino in the pictures. She could feel a blush rising up through her skin.

Instinctively she placed her hand on top of his where it rested between them on the stone seat. Just as quickly, she realised what she had done and withdrew it. He took her

77

hand back, enveloping it in both his own. He turned her hand over and cradling it in his, he bent his head and kissed her open palm.

She drew her hand away, afraid of the feelings that were sweeping through her and confused that in the midst of her grief for her father, she felt excited. The raw intimacy of what he had done shocked her, but thrilled her.

'I'm sorry. I shouldn't have done that. I couldn't help myself. I didn't mean to offend you' he said.

'It's all right. You've been very kind. I've said too much. You may be the only person I know here but I still hardly know you and I've been presumptuous in telling you so much. I've always been too open. Mother used to tell me that. I've told you half my life story. You instead have been more circumspect. You must think me very forward.'

'That I don't. It's my fault. I've not been honest with you. But I'm afraid if I tell you the truth about meself, you won't want to know me. After what I've done I don't expect anyone to think well of me.'

'I already know. I saw you.'

He twisted round in the seat and stared at her.

'What are you talking about? You saw what?'

'I wasn't spying on you. I promise. I just came upon you and I saw. I'm sorry. Look this is very embarrassing. I feel such a fool. That's why I was avoiding you. On the ship. The last few days.' The words tumbled out of her and he frowned, puzzled.

She said 'I didn't mean to say that. Oh what the heck? Why does it matter what you think of me? I've wasted enough of your time. I'd better go now.'

She jumped to her feet but he stretched out his hand and pulled her back down onto the seat beside him.

'What are you talking about? Mebbe I'm being very thick, but I just don't understand what yer saying.'

'You and that stewardess. I saw you.'

'Betty?'

She looked down at her lap where her hands were worrying away nervously at the fabric of his linen handkerchief.

He laughed and she turned towards him angrily. 'Yes laugh at me. I know you must think me a stupid fool. Did you tell her I invited you to come with me to a concert? Did you both have a good giggle at that?'

He frowned. 'Elizabeth, I don't know what you think you saw, but I can promise you there's nothing between me and Betty or any of the stewardesses on that ship – or any woman at all for that matter.'

'But you had her in your arms?' Her voice trailed away.

'Aye I gave her a bit of a hug. I were comforting her. Trying to cheer her up. Have you ever talked to Betty? Do you have any idea what her life is like? What she's bin through? Poor soul.'

'No.' Elizabeth's voice was barely a whisper. Her heart was banging against her ribs.

'She lost her husband in the war. He were killed in Mesopotamia. Buried out in Baghdad so she doesn't have a grave to visit. She's got five children under ten. The two eldest girls are being brought up by the nuns. Her two lads have been farmed out to her brother in Nottingham to bring up with his kids and her youngest is being cared for by her mother back in Liverpool. Poor Betty has to work on the ships to support the them all. She's a plucky woman.'

'I didn't know she was a widow. She wasn't wearing a wedding ring.'

'She'd not have her job if the shipping line knew she were a married woman. Widow or not. It's a tough old life for the likes of her and things would have been different if her husband had made it through the war. What price his sacrifice, eh? She'd told me as she knew I'd been at the Front. She needed a shoulder to cry on every now and then. You can't begrudge 'er that, Elizabeth. And there were absolutely nowt more between us. She's a full ten year older than me for starters.'

Elizabeth smiled. 'But she's a good looking woman.'

'I'll not deny that. But she's not a patch on you.'

She smiled up at him, feeling the happiness through her pain. She put her hand into his and as it folded around hers she felt safe, protected, better able to face the problems her father had presented her with. No longer alone.

And then she looked up into his eyes, frowning.

'So if it wasn't Betty, what did you mean when you said you hadn't been honest with me? You said if I knew, I wouldn't think well of you?'

He dropped his hold on her hand and his body stiffened. 'I did something that I'll never forgive meself for as long as I live and if you were to know you'd think differently of me and I couldn't bear that.'

'If you've made a mistake, you've clearly already suffered as a consequence. But you don't have to go on suffering for the rest of your life. No one should have to do that.'

'I should. I've destroyed me family and wrecked their future.' He stared at the ground beneath his feet and kicked at a pile of leaves, the gentleness of the mood between them replaced by awkwardness. The rapidity in which they had moved from strangers to confessors and, in his kissing of her palm, almost to lovers, embarrassed them now. As if by design, the sun had begun to sink in the sky, bringing a slight chill to remind them that this was indeed autumn.

She realised he didn't want to tell her more, but reluctant to let it go unresolved, she tried a different tack. 'Was it to do with the War?'

'No. It weren't the War.'

She could tell he wasn't going to take her further into his confidence and she felt hurt. They fell into silence. Elizabeth was the first to rise from the seat. She gathered her coat around her shoulders and turned to bid him farewell, taking refuge in formality.

'Thank you again for your kindness, Michael. You've helped me. I feel better able to face the funeral tomorrow.'

He took the proffered hand in a formal handshake, avoiding eye contact. 'I hope it won't be too painful for you tomorrow. I'll be thinking of you.'

'Thank you.'

They stood there awkwardly until she turned and started to walk away, heading back towards the waterfront pathway. She walked quickly, the tears brimming again. Then she heard him running after her and before she knew what was happening, he pulled her towards him and gathered her in to his chest, where he held her, against him. She buried her head in the roughness of his jacket. At last he spoke. 'I have to see you again.'

She nodded. 'Yes.'

'Tomorrow?'

'I have the funeral tomorrow morning.'

'I'll come with you. You shouldn't go through that alone.'

Elizabeth thought of the conversation she must have with Jack Kidd. She didn't want Michael witnessing that and hearing of her father's debts. Besides she had to explain to Kidd that her father's plan for their wedding would never be realised. She could not do that with Michael at her side.

'No. I want to be alone when I say my goodbyes to Father.'

'Then we can meet afterwards? I want to tell you everything. When you've heard what I have to say, you may decide you don't want to see me again, but I'll have to take that risk.'

He eased her away from his chest and looked down into her eyes. It was almost unbearable to see the pain in his eyes and at that moment it felt for her that there was nowhere else but here and now, with him and her mouth moved up to his. His lips felt soft and warm as they met hers and she closed her eyes. Just as the kiss became more urgent, he broke off, brushing his lips over her brow before holding her away from him at the end of his outstretched arms. He continued to hold her eyes with his.

'I killed me brother.'

Elizabeth gasped. 'My God! Why? What happened?'

'We were shooting rabbits and I were reckless. I didn't take enough care of him. I let meself get distracted and I shot Danny by mistake. I were trusted with his care and I abused that trust and now he's dead. He were only fourteen.'

Elizabeth reached for his hands and grasped them tightly.

'It wasn't your fault. It was an accident. You didn't mean to kill him.'

'If I live to be a hundred, not a day'll pass when I won't think of Danny and what I did to him. What I've done to me parents. It's destroyed me mother. I don't deserve to be happy meself. I came here to escape the look in me mam's eyes. That makes me a coward as well as a killer. I thought running away would at least give me some peace, but now you'll think ill of me too. I thought I knew what I were giving up when I left England and I didn't care. But now that I've met you… we've just met but I feel, I feel…'

'I feel it too'. She took his hand in hers and placed it against her cheek.

'You mean you still want to know me after what I've done?'

'Yes'. As she spoke, she leaned into his chest and raised her head to seek his mouth again. He kissed her slowly and tenderly and she let herself be consumed by his kiss. She drank in the smell of him, the taste of him and let out a little involuntary moan, which made him kiss her harder and she felt his body press itself into hers. Her arms gripped him tightly, squeezing, hanging onto him as though she were drowning and he her only hope of salvation. Here she was in the middle of a public place, kissing a man as she had never been kissed before, returning his kiss and wanting it to go on for ever. She wanted to cry out 'I love you' but a wave of rational responsibility washed over her. First she must sort matters out with her father and Jack Kidd, then she would be free to be with Michael.

'I have to go now' she said as she eased herself away.

'Tomorrow afternoon. Twelve o'clock.'

Then she left, and he stood watching her move quickly through the trees, her shape lit up in the last rays of the afternoon sun.

CHAPTER SIX

JACK KIDD

The church was empty when Elizabeth took her place alongside Mrs Little and her husband, in the front pew behind the coffin. She had not been allowed to look at her father's body: the lid was already nailed shut and the undertaker told her it would be too distressing for her to see him after five days in the water. The mysterious Mr Kidd had identified him by his clothing and fob-watch, his features having been unrecognisable.

She buried her head in her hands and leaned forward, trying to make herself pray. But prayer eluded her. In just a few weeks, her life had transformed – she made a mental inventory of what had happened. Against this grim sequence of events she had now met a man with whom she was falling in love, despite the brevity of their acquaintance. Embarking on a relationship with Michael might bring more problems, more pain and sadness, as he was clearly a troubled man. She shivered in the chill of the church, then the organ broke her reveries with its sombre dirge as she remembered she was here to bury her father. It was hard not to hope that this was a strange and terrible dream and she would soon wake up.

Her hold on religious faith had always been shaky, with what little belief she held stretched by the war and Stephen's death, and now by everything that had befallen her and her family. Yet she wanted to believe in an eternal life for her parents, even if that was more of an abstract concept than a vision of them hand in hand in front of an all-redeeming creator. Her father had been unhappy since her mother's death. He had stumbled along, searching for a meaning to life without her, but unable to find one. Elizabeth wondered what it would be like to love someone as much as that? So much that their loss took all meaning from living.

She thought of Winterbourne's sad eyes and knew exactly how his loss and grief felt. He carried a burden he feared to share with others. Just as she did. Her stomach made a little leap. How he could want her once he found out what Dawson had done to her? Michael's words twisted in her like a knife: *'When you've heard what I have to tell you, you may decide you don't want to see me again'*. Killing his brother was an accident. She could not hold him to account for that. But if he were to find out what had happened to her, would he want to see her again? Just as her sister had assumed fault on her part, so might he? An unmarried, older sister leading her brother-in-law astray?

She gave a little involuntary cry and Peggy Little patted her on the shoulder .

'There, there, my lamb, he's at peace now. He's with your Ma - he often talked of her you know.'

Elizabeth covered her face with her hands. The organ reached a crescendo, the melancholy notes reverberating around the almost empty church. She turned and saw the clergyman approaching, followed by a short man, in his late fifties, who took up a place in a pew across the aisle. Mr Kidd, she presumed.

The service was short, with a brief impersonal eulogy by the clergyman, who had evidently never met William

Morton. They made their way in a bleak procession into the adjoining graveyard, Mr Kidd a few paces behind the rest of the party. As the coffin was lowered, she placed on top the picture of her mother that had been among her father's few possessions and a flower she had plucked in the churchyard. Then she stood in the warm sunlight looking into the newly-dug cavity, before throwing in her handful of earth. She heard the quiet thuds as the Littles and Kidd did likewise and the priest droned his words of final ceremony.

When it was over Mrs Little led her away from the graveside. The man she presumed to be Kidd turned to her and spoke in a voice that sounded as though it had been dried hoarse by the Australian sun. His face was like tanned leather and covered in fine wrinkles, testament to an outdoor life. He held his hat in his hands, exposing a head covered with cropped, steel-grey hair. His legs were slightly bowed, as though he spent more time in the saddle than on his feet. He looked uncomfortable in his ill-fitting dark suit. Elizabeth wondered if it had been borrowed for the occasion. He didn't look like a wealthy man. Her father must have got it wrong.

'Miss Morton? Sorry about your father.'

'Thank you. You must be Mr Kidd?'

She held out her hand to him as Mrs Little interjected. 'I'm sorry Elizabeth, love; I should have done the introductions. This is your late father's friend, Mr Jack Kidd. Now you'll be coming back to the house, Mr Kidd, won't you, for a nice cup of tea and some light refreshments? It's all prepared - our Molly's been getting it ready while we're here.'

They walked the few streets back to the boarding house in silence, Elizabeth rehearsing in her head what to say to Kidd. She had never had to do anything like this before: find a way to tell a stranger that she could not accept his marriage proposal.

When they were all supplied with tea and a selection of sandwiches, she whispered to Peggy that she would like a few minutes alone with Mr Kidd.

'That's fine, my dear - but you won't get much out of him you know. Miserable old codger if you'll pardon my language.'

She nudged her husband and ushered him from the room, leaving Elizabeth alone to face her would-be suitor.

She took a deep breath, thankful that her father had not shared his matchmaking plans with his landlady.

'Mr Kidd, I understand you have paid for the funeral. I'm very grateful to you for doing that and for being a friend to my father. You have been very kind. I will repay you in full - but I'd be grateful if you would grant me some time. I must find employment - I hope to work as a music teacher but finding the right...'

He interrupted the rapid flow of her words, raising a hand in front of him as he spoke, as though halting traffic.

'You won't be teaching - there's no call for that where we'll be going.' He looked at the floor rather than addressing his remarks to her face. 'I've a trip to make but I'll be back in three weeks. We'll be wed when I return. Then we'll head up home to the Blue Mountains - there's plenty there for you to do, but won't be teaching music.'

As if exhausted by an unusually high outflow of words, he settled back in his chair and resumed eating, stuffing his mouth with the delicate sandwiches as if he hadn't eaten for a week.

'I can't marry you. It's out of the question. I only came here to join my father. I don't wish to be rude and I'm honoured that you should think me worthy of a proposal of marriage, but it is impossible for me to accept. We don't even know each other.'

Without waiting to finish his mouthful he answered her. 'It's all settled.'

'What do you mean? Now my father is dead I answer to no one.'

'You answer to me. That's the deal. Didn't your daddy tell you?'

'What deal? What should he have told me? He wrote to me that you'd offered to marry me and he sent the ticket for the journey here. I came because I wanted to start a new life here with Father. Now he's dead I'll just have to do it without him, but do it I will. I'll repay the funeral cost as soon as I can. I intend to start looking for a teaching position tomorrow.'

Kidd put down his plate. 'His debts were more than the funeral costs. He lost twenty thousand pounds to me at cards. And there's another twenty-five thousand he ran up with some other fellas that are a lot less understanding than I am. I paid them off too. So I get you in return. That's the deal.'

Elizabeth felt her blood freeze in her veins. 'Are you saying my father used me to settle his gambling debts?'

Kidd acknowledged the question with a nod.

'You're lying.' Her voice was chilly and she rose to her feet, summoning an imperious posture and expression, belying the rising panic within her.

Kidd looked up at her. 'Don't believe me. Believe him.' He reached into the pocket of his suit jacket and drew out a sealed envelope. As she read the letter the room began to spin around her.

My dearest Lizzie

There is no way to make this any better so I'm just going to write the facts. May you and God forgive me for what I have done but I could find no alternative.

I lost a fortune at cards to Jack Kidd and he offered to relieve me of my debts if I agreed to his marrying you. I had shown your picture to him during our games. I was so proud of you. I know now this was my own foolish vanity and I should have been more circumspect. He was very taken with your photograph. When my luck went against me he made an offer to marry you. Of course I refused and asked for time to repay him, but word had already spread of the other losses I had sustained, for which I had already borrowed large sums of money from some men with little patience and no scruples. To come to the point, dear Lizzie, threats were made and I feared for my life. I agreed to Mr Kidd's proposal, thinking it would buy me some time to find an alternative solution. I did not intend to involve you at all but Kidd stood over me while I wrote my letter to you. Since its dispatch – which he undertook himself – I have prayed every day that you would react as I would expect my Lizzie to do, by tearing up the ticket and concluding that your poor father had gone quite mad.

I have decided I can no longer bear the shame, guilt and unhappiness that have become my way of life. I will end it tonight. I am sending this letter to Kidd to give to you in the unlikely possibility that you do come to Australia. I have not told him what I am about to do – but he has probably guessed. If you are reading this now my prayers have been in vain. I have tortured myself trying to find another solution to my troubles – one that would keep you from having to fulfil my shameful debt. I cannot see any way out. I can only hope that your good nature will succeed where I have failed in prevailing on him to think again. May God have mercy on you – I deserve no mercy for myself, but I beg for your forgiveness and that of God and your beloved mother.

Your loving but unworthy father
William M Morton

Elizabeth folded the paper and raised her eyes to look at Kidd. 'Did you know he intended to take his own life?'

The man looked ashamed but said nothing.

'Mr Kidd, I appeal to you as an honourable man. Free me from this contract. Don't hold me to a bargain made by a man out of his mind with worry. I don't expect you to do me any favours, but can you do one for him? I swear I will do everything to repay every penny of his debt to you.'

'I'm not interested in money. I need a wife and I've chosen you.'

'You can find another wife - someone who wants to marry you - someone who would care for you. I don't even know you. I can never care for you. I'd be an unwilling prisoner. I'd make you unhappy. I'd be unhappy myself. Please! You must understand that?'

Kidd got up and went to the door. At the threshold he looked back at her. 'I'll take my chances. We'll marry when I get back.'

When he had gone, Elizabeth curled her feet underneath her on the chair and stared out through the sunlit window. She could not take in what had happened. Her father had sold her into slavery - dramatic as this sounded, it was effectively what had happened. Someone must be able to help? Mrs Little would know what to do.

The door opened and Peggy Little entered the room. 'My dear, Mr Kidd has just told me you're to be married! All very sudden, but I'm pleased for you - he's a very wealthy man. You'll want for nothing. I hope you'll be very happy.' The woman moved towards Elizabeth with her arms outspread to embrace her.

'Peggy, you have to help me. I can't marry that man. It's not my choice. Father owed him a fortune and in exchange agreed that we should marry. I can't be expected to go through with it. It's barbaric. I'll find some other way to repay the debt. I'll go to the church and tell the minister that the marriage is against my will then it can't possibly go ahead. Help me to convince Mr Kidd that it's crazy.

Please, Peggy, I need your advice about finding work - I'll do anything - domestic service probably pays more than music teaching? Or I could work in a shop? Whatever it takes. Anything's better than marrying that man.'

Peggy Little began to twitch at the corners of her apron as she had done the previous day.

'I can't help you. I'm sorry and I wish to God I could help but I've no choice. Your father owed money to me. Mr Kidd settled his debts - he's paid ten month's worth of lodgings on your father's behalf as well as your board for the next 3 weeks. If I were to help you, God knows what he'd do. He's a powerful man and my Fred would kill me if I crossed him. We have the children to think of too. We can't go against a man like Kidd. I'm really sorry, my love. It's not such a bad plan. He has plenty of money - mining interests they say and land as well. You could do worse, my dear. Better to have a home, you being all alone.'

'My God, I can't believe it. You are a woman for heaven's sake! Can't you understand I can't possibly marry that old man? Not only do I not love him - I find everything about him and what he's done to my father an abomination. Did you know my father killed himself? He left me a letter. He couldn't forgive himself for what he had done and he hoped that his death might force Kidd to show some compassion. Fat chance!' Her voice was shrill now.

'Now, now, my dear, don't upset yourself. Nothing's as bad as it seems. I'm sorry about your father - I'm not one to judge others - and no one will hear about it from me - as far I'm concerned it was a dreadful accident. Knowing otherwise won't bring him back and I won't speak ill of the dead.' She hugged Elizabeth to her ample bosom.

Elizabeth pulled away to speak again.

'Father was hoping I'd ignore his invitation to Australia - and I would have done... had not ... had not something terrible happened. I'd no idea I was walking into a trap. Jack

Kidd believes he's bought me like a piece of meat. Help me, Peggy.'

'Hush, dear. No point in tears. It won't do any good. I wish I could help, my lovely - but there's nothing I can do. You'll have to make the best of it.'

'No woman should be expected to marry a man she doesn't love.'

'Love?' Peggy sighed. 'That doesn't last long. They're all the same really, men – farting, belching and snoring and taking up most of the bed. Sleep, food and their conjugals - that's all they want. A wife's just there to wash, cook, clean and service his needs in bed. Never mind her own needs! Yes there may be many men more handsome than Jack Kidd, but there's few as well off - and believe me Elizabeth - you won't see what he looks like when the light's out!' She laughed bitterly. 'We women have a lot to put up with, young lady and the sooner you realise that the better. At least you'll never have to worry where your next crust of bread's coming from. The first two years I was married I never knew from one day to the next if I was going to be able to put a meal on the table. Love doesn't help when you're hungry. By the time my Fred was making decent money we'd forgotten our romantic notions. You settle into a steady old pattern. Get used to each other. Put up with the shortcomings – there's children to keep you busy and to care for. Jack Kidd may not be the man you dreamed of, but then the man you dreamed of wouldn't be that for long either. If you've no expectations, you'll never be disappointed.'

Elizabeth rubbed her eyes with her handkerchief, then saw it was the rough-spun confection that Michael Winterbourne had given her the previous afternoon. She breathed through the coarse cotton trying to recapture the scent of him - a mix of hay and warm tweed and the outdoors.

Her stomach lurched. It was already nearly noon and

it would take her a good half hour to get to the meeting place. He may never want to see her again when he knew her story, but she had to take the risk.

She jumped up, grabbed her coat and bade an astonished Mrs Little goodbye.

'Where are you off to in such a hurry?'

'I promised to meet someone I met on the voyage. I'm late.'

'I hope you're not thinking of doing anything foolish my love?' But Elizabeth was already out of the door and running along the street.

As soon as she left the Littles and retraced the steps she had taken the previous day, she ran into the crowds. She had never seen so many people. They were all heading the way she was and she was swept along in their midst. She began to panic as the pace slowed right down as the volume of people increased, merging on the same spot from all directions. She tried to turn back and find an alternative route, but the people kept on coming, pushing forward excitedly, many carrying flags and bags of confetti. When she tried to push her way back, a man elbowed her in the ribs and she stumbled and fell. Someone yanked her to her feet but in the crush she couldn't see who had helped her. The noise was getting louder, cheering and singing. She turned to a woman and asked her, 'Is someone getting married?' The woman looked at Elizabeth as if she'd lost her mind, shook her head and turned away without answering Over the heads of the crowd in front she saw a large building, with a portico and clock tower, the façade of the building hung with enormous flags – the Union Jack and the flag of Australia. She turned to another person and asked 'Where's everyone going? What's happening?'

This time a man answered her. 'To see the Digger Prince. Where've you been hiding darling? Up on the planet Mars?'

'The Digger Prince?'

'The future king himself.' The man assumed a hammy English accent: 'His Royal Highness, Edward, Prince of Wales. Look there he is – up there on the platform. The fella waving his hat at us.'

She pushed herself onto her tiptoes but the crowd was so dense she couldn't make out the figure of the Prince. She turned back to the man. 'How do I get through? I need to go down to the Harbour, past the Circular Quay.'

The man laughed. 'Not yet you won't. You'll have to wait your turn and follow the crowd. We all want to get a glimpse or even have a touch.'

'But I don't. Please. I don't want to see the Prince. I just want to get past.'

The people around her started mumbling in disapproval. The man spoke again. 'Did you hear her? She doesn't want to see the Prince! Her a pommie and all. Bloody unpatriotic I call it. You should be ashamed of yourself.'

Almost screaming in frustration, Elizabeth had to concede defeat and shuffle along with the masses in the slow, steady advance towards the Town Hall.

CHAPTER SEVEN

THE PRINCE OF WALES

Michael sat on the stone seat overlooking the harbour. The beauty and brightness before him contrasted with his own downcast spirits. The sun shone down through the trees and the water in the Harbour was deepest azure. In the branches of a eucalyptus tree a parrot flashed white against the dark of the leaves and screeched. He looked at his watch again. Where was she?

Yesterday, he had felt for the first time in his life that someone understood him. She sensed his feelings without the need for words, shared his loneliness and seemed to suffer from her own inner demons. He had seen the sadness in her eyes. He longed to comfort her.

But she had not come. She must have thought better of it. He wished he hadn't kissed her. It was too soon. She must have thought him presumptuous, a chancer. She was from another world. There had been something about being here in Australia that had led him to forget the class barriers that in England would have prevented them from so much as having a conversation, let alone sharing an embrace. Yet the memory of her lips against his, the warmth of them as she gave herself over to the kiss, belied his doubts. She had wanted him as much as he had her. He knew it to be true. But she was not here. What did that say?

He thought of the lads from Manchester and how they'd jeered at his pretensions towards Elizabeth. Hadn't they said she was out of his class? And the obnoxious Mrs Briars had made it clear that a man like him was unworthy to clean the shoes of the likes of her and Elizabeth. She must have been caught up in the moment yesterday, grief for her father getting the better of her judgement. In the cold light of day she must have realised he wasn't good enough for her. And how could she want a man who had killed his own brother?

He waited on the rocky seat they had occupied the previous day, until the sun sank and the huge sleeping bats that had been hanging motionless from the trees around him, awoke and started their swirling flights, ghoulish silhouettes against the darkening sky.

He walked through the dusk, to Woolloomooloo and into the bar next door to his lodgings, where he asked for a beer.

'Middy or schooner?' asked the woman behind the counter.

Michael shook his head, puzzled.

'Fresh off the boat?' She explained the difference between the measures and served him a schooner from one of the many beer taps all identically labelled Tooth's Draught.

He gulped the cold liquid down and asked for a second. The bar was empty, save for the woman who was serving and an old man at the far end of the counter. The woman, presumably the proprietor's wife, showed no interest in conversation, serving Michael's second glass wordlessly, before returning to polishing glasses.

He looked around. The pub was more like a public toilet than a drinking establishment. The walls were covered in white tiles and the floor was covered in sawdust.

He turned back to the woman. 'You know where I can get work?'

Without looking up she replied, her voice bored. 'What kinda work, mate?'

'Anything on the land or with animals.'

'Sheep or cattle?'

'Either.'

'Talk to Big Billy Carter. He's only in town one more day but he's hiring hands. Has a sheep farm up at Fairtown.'

'How'll I know him?'

'You'll know him. Built like a brick wall and more than six foot tall. Everyone knows Billy'

He asked for another beer. The woman poured it then looked at him.

'You from England mate?"

'Arrived yesterday. On the Historic.'

'So you don't know about the Six o'clock Swill?'

'I don't.' He didn't particularly want to either.

'It's the law. No drinks served after six o'clock. Better get them in now mate, as in a few minutes it'll be pandemonium and you won't have a Buckley's chance of getting another – they'll be ten deep at the bar. Moment the whistle blows at the dock they all pile in here. You won't believe how fast they get 'em down their necks.'

The prospect of the onrush to come was not an appealing one, but more to appease her than anything, he agreed to line up another pint. As she predicted, the place filled up rapidly and Michael's solitary corner was invaded, as the crowd pushed into all the available space. The noise was deafening and the woman behind the bar was joined by her husband and daughter and the trio kept up a virtuoso performance of high speed pint pulling.

He was about to move through the room to seek out

Billy Carter, but the words of the group around him filtered into his consciousness and he listened with growing interest. There were three or four men, about his age and one of them had just returned from a mining town, where he had earned substantial sums of money.

'I tell you, I never had it so good. They can't get the stuff out the ground fast enough and they'll pay a fortune if you don't mind going underground. They're so desperate for workers they're even bringing in Chinamen.'

'You don't say?'

'No word of a lie. I'm quids in. Reckon in another six months I'll have enough to buy a place for myself and I can say goodbye to the mines and be my own boss on my own land.'

'Isn't it a bit lonesome up in the mountains?'

'No, mate. McDonald Falls is a bonzer town. There's a railway, a new fancy hotel, stores, plenty of bars and plenty of women.' He gave an earthy laugh, which was echoed by his cohorts.

'What they mining up there? Coal or what?'

'Everything, mate. Gold. There's coal and bauxite and there's copper. Rocks are just full of the stuff. I tell you it's like digging money right out of the ground.'

Michael had heard enough. Thoughts of becoming a sheep-hand abandoned, he pushed his way into the group and addressed the young man at the centre.

'Where's this place and how do I get there?'

'McDonald Falls. 'Eighty miles or so from Sydney. They're laying on transport for workers. A wagon leaves tomorrow from Circular Quay at sun-up. Just show up and they'll find a place for you I reckon. You'll need a couple of quid for the fare.'

He appraised Michael coolly, then stretched out his hand towards him. 'Name's Burton - Fred Burton.'

'Michael Winterbourne.'

'Welcome aboard, mate! There's just time for your shout before six.'

Every day for a week, Elizabeth returned to the green sward where she'd met Michael, but he was never there. Everywhere she went throughout the city she was mocked by the flags and bunting hanging from buildings and lampposts to welcome the Prince of Wales. She cursed her stupidity in failing to notice the flags the previous day, at being so wrapped up in herself that the world and its events passed her by unremarked. Now she came to think of it, she remembered that Peggy had commented on the Royal visit over breakfast, but she hadn't been listening properly.

She asked why Michael's feelings towards her were so shallow-rooted that her failure to turn up on time had been enough to kill them? He must have heard of the Prince's visit so why hadn't he put two and two together? She'd had no means of contacting him, didn't know where he was lodging, so why hadn't he come back the following day? Or the day after that? Just as she was doing.

When she finally accepted he wasn't going to return, she continued her walks along the harbour, immune to the gentle warmth of the autumn sunshine and the beauty of the harbour, with boats dotted over its deep blue surface.

The passage of the time brought another worry. She had not had a period since two weeks before leaving Trevelyan House, more than two months ago. Although her slight figure still showed no signs of a pregnancy, she could not ignore the constant tiredness and occasional nausea. With dread, she acknowledged the possibility that she was expecting her brother-in-law's child. The thought was repugnant.

Marrying Kidd paled into insignificance against the

prospect of bearing Charles Dawson's child. Each morning she woke with hope mixed with fear, but the hope was dashed and the fear gained more ground. She wasn't sure if the spells of nausea were due to the pregnancy or her feelings about it. There could be nothing more that life could throw at her. Then she remembered that pregnancy was not a one-off event, but something she would have to live with every day for the rest of her life: a constant living reminder of the worst night of her life.

She began staying in her room, pleading tiredness. Molly brought food up to her. The child noticed her pallor and increasing withdrawal and told her mother. Peggy, who had been avoiding Elizabeth out of guilt at her inability to ease her plight, climbed the stairs and confronted her guest.

'Molly's worried about you. She says you're looking pale and she's absolutely right. Come on now. Pull yourself together girl. Moping all day long isn't going to make it better. There's worse things can happen to a woman than marrying a wealthy, old man.'

She started to chuckle, then saw the distress in Elizabeth's eyes. She gathered her into her arms and sat beside her on the bed rocking her.

'There, there, my honey. What's the matter? You frightened of Jack Kidd? Frightened about marriage to him? Are you nervous about leaving the city? I know you're far from home and with no family. Is that it? Tell me what's wrong.'

Elizabeth's words were almost a whisper. 'I think I'm going to have a baby.'

'Oh my good God! I knew there was more to it. You poor little thing! How long's it been?'

'Over 8 weeks.'

'Since the last time you've been with a man?'

'There was only one time. He forced himself on me.' She stiffened and drew away from Peggy. The look of horror on the older woman's face angered her.

'Yes I was raped.' She almost spat out the words.

'Who did it to you, lovely?'

'It doesn't matter who did it. It's enough that it happened. If I'm expecting a child I need to know. As well as being late, I feel sick all the time and seem to be drained of energy. And my breasts feel tender.' She almost choked on the words.

'Yes I reckon you're in the family way.'

'I can't possibly have this baby, Peggy! You have to help me.'

'Help you?'

'Yes help me to get rid of it.'

'I can't do that, my love. It's against the law and I know nothing about such things.'

'You must know. Surely? Please help me. I can't have it. I just can't. Tell me what I need to do. Where I can go?'

'I don't think it's a good idea, Elizabeth. Not for a lovely girl like you. It's not nice what they'd have to do to you. And it's risky.'

'I don't care about the risk. I've nothing to lose. If I can't get rid of this baby I'll kill myself. I've nothing to live for anyway.'

'Don't talk like that dear. Please.'

'My father did it, so I can do it too.'

'Stop that talk now. I know you don't mean it. You're far too sensible for that.'

Elizabeth lowered her head.

After a few minutes, the older woman spoke again. 'Mrs Reynolds two doors down might be able to help. I'll have a word. If she can, you'll have to go there on your own. I have a reputation to think of. And I'll not have her in this house. I'll try and catch her at the fish market tomorrow and if she's willing, you can go to her place and she'll sort you out. It'll cost, mind.'

'I have some money.'

'You sure about this, girl? It's not pleasant.'

Elizabeth nodded.

'Very well, leave it with me.'

Good as her word, Mrs Little made the necessary arrangements and Elizabeth found herself at the back door of one of the permanently curtained houses further down the street. The door was opened by a boy of about seven, who said nothing to her but shouted over his shoulder, 'Ma. For you.'

She went in. It was a small, scruffy kitchen, smelling of fried fish and overcooked vegetables. Two ginger cats were asleep under the large deal table that dominated the room. Mrs Reynolds, a scrawny woman who looked as though she needed a good meal, looked Elizabeth up and down.

'Quite the lady eh?'

'Mrs Reynolds?'

'Frank! Clear the table. Look sharp about it.'

Ignoring Elizabeth, she went to a cupboard and began to rummage around inside, gathering together equipment. Elizabeth stood there, a feeling of mounting horror sweeping over her as she saw the length of tubing and the collection of metal instruments, all of which the woman pulled out of a canvass holdall. The boy grabbed the dirty plates and breadboard off the table and dumped them in the sink on top of an pile of unwashed dishes, then with the side of his hand, flicked the breadcrumbs onto the floor, where the cats sniffed them disdainfully.

Mrs Reynolds turned to her. 'I need the cash up front. Did your friend tell you there's no refund if it doesn't work. But then it always works – one way or another. If anything goes wrong or you get ill and call a doctor you don't tell him about me. Clear?'

Elizabeth nodded. 'Where are you going to do it?'

'Here. Take your skirt, underwear and stockings off, and get on the table on your back, knees up and apart.' She turned to the little boy 'Hop it, Frank. Tell the girls I'm on a job and no one's to come in here till I'm done.'

102

Elizabeth felt herself shrinking and took a step backwards.

The woman narrowed her eyes. 'What's up? Get on with it. Get yourself up on the table. I haven't got all day.'

'It doesn't look very safe? Or very clean?' Elizabeth was speaking in little more than a whisper.

'Bugger off then - you poms are all the same. Always moaning. If you want clean, white sheets, then cough up and get yourself a bloody doctor. The price you're paying me is the same as all the working girls round here pay and you'll get the same service they do. I'm risking the law to do this. When you're desperate you can't be fussy. So make your mind up and stop wasting my time.'

Elizabeth jumped as she felt something warm brush against her legs. She looked down to see one of the cats rubbing itself against her ankle. A wave of nausea came over her and she stumbled to the doorway and out into the dark of the evening, gulping for fresh air.

Peggy Little looked up and smiled as she entered the room. 'Couldn't go through with it? I'm not surprised, my love. She's not a nice woman that Mrs Reynolds and it's not a nice thing to do. Dangerous too. There's many girls die. I did warn you.'

'It was horrible. It was so sordid. Her little boy was there and seemed to act as if it was normal and he was used to what was going on.'

'Well, she's kept busy at it. She used to be on the game, but since she had her little lad I think she's concentrated on helping out girls that way.'

'The place was filthy. The instruments she was going to use looked horrible. She was going to do it on the kitchen table with the dishes in the sink and the cats eating scraps off the floor. It was disgusting.'

'I don't like to say it, love, but I told you so!'

'What am I going to do now? I can't go through with what she wanted to do to me but I can't have a baby either!'

Then she remembered that her panic over the baby had not removed the other looming problem – Jack Kidd and his intent to marry her in just a few days.

'I'll tell Mr Kidd. He won't want to go ahead with the marriage when he knows I'm carrying another man's child.'

'Are you crazy Elizabeth? You'll do no such thing. You must marry him. You'll need a father for the child. Don't tell him. Say the baby came early. Men often don't get these things.' She pressed on. 'You have to do it. Otherwise what'll become of you? You've no money and no family and once you have a child you've no means of working. No, my love, in time you'll give thanks that Jack Kidd came along when he did. Every cloud has a silver lining.'

'I can't pretend the baby is his.'

'Worry on that when the time comes. You aren't showing yet – by the time he finds out it'll be too late for him to do anything about it.'

Elizabeth played with the corner of the coverlet, creasing it back and forth between her fingers. She weighed the older woman's words. With a new, hard edge to her voice she said. 'You're right. I have to marry him. I have no choice. I'll soon have a child I can only feel loathing for, so why not a husband I loathe too? It's almost fitting.'

'Don't say such dreadful things, dear. I'm sorry about what's happened to you, but it's not the baby's fault. Don't take it out on an innocent child. God bless it.'

'Don't be sentimental, Peggy. A man I hate forced this baby on me. I'll never look on it with anything other than revulsion. It'll be a constant reminder of the man and the humiliation and pain he put me through. It'll be easy enough for me to pretend that the child is Kidd's as I hold him in contempt too.'

As she prepared for bed that night, Elizabeth looked in the mirror and saw a new hardness in her eyes. The sad young woman who had stepped off the ship was now determined. The unquestioning optimism that had once characterised her was gone. She found it hard to imagine a time when she had woken each day without a care beyond what clothes to wear and who would partner her in a game of doubles. It was even harder to imagine that she had once had hopes for a future that was contented, if vaguely defined. Now her future was a life sentence she had to serve.

She slipped between the crisp cotton sheets, thinking about Michael Winterbourne. He was not the type of man she had been used to meeting in the drawing rooms of Northport. Many of those young men had gone off to fight the war and many, like Stephen, had failed to return or, like his friend Randolph Archer, had come back broken men, now closeted away because of "nervous troubles". Elizabeth had been saddened hearing the news of each, but in death they had become shadows, fading with each passing month. Even Stephen.

Her relationship with Stephen had been affectionate and close. She had believed it was love, but she knew now it wasn't. Her feelings for him had never involved the longing and need that she had for Michael. She had not known what it was possible to feel for someone, until it was too late.

She imagined Michael in shirtsleeves, walking across a field in the sunlight, arms strong and stride purposeful. It was hard to see him in an evening suit sitting in a box at a concert or sipping tea from a china cup. Yet she knew there was a depth to him. It was in his eyes - it was plain that he had suffered and was still suffering. The other men she had known lived life on the surface, inhabited the everyday world of commerce and social intercourse, never moving beyond these confines. They talked of politics, war and cricket, a ritual exchange of platitudes. They discussed plans and ambitions, but centred on actions and events, never feelings or emotions: so it was hard to believe that they had any. Michael's emotions were exposed, raw and visible. The hurt was in the lines that furrowed his brow, the longing and hope in his eyes. She could not have done anything to avoid being drawn to him. His pain at what had happened to his brother made her heart ache. She wanted to comfort him, reassure him, tell him she loved him.

She would never see him again, nor enjoy a moment's happiness with him. But she could never be disappointed or hurt by him. He could be hers forever in a way that no one could take from her. She could not change what had happened, wipe out the memory of Charles Dawson, nor escape a lonely future as the wife of Jack Kidd, but she could build a refuge inside her head and share it with Michael Winterbourne.

CHAPTER EIGHT

A WEDDING

The wedding service was mercifully brief. Peggy and Fred Little witnessed the ceremony and Molly was a charming but rather inappropriate last-minute addition as a brides-maid, carrying a small bunch of daisies plucked from the pots that graced the guesthouse windowsills. Elizabeth would have preferred to conclude the matter without an audience and the presence of the little girl and her evident excitement at the romantic ideal of a wedding was almost unbearable. She herself carried no flowers. Her dress was a simple green silk shift, one of the few garments stuffed hastily in her suitcase by her sister. She wore it under her woollen coat as, when the sky clouded over, Sydney could be surprisingly cold. As if in acknowledgement of her own low spirits, it was a day of heavy cloud, with a bitter wind and driving rain.

Jack Kidd wore the same ill-fitting suit he had worn to the funeral. From the way he fidgeted with the collar of his shirt, it was apparent that he couldn't wait to be released from it. Elizabeth avoided looking at him and whispered her responses so they were barely audible. She sensed him beside her and heard the heaviness of his breathing. When he placed the ring on her finger, she had to turn towards him, and she shivered as he held her hand ready for the ring. His hand was cold and dry, with callused fingers and dirt beneath the rough-edged nails. She glanced at his face, which was impassive. The wrinkles around his mouth and eyes were white against the tan of his leathery skin. She shuddered at the thought that soon she would be required to share a bed with him. There was no avoiding this either: not if she were to pass off the child as his.

There was no wedding breakfast. Kidd was keen to get on their way. The journey would take two days and he wanted to waste no time. Elizabeth was relieved: standing around making small talk with the Littles held no appeal. What would in normal circumstances be a joyful event was the start of an indefinite prison sentence. Despite Peggy's good intentions and efforts at kindness, Elizabeth didn't linger over her goodbyes. A new life lay ahead. It might not be the one she wanted, but she might as well get on with it. There was no going back.

They left Sydney in a pony and trap, the rear of which bore their luggage, such as it was. In Kidd's case, there was just a large canvas roll and in Elizabeth's, the bag her sister had packed. Her unplanned departure from England meant she had been ill-prepared for Australia, and the few garments she had were unsuitable for the life that lay ahead of her in the mountains. She mused on what it might hold for her as they trotted along in a silence for which she was grateful.

From time to time she glanced sideways at the man beside her, but his expression was closed and he kept his eyes fixed on the road ahead. His jacket, necktie and collar were consigned to the back of the trap in a heap under her luggage, and the top buttons of his shirt were now undone, under the protective cover of a large sheepskin coat.

After several hours, the road left the plains and snaked

its way through densely packed trees, curving with the line of the mountains ahead. The increasingly cold air was full of the scent of eucalyptus, which had an unchallenged dominance of the region. Mrs Little had told her that her journey would take her over the Great Dividing Range, into the Blue Mountains and that these had got their name from the blue haze that covered the hills. The road they were traveling on had been built with convict labour, in an engineering feat of about sixty years earlier, that was still the pride of New South Wales.

Few motor cars or other vehicles passed them on the road, which took them through several settlements, but Kidd showed no sign of stopping. He swigged from a water bottle, which he handed to her, signalling silently that she could take a drink if she wished. She shook her head. Thirst was preferable to putting her mouth around the bottle after his. She leaned against the wooden seat and let the motion of the trap and the steady clop of the pony's hooves lull her to sleep.

She woke with the realisation that they had stopped moving. The light had faded into dusk, so she must have been asleep for several hours. Kidd had unhitched the pony from the trap and it was a few yards away, feasting on a patch of grass by the roadside. Kidd was coaxing a fire, over which he had hung a frame to support a billycan. Elizabeth walked a short distance along the road ahead. The trees gave way to a space where the darkening sky was visible in a broad sweep. They were on the side of a ridge or plateau but the night was descending fast and she could only just make out the mountains, black against the dark grey sky. She would have to wait until morning to see if these mountains were as beautiful as Mrs Little had claimed.

Kidd called to her that the tea was brewed. When she reached him he spoke for the first time since they had left the city. 'I've made the brew. But it's the last time. That's your job. I like it strong with three sugars.' He handed her a chipped enamel mug with a dirty piece of string attached to the handle. 'Wash the things afterwards in the stream over there.'

He took up his own mug and walked away to sit against the trunk of a tree, curling back into his silence. Elizabeth sat down on the grass, leaning against one of the wheels of the cart as she sipped her tea. He had added sugar and she wrinkled her nose in distaste, but made herself drink the hot liquid. She realised she was hungry. She had eaten nothing since the slice of dry toast she had forced down that morning and then thrown up.

She finished the tea and walked over to collect Kidd's cup. 'Where we will be staying tonight, Mr Kidd?'

'Here. After we've eaten. There's some jerky and bread in the bag in the back. Fetch it here. Washing up can wait till morning. But do it quick. I want to move as soon as it's light.'

'We're not taking shelter in a guest house? We've passed quite a few.'

'I'm not paying to stay in someone else's house.'

'We can't sleep out in the open and there's no room on the trap,' she said.

Kidd jerked his head at the back of the cart and the rolled up pile of oilcloth.

'You mean we're to sleep in a tent?' There was disbelief in her voice.

'No tent. Under the stars in a swag.'

'What about wild animals? Where do I wash? Change my clothing? I can't sleep in the open.'

'Welcome to Australia, your ladyship. Wash down there in the stream. Water's cold, mind.' He pointed to where the ground sloped away under the trees.

Kidd unrolled the canvass swag bag, spilling a mix of pots, pans, boots and assorted items of clothing onto the ground. He showed her how to arrange the swag, the calico cover acting as a ground sheet with a couple of blue blankets on top and the clothing rolled into a makeshift pillow. Elizabeth shuddered at the prospect of sharing that grubby and likely uncomfortable sleeping accommodation.

After their meal of cold jerked meat, bread and another mug of strong tea, which in Kidd's case was supplemented with a large tot of whisky, he belched loudly then walked a few yards away, turned his back and urinated noisily and copiously. The man was a savage, but the sound of him made her realise she needed to relieve herself too, so she walked back down the road, out of his sight and hearing. Struggling to adjust her underclothing, in the now almost impenetrable darkness and chill air, she wondered what she had come to.

She looked around to see if there was some way she could avoid taking her place beside Kidd in his swag. She thought of lying down in the cramped space at the back of the trap and covering herself with layers of clothes, but Kidd called out to her:

'Get over here, woman. I'm not waiting all night. We've an early start tomorrow.'

Elizabeth reminded herself that she could not afford a delay in consummating the marriage, if she were to pass off the baby as Kidd's. She unlaced her boots and slipped under the rough blue blanket beside her husband, trembling with dread. Almost immediately he began to snore. She sighed with relief and tried to sleep herself. She shivered in the cold of the cloudless night, aware of the unfamiliar sounds of the bush. Terrified that a strange animal might come and attack them, she lay rigid beside the sleeping man, staring up at the stars. The constellations of the Southern Hemisphere were different from the stars she had grown up with. It was indeed another world and she was far from everything familiar. About to cry, she reached in her pocket and found Michael Winterbourne's handkerchief. Holding it in her hand she felt calmer and turned on her side, her back to Kidd and at last slept.

Sleep was short-lived. Kidd was pressing up against her, his body curved into the spoon of her back. His erection pushed against her and then his arm was over her, pulling her onto her back. He was half asleep. It was the middle of the night.

Consummating her marriage to Jack Kidd was a short-lived ordeal. He unbuttoned his trousers, pulled down her undergarments, spat on his hand and after rubbing it quickly between her legs, climbed on top of her. She closed her eyes and whispered 'Don't hurt me' then with a few thrusts it was all over. He rolled off her onto his side with his back to her.

After a couple of moments he echoed her words, ' "Don't hurt me" – that's rich! I've bought second hand goods.'

Before Elizabeth could respond, his snores were per-meating the quiet of the glade. She lay on her back and watched the stars. The first day of her married life was over. But Kidd knew she was not a virgin and would surely find out she was having another man's child. How stupid she had been to think he could be deceived. If he found out she was pregnant, he might throw her out. Only a few days ago she dreaded marrying him and now she was afraid of being abandoned. What would she do with no means of supporting herself and a baby? Her mind was in ferment as her anxieties crossed the divide from thoughts into dreams.

When she woke next morning, Kidd was nowhere to be seen. The sky was lightening and the clouds were tinged with pink. She scrambled to her feet and gathered the cups and plates they had used last night and headed over to the stream. The ground fell away in a steep descent. In front was a panorama of mountain ranges and valleys. A sea of eucalyptus trees covered all but the vertical sections of mountain, breaking the cragginess of the rock face. Over it all there was a hazy blue canopy, a sapphire mist. It was so lovely a sight that she wanted to cry out.

Australia was a beautiful and wild country. For the first time since leaving Trevelyan House, she felt hope and a sense of purpose. There on the edge of the mountain, in front of the vastness of the scenery before her, she squeezed the white cotton handkerchief and imagined Michael standing beside her, his hand holding hers.

Her daydreams were interrupted when Kidd shouted. 'Get a move on, woman.'

They resumed the journey in silence, the pony plodding on along the road through the mountains, passing small settlements and farmhouses, but never stopping.

Elizabeth stood on the threshold. The gloom of the interior contrasted with the brightness of the day outside, but the darkness could not hide the disorder of the place, nor could it mask the smell of mildew and rotting food.

Kidd had gone. He had dumped her in front of what was to be her home and with a crack of his whip and a mumbled statement that he would be back the following day, guided the pony and trap on down the dusty road towards what she presumed was the nearest town.

It was a large, single storey, wooden dwelling, with a makeshift veranda. It looked as though someone had tried to enhance the appearance of the place by tacking on the veranda decking, but had become bored or called away to other tasks before the job was completed. The wood was untreated and the railings only partly inserted, so it was sad and dilapidated. There was a hole in the planking where the wood had rotted and someone had put a foot through. It was hardly more than a hut: to call it a house was an act of generosity.

Elizabeth turned her back on the building, lacking the strength yet to face what might be inside, and surveyed the land surrounding the property. A well-worn dirt path led to a shed at the side that was probably a stable for the pony. There was another hut with a tin roof and a metal water pump. Between the house and the rough track Kidd had driven off along, there was a tangled mass of brush and a stretch of earth thinly covered in browned grass. Even to her untrained eyes it was clear there had been no rain for a considerable time.

At the back of the house the paint was cracked on the wooden slats and around the window frames. There was a water butt and a tree-trunk with a rather rusty axe embedded in its surface. Against the back wall was a pile of logs covered in cobwebs and a collection of long-dead bugs that looked like wood lice. The scrub stretched for a few hundred yards, before giving way to a dense growth of gum trees. Elizabeth walked back to the front of the house and looked in the direction Kidd had taken, but there was no sign of other dwellings, just the dusty track, a sea of scrub and the ubiquitous eucalyptus.

She moved her bags onto the veranda from the side of the track where Kidd had dumped them. Taking a deep breath and covering her mouth with her handkerchief, she stepped inside, leaving the door open. As she entered, there was a scuttling and scrambling. Mice, or worse, rats. Or more likely possums. She stepped gingerly across the room towards where she thought a window might be. The shutters were just a few boards hammered together and held in place by a bit of string tied at each side to a large nail. They were evidently intended to serve in place of curtains as well. She untied the string and lifted them down from the window. As the light forced its way through the grime of the windowpane, she looked around in disgust.

It was one big room. Everything was a jumble. Against

the rear wall was a large unmade bed, its covers slipping onto the floor. The bedclothes looked as if they hadn't been laundered in months. Beside the bed, a small table made from a tree-stump and a piece of plank, bore an oil lamp and a dirty glass. She picked up the glass and saw there was a thick culture growing inside on the residue of what might once have been beer. A table was shoved under another window, which had the same quasi shuttering as the other - this time propped on the table, there being no windowsill. She reached up and undid the string and lifted the wood to the ground. The windowpane was as dirty as its fellow, but with a crack running from top to bottom ending in a triangular hole. On the table was a bowl of dirty dishes, the remains of a mouldy loaf, an onion that was oozing liquid and competing with the bread, the dishes and the whisky glass in a mould-growing contest. A rag rug lay on the floor, pieces of grubby ribbon fraying at the edges. It looked as though whatever she had heard scuttling away when she'd entered, had been devouring the rug. A stove stood in one corner, its surface covered in grease and baked-on food. The only other furniture was a rocking chair, draped with clothing, and a large, battered trunk.

Depressed and dispirited, Elizabeth went outside and sat on the edge of the crumbling veranda, her head in her hands. She would not cry. She was past crying. She had no tears left. She thought bitterly of Peggy's words that at least she was marrying a rich man and would want for nothing. If Kidd was a rich man, he did not believe in flaunting his wealth.

When he'd left her at the roadside, telling her he would be gone for a day, she had enjoyed a short-lived pleasure at the prospect of being alone and setting up her home. But this shack was fit only as a home for a pig. But that was what it was. Jack Pig. She allowed herself a smile.

'Elizabeth Morton, you've led a cosseted life: servants

to wait on you; agreeable friends to amuse you; nothing too onerous to do, except teach a few charming but talentless children to play the violin. Now let's see what you're made of!' She jumped to her feet.

'I won't let him reduce me to living like a wild creature. I've never done housework before but by God I'll do it now. I'll make this hole a fit place to live if I die in the process!'

An hour later, the contents of the primitive dwelling were stacked on the ground in front of the veranda and Elizabeth, hair piled under a scarf, was at work with a broom. The dust was thick and the broom missing half its bristles. Her throat burned as she laboured, pausing every few minutes to cough. The floor could not have been swept in months, probably years.

Under the bed, amid a jumble of shoes, a dirty plate that had mould growing on the mould, and an assortment of socks and undergarments, she found a rolled up rug. After a hefty beating with a piece of planking over the rail of the veranda, it appeared in reasonable shape and wasn't too faded. It would add a welcome touch of colour to the otherwise drab interior. She consigned the other moth-eaten rag rug to a pile of items to be burned, then set about washing the now clean swept floor.

As the day progressed, she realised she was tired and thirsty. Her pregnancy made her tired after only moderate exertion. Even walking, a pleasure she had always pursued with a passion, wearied her now. She cursed her condition, then pushed the thought to the back of her mind. There was no point in dwelling on it. Better not to think about it. It was too painful to imagine the child growing inside her. With an effort of will, she pulled herself back on her feet and after drinking some water straight from the pump, she pumped a bucketful and set about washing the bedding and then the dishes. At least the effort stopped her from feeling the cold.

As the light began to fade, she stood in the doorway, hands on hips and surveyed her handiwork. The room was still spartan and ugly, but at least it was clean. She had done all she could with the materials available. A couple of old prints of some long-forgotten English town now hung on the wall near the table. She had found them in the bottom of a cupboard. The crockery was clean and neatly stacked on a shelf she had made from an upturned wooden box. When he returned, she would ask Kidd for a hammer, nails and some paint so she could make a more permanent solution. The bed was made up with clean sheets she had found in the trunk. The other sheets were hanging on the washing line. Her finishing touch was a brightly coloured shawl that had taken her fancy when the ship called at Tenerife. She draped it theatrically between a couple of nails across the wall over the bed.

There was one last task she wanted to do before turning in: to burn the pile of rubbish. She could cook the potatoes Kidd had left her in the embers and boil up water for tea. Cleaning the stove inside the house would be her task for tomorrow and meanwhile she would enjoy a meal under the stars tonight. She set about lighting the fire.

'What do you think you're doing, you stupid idiot?'

Before she could turn towards the voice, she was pushed out of the way and landed on the ground like a sack of flour. She struggled to her feet. A young man was pouring a pitcher of water over the still small flames of the bonfire. Discarded on the ground nearby were about half a dozen fish, tied together with string.

'You trying to burn the place down? And everything between here and town? And the whole town too? What the hell do you think you're doing?'

'How dare you!' she yelled. 'Who do you think you are? This is private property. I can burn a fire here if I choose.'

He looked at her, the nascent fire having been quenched.

117

'Don't you know about bush fires? We've had no rain in weeks and a fire could burn the whole county out and destroy everything in its path. If you want to light one, you dig a hollow first. Then you put in just enough to get it going and add more bit by bit so you can stay in control. Make sure the wind isn't going to blow the sparks straight in the path of a tree or a building. This place is all wood and it's dry as a dead dingo's donger. It'd go up like a box of kindling.'

He was little more than a boy: about sixteen or seventeen, but tall and already quite broad around the chest. His hands looked as though they had already seen a lifetime of labour. Bright white teeth and shaggy blonde hair contrasted with the warm tan of his skin. He wore a checked shirt and dirt-encrusted overalls.

He moved towards her, rubbing his hands down the side of his overalls then stretching one out to her. 'Sorry, Miss. I'm Will Kidd. I didn't mean to shout at you like that. But if you'd seen a bush-fire you'd understand why.'

She took his proffered hand. 'I'm Elizabeth. I didn't know that Mr Kidd had a child?'

'Not just me – there's Harriet too – Hattie we call her – and we've an older brother, Nat, but we haven't seen or heard from him in years. He may be dead'

'Where's Hattie?'

'She lives in town with the schoolteacher. Hattie's eighteen. She's been there since Ma died, five years ago. Pa said it wasn't suitable for a young girl living with us men. But who are you, Miss? Pa didn't tell me to expect a guest.'

'I'm not a guest, Will. Your father and I are married.'

The boy looked stunned. 'Married? Pa? He said nothing about getting hitched.'

'I'm sorry to surprise you like this. It must be quite a shock.'

'I never thought he'd marry again after Ma died. Never

seemed to show much interest in anything after she went.'

Elizabeth's capacity for surprise had significantly diminished since landing in Australia. 'I'm sorry Will. It must have been hard for you, losing your mother at such a young age. I lost my mother too just a couple of years ago.' Embarrassed and silently cursing Kidd for placing them both in this situation, she blundered on. 'It must be difficult to get used to your father marrying someone else after your mother. I can't think why he didn't tell you about me. Or me about you for that matter.' Her voice trailed off in embarrassment.

'You're very welcome here. I'm just surprised – though not that Pa should want to marry you – you're a beautiful lady.' He looked at her wide-eyed.

'I had no idea about you and your brother and sister, Will. I know next to nothing of your father and his circumstances. He was a friend of my own father; I met him only briefly before we married.'

The boy grunted, 'Didn't think the old man had any friends.' He was about to ask another question, then seemed to realise it would be inappropriate to enquire further.

Anticipating his discomfort, Elizabeth said, 'I arrived from England three weeks ago to join my father in Sydney, but he died just a few days earlier.' Her eyes welled with tears. She brushed them away and turned her head so the boy would not notice.

'That's real sad' he said. 'You coming all that way and getting here too late.' His voice was tender and he moved towards her. 'I expect you're feeling pretty low. I know I was when Ma died. Pa and I never had much to say to each other and since she went, we hardly speak at all. I miss her. And your Ma's dead too?'

Elizabeth frowned.

'I'm sorry. I didn't mean to pry. I always say more than I should. If Pa were here he'd tell me to shut it – or like as not belt me round the ears.' He smiled shyly.

'That's all right, Will. Call me Elizabeth. I do hope we can be friends.'

The boy grinned at her. 'I saw Pa in town today and he told me to get back here and clear the place up a bit. Didn't say why though. I'm sorry it's such a mess. I sleep in the hut there – I like to keep out of the old man's way – but I know the house is a bit of a tip. I'll get started right now.' He bounded up the step and stopped on the threshold, giving a long whistle.

'You've done a fine job – you must have worked real hard. It looks like a home. When Ma was alive she grew veggies at the back and flowers in front. She was always getting on at Pa to fix things up nicer. But he's never been one for spending money – and when she passed away the place went to rack and ruin. Pa and I never seem to have time and I don't think we'd noticed how bad it got – least not until now you've made it clean. All that dirt and mess just crept up on us. It's mostly just me here these days. Pa spends most of his time in town.'

Elizabeth smiled. 'It'd look better if I had some cleaning materials – I did this with just plain water. Once I get some washing soda and some soap – and a decent broom, I can do a proper job.'

Her tummy rumbled and she said 'I was about to cook some potatoes on that fire that you've doused into oblivion. How about digging me one of those hollows you were talking about and I'll fix us a meal and boil up some tea.'

'I'll gut the fish and we can cook them with the spuds.'

'Perfect.'

Before long they were seated side by side on the rug she had dragged out of the house, wrapped in warm blankets in the glow of the fire, sipping tea and enjoying the aroma of baking potatoes and river perch. The moon glowed behind the branches of the eucalyptus and cast a silvery sheen over the house, giving it a ghostly and yet beautiful appearance.

Elizabeth liked the boy already and marvelled at the difference between him and his taciturn father. He was a good-looking lad; both his personality and his looks must have been attributable to his mother as there was no trace of Jack Kidd in him. He chatted happily and freely and took her presence here for granted.

'What do you do all day, Will? Do you go to school?'

The boy laughed. 'Pa doesn't hold with schools or book learning. The only reason Hattie went to school was to keep her off his hands when Ma died and Miss Radley, the teacher up in town offered to take her in. Pa can read and write and Ma made sure Nat, Hattie and I could too. What learning Nat and I got came from Ma. When she died that was the end of it.'

'What a pity. Lessons are important. If you want to have a choice about your future, a good education is essential.'

'There's no time. Pa expects me to look after this place and since I was seven years old I've been working. We have sheep and a milk cow and there's veggies in the big plot down near the creek. There's always a fence to mend and things like that to do. Pa expects that my future's here. I know different, but there's no use telling him as there'd be trouble - like with Nat. When Ma was alive she spent all her time coming between him and Pa.'

'When did she die?'

'Five years ago – I'd just turned twelve, Hat was thirteen and Nat was sixteen. He left after she died. He and Pa fought real bad. I was glad he'd gone. It's quieter round here these days. Ma stopped them fighting but once she got ill it was terrible. They screamed and shouted and Ma was sick in her bed so she could do nothing. I hated it.'

'I'm sorry, Will. It must have been awful. Where's Nat now?'

'Who knows? He just buggered off. Took his horse and left and we've heard nothing since. I reckon he signed up.

Probably got himself killed over there in the war. There are people reckon he fell into the canyon. I don't miss him. He was real mean. I know I shouldn't speak evil of a brother but I can't help it. He was bad and I don't care if God strikes me dead for saying that.' He threw a stone into the dying embers of the fire.

Elizabeth reached out and touched his arm. 'I understand. I have a sister and I never want to see her or her evil husband again as long as I live, so I know how you feel.'

'You do?' He turned to her eagerly. 'We've got something in common then, Miss.'

'Elizabeth, please! Yes I suppose we have.'

As if gaining courage from her admission, Will swallowed hard and spoke. 'Lizbeth, why did you marry my Pa? You're a beautiful woman and he's a miserable old sod. It doesn't seem right to me. And this place isn't going to be much fun for someone like you. It's ten miles into town and when you get there there's nothing much there anyway. Why'd you marry him?'

'Don't ask me that, Will. It isn't right to speak of your father that way. I'm sure he's a good man really.'

'He's not. He's a miserable bastard. Soon as I save enough money I'm out of here too. In the meantime I keep out of his way, like Hattie does. I'm not as daft as Nat – better to keep my distance and avoid provoking him.' He threw another pebble into the fire. 'I reckon he left Hattie in town because he's hoping Miss Radley will turn her into a lady and he can marry her off to some rich fellow and get her off his hands. He certainly isn't educating her for her own good.'

Elizabeth sighed, acknowledging the probable truth of what the boy was saying. 'When do I get to meet Hattie?'

The boy shrugged. 'Who knows? She never comes out here – hasn't set foot in the place since they carried Ma out in her coffin. You could ask Pa if you want to meet her – but I can't see as he's likely to see the point.'

'Don't you see her?'

'I bump into her in in town sometimes. We don't have much to say to each other. I don't feel I know her any more. She used to be a bit of a wild child, always climbing trees and riding her pony. But she's a proper little lady now – with her nose in the air. She pretends she's not related to me and Pa. Can't say as I can blame her.'

'How sad. Were you close to her when your mother was alive?

He nodded. 'Me and Hat are just a year apart and we were scared of Nat and Pa so we stuck together. It's different now. Ma dying changed everything.'

She leaned over and pressed his hand. During the short silence that followed, Elizabeth leaned back and looked up at the night sky, seeing again that it was a different sky from the one she knew so well in England. The night was cloud-free and the strange constellations of stars were bright and clear.

'The stars are completely different from those at home.'

'Fair dinkum? you have a different sky in England? I love the stars; Ma taught me the names of some of them. There's the Southern Cross.' He pointed to the sky. 'See those bright stars one above the other - they're beta Centauri and alpha Centauri. If you look above them and to the left that's the Southern Cross.'

'We have the Plough and Orion back home. They were the only ones I ever knew. To be honest I didn't spend much time looking at them. I've never done anything like this before: eating a meal under the stars. I used to spend my evenings indoors – at concerts and parties or at home. Although I did love walking in the hills and on the beach in the daytime.' She sighed.

'What made you come to Australia, Lizbeth? It's going to be a very different life for you. I don't know if you realise that? Life here's pretty hard for a man, let alone for a woman and one brought up with city ways.'

'I didn't get along with my sister and I wanted to see some more of the world. I just hadn't banked on my father dying.'

The boy nodded.

'Tell me about the town, Will. Is it a big place?'

'Big enough and growing fast. People used to come and prospect for gold, but not these days. The gold's gone. There's coal and kerosene and stuff. Tourists come up here from the city because the air's fresh and the scenery's nice. It's popular for honeymoons. There's a fancy hotel and lots of guest houses and a few shops. And it's right on the edge of the canyon rim so there's pretty views across the valley. Cliffs and waterfalls and stuff like that. It's a good place I suppose. Oh and there's a railway too.'

'A railway? Up here?'

'Yes. Built by the Chinamen. They'd run out of convicts by then to do the hard work!' He laughed. 'It was convicts built the road from Sydney. I hope Pa lets you come into town with me some time. I think you'll like it there. A bit more for a lady to do and look at than there is out here.'

'What does your father do when he goes into town?'

'I don't really know about that. It's to do with the mine I think, but he doesn't tell me anything about that side of things. He just wants me to work here.'

'Does he visit Hattie?'

'If he does he never tells me about it. But he never tells me anything.' He gave a dry laugh. 'He got into the mining when Ma died. Everything changed then. Before that he used to talk a bit. Since Ma went it's just silence and cusses. This place was always pretty simple but at least it was like a home and not run-down. We never had much money but Ma was a good housekeeper and made the best of things and Pa made sure that she got what she needed. We had flowers in pots on the veranda and curtains at the windows. There was never much space but we managed. Since she died it's gone to hell – until today that is! You've worked a miracle.'

'If your father has mining interests he must be quite a wealthy man?'

'They say he's worth a fortune, but I've never seen a penny of it. I've no idea what he does with his money. He lives like he's not got a brass razoo. He spends most of his time in town, but I reckon he prefers it out here to whatever he does there. This is what he grew up with. I reckon, no matter how rich he could be, he'd still rather be sitting in the scrub, boiling up his billycan.'

Elizabeth smiled, then suddenly felt overcome with tiredness after her efforts of the afternoon. 'It's time I turned in for the night, Will.'

'Me too. I have to ride into town tomorrow to get that cleaning stuff for you.'

'Thanks, Will and goodnight.'

'Goodnight, Lizbeth. I'm glad you've come – at least for my sake I'm glad. But it's a shame for you.'

'Don't worry about me. I'm fine.' She leaned towards him and grazed his brow with her lips, then turned and went into the house. Will walked towards the little shack where he spent his nights, the deep flush on his face hidden by the darkness.

CHAPTER NINE

A NEW HOME

As soon as he climbed down from the wagon at the Black Water Colliery, Michael knew he'd made a mistake. The mine had an air of neglect that didn't square with the tales of untold wealth Fred Burton had spun in the bar. His instincts told him that no one was making a quick buck here. After years working at Berrywake Crag, he could sniff a diminishing mineral seam in the air. He saw resignation in the faces of the miners as they queued for the lift to take them underground. He saw it in the faces of the wives sitting outside their hastily put-together homes made from bits of bush timber and hammered-out kerosene cans. And he could see it in the scrawny bodies and tattered clothes of their children playing a half-hearted game of tag.

He turned accusingly to Fred Burton, who avoided his eyes and shrugged in apology.

'Look, mate. It's a job isn't it? These days any job's hard to come by. It'll pick up soon. This place will be boomtown again before we know it. You can always get digs in town if you don't mind the walk. Mind you, you're probably better off bunking out here when the weather's bad, mate.'

So here he was, nothing had changed. He'd substituted

the long walk down the dale from Hunter's Down to the pit at Berrywake Crag for a long trek through the bush from some miserable town to the Black Water Colliery. And he was going to be smashing up rocks for the rest of his life. If Minnie Hawthorn could see him now she'd be saying I told you so.

To make matters worse, it started drizzling: the kind of deceptively fine rain that soaks as thoroughly as a dip in the ocean. Michael pulled his cap down, turned his collar up and looked for shelter. There was none.

A fat man with a paunch and a badly fitting waistcoat came out of the site office, brandishing a clipboard and pencil. Telling the new men to line up in front of him, he squashed into a chair, protected from the rain by both the overhang of the office roof and a large umbrella. Michael disliked him on sight.

When it was Michael's turn to step forward, the man asked his name, age and marital status, then assigned him a number.

'Don't forget it or you won't get paid. You're on second shift. Start at 11 in the morning and finish at 7. Twenty minute break to eat your tucker. We don't like slackers round here so any sign of that and you're out on your arse, pom.'

He looked Michael up and down, lip curled, then cocked his head towards the mineshaft. 'Over there. See the shift manager. Tell him what you can do and he'll assign your work.'

He was detailed to go down in the cage with the next load of men, to work a side tunnel off the main seam. There were half a dozen men, a couple of whom had travelled up on the wagon from Sydney, and Michael had established an easy camaraderie with them, taking the inevitable jokes about his pommie provenance in good part. There wasn't much chance for levity down the pit though. The work was unrelenting, physically tiring, and the noise of the machinery prevented anything other than short, shouted instructions. The men knew what was expected of them and got on with wielding their pick axes and smashing the rock into smaller more manageable pieces that could be loaded into bags and dragged back up the shaft.

At the end of the shift, one of the lads offered to walk into town with him and introduce him to a landlady who could provide digs at a reasonable rate and was said to be a good cook. Anything had to be better than living out here in what was a glorified squatters' camp.

It was two days before Jack Kidd returned. He entered the shack without greeting and slung his bags on the floor. He made no comment on the transformation.

'Where's the lad?'

'Will's been working all day. Fishing and chopping wood I think. Supper will be ready in an hour.' She wiped her wet hands on a cloth and turned to him, ready to ask why he had neglected to mention his children, but he'd already left the room. Life as Mrs Jack Kidd was not going to stretch her conversational skills. Yet it was preferable to having to play the role of attentive wife. As long as she put food on his table and kept out of his way, it seemed that Kidd would expect little of her. But she would be expected to share the narrow bed with him: an uninviting prospect.

Her thoughts were interrupted by the return of her husband with Will close behind him.

'G'day Lizbeth.' The boy's voice was cheery, but he'd barely got the words out when Kidd cut in.

'Don't speak to her that way, boy. Show some respect.'

'I asked him to call me Elizabeth, Mr Kidd.'

'You keep your mouth shut.'

He pulled off his dusty boots and kicked them under

the bed. Undoing his shirt he scratched his scrawny ribcage and slumped into the chair.

'Bring me a beer, woman.'

'There is no beer.'

'In my saddlebag. Put away the rest of the stuff while you're at it.'

She went to pick up the bags that lay by the door, but Will got there first. He handed her the beer and assorted tins and supplies and she put them away on the makeshift shelf.

The evening passed slowly and in silence. As soon as they finished the meal, Will excused himself and went off to his quarters in the shed. Kidd continued to drink his beer, leaning back in the chair, staring at the rafters. She guessed these were not the only beers he had consumed that day and hoped the drink would lull him to sleep in the chair so she could enjoy another night alone in the bed. When she thought he had drifted off, she dimmed the lamp, crossed to the back of the room beside the bed and began to undress. Tomorrow she would ask Will to make her the frame for a screen. She could cover it with calico – she'd found a small stash in the bottom of the chest.

Fumbling for her nightgown, she realised Kidd was awake and watching her. She pulled the gown in front of her and sat down on the edge of the bed, trying to cover herself.

'Stand up.'

She froze.

'Stand up. I want to look at you.'

Still she sat, clutching the nightgown across her breasts.

'I won't ask you again, woman. Stand up.' His voice held a quiet threat.

Holding the nightdress in front of her body, she rose from the edge of the bed.

'Put that down.' Then, when she continued to stand

trembling behind her gown, 'Do as I say. Put it down.'

She laid the garment beside her on the bed and turned away from him.

'Turn around.'

She turned to face him, her hands automatically reaching in front to cover herself.

'Put your hands down. Now come over here.'

Her heart pounding, she crossed the room towards him. 'Closer.'

She stood in front of his chair, shivering, although the evening was mild. The lamp was dim, the wick burnt low. She felt ashamed standing there before him, exposed to his gaze. He didn't look at her eyes but focused on her body, slowly surveying every curve, from her breasts to her now slightly swollen abdomen. She turned her head away, feeling the blood burn in her face, longing to grab her clothes and escape from his scrutiny.

He leaned forward and put his hand on her belly. His palm was hard and rough, but warm against her skin and she flinched slightly at his touch. He stretched his hand out, flat against her skin and began to stroke her stomach with a circular motion. She tried to lean away but he placed his other hand on the small of her back and held her in position.

She closed her eyes and prayed for it to be over quickly, hoping he would be as fast in taking his pleasure as he had been when he rolled on top of her on their wedding night. But tonight Kidd was taking his time. He continued to massage her stomach with slow, gentle movements. His hand wandered up her belly and began to caress her breasts. She gave a long, involuntary shudder and began to breathe deeper, shorter and faster. Her breasts, swollen in response to the child inside her, ached as he touched them. Again she tried to pull away, but the hand pinioning her back held her in place. The other hand now moved back down her stomach, with slow circling movements that were beginning to arouse her. He rose from the chair and steered her back to the bed, still stroking her. She was gasping now. Ashamed that she was unable to control her own body, she tried to fight the warm and tingling sensation that was spreading through her and rolling in waves towards the wet area between her legs. He pushed her back onto the bed and slipped his fingers inside her and she cried out and arched her back. He was kneeling over her now, knees planted each side of her as he continued to work on her, and she felt her body respond to his fingers. She opened her eyes. He was looking at her. He pulled back from her and undid his belt.

'So you're carrying another man's child? Behaving like the Virgin Mary when all the time you've a little bastard growing in your belly.' His voice was low and, despite the words, seemed to bear no trace of anger.

Elizabeth felt a chill pass over her. 'How did you know?'

'I know the sign of a pregnant belly. I've fathered enough children to know that. Did you think you could trick me into believing it was mine?' As he spoke, he jerked his trousers off and positioned himself with her between his knees, pinning her shoulders against the bed as she tried to struggle upright. With a grunt he thrust himself inside her. This time her body responded as he entered her and she started to moan softly. He thrust slowly, holding his upper body away from her with his arms, which were planted either side of hers.

He spoke as he pushed into her. 'I don't care who fathered the bastard. As long as you keep it out of my way.'

She started to sob. 'I'm sorry. I don't want it. It was forced on me. I wish I were dead.'

Kidd ignored her and continued to pump away. 'You like this? Does it feel good? Bit of a whore aren't you?'

Elizabeth cried out as she reached her climax, then whispered, 'I'm not a whore.'

'Oh no?' He made a last thrust then rolled off her onto his back. 'Then how come you moan like one? And take your pleasure like one? And your bastard child can't have been an immaculate conception. My wife was a lady and I treated her like a lady. You're no better than the floozies at the flophouse up in town. But get one thing straight – your days of putting yourself about are done. You may be a whore but you're my whore, for the exclusive use of Jack Kidd.' He closed his eyes, put his hands behind his head and let out a loud beery belch.

Elizabeth rolled over and turned her face to the wall, ashamed and angry with her body for betraying her. It would have been better to have experienced pain than pleasure, when its source was a person who filled her with disgust and showed her nothing but contempt. She couldn't bear to look at him. Yet the feel of his calloused hands on her naked skin had aroused her. She had been unable to fight or resist it. Her body had taken over, had given itself up to the sensations that his slow, calculated caresses had provoked. Was she no better than a whore? Was the fact that she had been unable to control the response of her body proof that he was right? She thought about what he said of his late wife. Women were supposed not to take pleasure in such things. Her knowledge of such matters was limited. Her mother had never spoken of them. She thought of her sister. Sarah had produced two children with a third on the way. It was hard to believe that her sister actually took pleasure in her relations with Dawson, yet from her manner she could only surmise that she must do. The first time with Kidd had been hurried, ugly and undignified. Tonight she was embarrassed to her core, angry with her own body, fearful, yet unable to deny that she had found it strangely pleasurable.

Kidd's stentorian snoring filled the room as she lay beside him, trying to keep a gap between their bodies. Her

132

nightgown lay in a heap across the floor out of reach. She pulled the sheet higher and leaned into the wall.

Unable to sleep, her thoughts turned to Michael Winterbourne. She gave a shudder of pleasure as she imagined making love with him, feeling his arms around her, burying her head in his chest, looking into his eyes as he moved inside her, feeling again his lips upon hers. She stiffened and cringed that she had allowed herself to take pleasure from the touch of the man who lay beside her. Her love was and could only ever be for one man. A man she had met for so short a time, it was hard to believe she could love him. But she did. She really did – and she knew now it was a love that would last as long as she lived; a source of strength, even though it could never be returned.

She could not help smiling to herself in the dark as she thought again of Michael. His image was burned on her brain and she would never let it fade. It was better that she had met him so briefly and fallen in love, than that she had never had the chance to experience this feeling at all.

But tonight she had betrayed Michael by taking pleasure at her husband's touch. She stared up through the dark at the ceiling, where she could make out the ripples of corrugated iron in varying shades of darkness. Kidd stirred and turned over. The snoring stopped for a few moments then started up again.

If she had to live without the man she loved and must share the bed of a man she loathed, then why not take what pleasure she could from him? As his wife, she could not deny him her body, so was it not better that she should get some satisfaction from it? Compared with the violence Dawson had subjected her to, and the quick penetration of her wedding night, some physical pleasure from Kidd's touch was not such a bad bargain.

The next morning, when she woke up he was gone.

CHAPTER TEN

THE TOWN

It was almost two months before Elizabeth left the house to make the journey into the town. Every time she asked Kidd if she might accompany him, he refused. She grew annoyed and increased the frequency and intensity of her requests. The shack was a metaphor for her marriage: cold, bare and lacking much comfort and she wanted to escape from it if only for a few hours. She craved the sight of people: ordinary people going about their business, living ordinary lives and having ordinary conversations.

Instead, their married life had taken on a strange and perverse rhythm. Kidd was gone for days; overseeing whatever business he had in town. He would return home, usually for one night only, eat the food she put before him in complete silence, grunting or offering monosyllables in response to the attempts she made at conversation. After she had cleared away the dishes and Will had retired to his shed, Kidd would fall asleep in the chair or sit drinking a beer outside on the steps, until she started to prepare for bed – now undressing behind the screen that Will had made for her. Just as she had slipped beneath the sheets and was starting to drift into sleep, he would climb into the bed beside her, pull her nightdress up and lift his thin and wiry body on top of hers. Despite the sometimes perfunctory nature of his foreplay and the fact that she found nothing in him to attract her, her body usually responded. After a while she learned to accept this without recrimination. Since the first night they had spent together in the hut, he had never again compared her to his late wife or to the local prostitutes. Indeed he shared few words with her at all, to her relief. Theirs was a silent coupling, almost furtive, like a pair of animals rutting in the dark, a quiet, cold and unemotional centre to their marriage.

She found in Will the conversation that was absent with Kidd. They got in the habit of walking together when Kidd was away.

'Do you have any friends, Will?'

'Friends?' he laughed hollowly. 'You're joking aren't you?'

'But you're young. You should be with people your own age, not hanging about with an old lady like me.'

Will grinned up at her. 'You're not old, Lizbeth.'

'Don't you get lonely?'

'A bit I suppose. It's always just been the old man and me since Ma died. And he chews my head off. It's bonzer having you to talk to.'

There was a flurry of beating wings and a flash of colour rising from the vegetation in front of them.

'King parrots!' Elizabeth grinned and turned to the boy for endorsement.

'Right. You're getting good at this.'

'The birds here are so exotic. I've been used to boring old brown sparrows and starlings.'

'Come on then. We'd better get a move on if we're going to catch any rabbits today.'

'I'll watch you set the traps, but I'm not going to watch when you empty them. Poor little rabbits.'

'We've got to eat haven't we? I didn't notice you being

so picky when you tucked into that stew the other night.'

'I pretend they come from the butchers.'

Will laughed. 'Then you won't be wanting to watch me skin them later?'

'Not a chance.'

'If I get a load of them today I can sell the skins in town tomorrow.'

'You sell them?'

'Sixpence a skin. Don't tell Pa.' The boy tipped his head to one side and grinned at her. 'Mind you, I reckon the old man knows. That's why he keeps me on short rations. He's guessed I've got a profitable little line going. You can't get much past him.'

'You're not so daft are you young man? I bet you've got quite a stash of cash under your mattress haven't you?'

He winked at her. 'You suggesting something?'

'Just wondering what you're saving up for?'

'One day I'm running away to sea.'

She laughed and the two of them hurried off together, the boy carrying a burlap sack with the traps inside.

Most days, Elizabeth and Will took their meals together, Will always appreciative of the experiments she worked with the simple ingredients available to her. She lacked previous experience of cooking, but if the results were not always very appetising, Will never gave any indication. He ate heartily and enthusiastically and talked to her of the things he had seen or done that day: finding a dead joey, clearing ground to plant vegetables.

By contrast, when Kidd was at home, Will lost his tongue under the critical gaze of his father and barely responded to Elizabeth's attempts to draw him out. In the end she accepted this and stopped trying to make conversation, so the three sat in a silence punctuated by the sound of Kidd's jaws chewing and his occasional complaint about the quality of her cooking.

The days passed with Elizabeth learning the toils expected of the wife of a Blue Mountains smallholder including the weekly washing. When she dragged the big tub out, Will emerged from his shed.

'Let me help you.'

'Your father doesn't like you helping me.'

'I know – "Women's Work" – but I used to give Ma a hand – it's a heavy job for a lady. Besides, he's not around to see.'

Elizabeth gratefully accepted his help and they carried buckets of water to and fro until they had filled the big tub. She put the bedding and clothes to soak.

'I'll get the fire going in the washhouse' said Will.

Another large metal pail was put to boil over the fire and Elizabeth stirred and prodded the clothes back to cleanliness in small loads, each time dragging them back out to the big wooden tub to be scrubbed on the wooden washboard, rinsed and then wrung out. Will watched her, busy himself twisting wire to mend his snares.

She hung the washing on the line. 'I can't believe how hot I am.'

'It's the sun on the tin roof.'

'And the fire in the washhouse.' She wiped the perspiration from her forehead and smoothed her hands over her belly.

'I can't imagine what doing the washing will be like in the summer – and by then...' She stopped short, unwilling to think, let alone speak to Will, about her pregnancy.

But he spoke for her. 'It doesn't seem right for a lady like you to work like a digger, you being in the family way...' He studied his snare, brow furrowing.

Elizabeth blushed. She hadn't been sure he'd realised. She was embarrassed and decided to ignore the reference.

'Before coming to Australia I'd never done any washing.'

'No?' The boy looked at her curiously.

'I'm ashamed to say we had servants to do it for us.'

'Servants? That's not fair go. What did you do all day?'

'Not much now I think about it Will. And you're right it doesn't seem very "fair go" does it? I played the violin. I taught children to play it too.'

'You played the fiddle? Can you play it now? I'd love to hear you.'

'I left it in England.' She gave a rueful smile. 'I wish I hadn't. It would remind me of home. My mother and father loved to listen to me play.'

'Get the old fella to buy you a new one. Or I'll get you one with my rabbit money.'

'How can you run away to sea if you blow your ill-gotten gains on me? And I don't think your father likes music.'

'He used to. When Ma was alive he sang a lot.'

Elizabeth raised an eyebrow. 'Did he really? I can't imagine that.'

'He wasn't always a miserable bugger. Sorry – didn't mean to say that.'

'There's not much likelihood of him letting me take up the violin again. Where would I get one anyway?'

'In town. There's a shop sells musical instruments.'

'I'm starting to wonder if this mythical town exists. There's as much likelihood of your father taking me there as my being waited on by servants again!'

'Do you miss your old life?'

'It doesn't seem real any more. It's a faraway dream. My old self was a different person. And anyway there's no point in worrying about it. It's a closed chapter.'

'That's sad.'

'No it's not. If I'd stayed in England I'd never have met you would I?' She saw the blush creep up his neck and into his cheeks.

'Ask Pa to take you with him next time he goes to town. Wait till he's eaten and got a few beers down his neck and he'll be eating out of your hands.'

She laughed. 'You know that's not true, Will.'

'I know but you have to hope!'

But a thought had been planted, and the next evening, when Kidd had returned and they had partaken of their silent supper, instead of undressing and going to bed when Will retired and she had finished her tasks for the day, she sat down and set about darning and sewing from a pile of mending in a basket by the chair. This was a break in established routine. Kidd, dozing in his chair, realised that she was still sitting opposite him when she should have been warming the bed for him.

'What are you doing?' he snarled.

'Mending your socks and fixing a shirt for Will.'

'Go to bed.'

'I'm not ready yet.'

'I decide when you're ready. Go to bed.'

Emboldened by frustration at being a virtual prisoner, she put down her sewing and looked at him. 'I'm not going to bed until you agree to take me into town.' As she spoke she leaned back into the chair and parted her legs slightly.

Kidd looked stricken. He lunged towards her. 'Get in that bed right now before I take a belt to you.' His words were hard but his voice betrayed an anguish that told her that she had already gained a kind of supremacy. His need for her was greater than his need for control. He clutched at her breasts and tried to push his hand under her skirt. She pushed him away and stood up, her hands under her swollen belly.

'You'll do no such thing. If we want the townspeople to believe that this is your child, you'd better start behaving as though it is. I need a layette. And while we're at it, some clothes for me wouldn't go amiss. I had little enough when I arrived here and what I had is now ruined with all the scrubbing and cleaning I do. Not to mention straining at the seams in my condition.'

'Scrubbing and cleaning too good for you, woman?'

Impatience got the better of her and heedless of how he might react, she pressed on. 'I thought you were supposed to be a man of some importance. It's hard to believe it since you're ashamed to show me in the town and hide me away out here. I may be able to put up with it, but is it right that your child should? The baby should be dressed as befits the child of a man of stature. And this place needs fixing up properly. We need a room for the baby and it's not right that Will should be sleeping on a wheat bag in a shed built to shelter a pony. Why don't we all go in to town and get some provisions? Will can get some wood and nails to partition this room up – it's big enough to make two more small sleeping areas. I'll get some fabric and make something for the baby to wear and something for me. Nothing special – just something clean and practical. I could also buy some material for bedding and curtaining. It won't cost much if it's plain fabric and I can sew it myself.'

'Will's staying here. Do you think I can't afford to buy decent clothing? I'm one of the richest men in this town.'

'If you stand for something round here, show people you have a wife and a baby on the way. Most men would be proud of it.' She paused seeing the look of amazement on Kidd's face, then pressed home her advantage. 'Lots of men would envy you. More than fifty years old with a young wife and a baby coming. If you hide us away they'll think something's amiss. They'll realise the truth – that you forced me to marry you and the baby isn't yours.'

Kidd went white and lunged at her. She'd expected this reaction and parried his arm with hers. He stopped, as if seeing the sense in what she had said. He stepped back and looked her up and down. His tone was contemptuous.

'Think you're too good for me? You speak to me with airs and graces like I'm a dog at your feet. But that's not the way it is, is it? It's you who have nothing. Just the rags you're wearing. Where's all your finery now? No call for it here, with all that cleaning and scrubbing. I *own* you. Don't ever forget that.' He was shouting now. 'Everything you have is down to me. Including that baby as far as the world's concerned. I *will* take you to town, but only because I choose to do so. In fact we'll stay up in town until the little bastard is born.'

'That's wonderful,' she cried. 'Where will we stay? Will I get to meet Hattie?'

He ignored her and strode through the door to sit on the veranda with his beer, leaving her to go to bed undisturbed.

The trip into town took place in total silence. Will was left behind at the shack and Elizabeth was saddened that she might not see him again until the baby was born and they returned. Kidd had made that clear when she urged Will to lose no time in coming to see them.

'He's staying here. Understand that, boy? You've work to do and I'm tired of seeing you hanging around town selling bloody rabbit skins, when you should be working.'

'But Pa...'

'Shut your mouth and heed what I say.'

The boy bit his lip and kicked at the dusty ground. Elizabeth slipped down from the trap and went to hug him. 'Don't worry, Will. I'll see you soon. Look after yourself.'

The boy's eyes were sad and she could see the loneliness in them. 'You're a good friend to me, Lizbeth. I'll miss you.'

Before Kidd could raise a curse, she climbed up beside him and faced the road ahead. He flicked his whip and the pony shuffled forward. She turned as they reached the bend in the track and looked back at Will, but he was already walking away, his shoulders slumped.

The journey was uncomfortable. The road was bumpy and full of potholes that she was sure Kidd did not always try to avoid. She had one hand on her stomach to cushion the baby, the other on the side of the trap as it swung from side to side when they hit a pothole or veered around them.

After driving through endless scrub, the occasional houses and shacks grew in number, until they were a continuous development along the roadside, looking more established the nearer they got to the centre of the town. Many had well tended gardens and brightly painted signs offering guest accommodation, some just a bare space in front with a few chickens scratching around. Most of the buildings were single storey, raised slightly off the ground and constructed in painted wood panels. The town had an air of prosperity, but also seemed to have grown up in haste and not always with sufficient planning and attention.

They came to a house larger than most of its neighbours, set back from the road in extensive grounds. Kidd reined the pony into the driveway that ran beside the house, leading to a large stable. The front door of the house opened and a tall man walked towards them with his hand raised ready to help Elizabeth down from the trap.

'Good afternoon, Mrs Kidd,' he said. 'We've been watching out for you. Welcome to Kinross House. You must be tired, Ma'am. Let me take that bag.'

Anticipating that Kidd would not have supplied the information, he added, 'I am Oates, Madam. I look after things for Mr Kidd here at Kinross House.'

Elizabeth looked around her in astonishment. The house was very grand indeed. She could not imagine a greater contrast from the shabby shack she had been living in. Unlike its neighbours, it was built with two storeys and the front door was large and solid and set in the middle of a wide, covered veranda.

She turned to Kidd, but he was already turning the pony around to head back to the road in his customary cloud of silence.

'Come in, Madam. Come in. You should get some rest. Mrs Oates will show you your room.'

A plump, smiling woman was waiting on the doorstep. 'Welcome to Kinross House, Mrs Kidd.'

'I don't understand,' Elizabeth said as she followed the couple across the threshold and into a large hallway with a sweeping staircase. 'Whose house is this? Am I to stay here tonight?'

Mrs Oates raised her eyebrows and glanced at her husband. 'He never has much to say for himself does Mr Kidd, that's for sure. But I'd have thought he would have told you this much.' She shook her head. 'Kinross House belongs to Mr Kidd, Madam. It's your home. Come in, you look exhausted.'

The woman looked her new mistress up and down. Elizabeth was wearing the only item of her limited wardrobe that had not been ruined by the arduous life out at Wilton's Creek. The green silk dress had lain untouched since its brief outing for her wedding ceremony. While rather creased after the rigours of the pony and trap and straining slightly at the seams, it was a beautiful garment and should still pass muster in even the most elegant circles of this outback town, which was more than could be said for the other contents of her suitcase. She shuddered at the thought of the shabby dresses inside. What on earth would Mrs Oates make of them? Clearly she had no idea Elizabeth had been working as Kidd's kitchen skivvy.

'Your bedroom is the first on the right at the top of the staircase. There's hot water and towels laid out ready for you. I'll bring you up a cup of tea and some sandwiches in a few minutes and then Mary can draw a bath for you. At four o'clock Mr Kidd has given instructions for Oates to take you in the automobile to the Salon de Paris for a fitting.'

Elizabeth was dumbfounded. It made no sense. Why had Kidd put her through the ordeal of the last few weeks, when he had a fine house here in town? Why did he want to spend time at Wilton's Creek himself? While Will said his father preferred a simple outback life, it was inconceivable that he could own a place like this and keep his son scratching out an existence on a primitive small-holding in the bush.

She opened the bedroom door. It was an elegant, opulent room. The floor was polished wood; the enormous bed was covered with a blue, silk counterpane in luxurious contrast to the threadbare bedding at Wilton's Creek. Matching blue silk curtains hung at the tall windows. With a gasp, Elizabeth rushed towards them, overcome by the beauty of the view in front of her. The afternoon sun was lighting up spectacular crags and cliffs and beyond them a wide valley with mountains on the other side. The blue haze above the eucalyptus trees spread throughout the valley as the trees made a dense canopy in the bottom and reached high up the slopes and craggy walls. Waterfalls plummeted over the edge of the chasm. In the distance, she could see birds circling high above the trees. She had never seen a sight more beautiful and less expected. She knew she would never tire of rising in the morning to be greeted with this view. Her spirits lifted.

Even marriage to Jack Kidd was a fate to which she could be reconciled. The privations of the last few weeks must have been some kind of test. She couldn't imagine why he had wanted to put her through it, why he felt he had to test whether she was strong enough to cope with the hardships of outback life? A needless test, if she was to be mistress of this beautiful house, with its servants and exquisite objects. She gazed around her at the oil paintings on the walls, landscapes that mirrored the views outside the windows, at the delicately carved furniture and the fine bone china on the washstand.

There was a knock at the door and she turned, expecting Mrs Oates, but it was a maid, a young girl with an unmistakeable Irish brogue and the reddest cheeks Elizabeth had ever seen.

'Afternoon Ma'am. Here's your tea and some sandwiches. Mrs Oates said you were sure to be hungry.' She placed the tray on a small table in front of the windows. 'I'm Mary, Ma'am. Your bath will be ready in ten minutes. Please let me know if you need anything else?' With a smile that lit up her chubby, country face, she hurried out of the room.

When Elizabeth descended, refreshed by the tea and sandwiches and a long soak in the bathtub, Oates was waiting at the front door, with a gleaming maroon motor car ready in the driveway. He was wearing a peaked cap and holding a large pair of leather gloves.

She had not driven in an automobile since her father had sold his pride and joy before coming to Australia. Dawson's modest salary had never permitted him to aspire to automotive ownership and motorcars were still rare on the streets of Northport in 1920. Oates opened the door and helped her in, before taking his place in the front.

'I'm surprised to see a motorcar up here in the mountains, Mr Oates. How on earth did it get up here from the coast?'

'Ma'am, it's not the easiest of journeys. There are stretches where we needed horses to give us a bit of a helping hand. That was a few years ago. But now it only gets used around town and then not very often. Mr Kidd is not fond of motorcars. He prefers to use the pony and trap or to ride his horse. Most of the time the motor is in the stable. I take it out for the odd run to keep it ticking over. There are quite a few vehicles in the town, as well as a large motor coach to take the tourists around the mountains. Most people come up on the train.'

'Why did Mr Kidd buy a motor car if he doesn't like to use it?'

The man gave a slightly embarrassed cough before

speaking, 'I understand he didn't purchase it. I believe he er... 'inherited it' along with the house and all its contents. He has a lot of luck with the cards does Mr Kidd. I'm sure now you're here it'll get more use.'

They had reached the centre of the town. There was a large and imposing hotel, The Queen Alexandra, set back from the road on rising ground with sweeping driveways bounding each side of a large terraced lawn, thin and brown from the past summer's drought. The poverty of the garden did not detract from the splendour of the building. It was built on three floors with a turret structure at one end, and a balustraded wrought iron veranda at the front. The tiled roof contrasted with most of the other buildings clustered along the sides of the main street, which, like the shack at Wilton's Creek, were mostly roofed in corrugated iron.

'That's a fine-looking hotel, Mr Oates. Does it get much trade up here?'

'Why yes, ma'am. People come to the Blue Mountains for their health and for holidays as the air up here's fresh and clean. Some treat the town as a kind of sanatorium after they've been sick. Others come for the scenery and the excursions. It is a very popular tourist destination and a favourite for honeymooners.'

The car pulled up outside a shop-front that appeared a little grander than its fellows. It had a large double window with a pair of tailor's dummies displaying what must have been the latest fashions in New South Wales. Elizabeth smiled to herself. Northport was not exactly Paris, but it did seem to be a couple of years ahead of this place in acquiring the latest designs. Her green silk dress was of the minute, compared to the display in the Salon de Paris. But compared to the rags most of her clothes had become, the window display was tempting. As she got to the door, her heart sank. How was she to pay? Oates, as though reading her mind, moved to her side and held open the door. 'Just choose your purchases, Ma'am and Miss Godfrey will put them on the account. It's all arranged. I'll be outside waiting for you.'

A bell rattled as she crossed the threshold. A small pinched-face woman rushed forward to greet her.

'Mrs Kidd? Take a seat. I'm Miss Godfrey. I'll bring some selections for you to look at.' She paused and managed to appear both smug and slightly embarrassed, as she looked Elizabeth up and down, taking in the lines of the green silk dress and doubtless searching for signs of her condition. 'I understand Madam is expecting a happy event and will require some suitable clothes?'

Elizabeth blushed. Did the whole town know?

'Mrs Oates said you'd be calling in. When you're finished here you'll find a good selection of items at Motson's the Haberdashery and General Stores for when the happy event has happened.'

Elizabeth was irritated by her coyness. 'I presume you mean I can buy a layette there?'

The woman nodded and scurried away to the rear of the store, returning with an array of gowns in varying shades of drab.

'No thank you' she said before the woman could lay the dresses out before her. 'I'm having a baby, not attending a funeral. Something brighter please. Like this.' She leaned forward and fingered the hem of a deep-pink watered-silk gown.

'Madam, it's usual to wear something a little quieter and less obvious when one is in your condition.'

'My condition? I'm not ill.' She was about to add that she was not in mourning either, when she remembered that she ought to be. But she was not going to make public the loss of her father. She was done with mourning and clinging to the past; it was time for her life to go on. Her pregnancy was a source of shame to herself alone. No one else need know – as far as other people were concerned she was carrying ack Kidd's baby.

'I'm sorry, Madam. I didn't mean to offend'. The woman stared at the floor and shuffled her feet.

Elizabeth smiled. 'No offence taken. Now bring me something more colourful please. I'd like a shorter hemline than those, before you suggest otherwise.'

'All our apparel for expectant mothers is full length and the brightest colour I have in the maternity line is olive green.'

'Then, why don't you show me something for a larger lady who's not an expectant mother and maybe with a bit of alteration we can find something that will fit the bill.' She smiled brightly at Miss Godfrey.

'Very well, madam. Right away.'

Half an hour later, Elizabeth left the shop having ordered three day dresses and two for evenings, all pinned and ready for the alterations to be carried out with delivery promised for the following day.

Her visit to Motson's Haberdashery was more straight-forward and she was able to purchase a layette for the baby-to-be, without comment from the sales staff. She set off back to Kinross House with a sense of quiet satisfaction and achievement.

The girl was waiting in the drawing room when she entered, but Elizabeth didn't see her at first, as she was standing motionless with her back to the window, her brown school uniform dress merging with the brown bro-cade of the drawing room curtains. Elizabeth jumped in fright when she realised there was someone there.

The girl stepped forward, looking Elizabeth in the eye without smiling in greeting and offering no hand. 'You're younger than I thought you'd be.'

Elizabeth's instinct was to rush forward and take the hand of her stepdaughter but something made her hold back.

'You must be Hattie? How lovely to meet you. Will told me all about you. I'm so happy that we get to meet at last.'

Harriet Kidd turned away and gave her attention to the garden outside the window, where a couple of brightly plumaged lorikeets were screaming at each other in the branches of a bottlebrush tree. She was tall but slight of build, with narrow shoulders that sloped downwards from a slender neck. Her skin was pale and perfect, like the surface of a bowl of cream. Her face was framed by light brown hair, left long around her shoulders, its soft waves complementing slightly angular features. It was a face that would have merited the description of beautiful, had it been illuminated by her eyes. As she turned her gaze back to Elizabeth, they were lifeless and cold.

Elizabeth spoke again. 'Will you take some tea? I'll call Mrs Oates. Please sit down.'

The girl ignored the offer and turned again to the window. Elizabeth, tired from her shopping expedition, eased into a chair and slipped her hands behind her to support her back. 'I must sit down myself. I'm a little tired.'

The girl turned towards her. 'Do what you like. I'm not staying. I just wanted to find out what a gold-digger looks like.'

Elizabeth sighed. It was going to be difficult. The girl was as cold as her brother was warm. 'I know it can't be easy for you. It must have been very hard losing your mother.'

The girl interrupted. 'Don't speak of my mother. You've no right to talk to me about her. You're nobody, turning up out of nowhere and flashing your eyes at an old man to coax him into marriage, just so you can do his children out of what's rightfully theirs.'

'Just a minute, Hattie. I've no intention of doing you out of anything.'

'And don't call me Hattie; my name is Harriet. As far as I'm concerned you and the brat you're expecting can go to hell.'

She strode away, slamming the front door behind her and Elizabeth heard the crunch of her steps on the gravel drive. Almost immediately, Mrs Oates appeared. 'Everything all right, Ma'am? I see Miss Harriet has left?'

Elizabeth flushed, hoping Mrs Oates had not heard the exchange, but fearing she had. 'Yes. I offered her tea but she was in a hurry.'

'Don't you mind her, Ma'am. She's not the easiest of girls. She can be a bit rude. Rather full of herself, if you don't mind me saying? It's not my place to say so, her being Mr Kidd's daughter, but she feels the lack of a mother. Miss Radley at the school is too soft by half. I was saying to Mr Oates only last week that Miss Harriet needs a good talking-to and some strict discipline. She's too fond of getting her own way. Miss Radley's too timid to stand up to her. Can I get you some tea?'

Elizabeth smiled. 'Mrs Oates, you're a mind-reader. A cup of tea would be perfect. I'm a little tired and I have to admit my first meeting with Harriet didn't go as I'd have wished.'

'Don't worry. A good cuppa will make you feel better.' With a kind smile, the woman left the room.

Elizabeth knew what it was to lose a mother. She recalled her own spoiled and pampered existence back in Northport and, while she hoped she had never been as frosty as Harriet, she knew had not always been without fault.

She decided to call on the girl at Miss Radley's and try to make peace. She would look past the cold and unfriendly facade and try to discover the girl who had once been Will's little sister Hattie.

CHAPTER ELEVEN

THE SCHOOL HOUSE

Michael was on a late morning shift. He left his lodgings and headed for the centre of town. There was time before his shift to call into the post office and mail his first earnings to his parents. After paying the money for his digs there wasn't much left but he'd been careful and, at the risk of being tagged as unsociable, he'd resisted the invitation to join the other men for a few beers on payday. There wasn't a lot of time for drinking anyway, not with the alcohol curfew that was in force throughout the state.

It was barely eight in the morning yet the main street was thick with people. Outside the schoolhouse, children were enjoying their last few minutes of liberty, before the start of the day's lessons and clustered about the yard, playing hopscotch and follow my leader. As he passed by, a child gave a high pitched scream that was taken up by the other children and spread like bushfire, so that the happy playground became a cacophony of noise, as panicking children ran screaming for help.

He pushed his way through the people on the pavement. A small boy lay on the ground, surrounded by distraught children.

'It were a snake' a small girl cried, jumping up and down on the spot.

'Did you see it?' another child responded.

'It bit Johnny. It's gone behind the trees over there.'

'He's going to die!' More wailing and rising hysteria.

He didn't hesitate. He ran into the yard and took the child by his leg and bending low over his stricken form, sucked on the leg in an attempt to get out the venom. He realised at once that there was none.

'You'll live. The snake didn't get you.'

The door of the school opened and the schoolmistress emerged and pushed her way through the crying children. Cradling the boy in her arms, she asked Michael what had happened.

A child spoke before he could answer. 'It was a snake Miss. The man sucked out the poison.'

'I did nowt. There were no poison. Looks like a dry bite. Just a bit of a sting. But as well to 'ave the doc take a look at him. I don't know the snakes here.'

'Thank you so much, Mr…?'

'Winterbourne.'

She stretched out her hand and smiled. 'Verity Radley. I'm the schoolmistress. Thank you for what you did.'

She turned towards the crowd of passers-by and parents gathering at the edge of the schoolyard and called out.

'All's well, ladies. You can go home now. School will be starting as usual.'

Michael helped the boy onto his feet but was almost knocked aside by a woman who burst through the crowd and swept the child into her arms. She set him down again, grabbed him by the hand and led him away, the recipient of a quantity of advice from the crowd on home remedies and choice of doctor. As she hurried off to put some or all of these suggestions to the test, she called back over her shoulder to Michael. 'Thank you, mister. You saved my boy's life.'

'Get the lad to a doctor. He should be fine.'

Michael picked up his jacket from where he'd flung it on the ground and made his way through the dispersing crowd of onlookers. As they stepped aside to let him pass, one woman blocked his path. With a shock of recognition he looked into the face of Elizabeth Morton.

She was as astonished as he was. They stood rooted to the spot staring at each other in disbelief. Michael was paralysed, unable to move or speak, as the schoolyard, the crowd and the last straggling children were wiped from his consciousness and the world stopped. There was only her.

How many times he had dreamt of this moment? Now that it was a reality he couldn't remember the script. From the look on her face she felt exactly the same.

She pushed away a lock of hair that had escaped from her chignon. He wanted to take her in his arms. Her face was a mixture of joy and disbelief. He went towards her, half stumbling, his throat choked with emotion as he said her name.

As he reached for her, she stepped back and her hands dropped to her belly. He saw the ring on her wedding finger and his heart almost stopped.

Her face contorted as she struggled to speak and he realised she was not only married, but expecting a child. Her hands were gathering her open coat across her stomach as though she was trying to disguise the fact, but it was unmistakeable. He stood looking at her. Frozen. Dumb. Afraid. Eventually he spoke.

'You're married. And yer having a bairn?'

She nodded.

'That's why you didn't come to meet me? Did you think it were a bit of a joke? Were you toying with me? A way to pass the time on the voyage? A fine lady having a laugh leading me along? Slumming it?'

'It wasn't like that at all. Please ... let me explain.'

'What's to explain? I can see for meself.'

He paused, then shook his head. 'I waited four hours for you. I see now why you didn't turn up. You never intended to. I bet you had a right old laugh about the poor sod that was daft enough to think someone like you might feel summat for him? If you wanted to make me feel stupid, you succeeded.'

Elizabeth stretched a hand towards him, but he shoved it away. She said, 'I didn't want to hurt you and it's not as it seems. I can explain. I tried... I wanted...' She paused, suddenly at a loss as to what to say. Then as though she realised it was pointless, she bent her head and covered her eyes.

Seeing her standing there with her swollen abdomen, he felt as though he had been kicked in his stomach. The nerve endings in his skin prickled and there was a hollowness inside. Something was blocking his chest cavity, tightening, threatening his ability to breathe.

Elizabeth started to speak. 'I tried to get to you that afternoon, but...'

'I don't want to know.' He spat the words out, afraid he was losing control of his emotions. He wanted to be as far from her as possible. Away from the shock of seeing her with another man's ring on her finger and carrying another man's child. He began to run. He didn't look back, picking up speed. He ran past the post office, past the hotel in the centre of the town, past the neat rows of wood-panelled tin-roofed houses and on until he reached the edge of the town and had to stop where the land changed to a steep escarpment and the thick forest trees and undergrowth barred his way. Exhausted and gasping for air, he flung himself down on the grass and closed his eyes as the earth tilted beneath him.

He'd never expected to see her again. And certainly not here in a remote mountain town. He tried to piece together what had happened. She must have been pregnant when he met her? Married all along. Or if not, on her way to get married. There was no doubt in his mind. She had dallied with him, an on-board flirtation. It was probably common practice on those long sea voyages. He thought of how he had confided in her. How he had opened his soul to her and told her what he'd done to Danny. He thumped the ground with his fists. I'm a fool. I've been taken for the biggest idiot.

He didn't know if she were living in MacDonald Falls or passing through? It was a small town and he risked running into her again. Pull yourself together, mate. Get on with the job. Make some money then move on. Forget her. She wasn't worth it. Yet as he thought this, he knew he didn't really believe himself.

Elizabeth leaned on the schoolyard wall, fighting to hold back the tears. That afternoon on the Sydney harbour front seemed aeons ago, unreachable, a dream. Hopeless. A chasm had opened between her and the man she loved. She remembered looking into his eyes the last time they had met, knowing with certainty that he loved her. But today there was nothing. When she saw him in the playground she'd experienced a surge of joy. She'd forgotten her pregnancy until she saw the look in his eyes as he recognised her condition and a curtain dropped over his face and shut her out. His eyes had had a blankness. He had run from her. Actually run away, as though he was escaping a fire or a flood.

Panic swept over her. Helplessness at her inability to undo what had been done. Alone. Lonely. Cut to the quick by his coldness. She steadied herself against the wall and took some deep breaths. The baby kicked inside to remind her of its presence and she cursed it.

Suddenly aware that someone was watching her, she saw Harriet in the schoolroom door. Had she witnessed the meeting with Michael? The girl, seeing her looking, went inside without acknowledging her presence. Elizabeth abandoned her plan of calling on her. She was in no state for another difficult encounter.

She slipped her hand into her pocket and felt the familiar rough linen of Michael's handkerchief. For a moment she contemplated throwing it away, but couldn't bear to lose the last vestige of him. Despite the cruel look in his eyes and the way he'd run from her, this brief meeting had reinforced the strength of her feelings for him. She walked back to the waiting car.

CHAPTER TWELVE

A BIRTH

The pain started in the middle of the night. Kidd was beside her in bed. In the last few weeks he had left her alone, sliding into bed and falling quickly into a noisy sleep. Elizabeth was unsure whether this was out of consideration for her condition or fastidiousness about it. The bed was wide and very comfortable after the lumpy mattress at Wilton's Creek and so big that she was able to pretend she was alone in it.

The early contractions had been merely uncomfortable and she lay there quietly, counting between them, while Kidd slept. They went on for hours without seeming to get anywhere. The pain was dull and lasted only a short period each time it came. But then as the first light emerged below the heavy bedroom curtains, it changed. She never imagined it would be like this. She remembered the screams of her sister when she gave birth. In Sarah's case, the labours had been blessedly short and she showed little discomfort afterwards, so Elizabeth had put the screaming down to Sarah's desire for dramatic effect. But now, as her whole body felt as though it was being ripped apart, she could not hold back her own cries.

Kidd leapt out of bed, flung on a dressing gown and ran onto the landing to call Mrs Oates. The portly, but still sprightly woman was at their door in seconds, her husband dispatched to summon the doctor and Kidd relegated to the drawing room and the comfort of a bottle of whisky. Mary appeared at the bedside with a bowl of water, a pile of towels and a cheery smile. As Elizabeth sobbed and moaned, Mrs Oates was calm and authoritative and Mary full of chatter and reassurance, regaling them with stories of the birth of her numerous younger brothers and sisters. Elizabeth wanted to tell her to go to hell but lacked the energy.

Her body was wracked with pain and she prayed to die so that it would be over. Instead it got worse with each contraction. Sweat poured down her face faster than the attentive Mary could wipe it away.

Mrs Oates clutched her hand. 'Come on, Mrs Kidd, take a deep breath and try to relax. Breathe in now.'

Every time she tried to relax in the lull between the waves of pain, another contraction hit her in a crescendo of agony. The dawn turned to day and she was vaguely aware of the presence of the doctor, barking instructions at the two servants. It was February and the summer was unusually hot for the mountains.

Mrs Oates wiped her brow. 'Be glad you're not in the city. I'd not want to be in labour with the temperature it is in Sydney at the moment.'

Elizabeth was unimpressed. She barely took anything in, as the contractions came fast and furious, until she felt her body could take no more. But still her labour went on. Every now and then, Mary or Mrs Oates whispered words of encouragement, as if she were a small child who had done well at her schoolwork and deserved a pat on the back.

It finally came to an end. With an effort, of what seemed to her superhuman proportions, Elizabeth was relieved of the burden she had carried for so long. She lay back exhausted on the sweat-soaked sheets, while the doctor and Mrs Oates ministered to the baby. The child yelled with lung-bursting intensity. Mary, ready with fresh linen, prepared to change the bedding, but Elizabeth pushed her away.

'Please leave me alone. Let me rest.'

'Come along, Mrs Kidd. The sheets are soaking. You can't lie in a wet bed. Here I've done this side. Just ease over and I'll do the other. Now you're ready to see your lovely little boy. Just listen to him. A strong little laddie. Just like his Da. Mr Kidd's going to be proud of the little fella.'

Elizabeth groaned, sank back into the pillows and closed her eyes. The agonies of labour had left her exhausted and anxious. Now she must face what she had until now pushed to the back of her consciousness: seeing the face of Charles Dawson in the child. She broke into wracking sobs.

'There, there my dear.' It was the gentle voice of Mrs Oates. 'Doctor Reilly has checked this beautiful little boy and he's fine and healthy – just perfect. You can hold him now.'

Eyes still tightly shut, Elizabeth snarled. 'Take him away. I don't want to see him. I never want to see him.'

Mrs Oates stepped back, eyebrows raised but the young Irish girl spoke first.

'Come on, my lovely. You're just tired. You've been very brave and it's all over now. This little fella needs a feed and a bit of a cuddle from his mammie.' Mary was cradling the crying child in her arms. 'See what a little charmer you have here. I'll be off to make you a nice cup o' tea.'

With that the girl placed the small bundle in his mother's arms and left the room, leaving Mrs Oates standing guard at the bedside.

As soon as she felt him in her arms she was lost. He was so small and so light. It was hard to imagine that such a tiny creature had been capable of inflicting so much pain in his entry to the world. He had stopped crying and nuzzled up to Elizabeth's breast, making soft noises like a small animal. He had his own special smell. It was like nothing she had known before. She looked at his face and was overwhelmed with love. It was extraordinary.

His face was nothing like Charles Dawson's. As she gazed into it she didn't even think of the father. Her own face lit up with a smile. The baby's skin was soft, downy and flawless. His features were in miniature but all perfect. She had never seen anything so beautiful. She stared enraptured at his miniature fingernails and his little hands clenching and unclenching into fists.

'Let him have the breast, Ma'am. He'll know what to do.'

Elizabeth drew aside her nightgown and turned the baby towards her breast. The child began sucking with gusto as Elizabeth winced in discomfort, but smiled with pride at the greedy way he sucked.

She knew then that she would fight to the death for this child. Nothing would take him from her. He was hers and she was his. As she looked at him, the pain of labour was forgotten; the identity of the boy's father an irrelevance.

She would call him William after her father. Then she remembered Will. As far as the world was concerned the baby's father was Kidd. It would be absurd for a man to give two living sons the same name. The boy would have to take her father's middle name. William Michael Morton. Michael? It was a crazy idea. But somehow it was also very sane. It was still a link to her father, a means of honouring him as the man he had once been and the first step in trying to forgive him. But to bear the same name as Michael Winterbourne? What better model could she have for how she would like this child to grow up? Tall, handsome, strong, caring, independent, fiercely proud. Yes, she would name him Michael.

There was a knock at the door and Kidd entered. He

strode to the end of the bed. 'Let me see the brat.'

'Oh Mr Kidd he's beautiful.' Mrs Oates was beaming.

'Looks like all new-borns. Ugly little runts.' He glanced at the child and turned to go. Then paused. For a fleeting moment Elizabeth thought she detected a softening in his countenance, until the customary frown reasserted itself.

'Mr Kidd, I thought we could call him after my father, but obviously we can't call him William. Michael was Father's second name. I think that would be a fine name for him. Do you agree?'

'He should be named for me, John.'

'It would mean so much to me to remember my late father too. ' She gritted her teeth. 'Especially as it was through him that I came to be married to you, sir. Shall we say Michael John?'

'Call him what you like. I'm off now to Wilton's Creek. Don't know when I'll be back.'

'Please give my good wishes to Will. Tell him I can't wait to introduce him to his baby brother!'

Kidd ignored her and moved to leave the room, pausing by the dressing table.

'This is for you. But don't go near the bloody thing when I'm in earshot.'

He placed a large, brown-paper, wrapped parcel on the dressing table and left the room. The parcel's shape was unmistakable: a violin. The old devil had remembered she played. Life was full of surprises. She looked down at the baby, listening to the little noises he was making and wondering what he had made of his first moments.

'Welcome to the world, Michael John Kidd.' As she slid into an exhausted sleep herself, she realised she was actually happy.

The fellow he'd met in the bar had told him that what would take a year to earn on a sheep farm, could be in his pocket after a couple of months in the mines. But the promises had been empty ones. Michael had paid over the odds for a place on the wagon that brought him here, only to find that pay and conditions in the coal mines were nothing like the man described. There was discontent in the workforce and even talk of strikes, but with so many men out of work and the economy struggling after the impact of the Great War, they had little choice but to get on with it and take what they could get.

He had been lucky: he still didn't fully understand what it was about him that had taken the boss's fancy? One morning, as he'd been about to descend in the shaft to the coalface, the owner pulled him aside.

'What's your name?'

'Winterbourne, sir.'

'You're the Pommie then? Look lively. I've a job for you. Pick four or five men and get yourselves over to the North side. The pithead entrance has collapsed. I want you to shore it up and seal it off as it's out of use and I don't want any children or animals falling down the shaft. Do it as fast you can.'

Before Michael could ask for further instructions the mine owner strode back to the pit offices. The other miners looked at Michael dubiously.

'Get you, Pommie! Who's the boss's pet? How come he's picked you, mate? You've only been here five minutes and you don't know your arse from your elbow!'

'Aye, that's as may be, but I know *your* arse from your elbow and I'll give you a kick up it if you don't look lively, mate. I'll take you, Ned, along with Walt and Frank. Shift your arses, lads.'

'We don't get paid full whack if we don't go below,' one of the men protested.

'You'll get paid just the same.'

There was muttering among the men, but Michael cut in. 'You'll get paid the same. I've told you.'

Looking at each other doubtfully, the chosen crew gathered up their tools and followed Winterbourne to the disused shaft where they began clearing away fallen debris and shoring up the broken supports, ready to seal the opening. They'd been on the job about two hours when Robinson, the colliery accountant appeared.

'What the hell do you think you're doing? You should be down below. I'll dock all your wages for this.'

Michael carried on heaving a block of timber into position and replied with his back to the man. 'The gaffer's orders.'

'You're paid as miners and the pay is for going below, not for spending the day in the sunshine doing odd jobs. Get yourselves down number three shaft, like the roster says. If this job needs doing, then casuals can do it. And I'll make sure your wages are half the rate for the last couple of hours.'

'I told you. It were the boss's orders.'

'Right now the only boss around is here is the one in front of you. And I'm telling you to get yourselves down that shaft or you can collect what's owed to you and bugger off.'

The men looked at Winterbourne and grumbling "I told you so", were about to head back to the cage.

Winterbourne called out to them, 'Stay here, lads. We've a job to get done. Like the boss told us.' His voice was calm and the men glanced at each other then picked up their tools again.

Robinson looked about to explode. His face reddened and he tucked his thumbs into the braces that stretched to bursting point over his extensive potbelly. He looked like an inflatable balloon that had escaped its tether. Winterbourne continued to clear the rubble from the entrance.

Robinson's voice was angry. 'You're in big trouble. You'll all have your wages docked. The whole bloody lot of you. Wait and see. And you, Winterbourne, you can come with me now and collect what little's owed you and then you can shove off. You're sacked.'

Another voice spoke quietly. 'Leave the bloke alone, Robinson. He's acting on my orders. Get back to the office – I told you I want those numbers by the close of today.' Jack Kidd nodded to Winterbourne and walked off, a furious Robinson waddling in his wake. At the end of the shift Kidd called Winterbourne into the office and made him a shift foreman. The best part about it was seeing Robinson's face when he handed over Michael's now larger wage packet.

Word of Winterbourne's stance against Robinson spread quickly around the mine and he found himself treated with a new respect by the men, all of whom hated the accountant. Michael hated the mine and cared as little for the fact that he had made new friends as that he had acquired a new enemy.

To Elizabeth's delight, soon after the baby's birth, Kidd brought Will back to live at Kinross House. The plan was to have the boy work at the coalmine. He came into the drawing room, where Elizabeth was cradling the sleeping child. Will's nervous and curious looks at his surroundings made it clear to Elizabeth that he too had been ignorant of his father's other life and had never been inside Kinross House before.

'G'day Elizabeth.'

'Come and give me a hug. And meet Michael John, your new little brother.'

Will gave her a very tentative hug, careful not to press on the sleeping baby. Elizabeth pulled him towards her and kissed his cheek, amused to see that it was the cause of an attack of blushing.

'He's bosker, Elizabeth. So small. Just like a little

wombat.' If he had worked out that the birth of his step-brother was a couple of months too soon for him to have been his stepbrother, he gave no indication.

The baby stirred.

'Just hold your little finger out to him – he'll grab onto it.' She said.

Gingerly the boy did as she suggested, then started to laugh. 'He's got a fair old grip on him. Hey there Mikey boy! You've got a stronger grip than me, mate. Can I call him Mikey, Lizbeth? Michael John's a big name for such a little fella.'

'I suppose so – at least while he's a little baby. Now come and sit here by me and tell me all your news. How's the rabbit fund? What brings you to town at last? I'm so happy to see you. I've missed you.'

'The old man wants me to go into the mine. He says he might lease out Wilton's Creek. He's wants us all living together here. Maybe Hattie too. Do you know Elizabeth, God's honest truth, I'd no idea about this place. I thought when he was in town he stayed in a boarding house. Sometimes I wonder what his game is? I reckon he just likes to keep us all guessing about things?'

'Harriet knew. She called on me here one day.'

'She's as bad as he is. Secretive. But she isn't living here yet is she?'

'No. She called here just the one time and I'm afraid we didn't get off to a good start. It was a very short visit. I'm at fault I know. I meant to call on her later but she made it clear she didn't want to have any further contact with me. I should have persisted, but I was very tired before the baby was born and somehow I never got around to trying again. You know how your father is. I couldn't raise the subject with him – he's never even mentioned her to me. As far as he's aware, I might not even know she exists! Just as he never told me about you or about Kinross House. He certainly enjoys surprising people.'

'I don't know that he enjoys anything. Except being miserable and trying to make everyone else miserable too. He's an awkward old bugger – I'm sorry I shouldn't be using bad words with you, Lizbeth. I don't want to offend.'

She smiled. 'I think there's a good streak inside your father, Will. He's had a hard life and he struggles to show his emotions. But he can be kind. He certainly specialises in surprises.' She told him about the violin.

Will raised his eyebrows. 'Fair go. I shouldn't talk badly of him to you – you're married to him – though God knows why.'

The end of this sentence was muttered at the floor, but sufficiently loud for Elizabeth to hear. She chose to ignore it.

'I'm so happy you're going to be living here. I've really missed you.'

The blush spread across his face.

'How do you feel about going to work in the mine? What sort of work does your father want you to do? Is he going to train you to take over the running of the place?'

'You're joking! He wants me down there digging rocks and shifting loads. Learning the hard way, he says. Just like he did. 'Except he didn't, did he? Anyway he's got a new foreman. He'd rather trust a stranger than his own son. I'm just a workhorse as far as he's concerned.'

'You're being a little hard on him. I'm sure he has good intentions. He probably wants you to have the experience of hard work and doesn't want you to be spoilt by his money?'

Will snorted with derision. 'You think everyone is as good intentioned as you are. The old bastard certainly isn't. He wouldn't know a good intention from a didgeridoo.'

Elizabeth smiled. 'We'll just have to agree to disagree. I'm sure he wants you to get some experience that will ready you for taking things over eventually.'

'He won't let me take over anything. After what happened

with Nat, he won't ever let a son of his get involved in his business. Besides he prefers Hattie. She's more like him, even though she's a girl. He probably wants to marry her off to someone who can take over from him in the end. Either that or he'll wait till little Mikey grows up.'

Elizabeth was uncertain if there was an implication that Michael's parentage was in question, but the subject was dropped and she turned to quizzing Will about his rabbit trapping and the progress of the now abandoned vegetable patch at Wilton's Creek.

The following evening, while the baby was sleeping, Mrs Oates entered the drawing room with pencil and paper in hand. 'Is now a good moment to talk to you about the menu for tomorrow evening, Mrs Kidd? Or we can leave it until morning?'

'What's to discuss, Mrs Oates? I'm happy, as always, to leave the arrangements to you and Cook.'

Mrs Oates looked surprised. 'Have you forgotten, Ma'am? Tomorrow night we have company. I thought you'd like to discuss what Cook should prepare. I got the impression Mr Kidd wants a special effort to be made. But if you're happy to leave it to me that's quite all right? I know you must be tired.'

Elizabeth struggled to hide her embarrassment, and then decided there was nothing to be gained from pretending to be aware of her husband's plans. She was getting weary of his gamesmanship.

'Mrs Oates, I'm at a loss as to what you are talking about.'

A puzzled look flickered for over the face of the older woman. 'But, Mrs Kidd - the dinner to mark the arrival of Master Michael John.'

Elizabeth decided to lie rather than confess that Kidd hadn't told her. 'Of course. I was distracted – I'm getting forgetful with all these disturbed nights.'

'I keep telling you, Ma'am, we could give the child formula during the night so you could get some proper sleep. You need it.'

'No, Mrs Oates. I don't want to discuss this again. I want to nurse my own child.'

The servant shook her head in mild disapproval, but continued. 'There'll be six at table: you and Mr Kidd, Master William, Miss Harriet, Miss Radley from the school and Mr Winterbourne.'

'Mr Winterbourne?' Her words were little more than a whisper, and she struggled for breath. 'I'm sorry, I've forgotten. Who is Mr Winterbourne?'

'Why he's Mr Kidd's new foreman at the mine. He's recently come from England, just like you ma'am. He must have made a big impression on Mr Kidd. He took him on as a worker then made him foreman in no time at all.'

Elizabeth forced a laugh. 'Motherhood is indeed making me forgetful. Mr Kidd told me what a good job Mr Winterbourne's been doing. As to the menu, I'll leave it in your very capable hands.'

With an eyebrow raised almost imperceptibly in disapproval, Mrs Oates left Elizabeth staring out of the drawing room window.

CHAPTER THIRTEEN

THE DINNER PARTY

Kidd stood in the bedroom doorway, anger etched on his face. 'Get out of bed and get downstairs.'

'I'm not well. Something I ate at luncheon disagreed with me. Please make my apologies to our guests. Harriet will make a very congenial hostess.'

Her husband lunged towards her and grabbed her by the wrists. 'Get up now and get downstairs or I'll beat the living daylights out of you. I ask little enough, but what I do ask, I expect you to do.'

'I can't. I told you I'm not feeling well.'

With a sudden jerk of his arms, he pulled her up and made as though he were about to slap her across the face. Instinctively she ducked away from the blow that never came. The baby stirred in the cradle, then settled down.

Still holding her by the wrist he said, 'Put your clothes on and get downstairs. You'll not make a show of me in my own house. You'll sit at that table and you'll smile and be polite and talk your fancy talk to my guests.'

'Your guests? The guests you didn't even have the courtesy to tell me about. If you want me to play the chatelaine, then have the decency to tell me. Don't leave me to find out from the housekeeper.' She sobbed with anger.

'I won't say it again. And I won't be questioned. You can save those fancy foreign words for the guests, as they're wasted on me. Just remember this – you were penniless with a bastard in your belly. I've given you and the brat a name and a fine home. So you'll do what I ask. You're my wife.' He opened the doors of the wardrobe, pulling out dresses and throwing them onto the bed. 'All these fine clothes I've paid for. Put them on. Why do you think I bought them for you? So they can hang in a cupboard while you lie in bed and leave me to entertain the guests? I won't tell you again. Get downstairs. They'll be here any minute.'

Her heart beating like a hammer, Elizabeth entered the drawing room. She had splashed cold water on her face, chosen a dark blue silk dress and pulled her hair into some semblance of order. Despite the speed of her preparations and the argument that preceded them, she looked radiant. Motherhood had put a bloom on her face. Her hair had a gloss on it and was so silky that it slipped, as usual, out of the restraints imposed by the chignon she had hastily created, and formed little tendrils around her neck. She was a picture of calm beauty that belied her inner agitation. She took a deep breath before entering the room and was greeted by silence as the assembled company turned to look at her.

Everything blurred. Figures interchangeable and indistinguishable save one. Michael had his back to the door when she entered the room, but turned when the pause in the conversation signalled that the lady of the house had arrived.

She felt the colour rise up her throat to her face, and her skin burned hot as a bush fire. She tried to control the trembling that set her legs shaking and made her unsteady and dizzy. She clutched the back of a chair and took a deep breath. No matter how clearly his features were etched on her consciousness, each time she saw him, she saw him anew. The combination of joy and pain and the desire to rush across the room and fling herself into his arms was overwhelming. It must be apparent to the whole room? But the Kidds and Miss Radley were deaf to the thumping of Elizabeth's heart and the pounding of the veins in her temple.

Michael appeared frozen to the spot. Then he stepped aside to allow Miss Radley to meet their hostess first.

Elizabeth fixed her eyes on the woman and, stepping away from the support of the chair, extended her hand in welcome. 'How do you do, Miss Radley? I am so pleased to meet you at last.'

The schoolmistress smiled warmly in response. 'Delighted to meet you too, Mrs Kidd, and warmest congratulations on your happy event.'

Elizabeth turned to greet Harriet, only to find the girl had moved across the room and was talking quietly with Mrs Oates in the doorway. She turned instead towards Will. 'Will, how are you this evening?'

'I'm pretty good, Elizabeth.'

Realising that neither Jack Kidd nor Will was likely to proffer formal introductions, she stretched out a trembling hand to Michael. 'You must be Mr Winterbourne?'

His hand was warm in hers. As she felt the touch of his skin on hers she could not suppress a little gasp.

'Mrs Kidd.'

Their eyes met for just a moment, then he looked away and withdrew his hand. She stepped backwards, groping for the chair and using it again for support. When she lifted her eyes, he had already moved out of her space to join Will by the window. She saw Harriet was watching her. The girl was leaning against the door staring at her coldly.

'Mrs Kidd, might I see the new baby?' Miss Radley's eyes were bright and eager.

'Yes of course. I'll take you up to have a peek at him after dinner.'

'What have you called the little chap?'

'We've named him for both my late father and my husband.'

Miss Radley looked expectantly at her and Elizabeth realised the rest of the room had stopped talking. In a voice barely above a whisper she said, 'Michael John. His name is Michael John.' She didn't look at Winterbourne but she felt his eyes upon her and felt the heat of blood rushing up her neck and across her face.

'Two good solid names.' Miss Radley replied.

Harriet's voice carried across the room. 'Isn't your name Michael too, Mr Winterbourne?'

Michael acknowledged her with a slight nod of the head then resumed his conversation with William.

Just then, Mrs Oates opened the double doors. Still feeling unsteady on her feet, Elizabeth led the assembled company into the dining room. In line with convention, she and Kidd were at opposite ends of the table, Kidd between Harriet and Miss Radley and Elizabeth between Will and Michael Winterbourne. She prayed that Will would be in a talkative mood tonight, the distance from his father being enough to remove his usual inhibitions in his company. No sooner had they sat down than Kidd got up. 'If I have to sit at a table all night, then don't expect me talk to the womenfolk.' He strode to Elizabeth's end of the table. 'You sit down there. I can't be doing with women's chatter.'

Mrs Oates raised an eyebrow as she brought the food to the table. Mr Oates continued to pour the wine without changing his expression. As he reached the men's end of the table, Kidd thumped his fist down on the cloth. 'Take that stuff away, Oates. Keep it for the ladies – not too much mind – and bring us some beer.'

Elizabeth started to protest, but felt Miss Radley's hand gently placed upon her arm.

'Miss Radley, I apologise for my husband's behaviour.'

'Don't worry. They do things differently here. Men like their beer and they don't stand on ceremony. You'll get used to it. I'm from England too – though a good many years ago. I thought I'd never get used to life here, but I did.'

'What brought you to Australia?'

'I was sixteen when my mother died and my father decided to come out here. He'd already met my stepmother and it was her idea. She never settled to the way of life here and they went back to England a few years later. By then I was teaching in Melbourne and engaged to be married.'

Elizabeth hesitated to cross-question her guest, but Miss Radley needed no prompting to tell her story.

'He was a teacher too. We met at a concert. Bernard Evans was his name. He wasn't rich. He wasn't even handsome. But he was a good man and I miss him every day of my life.'

'What happened? Was it the War?'

'No. He died of diphtheria. It happened very quickly. All over in a week. It was just two months before our wedding day.'

'How dreadful.'

'It was. I didn't know what to do. I had nobody. Bernard had been alone here in Australia too. Born in the Welsh Valleys. We'd planned to come to McDonald Falls to open a school. He loved the mountains. I'd never been – we were to come here after the wedding, stopping off at a few places on the way as a kind of honeymoon: we didn't have much money and what we had was needed for the school. When he died I didn't know what to do with myself. I couldn't face the world. I didn't even want to eat. Then one day I was lying on my bed crying – I seemed to do that most days after he went – when it was as though I heard him speaking to me. "Get up, Verity" he said. "No good lying in bed feeling sorry for yourself or for me. There's children out there need teaching and who's going to do it if not you?" It was as if he were right there in the room beside me. It was the strangest experience I've ever had.'

'Did it happen again?'

'Never. I talk to him often – you'll probably think I'm crazy – but he's never spoken to me again. Just that once. Just to get me back on my feet. Next day I packed my bags and set off for McDonald Falls. And do you know? I've never left the place since.' She smiled. 'Everything I've ever wanted, aside from Bernard Evans, I have here. And I feel close to Bernard too, as this is where he wanted to live. It was the place he loved best and it's where he wants me to be.'

Elizabeth warmed to the small, thin spinster with the constantly smiling face. Her sunny nature belied the sadness that must have impoverished her life. After hearing the story of Miss Radley's fiancé, Elizabeth told her about the death of Stephen. The teacher's eyes filled with tears and she placed her hand on Elizabeth's.

'We have so much in common. I've now found contentment in my vocation as a teacher and you've found happiness with Mr Kidd and your little baby. We are both truly blessed.'

Elizabeth looked past the schoolmistress at Winterbourne, who was talking to Will, while Jack Kidd listened and solemnly drank his beer. She strained to hear what he was saying but the table was long and his voice was low. At least that meant he would not be able to hear her either.

She turned back to Miss Radley and said, 'Tell me about the school.'

'I had no money so I just gathered those children I could and gave them lessons in the shade of a tree here in town. I put a sign in the post office that I was willing to teach any children. At first only a few came but little by little the numbers grew. The town was growing fast then – although mostly menfolk working in the mines and on the railroad. They tended to leave the women and children on the coast at first, but as time went on, more and more of them settled here permanently. I like to think that having some proper schooling is what attracted so many people to settle in the town.'

'When did you get the school premises?'

'Ten years ago. Mr McDonald, who practically owned the town then – and owned the mine before Mr Kidd – built the schoolhouse and paid for the furniture and books. He was a great benefactor.'

'What happened to him?'

'He's retired and lives in Sydney. He sold the mine to Mr Kidd.'

Elizabeth realised this was the man rumoured to have lost everything at the card table to Jack Kidd, but she decided to refrain from mentioning this. Telling Verity Radley might diminish the schoolmistress's respect for her benefactor, while doing nothing to enhance Jack Kidd's reputation.

She looked again to the other end of the table; Kidd was munching his food and swigging beer, throwing the odd comment in Michael's direction. Harriet was eating in sullen silence on her left, next to Winterbourne. She had ignored Miss Radley's discourse, either from familiarity with its subject matter, or more likely to avoid being drawn into conversation with her step-mother.

When the dessert was served and Harriet had still not spoken, Elizabeth decided to take the girl on. She addressed Miss Radley, but leaned forward to include Harriet in the conversation. 'Is Harriet the only pupil who lives with you at the schoolhouse?'

'She is now, aren't you, Hattie? Until a year ago there were the Dunbar twins too. Their place is twenty miles out of town, so during the week they used to stay with us in town, but they've grown up now. Millicent helps out at home, as her mother is sick and can't do much these days and Pru got married a few months back to a young man from Katoomba, so she's gone to live there.'

'You must miss them, Harriet?' Elizabeth said.

The girl stared back at her in silence. Elizabeth flushed in anger but resisted responding, as Verity Radley had started to answer for the girl. 'Harriet's very different from the Dunbars aren't you?'

She added in a confidential tone to Elizabeth: 'Being twins they tended to stick together a lot – poor Hattie was left out a bit I think.'

Harriet spoke, stung into a response. 'Couple of outback ignoramuses. Good only for milking cows and plucking chooks.'

Miss Radley appeared oblivious to the venom in the girl's voice and smiled indulgently. 'Don't be mean-spirited. Not everyone is as clever as you, or shares your love of literature and music.'

'Literature and music?' Elizabeth seized on the information. 'Who's your favourite composer, Harriet?'

'I listen to music and I read books. That doesn't mean I want to talk about them with ignorant pommies.'

'Harriet! That's extremely rude! Apologise to Mrs Kidd.' Miss Radley spoke quietly but firmly, clearly anxious to avoid the male company overhearing.

Harriet was not accepting any reprimands. She scraped back her chair and jumped to her feet.

'I've had enough. Just because he's married her doesn't mean I have to talk to her. Or sit at the table with her.'

She ran out of the room.

At the sound of the front door slamming, Verity was about to go after the girl, but Jack Kidd's voice boomed.

'She wants to go so let her go.' Turning to Winterbourne he added. 'She's a chip off the old block. Can't do with fancy manners and chit-chat. I've had enough of sitting here like a stuffed shirt myself to be honest, mate.'

He reverted to the role of the mine gaffer, handing out orders to his foreman.

'Go and find her, Mick and see she gets back to the schoolhouse. Then if you fancy another drink come back here and join me. Will, see Miss Radley home then get to bed.'

Without another word, he rose from the table, took a decanter of whisky from the sideboard and went into the drawing room where he settled himself in an armchair.

Miss Radley made her goodbyes hurriedly to Elizabeth, then squeezed her arm and whispered conspiratorially. 'Harriet can be a difficult child. She still feels the loss of her mother. I hope you and I can be friends and I so want to see the baby. May I call on you after school one afternoon?'

When the schoolmistress left the room with Will at her side, Elizabeth realised that Michael had already gone, saving them both the awkwardness of a goodbye.

It took Michael almost an hour to track Harriet down. His heart wasn't in the task; his mind was still reeling after seeing Elizabeth. Nothing had prepared him for what happened. Unlike Elizabeth, he'd had no warning of their meeting. He'd accepted a dinner invitation from his boss, expecting a dull and uneventful evening, with perhaps the opportunity for a more substantial meal than his lodgings provided and if he were lucky, a little congenial conversation. If he had envisioned his hostess at all, it was as a plump, middle-aged matron presiding over her table – or as a pinch-faced harridan, a thin, wiry match for her husband. Never in his wildest dreams had he expected to meet Elizabeth at Kidd's table, let alone discover she was Kidd's wife and the mother of his new-born child.

When he finally caught up with Kidd's daughter he was in no mood for conversation, but the girl wanted to talk.

'Mr Winterbourne – or can I call you Mick like Pa does?' She didn't wait for a response but pressed on. 'Why do I get the distinct impression that you already know my father's wife?'

'I can't imagine, Miss Kidd, as I don't.'

'I saw you talking to her outside the school a couple of months back.'

'You must be mistaken, Miss.'

'I never forget a face. I think you're playing with me.' Her voice was coquettish and Michael was impatient to be rid of her.

He shrugged, then resisted her efforts to make conversation over the half mile or so back to the school.

Miss Radley was waiting on the steps of the schoolhouse so Michael made a speedy escape then walked the streets of McDonald Falls like a man possessed. By the time he got back to his digs he had decided to leave the Falls and resurrect his plan to try his hand at sheep farming. But the following morning, after a sleepless night, he had changed his mind again. Why should Elizabeth drive him away? He was damned if she was going to force him to give up a job that, since his promotion, paid him well when his parents needed the money. He tried to channel his feelings for her and the overwhelming sense of loss he felt at her betrayal into anger and contempt. Sometimes he even believed it was working.

If Jack Kidd had planned to bring Harriet to live at Kinross House, he abandoned the idea after the dinner. There was no mention of her leaving the care of Miss Radley. The schoolmistress took to visiting Elizabeth once or twice a week in the late afternoon, after lessons had concluded. Harriet never accompanied her. Miss Radley rarely mentioned her charge and seemed reluctant to answer any questions from Elizabeth about her progress. Elizabeth sensing this and relieved not to have a sullen stepdaughter under her roof, stopped enquiring.

She made it a rule every day to write something in her diary. Nothing profound or momentous. She didn't write of the loneliness of marriage to Jack Kidd, his lack of interest in her, other than in bed, where he grunted his way to a rapid climax, to which she felt like an incidental accessory. Elizabeth could not write of such things, so instead she recorded the progress of Mikey. The name Will had given the child had stuck within the household and no one gave him his full name, even Elizabeth.

The baby bloomed and grew rapidly, with a healthy complexion, bright eyes and a tendency to smile and gurgle happily at any attention paid to him. Elizabeth took joy in the little creature and was grateful that he was not a difficult baby, but the source of endless entertainment and pleasure. Every day she recorded his progress in her diary: the smiles of recognition, the angry cries when he was hungry or teething, his ever-stronger grip on her finger, the way he now rolled on his stomach trying to lever himself up.

One afternoon, she was taking tea in the parlour with Miss Radley, while Mikey lay on his stomach on a blanket, battling as usual to get into an upright position.

'He's going to have such strong arms. All that pushing and shoving will develop those biceps' said Miss Radley.

'I'd better make sure his father doesn't see or he'll have him out at Wilton's Creek chopping wood before he's talking.'

'Better that than sending him to work in the mine.'

'God, what a horrible thought. I'll never allow that. I hate the fact that Will is stuck there. I'm trying to persuade my husband to let Will stop working there – or to give him a job in the office, but I'm afraid Will's not cut out for office work any more than for mining. He likes to be in the open, setting rabbit traps and riding his pony. He told me last week he loathes going underground. It must be like going down into the bowels of hell. I think he's frightened by it. I know I'd hate it.'

Miss Radley shuddered. 'It sounds most unpleasant.'

'Yet so many men have to face it virtually every day of their lives. Like being suffocated: deprived of light and air. It's not natural.'

As she spoke, she thought of Michael, not of Will. He too must hate the descent into the Stygian depths, away from the world, from light and from colour, even from natural sounds – the relentless throb of the mining machinery and the clash of pickaxes against rock taking the place of birds singing and the everyday noise of the town. But he had been a miner in England and during the war so he must be used to it. She remembered how on board the Historic he had intimated that he wanted to do something different when he got to Australia.

She had asked Will if his father and the foreman ever went underground, hoping that the answer would be negative. Will told her that while his father rarely went below, Michael led by example and was usually first down and last up. She hated to think of him in that netherworld, battling his demons in the dark.

Miss Radley said, 'Men are tougher than we ladies, Mrs Kidd. They're made of different ingredients.'

Elizabeth laughed. 'Frogs and snails and puppy dogs' tails.'

'Exactly!'

'Miss Radley, may I ask you to call me by my first name? It's hard being Mrs Kidd to absolutely everyone except Will. I'd be so happy if you'd call me Elizabeth. You are my only friend in McDonald Falls'

The schoolmistress beamed. 'I would be honoured, Elizabeth – and you must call me Verity.'

'Delighted, Verity.'

'No one's called me Verity since my parents and my Bernard. I'm happy you think of me as your friend.'

'Now tell me what's been happening in the world? I'm starved of news here. There's no one to talk to except Will when he's around – but now he's at the mine he goes to bed early and rises early so I hardly see him. And, as you know, Mr Kidd is not a great talker.'

Verity smiled and said tactfully, 'He's not exactly renowned for conversation.'

'At least you get out and about and see people every day, Verity.'

'I see small children every day you mean. It's not exactly the same – and I'm rarely a party to their secrets being "The Teacher".'

'Come on now! There must be something to tell.'

'Well... I hear several young women are rather sweet on that nice Mr Winterbourne. He's made quite an impression in a short time. Mind you he's a good-looking man and quite charming to boot. Did you know he saved a little boy from a snakebite? He was so quick to act – it happened right outside the school. He's a hero among the ladies. I didn't get a chance to speak with him at dinner here, but he was very courteous when he brought Hattie home after she'd run off that evening. And his landlady, Mrs Abbott, sings his praises when I see her at church.'

This was not what Elizabeth had expected or wanted to hear. Verity had never mentioned Michael before. She felt the blood rushing to her face and cursed her lifelong tendency to blush at the slightest provocation. Trying to sound casual and hoping the quaver in her voice was not discernible she asked, 'Mr Winterbourne brought Hattie back to the schoolhouse that night?'

'Yes. Will walked me home and it was almost an hour before Mr Winterbourne arrived with Hattie. He had trouble finding her. She can be difficult when she chooses and when she doesn't want to be found she won't be found. Just the other day she was very moody when I asked her to go over her French verbs – ran off and didn't come home until almost bedtime. I should be stricter with her, but it's a hopeless task. The only person she ever listens to is her father and he rarely sees her. I should have been much firmer with her from the start, but with her dear mother passing away so suddenly, I made more allowance than was good for her. She's a good girl really but she is a little wayward at times.'

Elizabeth was desperate to hear more of Michael yet hesitated to bring up the subject again. 'Don't talk about Harriet,' she said. 'I've given up trying with her. I made a big effort to befriend her, but she's made up her mind to dislike me.'

'I'm sorry, Elizabeth. It must be hard for both of you. She probably can't help but see you as someone who has taken her mother's place in her father's affections.'

Elizabeth snorted, then tried to cover it up by coughing exaggeratedly. The sidelong look Verity Radley threw her indicated she was not deceived.

'I'm sorry, Verity, but if we're to be friends we have to be honest with each other. God knows, I have no one else to be honest with any more.'

'What do you mean?'

'It must be as plain as the nose on my face, that I've not replaced the late Mrs Kidd in my husband's affections.'

The schoolmistress looked shocked.

'Come on. You said it yourself,' said Elizabeth. 'He's no great conversationalist. It would not have been an exaggeration if you'd added that he's an uncouth, morose, miserable, old curmudgeon who shows no interest in anything other than the mine and his clapped-out old pony. He has no time for his children. He ignores Will and indulges Hattie – probably to compensate for largely ignoring her too. He shows no interest in Mikey. As for me?' She gave a hollow laugh.

'Elizabeth, you don't mean it.'

'Yes I do. I do. I do.'

'Then why did you marry him?'

'I had no choice. Believe me if I had, I would have done otherwise.'

She wished she could retract her words as soon as they were out. She'd broken her promise to herself to make the most of her lot and get on with life without complaining to others. Verity's friendship and the mention of Michael Winterbourne's effect on the women of the town had proved too much for her. But this was not what she had intended. She didn't want the mask to slip, not even with Verity.

'I didn't mean what I just said. Mr Kidd is a good husband and I'd no intention to speak ill of him. I don't know what came over me? It must be lack of sleep. I've a headache and it's making me grumpy. Mikey is cutting a tooth and I've had a series of disturbed nights with him. Please forget I said it.'

'I understand. I've forgotten already.' She smiled kindly, but her eyes told another story and something had changed profoundly in their relationship with this brief slip of Elizabeth's mask.

Elizabeth would have liked to confide fully in her new friend, but felt it was a betrayal of her father. She knew William Morton had lost something fundamental in his character, distorted by grief at his wife's death and despair at his own failings. She, his daughter, couldn't bear to confront the truth herself that he had gambled her away like a stack of chips, let alone confess it to someone else. Her father may have faltered in his loyalty to her, but she would not weaken in hers to him. And there was Mikey to think of. She wanted him to grow up with a chance of a good life, unsullied by her own sad history. That meant him being accepted as Jack Kidd's youngest son and growing up to respect his father. If she were to speak the truth of how she felt about Kidd, even to Verity, it would risk this.

Verity quickly tried to move the conversation back to what she thought was a safe and banal footing. 'I was telling you about Mr Winterbourne. Many's the time I've gone into the draper's to find a gaggle of ladies extolling his virtues. It's not often that a single man arrives in town as handsome and polite as him. And that lovely accent! They're all vying for his attention.'

'Really?' Elizabeth felt constrained from changing the subject when she had already steered the conversation away from one dangerous area.

Verity was unstoppable now, relieved to be on what she thought was safer ground. 'I'd be joining the queue myself, but I don't delude myself that a fine man like him would be interested in an old maid like me.' She gave a dry laugh. 'And after my Bernard there can never be anyone else.' Her voice dropped to a confidential whisper. 'Mind you. Hattie's not immune.'

'What are you talking about?' Elizabeth's stomach churned.

'He's a little old for her, but that's not always such a bad thing. My Bernard was quite a bit older than me. And she does seem to have taken to him. What do you think? I'm sure Mr Kidd would be delighted for Harriet to marry a young man like him.'

'Marry him? That's preposterous! Harriet's barely eighteen. He's almost twice her age. It's a ridiculous notion.' Her voice was sharp and she tasted bile in her throat.

Verity Radley saw at once she had upset her hostess.

'You're quite right, Elizabeth. What was I thinking? It's a schoolgirl crush. It will pass.'

'If it's a crush at all.' There was frost in Elizabeth's voice now. 'You must be reading too many silly, romantic novels.'

The schoolteacher blushed to the roots of her hair. Seeing her crestfallen expression, Elizabeth softened and smiled. 'I'm sorry – I didn't mean to be cruel. It's that head-ache again. I am out of sorts today. I definitely need an early night. Please forgive me.'

With a sigh of relief, the older woman nodded and the two of them turned their attention back to the small child playing on the rug.

Working alongside Will was the bright spot in Michael's life at the mine. The boy was intelligent and personable and Michael couldn't help but like him. Will introduced him to the beauty of the area surrounding McDonald Falls. In their free time, Will took to calling at Michael's lodgings and the two would wander happily and aimlessly, along the rim of the gorge, exploring the rugged sandstone escarp-ments, the narrow rivers and the dense forests of eucalyptus. Weathered rock formations rose through the vegetation in an often spectacular landscape of gorges, caves, and deep canyons.

'The aborigines made up crazy stories about these rocks. They thought they were people or animals and got frozen into those shapes. They reckoned the sun was a campfire made by some kidnapped girl who was put in the sky by her ancestor spirits.'

'How do you know all this stuff, Will?'

'Used to be an old black fella lived in the bush near our place at Wilton's Creek. When I was little I used to sneak off and go hunting with him. He told me how the earth was made by the great rainbow snake.'

'You're joking, mate? A bloody snake?'

'No the abos really believe it. The rainbow snake made the world. It's meant to have the head of a kangaroo, the tail of a croc and the body of a python. It brings the rain. It made all the rivers and the mountains and the animals and the humans. When it gets angry or when people do bad things it sends storms and floods to punish us. There are some rock paintings a few miles from here – I'll take you and show you. The stories go back gazillions of years.'

These trips into the bush with Will were a welcome release from the gloom of the mine and the darkness of Michael's thoughts. On entering the pit, he threw himself into the day's tasks with a blind energy, seeking oblivion in the ritual of hard, physical work. Although in a supervisory role, he still undertook a lot of manual labour, preferring to bring on the exhaustion that led to sleep at the end of the day. This, as well as his stand against Robinson, earned him the respect of the other men.

Harriet was standing in the open doorway to the garden, her back to the room.

'Harriet, we need to talk.' Elizabeth tried not to sound nervous or desperate, but knew she was not succeeding. The girl was barely eighteen but her frosty manner and air of superiority made Elizabeth feel like a naughty child.

'What do we have to talk about?'

Elizabeth took a deep breath. 'We would like you to live here with us. Your education has finished and much as I know Miss Radley enjoys your company, it's better that you live here with the rest of the family.'

'The family!' she snarled scornfully. 'I hope you're not including yourself and your brat in that description!'

'Harriet, please. There's no need to be unpleasant. Mikey has done nothing to deserve that.'

'If my father wants something he asks me. What I do has nothing to do with you. Where I live is none of your business. You're not my mother.'

'I know I'm not your mother, but I want the best for you. I don't understand why you're behaving this way towards me.'

The girl turned to face her stepmother. 'I can't help it that Pa has married you, though I don't understand why. He should have been able to tell you're a fortune hunter. It's obvious. There's no other reason you'd have married him. You may have snared him in your trap but you'll have nothing to do with me or where I choose to live. I'm staying with Miss Radley and that's final.'

She flounced through the doorway and into the garden, leaving a shaken Elizabeth staring after her.

A few hours later, Elizabeth was practising her violin: struggling to reacquaint herself with a difficult passage from Elgar's Enigma Variations, when Mrs Oates showed Verity Radley into the room. They greeted each other warmly, then Elizabeth refused Verity's request that she continue to play.

'It's quite enough for today. It wasn't going well anyway. I'm so out of practice that it will be a while before I let anyone hear me play, even you, dear Verity! Now come and sit down and have some tea.'

'I'm sorry to arrive unannounced, Elizabeth, but I understand Harriet had words with you this morning?'

'She told you?'

'Very little. Just that you asked her to move to Kinross House but she wants to stay at the School House. I've told her I think it's better for her to be at home with her family, but...'

'But she told you she had no intention of living with a greedy fortune hunter?'

Miss Radley blushed and looked away.

Elizabeth continued. 'I suppose that's what everyone in McDonald Falls thinks of me, isn't it?'

'Of course not!' Verity was indignant.

'Come on Verity. It's not surprising.'

'There'll always be some ignorant people who'll speak badly of others, but anyone who knows you well, Elizabeth, would never dream of imputing such motives to you.'

'I'm not daft, Verity. Harriet may hate me but I imagine she's not the only person who wonders how my husband and I came to marry?'

'There were one or two people who had their noses put out of joint by your marrying Mr Kidd. He may not be in the first flush of youth but there's many saw him as quite a catch.'

Elizabeth raised both eyebrows. How could anyone seriously harbour a desire to marry an ugly old man with a bad temper, an absence of manners and an inability to communicate? To her, marriage for personal advancement was an alien concept. She had not lacked money during childhood and early adulthood and had been oblivious to the advances of many a wealthy suitor until she accepted Stephen. Charles Dawson exemplified for her the worst qualities of the fortune hunter, although even in his case, she had to acknowledge that her sister had been a more than willing participant in the marriage.

'You must have wondered why we were married away from McDonald Falls and only moved here when I was expecting Mikey?'

Verity blushed. 'Yes, I suppose so. But Mr Kidd never discusses family matters with anyone else, and he was in Sydney so often over the recent years. I presumed he was lonely after the first Mrs Kidd passed away.'

'Mr Kidd was a friend of my late father.' She swallowed as she forced the words out. 'It was Father's wish that we marry. When he died, I felt obliged to comply with what was effectively his last wish. His death was sudden and I'd no one else. Mr Kidd offered me a future.' She paused for a moment looking at Verity, trying to read her reaction, then carried on. 'He has been good to me.'

Verity placed her hand on hers. Elizabeth carried on speaking. 'Tell me about the first Mrs Kidd. I don't like to ask my husband about her.'

'I barely knew her. She never lived in town. It was before Mr Kidd bought the mine. They lived out at Wilton's Creek and Mrs Kidd only came in once or twice a year. I asked her to send Nathaniel and Harriet to the school here but she and her husband preferred for her to school them at home. She said they couldn't afford to pay the fees. Mr Kidd was just a smallholder then, scratching a living in the bush. They were both from humble backgrounds. She was born around here, the only child of a labourer in the bauxite mine. I don't know where Mr Kidd was from, but he was a good ten years older than her.'

'How did she die?'

'She lost several children, one or two stillborn between her elder son and Harriet, then two or three more after Will. She was frail. When she was expecting another child she was taken ill in the influenza epidemic and died along with the unborn child.'

'How dreadful.'

'Indeed. She was close to term. Will was only eleven. Mr Kidd was away when it happened. The two younger children were at home with Mrs Kidd and Will went on his pony to fetch the doctor but it was too late. She was gone by the time he arrived.'

'So Harriet was alone with her when she died?'

'Yes, poor girl. She was out of her mind with grief and guilt. She felt she had not done enough to help her mother. All nonsense of course. The doctor said there was nothing anyone could have done for the woman, including him.'

'Poor Harriet.'

'When Mr Kidd returned he was in a rage. He cursed

everyone. After that he drank a lot and became the way he is now. Before then I gather he was quite a cheerful man. Used to sing. Always had a friendly word for folk. Not after she died, though. Who can blame him?'

'Did he blame himself for not being there?'

'Who knows? Given Mrs Kidd's history and fragility, perhaps he did regret leaving her. But what was he to do? He had to make a living and the baby wasn't due for another month. Life in the outback can be hard. Susanna Kidd wasn't the first and I daresay won't be the last young woman from round here to die before her time.'

After Verity left, Elizabeth couldn't stop thinking about the death of Susanna Kidd and the grief, guilt and anger it must have caused in father and daughter. Maybe she was too harsh in her antipathy towards the girl, but the story did little to abate her hostility towards her husband.

CHAPTER FOURTEEN

THE PIT

Will was never going to fit in at the Black Water Colliery. As the boss's son, the men treated him with suspicion, fearing he was his father's eyes and ears. After a few months, when they saw that Jack Kidd showed no favours to his own son and that Winterbourne, whom they all liked and respected, was clearly fond of the lad, they showed him grudging acceptance. He wasn't sure which was worse: being cold-shouldered or being the butt of their jokes. He sensed that his workmates knew he was afraid of the mine and that as, a result, he'd never really be one of them.

Michael understood how he felt. Not the fear, but the dislike of being down the pit. The Englishman had worked underground all of his adult life so, while he hated it, he didn't fear it. For Will though, every time he stepped into the metal cage and heard the winder and the ironbark beams creak as the cage descended into the shaft, a wave of nausea swept over him despite his empty stomach.

The men didn't eat much below ground: just some bread and jam, washed down with water. Eating too much heavy food gave them heartburn – no fun when crawling along the tunnels or bent double, hacking at the rock face. Will hated the way his feet got wet, no matter how well he fastened his boots or how thick his socks were. If it wasn't the surface water, it was his own sweat.

Michael was working with them underground today. He liked the spirit of the men and the sense of belonging and the misery of the pit was preferable to sitting in the office with Robinson and his snide comments. Seeing Michael walk towards the cage instantly cheered Will: the shift was more bearable when his friend was beside him.

They were working in a detail of half a dozen men, with a couple of pit horses to help haul the rock back to the base of the main shaft. The mine wasn't fully mechanized and there were dozens of horses employed. The animals never saw the light of day again once they went down into the pit. They were stabled underground. Moving them back to the surface was too much of a logistical complexity to be considered except in emergency. Accustomed only to the dark underworld, they would be uncontrollable if brought to the surface. The prevailing philosophy was that what they'd never known they wouldn't miss. Each horse worked with one designated miner, a bond of trust growing between them.

Will loved the horses. Compared to them, his own plight seemed trivial. At least he got to return to the surface at the end of his shift and had days off to enjoy the sunshine and breathe clean air. So he spent time at the beginning and end of each shift talking to the animals and feeding them the odd carrot when he could avoid the eyes of the miners who partnered them. He was hoping that before long he too would be assigned a horse to care for. The role of pit pony minder was not one trusted to rookies but after a while he hoped to convince Michael to give him a chance. There was no point asking his father.

They were half way through the shift when the two horses started whinnying and refused to move forward.

Michael pushed his way through. 'Move back down the tunnel, lads. Take it slowly. Don't raise yer voices. Be careful.'

As he spoke, there was a rumbling noise and a section of the tunnel roof collapsed in front of them, covering one of the men and his pony with rubble. Thick dust and debris surrounded them all, blinding them and bringing on violent coughing. The electric lights were pulled down by the roof fall. Michael took control, calling out instructions in the darkness.

'Kelly, take the other horse back and get it stabled. Eddie, go back up and bring torches and another crew to help. Tell them to bring some props so we can shore up the roof once we've got Jim and the horse out. Will and Rod, help me shift this lot.'

Michael, Will and the other miner worked in concert. The dust was choking and it was hard to see what was happening in the darkness. No one spoke. They rolled away the last boulders and pulled the unconscious man from the rubble. His face was covered in blood and his left arm and leg were obviously broken, twisting away from his body in an unnatural angle. The shinbone had burst through the skin and stuck out in a jagged edge. Will tasted metal and realised he was going to be sick. He pushed Rod out of the way and threw up behind a pile of rubble. He watched, pale faced, as Michael splinted the legs and arm, using the shirt off his own back and some wood that been brought by the rescue party. As Eddie and a few other men from the other shift carefully carried the man back along the tunnel in a stretcher, Will hoped Michael had not seen him vomiting.

'He should be all right if they can get him to the doctor quickly and the wound's not infected. Now let's get this pony out,' said Michael.

The horse was not so lucky. The animal had taken the full force of the collapse. One of its hind legs was crushed under a wooden roof beam. It was crying in pain and confusion and struggling with the impossible task of pulling itself upright. With its handler gone, it was clearly distressed and Will lay down on the rubble beside it, stroking it and trying to calm it, as the poor creature vainly attempted to rear up. Its pain was evident and its screams visceral. Michael called back down the tunnel behind him.

'Get a vet or a doctor. This horse has to be put down.'

'No!' Will looked at him in anguish.

'She's in pain. She can't be fixed. It's not right that she should suffer.'

'I can't stand it. Not to just kill her in cold blood. Please!'

'I don't like it any more than you do, mate, but it's got to be done.'

A voice called through the darkness to them. 'Doc's gone with Wingo to the hospital. It'll take at least an hour to find the vet and get him out here.'

The pony was foaming at the mouth now and its eyes were rolling.

Michael called back 'Get me a detonator and some wire then – and some whisky - and make it quick.'

He turned to Will. 'Sorry, mate, it's got to be done. I need you to help. We have to get her as calm as possible. Can you hold her down? Lean on her neck so's I can get at the head. We need to do it fast and put the poor girl out of her misery.'

Will lay across the horse's neck, using the weight of his slight body to keep the horse from struggling against the rubble to get to its feet. Michael poured the whisky down its throat. Will began to whisper into the creature's ear and kept up a constant stroking of its neck and the pony began to calm a little.

'Look away, mate.' Michael pushed the detonator into the horse's ear and fired. As the shot rang out, a last spasm went through the animal, then it lay still.

Will blinked back his tears. It wouldn't do for the other

men to see him crying. Especially over a pit horse. He looked at Michael. The older man had an expression that Will had not seen on his face before: a blankness, a cold determination, and a deadness about the eyes. He put his arm round the boy's shoulder and led him back to the main shaft. He called out orders to clear the rubble and the dead horse and shore up the tunnel, then turned to Will.

'Get yourself over to the Number 2 line and tell Watts to come over here. You take his place and help them load up the tubs.'

When the shift ended, Michael invited Will to join him in town for a beer. It was the first time he had done that. Will was not of an age to drink, but Michael passed him his schooner and put his hand on his shoulder.

'That were bad today, mate. You deserve a pint.'

'I hate it, Michael. I can't go back down. Please speak to Pa. Tell him I'm no good. I'm not cut out for the work. I can't stand it. The other men know it too. I can see them talking about me and how useless they think I am. I've tried. I've really tried but I can't take it any more. Today was the last straw.'

'I know, mate. It were a tough one. No one likes to see what we saw today or do what we 'ad to do. But we 'ad to do it. You see that don't you?'

'I know the horse had to die. But it doesn't make me like it.'

'Christ, mate do you think I did? No one loves animals more than me. I couldn't let her suffer. Not when there's no hope.'

'I know.'

'And if it helps, Will, I'd like to get away from the pit myself. That were the whole point of coming to Australia. I'd enough of tunnelling under the bloody ground – sixteen year I've done it and when I came out here it were to work on the land. I wanted to be a sheep farmer. Instead I'm still smashing rocks and splinting legs and now I'm killing bloody horses instead of riding them.'

'Why don't you leave then? I'm stuck here 'cause of the old man, but you could just bugger off.'

'Aye. I were going to, but he's given me another promotion this evening. Soon as I came up the shaft he were waiting and told me he's making me Deputy Manager – another couple of quid a week. I can't say no to that. Not when I'm trying to get enough to bring me folks out here – or at least enough for me Da to stop having to work. He's a miner too. Smelter. Bloody filthy job. And dangerous. Me Mam worries herself sick about him, so I reckon I just have to get on with it a while longer.' Then he smiled. 'And mebbe it were worth it to see the look on Robinson's face when yer Da told him I were to get more in me pay packet!'

Harriet stirred and stretched out on the bed, poking her toes through the bars of the bedstead.

Her friend Miranda perched on a chair beside her. 'That bed's too small for you. It's a child's bed. You've outgrown it, Hattie Long Legs. I can't understand why you won't go and live with your family in that huge house. I'd have thought you'd have had enough of school and Miss Verity Virgin by now.'

'Miss Radley's all right. Anything's better than being under the same roof as the Witch.'

She swung her long legs off the bed, tucked her feet into her slippers and examined her reflection in the mirror, frowning in irritation at the black spots where the mirror's silvering had worn away. Despite the mottled effect, she liked what she saw. Her long hair shone and her nose was straight with a slight retroussé upturn at the end. Her skin was smooth and unblemished, and her avoidance of the sun rewarded by a clear pale complexion. Not beautiful perhaps, but certainly pretty.

'It's so unfair that I'm shut away in the back of beyond in this town.' She added a theatrical groan.

Miranda joined her at the mirror so that they could talk to each other's reflections. 'Why not come to Sydney?'

Miranda had recently married her cousin's best friend and moved to Sydney, and had spent the best part of the morning regaling Harriet with stories of her life there.

'It's all very well for you, Randa; you've got a rich husband and a nice house. Here am I stuck in the schoolhouse like a no-hoper. It's not fair.'

'Don't sulk, Hat. Come and stay with us.'

'That'd make it worse. Then I'd really know what I'm missing.'

She twirled a lock of hair around her finger and looked into the mirror again.

'I'm going to get my hair shingled,' she said.

'Your hair's beautiful, Hat! Don't chop it off.'

'It'll really annoy Pa, Miss Radley will disapprove, and I'll look older and more sophisticated. If I can't get out of this dump, I may as well make my mark on it.'

She rummaged though a pile of magazines under the bed and pulled one out. 'What do you think of this? How would it look on me?'

'You wouldn't dare! It's frightfully short.'

'It's perfect. Lulu can copy the style.'

Miss Lu Yong ran the hairdressing salon behind the community hall.

Miranda giggled. 'You'll be the height of glamour, Hat. There's no one in the Falls with hair like that. Just like Gloria Swanson. Michael Winterbourne will be powerless to resist.'

Harriet snorted. 'That old man!'

'He's not that old and he's very handsome. Everyone's after him.'

'He's a Pom.'

'You're just peeved because he's never paid you any attention.'

Usually all she had to do was raise an eyebrow or lick a lip and the stupid young men in the town were putty in her hands. But Winterbourne was proving a tougher nut to crack. She had hoped, when he walked her back to the schoolhouse after that dreadful dinner, that he might pay her some attention instead of treating her as a child. She'd led him a dance that night, deliberately making herself hard to find, until there were was no risk of Miss Radley catching them up and tagging along for the trip. But she wasn't going to confess that to Miranda.

'He's paid me more attention than he has anyone else. He's just a miserable bloody pom.'

'Hattie, language!'

'It's true. He walked me home after supper in complete silence. He's as bad as my father.'

'You know how to get your own way with your Pa - a handsome man should be no trouble for a girl like you? If I weren't happily hitched to Robbie I'd make a play for him myself.'

'You'd be welcome to him.'

'Not just me. Half the town's got their eyes on him. I don't get you.'

'Actually I'm sure there's something going on between him and the Wicked Stepmother.'

'You're not suggesting..?'

'I'm sure they know each other. They're both from England. They turned up here within a couple of months of each other and I saw her talking to him outside the schoolhouse but she pretended she didn't know him when they were introduced at dinner.'

'And...'

'You may have given me an idea for throwing a spanner into wicked step-mother's works!'

'Oh dear, I smell trouble. What do you have in mind?'

'I'm going to take your advice, Randa, and start batting my eyelashes at the Englishman. A new haircut and a bit of flirtation – the perfect way to get everyone in town green with envy and, most importantly, upset the Witch.'

'Is that fair? On him I mean?'

'It's not like I'm going to marry the man, for heaven's sake. I've set my sights much higher than him – but a bit of a flirtation to annoy her ladyship, followed by a ceremonial dumping, is an irresistible opportunity.'

'You're a bad girl, Hattie Kidd.'

'Race Week's next week. He's bound to be there.'

The McDonald Falls Spring Race Week: not quite the Melbourne Cup, but still the perfect excuse for a girl to show off a new hairstyle and a well-shaped pair of ankles.

CHAPTER FIFTEEN

THE RACES

Until 1813, when three explorers, Gregory Blaxland, William Charles Wentworth and William Lawson found a way across the previously impenetrable Blue Mountains, the area that included McDonald Falls was enjoyed exclusively by the Aborigines. The Dharug tribes were hunter-gatherers, thriving on fruits, roots and berries, supplemented by the odd possum or wallaby. Once the explorers arrived and opened the mountains up to cultivation and commerce, the Aborigines were soon wiped out by disease and the collapse of their way of life. By the late 1800s McDonald Falls and its surrounds were the exclusive domain of the colonialists.

The town enjoyed rapid population growth once the roads and railway opened up the mountains. The wealth of minerals - gold, bauxite, coal and kerosene shale brought incomers to the area, as well as the cool mountain air and beautiful scenery which attracted rich Sydneysiders to build country retreats there.

A varied programme of cultural and social activities flourished in the town, but Jack Kidd was immune to the attractions of the dramatic society, the choir, the various churches, the debating club and the cricket team.

Elizabeth, while harbouring no wish to project herself into society, was tempted by the prospect of accompanying the Choral Club with her violin, but Kidd made it clear that any attempt to join in the life of the community would not be well received. He expected her to be in her place at the end of the table whenever he deigned to appear for meals at Kinross House and liked to see her quietly occupied with sewing or reading in the evenings.

An exception to Kidd's self-imposed social isolation was the annual McDonald Race Meeting. Although gambling was prohibited on racetracks, the local police quietly ignored this annual event. Martie Lennox, the publican of the Lawson Arms, ran an unofficial tote. While not one for socialising, Kidd treated Lennox as the nearest thing to a friend in his life. The friendship consisted largely of the exchange of pound notes across the counter in the bar and the odd shared horse racing tip.

The race meeting took place every autumn. It attracted large crowds: virtually everyone living in and around the town, as well as visitors from neighbouring Blue Mountains towns and those from Sydney seeking a day or two away from the city. There was no social divide. Rich and poor, young and old, flocked to watch the races and to have an unofficial flutter on the horses.

Elizabeth had never been to a horse race and had no desire to do so now. The fact that it was also an excuse for gambling made it less attractive still. The week before the races she was contemplating how she might manufacture an excuse from attending, when Mrs Oates interrupted her reverie.

'Mrs Kidd, would you be willing for us to close the house on the day of the picnic races so that the servants can go? Mr McDonald permitted it and we all look forward to it. It's a big day for the whole town.'

'You're welcome to go. I plan to stay here with Mikey anyway, so I'll hold the fort.'

The housekeeper looked crestfallen. 'In that case, Ma'am, I will stay behind too. I'll ask cook to leave some cold cuts for lunch if that's acceptable, then she can go. Mary had better stay back as well if the baby will be at home.'

'There's no need for that. Mikey and I will be fine on our own. I don't want to go to the races.'

The housekeeper looked at her with a sceptical expression. 'A word of advice, Ma'am, if I can be so bold. I don't think Mr Kidd would like you missing Race Day.'

His voice barked out and Kidd entered the room. 'No I wouldn't like that at all. You're going. The boy can stay behind with Mary, but you're coming.'

'Horse racing is of no interest to me.'

Before Kidd could reply, Mrs Oates interjected.

'Mrs Kidd, it's the most important weekend of the year. The whole town will be there. Everyone in Sunday best. It's a grand day out. It's not just the racing, there's things for everyone to do – a great big picnic. You'll enjoy yourself.'

Kidd spoke then. 'Buy yourself a new dress. It's time you were out of those baggy things.'

She had regained her figure quickly after the birth of Mikey and her maternity clothes hung about her loosely, but as she never went anywhere, she had not got around to having them altered or buying anything to replace them.

'I can wear the green silk. I can fit into it comfortably now.'

But Kidd was having none of it. 'You'll not show me up by wearing something old.'

'It's hardly old - I've barely worn it.'

'Buy something new.' He looked at her appraisingly. 'And not green. Blue suits you better.' With that he left the room, leaving her open-mouthed.

So it was off to face Miss Godfrey again at the Salon de Paris. After waving away the pastel blues that were first shown to her, Elizabeth settled on a dress in a deep sapphire silk, with a matching hat, simple but elegant.

They were to go to the races in the car. Not Kidd: he'd make his own way there, via a session in the Lawson Arms, but Elizabeth was to be driven by Oates to the school where they were to collect Miss Radley and her charge.

Verity emerged looking flustered.

'I'm sorry, Elizabeth, but Harriet and I had words this morning. She's had her beautiful hair chopped off. Mr Kidd will be very angry when he finds out.'

Elizabeth smiled. 'He'll get over it. Tell her to get in the car.'

'She's not here. I told her that you'd be coming for us in the motorcar but she said she'd made other arrangements. She left half an hour ago.'

'Her father will be annoyed about that.'

'You know what's she's like when she has a mind to it. She won't listen to anything I say and now she's a grown woman it's hard to influence her. I can't chain her up!'

'It's not your fault, Verity. She's wilful and yes, she is a grown woman. You can't be expected to discipline her like a naughty schoolgirl – even when she behaves like one. Come on. I've been dreading today. Let's get it over with!'

Oates manoeuvred his way carefully onto the part of the park set aside for ranks of motor vehicles. He deposited the two women at the edge of a gravelled pathway that led directly into the race meeting, where a large crowd was milling. Mrs Oates had been right about the whole town being there. Everyone decked out in their best clothes: young and old, small children, miners and Sydneysiders, people from all the surrounding towns, dressed up to the nines. The race course, on the only area of flat ground near the town, consisted of a neatly mown track, lined with wooden posts. There was no viewing stand: the crowd gathered at the side of the track and around the roped off ring that formed the winners' enclosure. The jockeys were all amateurs, but kitted out in racing colours, like professionals. The sun shone brightly and the air was warm and Elizabeth picked up the contagious good spirits of the crowd. The smell of newly mown grass mingled with the scent of sweating horses and the warm smell of manure and she was glad she was there.

'Come on, Verity. Let's watch a race.'

The schoolteacher smiled and spoke conspiratorially. 'Shall we have a little flutter? I usually do on race day. Just a shilling each way on the McDonald Cup.'

Elizabeth smiled. 'You go right ahead, but forgive me if I don't join you.'

'Do you think I'm awful?'

'Of course not. Having a few bob on a horse once a year is not going to set you on the path to oblivion, but I have my own reasons for hating gambling – in any form. Don't let that stop you.'

'Maybe later. The McDonald is the last race of the day.'

They worked their way through the crowd and found a spot beside the track, where they watched a few of the races with mounting enjoyment. Elizabeth, while unwilling to place a bet, was happy to choose a runner and to call out her support as it raced around the track.

'What a shame you didn't actually have a bet on that one. It was 7 to 1 – you'd have won a few shillings. You know how to pick a winner. That's two out of three. Maybe you can pick mine for the McDonald?'

Elizabeth smiled. 'It's a deal! Let's go and see what else is going on.' She slipped her arm through Verity's.

The women looked around for Will, Kidd or Harriet but could see none of them in the crowd. They wandered towards a cordoned area in front of a marquee, which seemed to be a reserved enclosure for the great and the good. As they drew near, Will bounded up, eager as a puppy dog.

'G'day Lizbeth, you seen Hat? She's only gone and had all her hair chopped off. She looks a right Drongo!'

'No I haven't, Will, but I'm sure she looks lovely and you shouldn't be so rude about your sister. Someone might hear you and Harriet would be mortified.'

'She doesn't care. She's far too busy trying to yack to my cobber. Michael was just shouting me a beer when along she comes and starts hanging on his arm. She's all "Michael this and Michael that". He's too polite to tell her to rack off.'

Just then the crowd surged forward for the next race and Elizabeth saw her stepdaughter about fifty yards away. Harriet's hands were clasped behind her back, her hatless head, with its newly shingled hair, tipped to one side and her body language sending unmistakable signals that she was flirting with Michael Winterbourne.

Elizabeth's stomach gave a little lurch. She cursed the fact silently. The effect he still had on her. Anxious to avoid an encounter with either Michael or her reluctant step-daughter, she steered Verity towards the refreshment tent, hoping they might find a cup of tea there. Kidd emerged from the tent, a brimming mug of beer in his hand.

'Where's Harriet? Why isn't she with you?' He was frowning.

When he realised that his daughter had not only come to the races alone, but was wandering unaccompanied around the race grounds, he was furious. Elizabeth told him she was with Will and his friends from the colliery.

'I haven't paid a small fortune for her to get all dolled up, just to hang around with the men like a larrikin.'

He turned on Verity. 'Is that why I've paid you so much damned money to give the girl an education? So she can drink grog with a bunch of fellas?'

Before either woman could respond, Harriet appeared, dragging Winterbourne by his arm, with Will beside them.

Kidd almost spilled his beer. His face was rigid with anger. 'What the hell do you think you've done? Where the bloody hell's your hair?'

People turned around and looked with interest at the emerging drama.

'You look a bloody disgrace.'

His voice was raised. A growing crowd looked on, nudging each other that something was about to happen.

'This isn't the time or the place.' Elizabeth placed her hand on his sleeve and tried to draw him back into the beer tent. Kidd brushed her away.

'She's my daughter and I'll handle it the way I want to handle it.'

'It's the latest fashion. It's the cut in all the magazines' said Harriet.

'I don't care if you copied it from the bloody Queen of Sheba, it's not how I expect a decent girl to look and certainly not my daughter.'

He grabbed Harriet by the arm and pulled her behind him through the parting crowds, back to the edge of the park, where Oates was snoozing behind the wheel of the motorcar.

'Get in.' He shoved her into the back of the open-topped car and turned to Elizabeth. 'Get in with her. She's going back home with you, and going right now.'

Verity Radley seemed to shrink in on herself as the man's wrath switched to her. 'As for you and your fancy education, much bloody use that was! Go with them and get her bags packed and out of that schoolhouse. She's moving back under my roof now and she's going to stay there.'

Harriet slumped in the back of the car, tears of anger and humiliation streaming down her cheeks. Her ordeal was not over yet. Winterbourne had followed them and was standing beside Will with a look of astonishment. The girl shrank back into the leather seat, leaning away from Elizabeth and covering her face with her hands. They drove off, past the merry go-round and the picnic area, past the happy smiling people and the paddock of waiting horses.

As they turned out of the race grounds, Elizabeth looked back. There was Michael Winterbourne, rooted to the spot, watching them drive away.

Harriet's removal to Kinross House changed little between her and Elizabeth. They were in each other's presence daily, but might as well have been on opposite sides of the ocean for all the conversation that passed between them. Not for want of trying on Elizabeth's part – she went out of her way to give the girl some space and tried to engage her with some uncontroversial conversational gambits. The girl was immune to all such advances. When her father was present she replied to Elizabeth with a simple yes, no, or don't know, and when he was not, she acted as though her step-mother were not there, completely blanking her out. After a while, Elizabeth gave up and hoped that eventually the girl would outgrow this folly.

To Will, Hattie was friendlier than ever. It was if she hoped that by talking frequently and loudly with her brother, her father would fail to notice that she was ignoring her stepmother. Elizabeth suspected that her volubility with Will was also intended to make the silence between them more pointed. Easy-going Will was oblivious to his sister's calculations and welcomed the improvement in their relationship without question. Kidd never again referred to the girl's hair, either because he no longer cared, or had got used to it. The argument at the race day was not mentioned again. From time to time Elizabeth tried to broach the subject of Hattie's future, but he would not be drawn.

'She'll be married when I find the right fellow for her. I don't want to hear a word on the subject from you.'

'She's a clever girl. She could study at the University.'

'I'll not have a daughter of mine turn into a bloody bluestocking.'

'She can't just hang around the house all day. Her only friend is in Sydney. She has no social life. How on earth are you going to find her a husband? You never meet anyone! And a girl can't have her father choosing her boyfriends for her. She has to get out and meet young men herself.'

'I won't have you filling her head with romantic notions. That bloody Radley woman has done enough of that already.'

The chance of Elizabeth filling Hattie's head with anything, let alone romantic notions, was remote. As to the choice of husband, she didn't care. She hoped Kidd would get on with it and make a decision soon, as the presence of the girl in the house was becoming more irksome every day.

Despite the house being fuller than when she first arrived, Elizabeth was more lonely. Miss Radley rarely visited: the humiliation she had suffered from Kidd at the races proved too much for her to risk a repetition, so they only met when Elizabeth could visit the schoolhouse. Will was at work in the pit and seemed to spend all his free time with Michael Winterbourne. He was usually at home for supper and took the opportunity to talk with Elizabeth then, but the presence of Harriet and Kidd inhibited openness in their conversation. Elizabeth sensed a growing sadness in Will and presumed it was due to his loathing of the mine. Apart from a bit of banter with Mary and Mrs Oates, Elizabeth's days were devoid of adult conversation, but she exulted in her time with Mikey, who was growing so fast and managing his first words. Needless to say, he mastered the word mamma long before dadda. She wondered if he would have managed dadda at all, were it not for her constant repetition. Kidd showed no interest in the child.

As for Harriet, it was a while before she ventured out, after her public humiliation. Her aim of looking sophisticated and modern, a cut above the rest of the town and her former classmates, had backfired. She seethed with resentment at her father. She'd always been ashamed of his rough appearance, gruff manners and country ways. Their long separation had made her despise him more, except when trying to persuade him to part with money for new shoes or a silk blouse. But this time he'd gone too far. Shouting and bullying her in front of the whole town. Any thoughts she had entertained of impressing Michael Winterbourne were shattered. He'd see her for what she was: a naïve and gauche girl with a bully for a father. She lay on her bed wishing she were dead.

Harriet's passion for a dramatic and early demise faded soon. There were only so many tears of anger and frustration she could cry. When Miranda Appleton made one of her occasional visits from Sydney, Harriet accepted the invitation to visit her. She was bored of the four walls of her new bedroom and at least Miranda hadn't been present at the scene of her public humiliation. They sat together in the garden of Miranda's mother's house.

'I don't know why you care what people here think about you? Come to Sydney.'

'God, Randa, you've no idea how I'd love to do that. I'm so sick of this town and its stupid people. I'd like to escape and never have to look across the table at the Witch any more.'

'Surely she's not that bad, Hat?'

'She's taken my mother's place. That's enough.'

'Your mother died a long time ago. It's understandable that your Pa would want to marry again.'

'My mother was only thirty-four when she died. Her life was constant drudgery and struggle out in the bush but the Witch just swanned in and got to live a life of luxury in town. It's not right.'

'Your Pa's rich. You can't expect him to live the way he did before.'

'He was happy to carry on living like that until she came along. He stayed out at Wilton's Creek. But that's not good enough for the Witch.'

'Hat, you wouldn't want to live out there yourself. Not any more.'

'Too bloody right I wouldn't. I'm glad Pa's got lots of money now. But that doesn't mean I'm happy that someone else gets to benefit instead of my Ma.'

'You can't blame your step-mother for your Ma not being around any more.' Miranda's tone was tentative. She knew how volatile Harriet could be, especially on the rare occasions when her mother was mentioned.

Harriet looked away, preoccupied. Eventually she spoke. 'I think Pa wants me off his hands. He's been yelling at me a lot and complaining that I'm too fond of fancy clothes and French perfume. He doesn't care about me. But there's never any problem with him spending money on her.'

'Do you think he wants you to get married?'

'Who's going to look at me, when my father potters about in a ridiculous pony and trap with dead rabbits hanging off the back.'

Miranda giggled.

Harriet looked up in annoyance. 'I have a horrible feeling he'd prefer me to be shacked up with some poor old digger without two brass farthings to rub together and a house full of screaming brats.'

'How vile.'

'I want someone from the country club: a rich Sydney-sider who only comes up for the weekends or a few weeks in the summer. I'd like a big house here in the mountains – in Leura or Katoomba – that I could visit once or twice a year when it's too hot at the coast and an even bigger house in Sydney. I'd entertain the cream of Sydney society.' She sighed with longing.

'If you stay in McDonald Falls that's never going to

happen. You're not even a member of the country club.'

'Don't remind me!' she groaned. 'Those fellows from the country club think my father's a rough old swagman. I need a fresh start, away from here, where he can't embarrass me.'

'You can't just go off to Sydney alone. Your Pa would do his block. You can stay a few days with Robbie and me, but that's not going to be enough, is it?'

'No. And the trouble is I've no money of my own. Instead of giving me an allowance, I have to plead with Pa and justify why I need every penny.'

'Sorry, Hat, you may have to make the most of life beyond the black stump.'

Harriet scowled and made a mental note to be unavailable next time Miranda graced McDonald Falls with her presence.

As for Michael Winterbourne, since the race meeting, she couldn't even bear to think about him and how he had witnessed her humiliating exit from the park. She cringed with embarrassment. If her mother were still alive she'd scold her and tell her that it was no more than she deserved. That was why she didn't like to think of her mother very often - she knew she would not be happy with the way she'd turned out. *It's not my fault Ma - you should never have left me.*

Jack Kidd took little interest in the workings of the coal mine. It was a means to an end: the source of his wealth and the power that went with it. He was a countryman who loved fresh air, felt claustrophobic underground and hated being enclosed in darkness and damp. Before Winterbourne showed up, he had worked his way through a succession of foremen, without trusting any of them. The new man swiftly proved his competence, despite his lack of coal-mining experience and Kidd immediately trusted him. Coal was different from lead, but when it came down to it they both had to be dug out of the rock. Kidd also saw him as a bit of a kindred spirit. The Englishman spoke little, but told Kidd enough to let him know that he shared a love of the outdoors and came from a humble background. Kidd liked that. He knew he had served in the Great War and seen a bit of action, but he didn't seem inclined to talk of it and Kidd was not inclined to listen anyway. Winterbourne told him enough to reassure him that his wartime experience building and maintaining tunnels between the trenches and the rear lines gave him enough technical grounding to understand the mechanics of sinking a coal shaft and tunnelling safely.

The mine had seen better days. Kidd still made an income from it, but it was not the money-spinner he'd hoped when he won the title deeds from John McDonald, as the culmination of a series of increasingly high-staked poker games. The price of coal had plummeted since the War and the demands of the workforce were getting louder. The last thing Kidd wanted was a strike on his hands. He'd sell up if he could only find a buyer. He was hanging on in the hope that the market would pick up and he could negotiate a deal. The money itself didn't bother him. It was what it represented. The standing it gave him in the town. The fact that he didn't have to grovel to anyone.

He needed little for himself and only put up with living in Kinross House, with its fancy furnishings and servants, as he thought it might help him when it came to settling his daughter with a husband. It irked him though. He wished the girl took after her mother more, showing a bit of humility and understanding what a hard day's work meant. He knew Susanna had wanted a better life for her daughter and that was the only reason he'd gone along with the whole education charade.

But this morning Kidd had woken with a plan. As soon

as he thought it through, it struck him as the perfect solution to all his problems. Winterbourne could marry the girl. He rubbed his hands together with satisfaction. He could join the family and eventually take control of the mine. Will was never going to be up to the job. The boy had shown no inclination to learn the business and had an antipathy for going underground that was greater than Kidd's own. Winterbourne, on the other hand, was respected by the men and a hard worker. Kidd could get him more involved with the financial end of things. He could do a stint in the office. Robinson wouldn't like it, but he'd have to lump it. Harriet wouldn't want to be married to a man who came home with coal dust round his collar. After a while Kidd could liberate himself from the mine altogether. He could give the newly weds the house in town and move back to Wilton's Creek and do what he really wanted to do: farm the land. He'd need to invest a bit of money to build a proper homestead out there. Not for himself – he didn't care two hoots about his surroundings, but Elizabeth and the child needed more comfortable surroundings. And he could buy more land and farm it seriously.

Excited and feeling the energy surge in his body, he walked towards the foreman's office shouting, 'Mick! Get over here man. We need to talk.'

CHAPTER SIXTEEN

COURTSHIP

Will looked more down in the mouth every day. One evening when he returned from his shift, Elizabeth asked him to join her for a walk around the large garden. They walked in silence at first then, when they reached the boundary fence, they stood side by side, leaning against the palings, looking out at the fern-covered crags, listening to the sound of the distant waterfall. She breathed in deeply, filling her lungs with the unpolluted mountain air, then put her hand over Will's where he had placed it on the fence.

'What's wrong, Will? You're not yourself these days.' She took her hand away and placed it on his arm instead.

'You know it often helps to share a trouble.'

'Not in this case, Lizbeth. You can't make it better. It's not like Mikey grazing his knee.'

She put her hands on his shoulders and looked him in the eye. 'Spit it out. I want to know. I'll follow you round the garden until you tell me!' She was smiling.

Will frowned. 'It's the mine. I can't take it any more. There was an accident a few weeks back. Since then I keep thinking every time I go under that it's all going to come down on me and I'll die.'

She squeezed his hand to encourage him to go on.

'I'm not scared of dying itself. When your number's up, it's up. What scares me is being trapped and buried alive. I've been having nightmares. The tunnel collapses and I'm stuck under a ton of rubble and they all think there's no one there and close up the shaft and leave me to die – slowly and in terrible pain.'

Elizabeth pulled him towards her and held him, stroking his hair gently. 'It's only a dream, my darling. It's not going to happen.'

'I know. But it's getting worse. All the time we're underground I'm a bag of nerves, jumping at any sound. The men are starting to notice. If it weren't for Michael, they'd refuse to do the shift with me. They say I give them the willies. That I'm a big wuss.'

'A wuss?'

'A coward.'

'You? You're one of the bravest men I know, Will Kidd. Living on your own in the bush, looking after yourself. You're as brave as any of those miners. You just dislike being underground. Goodness, I'd hate it if it were me. You wouldn't be able to drag me into that lift cage! I think you should talk to your father. Ask him to let you work in the office or do some other work on the surface.'

'I'd rather go back to the Creek – apart from not seeing you and Mikey so much. And Michael. But I like being on the land. It's not natural being down there. And since poor Wingo copped it.'

'Wingo?'

'The fella who was trapped when the tunnel fell. He almost died. His leg got infected. He'll never work again. Crippled. They amputated his leg below the knee. Poor blighter.'

'I'm sorry, Will.'

'And then the horse dying. I could never have done what Michael did that day. They're right. I am just a big wuss.'

Elizabeth wasn't sure she wanted to hear any more, but

215

Will was visibly relieved at the opportunity to unburden himself.

'He had to kill a pit pony. Right there in the shaft. Fired a dynamite charge through its head. I know he was putting her out of her misery. She was in terrible pain and we'd never have got her out and her leg was broken and it looked like her spine too. He was right to do it. But he was so calm. I was a nervous wreck.'

He looked at her as though weighing up whether to continue or not, then carried on.

'I threw up, Lizbeth. In a pile of rubble and I couldn't stop blubbing like a baby. Michael was calm. He told me to hold her head while he put the detonator in her ear.'

'How horrible!'

'It was the worst thing. Bad as the day Ma died. I think he was pretty shook up too. We went for a beer afterwards. But don't you see, Lizbeth? That's the difference between him and me. He knows exactly what to do and he gets on and does it. He hates the mine too. He's told me so. But it doesn't stop him being good at the job. The men love him. They think I'm pathetic and they only put up with me because he stands up for me. How does that makes me feel?'

'Well, I think they're pathetic and you're a very brave man. I'm proud to know you.' She leaned forward and kissed him in the middle of his forehead.

Will reddened but couldn't help grinning. Elizabeth reached for his hand.

'Come on. That was the dinner gong. Promise me you'll talk to your father about changing your job?'

The boy's mouth hardened but he nodded and they went into the house together, hand in hand.

The sound of the violin was unlike anything Michael had heard before. He'd only known the cheerful and raucous fiddle playing that accompanied harvest suppers, weddings and miners' galas at Hunter's Down, in the days before the War robbed the village of so many of its men.

The plangent, haunting music was coming from the room next door. The notes rippled in the air in a bittersweet mixture of beauty and sadness. He'd never heard anything so moving or so sad. He stood beside the window looking out onto the garden, where the sunshine dappled the lawn, feeling a little melancholy as a picture came into his head of his parents sitting like bookends on either side of the fireplace in their humble cottage. He rarely thought of home these days. It was too painful, but the music carried him back.

Then he remembered what he was here to do and wondered momentarily if the musician was Harriet; but he knew it could only be Elizabeth. The virtuosity of the playing couldn't come from one so young as Harriet. He caught himself as he mentally added 'one so shallow'. He was not going to let himself think of Elizabeth any more in any context other than as his employer's wife. As for Harriet, he'd softened towards her since witnessing her father's humiliating treatment of her at the picnic races. Yes, she was vain and probably shallow, but she had spirit and hadn't deserved to be treated that way in front of half the town.

When Kidd mooted that Michael court his daughter, his initial reaction was outright resistance. The girl was too young and he had no wish to marry anyone, now that Elizabeth was beyond his reach. But Kidd brooked no opposition.

'A man your age needs a wife. I like you, Mick. You'll be a good match for Hattie. She needs a firm hand. She's taken against the missus and spends her life in her room sulking. You can take her out and get to know her and then we'll see what happens.'

'I'm not in a position to take a wife, sir. I have to support me parents. They need the money I earn here. If I was to have a wife I couldn't send them so much. They're getting old and me Da's not been able to work since...'

Kidd interrupted. 'Don't you worry about that, mate. If you marry her I'll see you both right.'

'What about Will?'

'I don't need you to tell me how to do right by my own son. I'll be getting out of town as soon as Harriet's wed. You can have the house and the bloody servants. Will can stay there if he wants, but I reckon he'll come back to Wilton's Creek. He'll never make a miner.'

'What'll you do?'

'Back to the Creek with the missus and the kiddie. I hate it in town. Can't be doing with all the crap people talk here. I hate having bloody servants creeping around after me, expecting me to live like a bloody snob. I'll have to polish the Creek up a bit for the wife but she knows what to expect. She'll be all right there. Not that she's got a choice. When you marry, I'll settle some cash on Hattie - Will too when he comes of age.'

Michael was torn. Elizabeth's betrayal was so absolute that it made no sense that she still had a hold over him. He hated himself for that. But try as he might, he could not hate her. He was too angry to admit to love for her either. He wanted to wrap her up and lock her away in a closed part of his brain, along with Danny and his parents. Thinking of her and them was just too painful.

His reverie was broken when the door opened and Harriet entered.

'Mr Winterbourne. Are you looking for my father?' Her tone was tentative. The brash confidence of their previous encounters was replaced with a demeanour that Michael would have mistaken for shyness, had he not met her before. Her father's public treatment of her must have humiliated the girl and dented her pride.

'Miss Kidd, I was wondering if you'd join me this afternoon for a walk?'

She could not hide her surprise. 'I don't think my father would like that.'

'I've spoken with yer father and he's agreed as long as I don't keep you out too late or take you anywhere dangerous.'

'I see.' She looked at him in silence and Michael was conscious of the poorly cut suit that was his Sunday best. He pushed away the thick lock of hair from his forehead and fixed his brown eyes on her.

'Well?'

'Wait a minute while I get my coat.'

She left the room, banging the hall door behind her. The music stopped and Elizabeth put her head around the other door, her violin and bow in her hands. She stopped short when she saw him, her face showing surprise.

Michael said, 'I couldn't help hearing you playing. It were a beautiful thing.'

He noticed her face turning slightly pink and she looked down, avoiding his eyes.

'Thank you. I was just practising. I'd no idea there was anyone in here.'

'What were you playing?'

'Edward Elgar. From the Enigma Variations.'

'It was beautiful, but sad. Made me feel I was back in England. Reminded me of the Dale.' He paused, then shrugged and his voice sounded colder. 'But then I'm ignorant where music is concerned. Someone once offered to help put that right but it came to nowt.'

The pink in her cheeks was now scarlet and she looked away again.

'Mr Winterbourne, is Mrs Oates looking after you? My husband is not at home. If it's an urgent matter, Oates can take you to him in the motor car.'

Michael took a deep breath, pulled his shoulders back and nodded towards the other door. 'Mr Kidd knows I'm here. I've come to take Miss Kidd for a walk.'

'I see. Does Harriet know you're here?'

'She does.' The voice was Harriet's. 'Come on; let's get out of here. It suddenly feels stuffy. I need some air.'

Nodding to Elizabeth, Winterbourne followed the younger woman out of the room. They left the house in silence and headed towards the large park in the centre of the town. As they went through the cast iron gates, Harriet turned to face him.

'Mr Winterbourne, is there something you want to speak to me about? Is it to do with Pa? Or Will?' She was hesitant.

'No. Nowt in particular.'

'So may I ask why we're going for a walk?'

'Just thought we could get better acquainted.'

'I see.'

They walked on in silence again, heading towards an ornamental lake on the far side of the park, away from the small crowd seated around the bandstand, where a group of men were playing a chirpy military march. They walked round the lake, alone apart from an elderly couple feeding bread to the ducks.

They began to speak at the same moment, and Michael gave way.

She started again. 'My father treats me as a child but I'm not, you know. I've never been so embarrassed in all my life as that day at the races. I'm not a little child. It's not fair. I'm eighteen. I'm an adult.'

'He were just a bit shocked at you getting all yer hair chopped off. No need to feel bad about it. Everyone understood.'

'I do feel bad. They were all laughing at me.'

'No they weren't. I were there. And yer new haircut's lovely.'

'Do you think so? Really?'

He looked towards the pond. A group of large pied

currawongs moved in on the ducks and grabbed the bread as the old couple tried to wave them away. Then he turned back to look at her again.

'Aye. It suits you.'

She smiled at him. 'Thank you.'

She looked prettier when she smiled. It was a shame she always had such a crab apple face on her, sulky and frowning. He wondered if being brought up by the schoolteacher and separated from her family had heightened her insecurities? Maybe that excused it but she was still hard work. He struggled to think what to say next and she showed little inclination for conversation. Like father, like daughter.

'What do you do with yerself to keep busy, Miss Kidd?'

'Nothing much.'

'I expect you help out with the wee lad do you? He's quite a handful I imagine?'

'You must be joking! I can't bear the sight of him.'

'Now then, that's not nice. Will says he's a lovely little fella. Mebbe you don't like children?'

'Can't say I do, but that one is worse than most – a spoilt brat. It's horrible that my father's started a new family at his age with that awful woman. It's just not right.'

He wanted to change the course the conversation was taking, but struggled for another topic. She was just getting into her stride.

'I bet she's hoping to get banged up by him again so she can give him a brood of ugly children and steal what's rightfully mine and William's. I call her the Witch. She's my Wicked Stepmother.' She laughed. 'Am I shocking you? I am, aren't I?'

'Aye. I'm not comfortable hearing that kind of talk, Miss Kidd.'

'It's all right for you. You're not affected. It's disgusting. What kind of woman is happy to marry an old man like my Pa? It's not normal. It's obvious she's after his money.'

'I don't think this is something we should be talking about.' He looked around desperately.

'Do you like the moving pictures?'

'Doesn't everyone?'

'Mebbe we could go together some time? If your father's all right with it. P'raps at the weekend? They put a new flick on each week at the picture house. I've not been there before, and I'd be glad to see a good picture meself.'

'Depends what's on. But yes I suppose so.' She was frowning again.

'Not if you don't want to?'

'Does this mean you're courting me, Mr Winterbourne?'

He looked down and swallowed before replying. 'I suppose it does. Is that all right with you?'

She shrugged. 'I said I'd go with you, didn't I?'

Then the frown transformed into a radiant smile and she put her arm through his and steered him towards the crowd at the bandstand.

'Yes, Mr Winterbourne, it's quite all right with me.'

They went to see a cowboy film. It was pretty tame stuff, Michael thought. Mexican bandits were never as scary as Indians, but in the dark of the theatre he could hear the indrawn breath of women as they clung onto the arms of their beaus in feigned or real fear. He wondered whether it was a ploy to permit closer physical contact? If so, it was one which Harriet didn't use. She sat bolt upright, eyes fixed on the screen, absorbed in the story.

Michael enjoyed the picture, apart from the scene when Tom Mix's character told the woman he loved *"I aint fit to graze in the same pasture as you, so I'm saying goodbye."* It made him think of himself and Elizabeth. Real life was so different from the moving pictures. The cowboy had got his girl in the end: she'd driven in her fancy car to save him from execution by paying his ransom.

When they emerged, Harriet put her arm through his as they walked back to Kinross House.

'Suffering coyotes! That was a bore!' she said.

'I like Tom Mix better when he's got a few Indians to contend with.'

'I hate cowboy pictures. All of them.'

'You should have said. We could have gone another time when there was summat else on.'

She spoke sneeringly. 'It was a ludicrous story. Poor cowboy marries rich rancher's daughter. She should have had more sense. And it's a shame those Mexican bandits didn't get to *"keel"* him after all.'

He was surprised by the harshness of her verdict and said, 'It's just a bit of fun. The flicks always have a happy ending. You wouldn't really want it to have ended sadly, would you? You wouldn't have wanted him to be shot?'

'Life doesn't have happy endings – why should the pictures?'

'That's a cynical view for a young woman.'

'Don't patronise me, Mr Winterbourne.' Her voice was slightly shrill and she jerked her arm out of his.

'I'm sorry, I didn't mean to offend. It were just that I'm disappointed you didn't have a better time.' He wished he'd never agreed to Kidd's plan. It was never going to work between them.

She countered. 'Did I say that? I just said it was a ludicrous story. I didn't say I didn't have a nice time.' She turned her face towards his and gave him a smile that would have melted the heart of a Mexican bandit and slipped her arm into his again.

Just before they reached Kinross House, she stepped out of the reach of the streetlight into the shadow of a gum tree, pulling Michael with her. She lifted her face to his and kissed him on the mouth. He was taken by surprise and found himself kissing her back but, just as quickly, she pulled away from him.

'I wanted to get that out of the way. I didn't want to have the prospect hanging between us and us both wondering when it would happen,' she said.

He ran his hand through his hair and stared at her.

She pressed on, her voice brisk and businesslike. 'You know what I mean don't you? You were probably thinking *Do I? Don't I? What will she think if I do?* And I was wondering is he going to kiss me or not? And I hate not knowing what's going to happen next.'

'I see.'

'You're annoyed aren't you?'

'Mebbe. A bit. It's not very romantic to reduce it to that.'

'Romance is tosh!' Then seeing his frown, she added, 'I suppose you're going to say I'm cynical, aren't you?'

'I wouldn't dream of it. I wouldn't dare!' he laughed bitterly.

'You need to understand, if we're going to be courting, I like to know what's coming next. I hate surprises,' she said, and then giving him a little wave, she ran into the driveway of Kinross House.

There was a good turnout for the annual colliers' cricket match, with the miners up against a team of railway workers. A large crowd spilled out of the Lawson Arms to watch the game: anyone with a fondness for cricket or an empty stomach – Kidd was reluctantly keeping up Mr McDonald's tradition of laying on an elaborate picnic, catered by the Queen Alexandra Hotel.

The railwaymen batted first and were all out for 133. Will and Michael sat side by side under the shade of a tree watching the first two members of their team head for the crease.

'We'll likely have a long wait before we get on to bat. Fred Burton's red-hot,' Will said. 'He may be getting on a bit now but he's a hard man to shift and he'll hit a few sixes I reckon.'

'Who's the other lad. Not seen him at the mine before.'

'Bruce Walker's eldest. Works in the post office at Katoomba. Pretty good cricketer too.'

'I'll bet you're handy with a bat yourself, Will? You did a good job fielding. Two out and I swear the umpire should have given LBW against the fat chap with the red hair.'

'Yeah I was robbed, mate! I could spit chips. You weren't so bad yourself. You ran the fat bastard out.'

'Come on, mate. Me granny could've run that fella out. He were nobbut a big lump of blubber.'

The crowd clapped as Fred Burton smashed a ball over the boundary. Will said, 'You getting serious about Hat, Michael?'

Michael rolled a cigarette, taking his time to answer. 'Yer old man wants us to get hitched.'

'What do you want, mate?'

'To be honest, Will, I don't know.'

'Mate, it'd be bonzer if you were in the family. But I can't say as I'd blame you if you weren't game for taking Hat on.'

Michael laughed and drew on his cigarette. 'I have to get married some time. I could do a lot worse than her. She's a very pretty girl.'

'Maybe. When she's a mind to be. But she can put a grim face on and act as miserable as a bandicoot on a burnt ridge. Half the time she looks like she's swallowed poison.'

'Give the lass a break. She's yer sister!'

'Doesn't feel like it, mate. We've lived apart for years. She's like a stranger to me. I'm closer to Lizbeth. I can talk to her about anything. She's…'

Michael interrupted him and pinched his cigarette out. 'Harriet's young. I'm not sure she'd have an old fella like me anyway.'

'You're not old! You're my cobber and I'm younger than she is!'

'Eleven years is a big gap. She'd be better with a lad her own age.'

'Pa doesn't think so. He's encouraging it. And look at him and Lizbeth.'

Back to her again. It always led back to her. He decided to stay with it. It cut him to the core every time he saw her with Kidd but if he were to marry Hattie that would be happening all the time, so he might as well confront his demons.

'You reckon they're happy?'

'The old man and Lizbeth? Can't imagine so. He's never happy about anything. He's like Hat. But I can't think how anyone could fail to be happy married to Elizabeth. She's so beautiful. She's kind. She's friendly. She's clever. She's…'

'Alright, I get the picture.'

The boy shrugged. 'Don't know what she saw in Pa enough to marry him. It was strange. She just showed up from nowhere. Pa's always been a dark horse, but marrying her took the biscuit. And our Hat's horrible to her. She won't even give her a G'day. Miserable cow.' He realised he might have overstepped the mark and quickly added, 'Sorry mate. I know she's your girl and all. But then she is my sister so I s'pose I can!'

Michael laughed and cuffed him lightly on the arm. The crowd erupted as Fred Burton hit another six.

On the far side of the pitch Elizabeth brushed a fly from her arm and glanced at her watch. She'd always found cricket boring and was not happy that Kidd had insisted on her presence this afternoon. There was no sign of him. He was doubtless holed up in the beer tent. It seemed he had even less interest in the game than she had.

Harriet had pleaded a headache and Kidd for once had let her stay at home so Elizabeth was on her own. It meant she was able to read surreptitiously: her handbag was open to accommodate the book should Kidd emerge and she need to conceal it. She didn't want him thinking she was showing disrespect to the players or sneering about her reading habit. Now and then she looked up from the pages and swept her eyes around the pitch to keep a general sense of what was going on. Cricket reminded her of Stephen and that summer before the war when she'd often sat on the boundary pretending to watch him play, while chatting to her friends.

A roar from the spectators and the cry of 'Howzat!' signalled a dismissal and she looked up to see a new batsman making his way to the crease. He was tall and she noted his broad shoulders and narrow hips and easy, confident stride. His sleeves were rolled up and the tanned skin on his arms stood out against his cricket whites. When he turned at the wicket and pushed the hair back from his eyes, she saw it was Michael Winterbourne. She tried to force herself to read. Damn him! How could he still do this to her? But the words on the page might as well have been hieroglyphics, so she gave up and started to watch.

Michael and the Walker boy made a formidable pairing and the runs kept coming. Elizabeth was soon hooked by the action on the field. She found herself jumping out of the deckchair as Michael hit yet another ball over the boundary. The noise of the crowd penetrated the beer tent and a group of men, including Jack Kidd, came out, pints in hands, to watch the play.

Will never got his chance to bat. The Winterbourne-Walker double act proved impossible to get out and as the sun began to sink, the umpire declared the miners the victors, 226 for the loss of just one wicket. His teammates gathered round Michael, clapping him on the back. Kidd took Elizabeth's arm and steered her to a table. 'You can hand the trophies over.'

'What?' Her jaw dropped.

'A cup for the team and a medal for each player.'

'I can't do that!'

'Shake each bloke by the hand and give him his medal and hand the cup to Fred Burton for the team.'

'I don't know what to say! I haven't prepared a speech.'

'Who's asked you to make a bloody speech. They don't want to waste drinking time listening to you! Give them a big pearly grin, shake their paws and hand over the medals.'

Mortified, she stood behind the table as the men lined up to collect the spoils, Michael and Will at the back of the line. As she lifted the large silver cup and presented it to the captain, she saw, out of the corner of her eye, Harriet run onto the green clutching her straw hat to her head and heading straight to Michael. The pair began to talk and Harriet flung her arms around him. He leaned forward and kissed her lightly on the forehead then slipped his arm around her waist proprietorially. Elizabeth felt sick to the pit of her stomach.

CHAPTER SEVENTEEN

CONFRONTATION

Will was lying on his back on the drawing room floor, while Mikey happily bounced around on his stomach.

'I hate it here, Lizbeth. I want to go back to Wilton's Creek.'

'Did you talk to your father?'

Will gave her shamefaced look. 'I bottled out. I told you I was chicken.'

'Oh, Will. If you can't bear it you must speak to him.'

'Don't get me wrong - I like all the fellas - especially Michael. He's a good mate and the other blokes are all right most of the time, but I can't stand not seeing the sky for so long. And I can't stop thinking about the tunnel caving in. I know it's daft, and I've really tried, but I can't help it.'

'Does your father mind going underground?'

'He's the same as me. Hates the darkness and misses the sky, but he doesn't have to go down if he doesn't choose to and he does it less and less, now he's got Michael to do so much.'

'Does Mr Winterbourne like being in the mine?'

'Nah! He hates it too. He likes being outdoors - being in the bush, in the fresh air. He used to work down a lead mine in England, so he's used to it, and he earns loads more money, now Pa's made him his deputy.'

'I see.'

'Not that he spends it. He sends most of it home to his folks back in England.'

'That's very creditable.'

'He won't have to worry about money soon. Pa'll see him right when he marries our Hat.'

Elizabeth almost choked on her cup of tea.

'Didn't you know that's the plan? Pa wants them to get hitched and then move in here and you and he and Mikey's going to move back out to Wilton's Creek.'

'What?' She put the cup down, spilling a large quantity into the saucer.

'Hasn't he told you?'

'No he hasn't. And what do Hattie and Mr Winterbourne think of this plan? I presume I'm the only one not party to all these arrangements?'

'I don't think Hattie knows either. Michael wasn't too happy at first, her being such a moody cow, but I think he's going along with it now. She seems to be on her best behaviour with him. All smiles and sweetness.

'I'll be made up to have him as a brother-in-law. I want to go back to Wilton's Creek with you and Pa and Mikey though. Could you ask Pa for me? He's more likely to listen to you. He says the mine is good experience for me, but I don't know what for? He'll never put me in charge – and I couldn't handle it if he did. Ask him will you, Lizbeth?'

She nodded distractedly. 'So Michael, er Mr Winterbourne, has agreed to marry Harriet?'

'He hasn't asked her yet but he's going to soon. Pa wants it sorted soon as possible. He wants to get out of town.'

'Does he?'

'Won't be much fun for you out there in the bush with just Pa and Mikey. If I could come too it would be bonzer.'

She thought about the prospect of Michael Winterbourne becoming a close relative. Her son-in-law for heaven's sake. Isolation in a shack in the bush would be preferable to living at Kinross House with Michael and Harriet under the same roof.

She waited until they were in bed. Kidd had just climbed in beside her and was stretching a hand out to lift her nightgown, when Elizabeth drew away from him. 'We need to talk.'

'Talk away.' He yawned and rolled towards her, again making to lift the hem of her nightgown.

Elizabeth pulled herself upright and drew her knees up in front of her. 'I understand you're planning for Harriet to marry your foreman.'

'That's right.'

'I don't think it's a suitable match. Harriet's had a good education and can do better than a mining foreman. I think she...'

He interrupted her. 'I don't care what you think. She's my daughter and I've made up my mind. She'll wed Mick Winterbourne.'

'What does Harriet think of this plan? Or haven't you seen fit to share it with her?'

'We'll bide our time till the lad asks her. They've not long been courting.'

'And is Mr Winterbourne aware that you expect him to marry your daughter?'

'He is.'

'He agrees?'

'He does.'

'It's preposterous!'

'You and your long words.'

'He's come from nowhere. We know nothing of him and

his family. How can you marry off Harriet to him like this?'

'This is Australia. We don't fret too much about people's family history. Now are you finished with your damn questions?'

'And we're to live in Wilton's Creek?'

'Who's told you that? You afraid of scrubbing floors again?"

'I'm not afraid of hard work. I'm just not relishing the prospect of being stuck in the middle of nowhere. I don't want Mikey growing up like a savage. He'll be lonely out there. Miles away from town.'

'We'll just have to make sure he has a brother or sister won't we? That'll be company and occupation for both of you. It isn't going to happen if you sit there like a bloody statue with your legs crossed. It's time you gave me a child of my own.' He put his hands on her hips and pulled her back down the bed.

Elizabeth stood at the bedroom window, a cup of tea in her hand, looking at the garden below. Will and Michael Winterbourne were kicking a flabby leather ball, while Mikey wobbled unsteadily between them, trying to intercept it, but failing, then toppling over and landing on his bottom. Each time, before the tears could start, either one picked the child up and set him back on his chubby legs, causing the incipient tears to turn to laughter, until another tumble set the cycle off again.

She watched, entranced. Neither Will nor Michael showed any sign of impatience: they teased and encouraged the little boy by turns. Mikey for his part was overjoyed at being the centre of attention and threw himself exuberantly into the game.

Michael feinted as Mikey ran towards him at speed, falling as though mortally wounded. He lay on his back motionless. Will gave a theatrical cry. Mikey looked bewildered, then teetered unsteadily over to the motionless body of the man, his face puzzled. As he arrived, Michael burst back to life and grappled the little boy, tumbling him into his arms and lifting him into the air. The child chortled, his momentary fear transformed into joy: a privileged participant in an exciting grown-up game.

This was a side of Michael Winterbourne that Elizabeth had never seen before: exuberant and playful. The two men now slumped together, breathless, against the garden wall while Mikey tried to pull them back into the game. She thought how things might have been different and she might have been watching Michael Winterbourne play with their own child.

She turned away from the window and slipped her wedding ring off her finger, dropping it into the empty porcelain dish on her dressing table. She pulled open the top drawer and took out a small box covered in faded black velvet. Inside was another ring, her mother's. She slipped it onto her finger and went back to the window. The three were still on the lawn: now Will was carrying Mikey on his back, horseback style, while Michael pretended to lead them: holding a thin belt, the other end of which was wound loosely round Will's neck.

As she watched the horseplay, she reflected that this was now her family. A boy, once a stranger, now her stepson; a small child she had never wanted to conceive and had thought to abort but whose very bones she loved; a man she had fallen hopelessly in love with, now to be her son-in-law. And the family she had once had were all gone: parents dead, her sister as good as, and her nieces lost to her for ever. She stood watching until the dinner gong, then she slid her mother's wedding ring off her finger and replaced it with her own, returning her mother's ring to its case and locking the drawer behind it. Taking a deep breath she went down to dinner.

Harriet was slumped in the only armchair in Verity Radley's tiny drawing room. Verity was seated at the small table where she marked her school papers and took her meals. She smiled at Harriet, thinking how pretty the girl looked, despite the heavy frown that marked her brow and broke the smoothness of her marble skin. It was so nice to have her company again: she was lonely without the company of Harriet and somehow diminished by no longer having someone to be responsible for.

'Sit up, Harriet. It's not ladylike to slouch like that.'

The girl sighed. She pulled herself upright and smoothed the front of her dress down where it had started to ride up above her knees.

'I can't take it much longer. I hate her. I don't know how you can bear to talk to her. I hate that you go to visit her rather than me.'

'For goodness sake! I go to visit you both. It saddens me greatly that you won't even enter the room if your stepmother is present.'

'Don't call her that. Not unless you insert the word wicked in front.'

'Harriet!'

'You know I loathe her. I wish she'd take her brat and go back to Sydney or England or whatever place she came from, and stay out of our lives.'

'I don't understand. Elizabeth has been kind to you. She made an effort to befriend you and she has your interests at heart. Why do you dislike her? It pains me that you behave like this towards her.'

'I've told you – she's a fortune hunter. She trapped Pa into marriage and she wants to take the place of my mother.

Ma worked hard and never had a penny to her name. Pa was poor when she was alive. Now this woman gets to enjoy his money. She struts around in fancy clothes and does nothing all day except scrape away at the violin and play with her horrible baby. My mother had to take in washing to get by. She should have lived to enjoy Pa's wealth.'

Verity had listened to this diatribe many times before and knew that nothing she could say would make the girl view Elizabeth any differently. 'Don't speak like this behind her back. I won't listen, Harriet. Elizabeth cares about you. She wants the best for you. And she never struts.'

The girl curled her lip and sank back into the depths of the chair.

'Anyway I don't want to talk about her any more either. There's something else I need to tell you. Michael Winterbourne asked me to marry him yesterday.'

'Goodness me, that's wonderful news! Mr Winterbourne has always seemed to me an exceptionally nice man.'

'I've decided to accept his proposal.'

'So you love him!' The teacher clasped her hands together in delight.

'Don't be ridiculous! He's a good-looking man and I do enjoy the fact that half the town is in love with him. But I'm certainly not in love with him myself.'

'Why do you want to marry him?' the older woman spoke nervously.

'He's my ticket out of this town and away from that woman.' She paused and looked away. 'And because she doesn't want me to.'

'She doesn't want you to?'

'She spoke to me yesterday. Said I was too young to be marrying. Told me if I didn't want to go through with it she'd speak to Pa on my behalf. The cheek of the woman. As if I can't speak to my own father!'

'Mr Kidd can be a difficult man.'

'That's nothing to do with it. I know she doesn't want me to marry him. So that's exactly what I'm going to do.'

'Harriet really! That's no basis to accept a marriage proposal. If you don't have feelings for Mr Winterbourne then you mustn't marry him.'

'Of course I can and I will. Besides Pa says I'll get Kinross House and that woman will have to move out with her horrid little child. Pa has promised to settle some money on me, so at last I can do as I like. My problems solved in one stroke! I intend to spend most of my time in Sydney. And the rest of the time I'll be mistress of my own house – the largest house in McDonald Falls. I have such plans!'

'Harriet! Please! And Mr Winterbourne? What does he have to say about living in Sydney? His work is here.'

'He doesn't know yet – but he won't care. He's at the mine most of the time. He'll let me do as I please. I'll stay in the city and he can stay up here. Perfect! He never says much anyway. When he's at the house he talks to Will not me. But then that's like Pa, so it's no change.'

'Does he have feelings for you? It seems cruel to enter into a marriage if you don't share his affections.'

'I don't suppose he cares any more for me than I do for him. I'm sure he thinks I'm pretty and I suppose he reckons he's got a good deal. Pa's promoting him to Mine Manager and giving him a big pay rise. He won't have to live in a nasty little lodging house any more. Not bad for a man no one had even heard of a couple of years ago and didn't have a penny to his name.'

'Harriet I'm shocked at how calculating you sound! It pains me greatly to hear you speak like this. It also saddens me to think of you entering into matrimony for reasons other than true feelings of affection. When I think of how happy I was when my darling Bernard proposed to me...'

'I don't believe in all that romantic tosh. It never lasts. Look at you!'

Verity blushed.

'I don't mean to be cruel, but romance is for fairy tales and the flicks. I'd rather have money and freedom.'

'Does Mr Winterbourne know you feel this way?'

'I haven't a clue. I told him I need time to consider his proposal. I don't want him to think I'm swooning at his feet like all the others.' The girl paused, then spoke: 'Has that woman ever told you she knew Michael Winterbourne? You know, before either of them came here?'

The schoolteacher looked taken aback. 'No. What on earth makes you ask that?'

'She behaves oddly around him. And so does he with her. They avoid each other. I noticed it that day outside the school when he sucked the snake poison out of that little boy. She was there. You didn't know her then and you'd already gone inside. They spoke to each other and I got the distinct impression they knew each other. The first time he came to Kinross House I could tell he was surprised to see her and they went out of their way to avoid talking to each other. Something's gone on there. The fact that she doesn't want me to marry him makes me all the more certain – and all the more determined to do so!'

'Your imagination is running away with you, dear. If Elizabeth knew Mr Winterbourne before she would have mentioned it.'

'Think what you like and so will I. It won't change my view and it won't stop me marrying him. And there's not a thing she can do to prevent me.'

Michael was halfway back to his lodgings from Kinross House when he heard someone running behind him. He stopped, thinking it was the young Irish maid or possibly Harriet herself. But it was Elizabeth.

She caught her breath, then spoke in a rush. 'Don't do it. Don't marry her. You know it's wrong.'

'What are you talking about?'

'Harriet doesn't care for you. She's very young. She's only marrying you to please her father.'

'What's it to you?' His eyes were cold.

'I don't want you to make a terrible mistake. Either of you.'

'The terrible mistake was made by me on Sydney harbour. Fresh off the boat and soft in the head.'

'It wasn't like that.'

'I'm not interested, Mrs Kidd. It's plain and simple. I don't see the problem. You married the father now I'm going to marry the daughter.'

Elizabeth choked back her tears. 'So this is about me? You're trying to punish me?'

'Don't flatter yerself.'

'Then why are you doing it? You don't care for Harriet. You'll make each other miserable and ruin any chance of happiness either of you might have in the future.'

'What do you know or care about me future happiness? You know nothing about me or about the girl. Just mind yer business. The matter's settled and I reckon if either Harriet or her father knew you were here talking to me like this they'd not be pleased.'

'Michael, I beg you. Harriet doesn't know her own mind. She's only doing this to please her father and probably to get away from me. As for my husband, I think he believes this is the best way to protect his financial interests and keep you at the mine.'

'Mebbe his financial interests and mine have a lot in common.'

'That's why you're marrying her?'

'Mebbe it's the same reason you married her father? Perhaps we're both after the main chance?'

'You know that's not true. Of either of us.'

'I'm not sure I know what the truth is any more. And I'm not sure I care.'

He walked away from her, anger rising. As the blood rushed into his face, he increased his pace, but as he reached the turnoff to the street where he lived, he kept walking, wanting to burn off his temper before he returned home and faced Mrs Abbott and the supper she'd have waiting for him. But as he walked, his heart was thumping a drum tattoo inside his chest and it wasn't from anger so much as desire. He had wanted to sweep her into his arms and promise he would never marry Harriet and beg her to run away with him. He knew he was a damned fool still to be beguiled by her. But he couldn't help it. He tried to hate her, but knew that he wanted her and always would.

As he pounded the deserted streets of McDonald Falls he told himself that Elizabeth's betrayal was a punishment for what he had done to his own family. Why be angry with her when he had no right to expect the happiness he so desired?

He made his mind up. He would marry Harriet. The consequent improvement in his finances would help his parents and that was the only consideration. Yet, despite the rational voice in his brain telling him that Elizabeth had toyed with him, his heart would not believe it. Her eyes when she looked at him were full of pain and longing.

Elizabeth walked home, eyes stinging from the tears she was trying to hold back. She had wanted to tell him everything, to explain all the messy details of how she had come to be married to Kidd, but she couldn't have done that without disclosing the true parentage of her little boy. That was not a risk she was prepared to take for anyone, even the man she loved so much. She also felt a debt of gratitude to Kidd for taking her in and acknowledging her son as his own. And it was too late anyway to undo any of this sorry mess, so what was the point of raking it all up? Her life had not turned out as she wanted, but it could have been much worse if Kidd had not married her: destitute and abandoned in a strange country with a child and no means of supporting herself.

One thing was clear. She could not live under the same roof as Michael and Harriet. Exile to Wilton's Creek was a far better alternative.

CHAPTER EIGHTEEN

ANOTHER WEDDING

Michael had pre-nuptial nerves. No matter how often he told himself to forget Elizabeth, he couldn't stop thinking about her. As soon as the date for marrying Harriet was set, he started panicking. Marrying her was wrong, very wrong. He tried to be cynical – he'd be a wealthy man and could afford to bring his parents out to Australia. He tried to be pragmatic – Harriet was an attractive woman and he had no desire to stay a bachelor. He tried to be angry – it would be sweet revenge for Elizabeth's betrayal. But none of it worked. He knew in his heart it wasn't right that he marry a woman he felt nothing for. And doing it in circumstances that would tie him forever to Elizabeth was worse.

The night before the nuptials was his last chance to pull out. He'd tried to refuse a buck's night, but the men at the colliery and Will were immoveable on the subject. Jack Kidd offered to stand them all drinks in the Lawson Arms so there was no chance they would let Michael slip off for a last quiet evening alone at his lodging house.

Kidd left early, after one drink, but everyone else was in a party mood. Michael endured the ribbing and ribaldry and nursed his pint with a growing sense of melancholy, escaping the crowd at the bar as soon as they were drunk enough not to notice. He sat down at a table beside Will.

Will slapped him on the back. 'How ya going, mate? That lot over there will be full as a boot before long with all that grog. But Hat'll do her block if I let you get sloshed the night before her wedding!'

Michael stared gloomily into the depths of his beer. 'I'm taking it slowly.'

Will looked at his friend curiously. 'You all right, mate? Having cold feet? Don't blame you!' he said, then punched Michael lightly in the ribs. 'I know Hat's a bit of a battler, but if anyone can sort her out, you can. She's been a bit of a grumpy cow since Lizbeth married Pa. She'll get over it once she's married herself and pushing out bubs. Her nose was put out of joint when she heard that Lizbeth has another on the way. Worried she'll be disinherited. But she perked up when the old man told her he's giving her a ton of money when she marries you. Once she's in the bub club herself she'll be happy.'

Michael paused with his beer midway to his mouth and put it down again on the table.

'Your father and Mrs Kidd are having another child?'

'Didn't you know? I thought Hat or Pa would have told you. Dad's made up. He never seemed that thrilled when she was expecting Mikey.'

'And Mrs Kidd?' Michael could hear the tremor in his voice and hoped Will wouldn't notice above the din of the bar.

'Pleased as punch. Hoping for a girl. I am too. As long as she's an improvement on Hat!' He poked Michael in the ribs again. 'I'm only ragging you, mate. Hat's all right.'

Michael threw the contents of his schooner down his

throat and banged his glass down. 'Time for another, Will. Let's make the most of me last night of freedom.'

Elizabeth sat at her dressing table, delaying the moment when she would have to take her dress off the hanger and put it on. It was a beautiful frock: a blue shantung silk with midnight blue satin ribbons outlining the V-neckline and falling loosely to meet the dropped waistline. With a sigh, she slipped it on and contemplated her reflection in the glass. She smoothed her hands down the sleeves, feeling the slight roughness of the silk as it flared below the elbows. The cloche hat trimmed in the same blue satin finished it off perfectly. Any pleasure she might once have felt at wearing such a garment, was cancelled out by her dread at what lay ahead.

The announcement of the wedding had failed to thaw relations with Harriet. The girl continued to treat her with contempt and Elizabeth counted the days until she, Kidd and Mikey could head for Wilton's Creek. When she'd first seen that place she'd never imagined that one day she'd look forward to returning there. She didn't relish the prospect of isolation, but the simplicity of life there held no fears. Kidd had arranged for some long overdue improvements to be made to the house and a detachment of workers had extended it at the back, partitioned the room and painted it. Kidd had fixed up a generator and had added a wood-burning stove. Elizabeth would have to get used to pumping water and chopping logs again but she didn't care. As long as she was away from Harriet and Michael, hard work was no punishment. She'd miss seeing Verity and Will, but she was sure Kidd would let her accompany him for the occasional day trip to town.

Kidd entered the room. He was wearing a new brown

suit with a sprig of red bottlebrush jauntily decorating the buttonhole. She'd never seen him dressed so smartly – certainly not on their own wedding day. His short hair was plastered flat, glistening with brilliantine and parted in a sharp line. He actually looked quite dapper. She resisted the urge to laugh: his frown telegraphing that he was not comfortable in his new garb and any comments from her would not be welcomed.

'The car's waiting. Get a move on. Oates needs to come back for me and Harriet.'

'There's plenty of time.' She was reluctant to leave the house, to leave this part of her life, to relinquish her faint claims on Michael Winterbourne. To witness him marrying Harriet: to finally forego any claim of her own.

She looked at Kidd again. The hair cream was not to her taste, but it added sleekness to his normally rough and spiky hair. He was cleanly shaven, with no trace of the usual dark shadows that crept over the lower half of his face. He smelt fresh, the scent of bay rum replacing the mixture of fresh sweat and slightly stale tobacco that usually lingered about him.

She felt an unexpected rush of tenderness for him. She raised two fingers to her lips then placed them on his. Kidd stepped backwards in surprise, and coughed nervously. He pulled himself up to his full height, which still fell short by at least an inch from Elizabeth's.

'You look very smart, Jack.' It was the first time she had used his given name.

He flushed and coughed again, frowning. 'Motor's waiting.' Then rapidly: 'Get moving. Where's the boy?'

He opened the bedroom door and called out onto the landing, 'Will! Where the devil are you? Where's the child? Get in the motor. It'll look bad if you're late.'

Closing her eyes and breathing deeply, Elizabeth

headed down the stairs towards her small son, her stepson, the waiting motorcar and the wedding she dreaded with every atom of her being.

McDonald Falls had never seen a wedding like it. Kidd had decided to spare no expense for his only daughter. Half the town was invited and the big stone church was packed to capacity.

Elizabeth, in the front pew, sandwiched between Will and Mikey, clutched her little boy's hand all the way through the ceremony. She kept her head down, her eyes closed and tried to shut out the goings-on in front of her on the steps of the altar.

Harriet was wearing ivory silk, encrusted with tiny seed pearls, with more pearls woven into the fabric of the veil which swept down to the floor from her pearl-encrusted satin skull cap. The dress had cost a small fortune and looked it. The shape was fashionably loose and fell flatteringly over the girl's slender figure, revealing a pair of trim ankles enclosed in white silk stockings and ivory satin shoes. When she walked up the aisle on her father's arm to the sound of the creaking organ, Elizabeth heard the gasps and whispered admiration. They did indeed make a handsome couple.

Keeping her eyes lowered, Elizabeth remembered her own wedding, three years earlier. She looked at her husband in his smart brown suit and remembered the shabby garments, the un-oiled hair, the rough hands and the dirt under his fingernails. Married life had effected some improvements.

The minister had reached the exchange of vows. Elizabeth dug her nails into the palm of her left hand, while clinging to Mikey's hand with her right. The little boy wriggled and tried to pull away, forcing her to relax her grip. She bent down to settle him, stroking his blonde hair, grateful for the distraction from the ceremony. She shivered when Michael's voice, with its still strong North Country burr, spoke out confidently in response to the prompts. Then Harriet's, softer, but clear enough for all to hear. Elizabeth swallowed, realising she'd been nursing an unvoiced hope for divine intervention. The minister pronounced the couple man and wife. There was to be no reprieve.

Elizabeth was standing on the steps of the church while the photographer fussed with his equipment, when Mikey, tired and hungry, started to cry. She was about to slip away with him, but she felt Kidd's hand on her arm.

'Leave the child be. Mary can take care of him.' On cue, Mary stepped out of the crowd and swept Mikey up in her arms and carried him away.

The formal reception of guests and the interminable wedding breakfast were followed by dancing. The celebrations were held in the vast formal dining room of the Queen Alexandra Hotel. It was a very grand building, looking out over the gardens to the town. Elizabeth was surprised at the grandeur, relative to the size of the town, but remembered that there was plenty of money pouring into the mountains from wealthy tourists and weekenders who expected the same high standards they enjoyed in Sydney. The ceiling was decorated with elaborate cornicing and two enormous glass chandeliers. Romanesque arches ran down each side of the room and ornate columns supported the high ceiling. Kidd must have bought up every florist in Sydney and the room was filled with the scent of flowers.

Elizabeth was conscious of Michael sitting beside her at the top table. Will was on her other side and she talked to him animatedly, desperate to avoid the need to turn to her left and speak to her new son-in-law. She need not have worried, as Winterbourne showed no inclination to talk. Sitting so close to him was like a slow torture. Her leg was a couple of inches from his and he accidentally brushed against her when they sat down. His leg sprang away as though electrocuted. Did he really hate her so much?

It was all such a terrible mess. She cursed herself, cursed the savage gods, whoever they were, for arranging things so cruelly. Then she thought of Mikey and told herself she could face anything as long as she had him. He brought her joy every day of his life and his presence helped wipe out the memory of his conception.

The party moved to the large ballroom where the dancing began, led off by the newlyweds. The second dance was between father and daughter and Elizabeth, to her horror, was pushed towards Winterbourne by Kidd and Will, urged on by the crowd who gathered around the dance floor, eager for the dancing to be opened to all.

When the musicians struck up, Kidd shuffled uncomfortably around the room, led by his daughter rather his own footwork. Michael took Elizabeth's hand for the dance, a waltz. He looked like a man going to his execution. Elizabeth held herself stiffly, feeling awkward and embarrassed, but as he held her, the music swept them up and she felt herself relax. Maybe it was the effect of the champagne, but she felt that she would rather be nowhere else. The smell of Michael, the feel of his skin against hers as their hands clasped, the light touch of his other hand against her spine. It was a long time since she'd last danced. Not since Stephen died. Their bodies moved together and the music moved through them as though they were one single being. She didn't want it to stop. She didn't want to let go of him.

The music ended and they stepped apart. For an instant he looked into her eyes and she felt the old Michael Winterbourne had returned. The moment passed, his body stiffened, his eyes narrowed into a frown and, nodding curtly, he stepped away to reclaim his new bride from her grateful father. Not a word had passed between them.

Elizabeth saw Verity across the crowded room and went to join her, glad to sit with her back to the dancing and the newlyweds. Out of the corner of her eye, she saw Harriet making a circuit of the room to show off her gown and her rings to the many former school friends present. Verity smiled. 'Doesn't she look a picture? You must be proud.'

Elizabeth nodded. 'She does indeed look lovely.'

'She's in her element with her old classmates. She'll be thrilled to be one of the first to be married – and to such a handsome man. She looks quite the lady now.' She paused, looking embarrassed. 'I mean… not that she hasn't always been lady-like…'

'I know what you mean, Verity. She's suddenly grown up.'

'Indeed. That's exactly what I meant. She looks so sophisticated and elegant. And Mr Winterbourne looks so handsome. They make a lovely couple.'

'They certainly do.' Elizabeth forced some enthusiasm into her voice.

When he came back from the bathroom, Harriet was sitting up in bed thumbing through the pages of the Sydney Morning Herald. She dropped the paper onto the floor, flicked off the switch on the night-table lamp and slid down beneath the covers. Michael climbed into the bed beside her, and then as he reached for her, she spoke.

'Can we get it over as quickly as possible?'

He removed his hand from her waist and went to switch the light on again.

'No, leave it off. Just get on with it please. I know it's going to hurt, so do it as fast as you can.'

Michael started to laugh.

'Why are you laughing at me? What's so funny?'

'I don't expect Rudi Valentino's ever got fed a line like that.'

'This isn't the pictures.' She was sounding sulky now. 'I know what happens. My friend told me. It's horrible for women. So I want to get things clear from the start. Do it if you must but I don't want to discuss it.'

'Harriet, for heaven's sake! Go to sleep.' He turned on his side away from her. As he lay there trying to sleep, she started sobbing quietly and feeling suddenly sorry for the girl, he rolled over and took her in his arms.

'Hush now. It's all right; you don't need to be scared. I won't do 'owt to hurt you and I won't do anything you don't want me to.'

'I don't want to die.'

'What?'

'Like my mother.'

'What're you talking about? What happened to yer mother?' He felt her hot wet tears in his hair.

'She kept on expecting babies and losing them and then she died. It was horrible. I couldn't do anything to help. Pa was away and Nat, my older brother, went off and I couldn't find him and Ma was really ill with the influenza and then Will went for the doctor but the baby started coming and I didn't know what to do and she was screaming and there was blood all over the bed and then she looked at me all sad and then she died. I don't want that to happen to me.' The words tumbled out almost unintelligibly.

'Harriet, that's not going to happen.'

'All she did was have babies or lose babies. Pa didn't let her alone and she wasn't very strong. She was always tired. She worked really hard. I miss her so much. It was my fault she died. I didn't know what to do. I couldn't help her. I had to watch while she died. It was horrible.'

Her body shook as the sobs convulsed her. Michael cradled her, stroking her hair and whispering what he hoped were words of comfort, until she drifted off to sleep.

The next morning a shutter had slammed down over her emotions. When Michael woke and reached for her in the bed she wasn't there. She was dressed and sitting at a small table in front of the hotel window, reading the newspaper.

'You're up and about bright and early. Don't forget we're on our honeymoon. There's no need to be rushing off anywhere.' He patted the bed.

She ignored him and said, 'I've made plans. We're calling on friends of mine. We have to make an effort if we're to be invited to the best places. And we must go to the theatre. Everyone who's anyone will be there. And there's a concert tomorrow night: the London Philharmonic are visiting.'

'Hold your horses, Hattie.'

'I've so much shopping to do. I need new clothes and the furnishings in Kinross House have to be changed.'

'Whoa! Harriet. I'm not spending my honeymoon watching you shop and being paraded around Sydney like a prize bull. I'd in mind that we'd spend our honeymoon together. Just the two of us. Isn't that the point of honeymoons?'

She didn't answer, but went on flicking through the pages of the newspaper.

'I thought we could travel up the coast? I've been underground for months and I'm longing for a bit of sea air. We could do some walking. Enjoy the scenery. Mebbe take a picnic. Go on a boat trip round the Harbour. Take the ferry across to Manly and have a bit of a look around. It'll be the first chance I've had to explore. I don't want to be stuffed into me best bib and tucker, making polite conversation with a bunch of high society folk who'll be looking down their noses at us.'

'At you maybe. No one will be looking down on me.'

'That's as mebbe... but surely you want to spend some time together? It's our honeymoon. There was me thinking it were women who were the romantic ones!'

'I've told you – we're not living in some stupid Hollywood picture. Romance doesn't enter into it. If you must know, I only married you to get away from my dreary life, my wicked stepmother and most importantly to get Pa to settle some money on me. I intend to spend most of my time in Sydney. It's as simple as that. You're a means to an end. I'm sorry to be blunt, but I've no wish to sit dandling on a porch swing with you or walking hand in hand into the sunset.'

'I see.'

'Don't look like that! You know as well as I do that this marriage suited us both. I get my freedom and we both get to spend my father's money. You can go back to work next week and I'll stay on for a couple of weeks. I'll come back to sort the house out and keep up appearances, but otherwise you're free to get on with your life. Once I've found a place here you're welcome to come down for the weekends if it makes you fell better. Entirely up to you.'

'You've got it all worked out then?'

'Of course I have. I'd nothing else to do but think about my future while I was shut up in that house avoiding the fortune-hunter.'

'Don't speak of yer stepmother like that.' His voice hardened.

'And what's it to you if I do?'

'It isn't respectful.'

'She deserves no respect. She's a money-grabbing witch, who's taken advantage of my poor old father.'

'Yer father's big and ugly enough to take care of himself.'

'No he's not. I'm sure she got herself knocked up with a baby to trick him into marriage. She's probably just a common prostitute. I'm not even sure the brat's his.'

Michael lunged across the room and grabbed her by the wrist. 'Don't you dare say that about her.'

'Why should you care? What's she to you?'

'I won't tolerate you calling yer father's wife a prostitute.'

'Let me go. You're hurting me.'

His contempt was palpable. 'You're disgusting.'

'You knew her already, didn't you? You'd met her before? I knew it! Did you plan this together? Did you cook the whole thing up together back in England?'

'Don't be ridiculous.'

'It's true isn't it? I can tell. You and she are in this together. Oh my God, I must tell my father.'

Michael sank back onto the bed. 'Believe what you want but it isn't true. Yes I met Mrs Kidd once before. We were on the same ship and we ran into each other again after we docked in Sydney. I'd no idea she was married to yer father and I'd no idea she was in McDonald Falls, so I was surprised to find out she were married to the gaffer. I'm sorry about what happened to your mother but maybe you have to accept that yer father, much as he loved her, wanted another wife.'

'That's rubbish. Pa would never have wanted …'

'Mrs Kidd's an attractive woman and it's understandable yer father would want to wed her. It's hard for a man to be on his own. Believe me, I know.'

'I hate her.'

'Hate away, but it won't change anything. Your father's made his choice and he seems happy with it. There's many a man in McDonald Falls wish they were in his shoes.'

'You too no doubt.' She spat the words at him. 'So that's it? You're carrying a torch for her.'

'Stop it, Hattie. It's all in your head. You're making up stories. I'm married to you aren't I?' He moved towards her and took her face between his palms. It was a pretty face, but the temper tantrum had mired it with frown lines and she had a petulant air that was unattractive. Michael ran his palm across her forehead as though to smooth the frown lines away, but the girl pulled back from him.

'Leave me. You'll smudge my makeup.' She reached into her handbag and pulled out a mother-of-pearl powder compact and began to touch up her face, then snapped the compact shut.

'We're expected at the Appletons this afternoon and I need to buy a new hat first.'

'All right Hattie. I'll come with you to meet yer friends today and mebbe we can go to a concert, but then please let's get away out of town and enjoy ourselves. I don't want to fight.'

'You can do what you want, but I'm not going with you. I'm staying in the city and you're not going to stop me. I'll wait for you downstairs.' She pulled on her hat, grabbed her clutch bag and left the room without a backward glance.

After a day trailing in Harriet's wake, as she explored the treasures of David Jones and Farmer's department stores, he persuaded her to take a stroll through Hyde Park and from there down to the Domain. As they walked by the edge of the water, he wished they weren't there. The scene brought back the memory of meeting Elizabeth and the misery of the day after, when he had waited in vain for her.

Harriet was in a good mood, buoyed up by the success of her shopping expedition. She'd bought so much it had to be sent to the hotel in a taxicab. Now she was busy planning their evening.

'We have cocktails with Miranda and Robbie. They haven't mentioned dinner - so I want you to suggest we take them on to a restaurant afterwards. They'll refuse, of course, but they'll feel obliged to invite us to stay for dinner. I know for a fact that they entertain at home almost every night. They obviously want to check you pass muster before they extend us an invitation. It will be an excellent opportunity to meet some interesting people. For God's don't tell them you're a coal miner.'

'Why do you feel the need to scheme so much? Can ya not let life come along and take you as it finds you? You're only eighteen – there's time enough to worry about yer social standing. Just try and enjoy yerself. Please!'

'You don't get it, do you? Try not to let me down or embarrass me. Keep quiet and only speak if someone speaks to you. Steer clear of saying what you actually do, just say you're helping develop my father's business affairs. Have you got that? If not, it's better you stay behind at the hotel and I'll make your excuses. I don't want you showing me up by talking about coal and nasty things like that.'

It wasn't worth answering. He wondered whether to take her up on the offer that he stay behind, but he needed to play along if there was any chance of getting her to compromise about the rest of the honeymoon. He leaned against the wooden bench and looked up at the trees. The huge fruit bats were there, densely packed, dangling upside down in the foliage. Used only to seeing the occasional tiny pipistrelle under the eaves of the cottage in England, he was amazed by the size of these, and their presence in the heart of the city. The ibises too surprised him with their exotic, long curved beaks. Everything was larger than life. Even after three years, he thought he would always feel like a stranger in Australia.

Harriet wasn't interested in bats or ibises. She prattled on about her plans and aspirations, and Michael wondered how he was going to survive his marriage. The *Little Girl Lost* of the race day and the tearful daughter of their wedding night were a replaced by a social-climbing martinet. Her suggestion that she spend most of her time here without him was appealing. It would anger Jack Kidd – but did he need to know? He was planning to live out at Wilton's Creek and would only be in town occasionally. With a bit of cooperation from Harriet, they might be able to work it that she would be in McDonald Falls whenever her father was.

He gazed at the bats, watching as the odd one broke away from its arboreal dormitory to make a lazy swoop through the air to alight on another tree.

They had finally consummated the marriage. Their delayed wedding night did not augur well for the rest of their marriage. All Michael's efforts to get Harriet to relax were in vain. She lay inert under him; giving a little cry of pain when he entered her, then lay there like a human sacrifice, her face set in a frown of discomfort that killed any ardour in Michael. He had hoped that once her virginity was dispatched, she might be able to relax and enjoy what he was doing to her, but this morning when he had tried to make love again, he'd felt like a rapist. She was rigid, with fear or, more likely, distaste, her eyes screwed tight shut and her mouth set in a hard line. Afterwards, she told him he was not to expect conjugal relations more than once a month.

She stretched her feet out in front of her as she sat beside him on the bench, admiring her new, shiny, bar shoes, tilting her ankle so she could take in the full glory of their neat little heels.

'I'll wear the pink silk tonight.'

She looked at her watch. 'Time to go. I want a bath before we go out.'

CHAPTER NINETEEN

LORIKEETS

The Kidds moved to Wilton's Creek while the honeymooners were still away. Will had made a series of trips with a wagon to transport their packing and provisions and was waiting at the small homestead along with Mary who, Kidd had finally agreed, would accompany them to help with Mikey.

Elizabeth had tried to convince Kidd to let Will live with them and help develop the land into a viable farming enterprise. Kidd would not relent. 'The mine will toughen Will up. He needs to grow up. I've already got a spoiled, lazy daughter and I don't need my son to turn into a bludger. He's got to learn to look after himself.'

'He hates the mine with a passion. He loves the land and he could be such a help to you. And he's not a bludger, as you call it – he's a hardworking lad.'

'Stop interfering. It's up to me to decide what's best for him. He'll move here soon enough, but not till I say so.'

She knew enough to bide her time for a better moment. It was a war of attrition, but she was confident she could win it.

They fell into a routine. Kidd rose early and was gone

before she got up. One evening she looked up from her sewing and said 'I have no idea what you do all day.'

Kidd grunted.

'Why don't you tell me? I'm interested. You ride off on the pony with your bags behind you and I haven't a clue where you go or what you do. Then there are the days when you take the truck to go into town. What do you do there? Is it the mine?'

'Sometimes.'

She stabbed the needle into herself in frustration and jumped up to wipe the blood off. When she sat down again she was all the more determined to pin him down.

'Not every time?'

'I have meetings.'

'Meetings?'

Kidd swigged his beer and replied impatiently. 'I meet with grain merchants and livestock breeders. I talk to land surveyors and other farmers. I have a few beers at the Lawson. And I don't expect to have to bloody well account for my movements to my wife.'

'I'm not asking you to account for your movements. I'd like to know more about your business. When I was a child, my father used to talk to me about the coffee business. It was interesting. I haven't a clue what you're even farming? You never talk about the mine, but I thought you might at least tell me about your work out here. I know you've bought more land, but you've never said what you intend to do with it.'

'And you're some kind of expert on land usage are you?' He got up from the chair, kicked over his empty beer bottle, and grabbing another bottle, took himself outside to sit on the veranda in splendid isolation.

Elizabeth sighed. Despite his surliness, she had begun to find a kind of accommodation with him, that could almost be described as fondness. But each night, as she looked across the room at him, she marvelled that it had come to this: being married to this short, tanned, weathered man who made no conversation and showed little or no capacity for affection or emotion. He was not untypical of men in and around MacDonald Falls. They shared his impatience with talk, communicating only what was vital and preferring the hard grind of physical work, washed down at the end of the week with a few schooners of beer. It was hard to believe she was the same woman who had sat in the stalls at the Liverpool Philharmonic, impatient for the orchestra to strike up; a woman who threw her tennis racket in a bag and rushed out of the house for a game of doubles. Tennis and symphonies were now alien concepts.

By rights she should have been bored, here in the middle of nowhere, a good hour's drive from town, deprived of company except Mary and Mikey, yet she liked the peace of the place. Time moved more slowly, as though operating by different laws.

Now that there was electricity and more space at Wilton's Creek, life was easier than in those first weeks of marriage. Mary now undertook the weekly washing ritual, her strong Irish muscles being well-fitted to the task of carrying the water to fill the wash tub and making light work of wrestling the clean sheets through the mangle and onto the washing line.

Kidd came home unexpectedly one morning, when Elizabeth was sitting on the porch with Mikey. She had a large volume on the birds of Australia and was listing them in a notebook as Mikey identified them. So absorbed were they, that she didn't hear Kidd approach.

'What's the one with the bright red head and tummy, Mikey?'

'Honey birdie.

'That's right, my love. The scarlet honeyeater. Do you remember what scarlet means?'

'Red!' He shrieked his response in delight.

'Are you sure? Don't you mean green?'

'No, Mummy – red!'

'Ooh, I thought it was yellow.'

'Silly Mummy – it's red!'

'You're just too clever for me aren't you, my little chap?'

'Look, Mummy – over there – my best birdies.'

A flock of rainbow lorikeets flew up in a bright, multi-coloured display.

The little boy cried out in excitement. 'Lollykeets – they's lollykeets!'

Kidd stepped forward and shouted to the distant Mary, who was pegging out sheets.

'Mary, come and take the boy and do something with him. He's under his mother's feet. That's what I pay you for.' He picked up the heavy volume of Birds of Australia and threw it carelessly onto a chair.

As the child was led away by Mary, Elizabeth turned on her husband.

'For heaven's sake. Am I not allowed to spend any time at all with Mikey? What's wrong with you?'

'He's hanging off your apron strings. It's not good for the lad. He'll grow up soft.'

'And why shouldn't he? I love him. It would do no harm if you showed him a bit of affection too.'

'He's not my child.'

'Keep your voice down. He must never know that. How could you?'

Kidd sighed and laying the book on the floor, lowered himself into the chair. 'Maybe I'll feel different when we have one I can really call my own.'

'What? Like Will? I don't see you showering Will with affection. You keep biting his head off. When the baby comes why is it going to be any different?'

'Leave Will out of it.' He kicked the book towards her then got up and went inside for a beer.

She followed him into the house and took him by the arm.

'Listen to me, Jack. When the baby comes I don't want you treating it differently from Mikey.'

'It'll be mine.'

'No it won't be yours. Children aren't possessions. He or she will be its own person. Just as Mikey is. I want you to love the child when it comes, but I want you to love Mikey too. Or at least put up a pretence of doing so and treat him fairly. He adores you. Even though you have no time for him. He's a little scared of you, but he worships the ground you walk on. He's always asking where Dadda is. He's desperate for your approval and affection.'

She saw surprise in Kidd's eyes, as though he was absorbing what she had said and finding it not unpleasing, but he turned away with a shrug of his shoulders.

She knew expressing his feelings was well nigh impossible for Kidd. He'd spent the years since his first wife died suppressing them. When, just before Harriet's wedding, Elizabeth had told him she was expecting his child, he'd made no comment, other than a nod and a grunt, but she took this to be of satisfaction. And that night in bed he'd made love to her with an unusual tenderness and afterwards, instead of turning away from her towards the wall, he had curled his body around hers and fallen asleep with his arm circling her waist.

Her words of reproach must have hit home as the following morning, Kidd spoke directly to Mikey, asking him what he planned to do for the day, then said, 'You're old enough to come fishing. You can help me catch a few trout. Maybe I'll let you hold the net. What do you think?'

Mikey's eyes were like saucers. He laughed his gurgling laugh.

'Yes please, Dadda!'

'He may be a bit small for that, Jack. He can barely walk.' Elizabeth said.

'I'll give him a piggyback if he gets tired. It's not far to the creek.'

Elizabeth laid her hand on his. 'Thank you.'

He shrugged her hand away and got up from the table and left the room without another word.

That night, Elizabeth felt as though she were part of a real family for the first time, as the three of them and Mary tucked into a supper of freshly caught trout and vegetables from the plot. She was incredulous that Kidd had spent a whole day with Mikey, ignoring the demands of the mine or whatever else it was that usually occupied him.

He laid down his knife and fork after the meal and belched in contentment. Elizabeth fought the urge to wince.

'We'll drive into town tomorrow for the doc to give you the once over again. I want him to keep an eye on you.'

'Everything was fine the last time. There's no reason why it shouldn't be this time.'

Mary interjected, 'Second babbies are always easier. The more you have the more they just slip out like butter – at least that's what my mammie used to say. It was true in her case and she should know as she had twelve of them!'

Kidd ignored the Irish girl. 'We'll stop in town after you've seen the doc. I need to go to the mine and see what Mick's been up to. You can find out Hattie's news – let's hope it'll not be long before she's having a bub too. It'll make her think about someone other than herself.'

She lay awake in the dark, thinking of seeing Michael and Harriet for the first time since their marriage. Beside her, Kidd slipped quickly into a deep, snoring sleep, oblivious to her anxiety. She still carried Michael's handkerchief with her every day. She pretended there was no significance to this, but several times a day she slipped her hand into her pocket and touched the coarse cotton, rubbing the fabric between her fingers like a talisman. She did it to reassure herself that what had happened between them at Sydney Harbour did indeed happen, hard as it was to imagine now. She clutched it tightly in her hand, falling at last into a deep sleep.

Doctor Reilly assured her all was in order. She was relieved that this time she'd be giving birth in the winter. She left the doctor's and, keen to postpone seeing Harriet, asked Oates to drop her at the schoolhouse and collect her later. Kidd would be annoyed, but that was preferable to sitting around while Harriet ignored her.

Verity was overjoyed to see her. She regaled her with stories of the school and her pupils and Elizabeth shared anecdotes about Mikey and his more charming expressions. Her biggest challenge, she told her friend, was preventing the impressionable little boy from picking up Jack Kidd's choicest language.

When they'd exhausted their news, Elizabeth went over to the fireplace and leaning back against it, said 'There's something else, Verity. I've been meaning to tell you but haven't seen you for so long. I'm expecting another child.'

The older woman clapped her hands in delight and quizzed Elizabeth about dates and her plans for the future. 'Won't you move back into town? I fear for you with a little baby and a small child out there in the bush. And selfishly I wish I could see you more often.'

'That's out of the question, I'm afraid. Mr Kidd is very occupied with the land. Today's the first time in ages he's been to check on the colliery. Anyway, we've nowhere to live in town now that Harriet and her husband are in Kinross House. I couldn't live like a guest in what was once my own home. Apart from the odd night like tonight. Although, to be honest, I'd rather have gone back tonight to the Creek, but you know Mr Kidd when his mind is made up. Anyway, I like it there. It's peaceful and safe and Mikey loves it. He's become quite an expert birdwatcher. And his father is teaching him to fish.'

Verity clasped her hands with delight. 'How wonderful. I do wish we could see each other more often though. Have you seen Harriet yet?'

'Not yet. To be honest I'm dreading it. I hope marriage might have mellowed her but I fear it won't have done.'

'You don't know?'

'Know what?'

'She's hardly ever here.' The schoolmistress dropped her eyes. 'She spends most of her time in Sydney.'

'How can she do that when…' she hesitated to use his name, 'her husband has to be here at the mine?'

'*He's* here. Rattling round that big house on his own. Such a pity! I tried to talk to Harriet when she was here last week. It was just a couple of days for a function at the country club. Elizabeth, it doesn't seem right! She should be with her husband. She seems to have fallen in with a bad set of people and can't see past the fact that they're all rich and well connected. She was never invited to the country club before and it upset her. Now she's like the cat that got the cream.'

'I had no idea. I don't believe Mr Kidd has either.'

'He'll find out tonight. Hattie went back to Sydney a few days ago and won't return until the end of the month.'

'They're both adults, so how they choose to run their domestic arrangements is up to them, but I think my husband is going to be very angry.'

Elizabeth was proved right on that count as soon as she walked through the door of Kinross House. Kidd's voice boomed from behind the drawing room door. She hesitated, then pushed the door open. Kidd was pacing up and down. Michael was standing by the window. She was taken aback. She'd forgotten how just the sight of him could move her. He looked away without speaking, acknowledging her arrival with a slight nod.

Kidd ignored her and continued with his tirade, 'Are you a man or a mouse? Get yourself down there, knock some sense into her and bring her back. You're her fucking husband, man.'

'And you're 'er father.'

'What's that got to with it?'

'If you hadn't given her more money than she's got sense she wouldn't be able to swan round Sydney pleasing herself.'

'Tell her she can't! Who the bloody hell does she think she is? A bloody suffragette? I'll take the money off her. That'll teach her.'

Elizabeth knew he could not reverse the transfer of money. His daughter was free to do as she pleased. He stopped pacing up and down and turned to Winterbourne again.

'You've only been wed five minutes and already she wants to get away from you. What the hell've you done to her, man? Can't keep her happy? Don't you know how?'

'I've tried to reason with her but she won't listen.'

'Give her a good slapping, man. She's your wife. She should be here, running your bloody house and keeping your bed warm, not gadding round the city with her mates.'

Elizabeth interrupted, 'Jack, please don't swear. The servants will hear you. Calm down! You'll say something you might regret.'

'Pull your head in! I'll say what I want in my own home.'

'It isn't our home any more. We have to respect that.'

Kidd spun round, his rage out of control. 'Respect? You talk about respect?' He was screaming. Before she could move out of the way, she felt his hand crack across her face, leaving her cheek stinging and knocking her sideways so she stumbled and tripped on the edge of the hearthrug. Winterbourne caught her fall and helped her into a chair, then turned on Kidd, grabbing him by the lapels and ramming him against the marble fireplace. 'If you lay a finger on her again I'll kill you.' He pushed Kidd back into a chair then stood over him. 'If you want to hit someone, hit me. What kind of man are you to strike a woman?'

To the astonishment of both Winterbourne and Elizabeth, Kidd began to cry. They looked at each other in amazement as he leaned forward and clasped his head in his hands. 'I'm sorry. I'm sorry. It's all my fault.'

Elizabeth did not know whether to comfort him or castigate him. Instead she watched helpless as Winterbourne left the room, slamming the door behind him.

Kidd pulled himself together and told her he was sorry again. She helped him to his feet and led him outside to his truck, calling out to Mrs Oates that they'd not be staying after all. He drove in silence, the expression on his face impenetrable. When they got back to Wilton's Creek he led her to sit on a tree trunk that lay between the house and the wash house and was Mikey's favourite seat. They sat in the darkening, still warm, summer evening and he took her hand.

'I'm sorry, Elizabeth. I don't know what came over me. I should never have hit you. Can you forgive me? Please say you'll forgive me. I'd rather chop off my own hand than lay a finger on you. It's just that when he was telling me about the girl, I knew it was my fault. Her older brother was bad and she's turned out the same way. I must have done something wrong. It wasn't their mother. She was a good woman. But there's bad blood somewhere. I'm scared Will'll turn out the same way. It's not Winterbourne's fault. I couldn't control Hattie myself and I was stupid to let her persuade me to give her that money. And now she's buggered off and there's not a Buckley's chance of her listening to a word he or I have to say. I'm sorry.'

She put her hand over his and then led him inside the house.

It was three weeks before Harriet returned. She made it clear to Michael over dinner that night, that she intended to go back to Sydney within the week.

'You can't expect me to stay here. It's nearly autumn and I can't stand the cold. There's nothing to do. I'm not a tourist. I've no interest in going for charabanc rides into the bush or exploring the Jenolan Caves. For heaven's sake – I've lived here all my life and this is the first chance I've had to get away so I'm taking it.'

'Yer old man isn't happy.'

'Don't call him that. It's impertinent.'

'If you're so keen to show yer manners, you should go to Wilton's Creek and see him. Tell him why you've chosen to spend his hard earned cash running round Sydney with the fast set.'

'They're not the fast set. Not that I'd expect an ignorant pom like you to know that. And his cash is not hard earned. He won it gambling. So there.'

'Please, Harriet. I don't want another row. It's not too much to expect for a husband and wife to live under the same roof, even in Australia.'

'I'm here now aren't I?'

'You know what I mean.'

'I don't want to be anywhere near that woman.'

'For Pete's sake, Harriet, you've driven her out of her home – isn't that enough?'

'No it isn't.' She spoke petulantly. 'I wish she'd die and leave my father alone. He's under her spell. I hope having another baby kills her. Just like my mother.'

Michael frowned. 'Harriet, stop dwelling on what happened to yer mother. It were a tragedy but it were the flu as killed her not the baby. Isn't it about time we thought about trying for one ourselves? That'd give you something to keep you busy – even up here in the mountains.'

'That's not going to happen.'

'What do you mean?'

'I don't want babies. I told you. I'm not going to go the

same way as my mother. Always pregnant and always sick and then dying. No thank you very much. I intend to keep my figure. Having babies makes you horribly fat and flabby. Ugh!'

'Grow up. You're talking like a school child.'

'No wonder I don't want to be around you. I can't help it if you're practically an old man. There was a baby but I got rid of it, so there!'

Michael put down his knife and fork and looked at her in astonishment. 'What are you talking about?'

She looked down for a moment, then defiantly raised her head and looked him in the eyes.

'Exactly what I said. I was expecting a baby and now I'm not. I got rid of it last week.'

She looked nervous, as though sensing she'd said too much.

'I wasn't going to say anything, but it's only fair to let you know what I've decided. If you want babies we can divorce and you can find another wife to have them with.'

Michael pushed his plate away. 'You were having our baby and you got rid of it? What the hell did you do? Wasn't it worth telling me? Before you did it not after?'

'It's my body so it's only fair that I decide. I've never wanted babies. I don't want one now and I don't want one in the future.'

'You stupid, little fool! You talk about babies killing your mother but getting rid of a baby is far more dangerous than having one.'

'Not if you're careful. I had a good doctor. Jolly well should have been, the price he charged. It was very discreet. Don't worry about that. You don't think I'd have done it with a knitting needle and a bottle of gin in a back street, do you? I'm not stupid – even if you treat me as if I am.'

'As the father, didn't I have a right to be consulted?'

'I told you. It's my body so I get to choose. You were

quick enough to give me the damn baby in the first place. If you want to foist yourself on me you have to be prepared for me to deal with the consequences. Anyway, the doctor's given me lots of tips on how to avoid it happening again…'

'It won't be happening again.'

'Do you mean you won't be bothering me again?'

'Bothering you?' He scraped his chair back noisily and got up from the table. 'This isn't a marriage. It's a joke.'

'I don't hear you complaining about living in this house. About being the boss of that dreadful mine and getting paid lots of money for doing it. It's a marriage that benefits you as much as me.'

'No it doesn't and I'll have no more of it. How the hell do you think it makes me feel to know me wife doesn't want me in her bed? To know she prefers being with her shallow friends to being with me? To find out she's got rid of our baby as if it were a bad cold and hadn't the decency to tell me beforehand? What else do you want to tell me? Come on, get it all out! I s'pose you're also having an affair with one of those brainless rich boys you're so fond of?'

'I'm not, but you'll be the first to know if I do – well the second I suppose…' she laughed shrilly at her very lame joke.

Michael waited for no more. He slammed the door as he left the room and headed out of the house to find some beery consolation at the bar of the Lawson Arms.

Giving birth to Susanna was less of an ordeal than Mikey's birth. She was overjoyed at having a sister for Mikey and even Kidd looked proud when he saw the child. She bridled a little when he said 'They all look the same when they pop out. Ugly little runts, but I'm sure she'll end up a looker like her mother.'

A few days after the birth, Kidd said, 'Hattie's buggered off for good to Sydney and they're talking divorce.'

'Divorce? That's unthinkable!'

'Not in New South Wales it isn't. She's wilful but I blame him. He should have shown her a firmer hand. Not literally…' he hastened to add.

'But divorce?'

'She won't get a penny more from me. She's had her lot. I can't take back what I've already given her, but she'll get no more when I'm gone. I put the house in Mick's name, but he doesn't want it. Feels bad I reckon. He's moved back to his lodging house. I've told him to try again to reconcile with her. He's promised to go down to the city and have it out with her. He wants to make a go of it, even if it's hopeless. I can't fault him for that.'

'What will happen to Kinross House if they part?'

'He wants to transfer it back into my name. He's an honourable man at least. What worries me though is whether he'll stick around. Can't see it myself. It's a bloody nuisance. I need him at the mine. Will's not up to it and I don't want to do it. I've a mind to sell but I'll not get the price for it.' He paused, 'I don't know why I'm telling you all this. It's not for you to worry about.'

'Why won't you get a good price for the mine? It's still producing coal isn't it?'

'Shut up and go to sleep. I don't know why I started this. I won't talk business with my wife. Come here and keep me warm. That's what a wife's for' He curled himself around her and tucked his head against the back of her neck and before she could speak again he was asleep. She marvelled at the way he was always able to drop off the moment his head hit the pillow, while she lay restless, her head milling with thoughts and questions.

She was worried about Mikey. He'd been fretful and out of sorts all afternoon and Mary put him to bed early. He went to sleep without protest, tired out, but woke in the night with a fever. Elizabeth spent the night at his bedside, sitting in the nursing chair, holding his tiny hand as he lay in his cot, leaving him only when the baby woke for her feed.

She slept fitfully, conscious of the boy's restlessness, constantly checking his brow in the hope that the fever had abated.

Mary appeared at dawn with a tray of tea for Elizabeth and a glass of milk for the child. Ignoring the tea, Elizabeth propped her son up with pillows and supported his head as he tried to sip the milk. He began to cry and was reluctant to swallow. She opened his mouth and saw his throat was badly inflamed.

She called out, 'Mary! Jack! Fetch the doctor. Mikey's still unwell.' As she reached out to her son he began to vomit.

She screamed 'Bring me a bowl he's being sick! Hurry!'

Jack Kidd appeared in the doorway, pulling his dressing gown across his wiry frame and rubbing his eyes. 'What's the noise for? I've a head as thick as a wombat's arse this morning and you've woken the baby.'

'Mikey's vomiting and has a temperature. It may be tonsillitis.'

'Keep him away from me then.' He went back to his bedroom.

Mary rushed in with a towel and bowl. 'Dear, dear! Poor wee lamb! I'll fetch fresh sheets and some hot water to clean the little laddie up.'

As she spoke he was sick again. His face was deathly pale and Elizabeth was becoming increasingly anxious.

'Jack, get the doctor *now*!' Her voice was rasping. 'It's serious. Get the damn doctor!'

Kidd reappeared, buttoning up his shirt. 'I'm going. I'll be as quick as I can.'

'What do you think's wrong?' Mary was at the foot of the bed.

270

'He has a fever. Perhaps it's a chill, but his throat is inflamed. Bring me some cool water, a flannel and more towels.'

'The poor mite. He must be so frightened' said Mary.

The two women cleaned the child up and laid him back down in his cot. He was listless and barely conscious. Elizabeth prayed silently as she kept a vigil by the bedside while Mary took care of Susanna.

Eventually the doctor arrived, with Kidd behind him. It was the same man, Dr Reilly, who had attended the births of both her children.

'Now then, ladies, let's have some space. Can I ask you to make me one of your nice cups of tea, Mary? Mr Kidd, would you step out for a moment. We don't want to crowd the little fellow, do we?'

He leaned over the bed, parted the boy's pyjamas, and placed his stethoscope on the pale, skinny chest. Dr Reilly had the inscrutability learnt from a lifetime's care of the sick. Removing the stethoscope, he opened the boy's mouth and looked inside, then shook his head.

'Is it tonsillitis, Doctor? His throat's very swollen.'

The doctor looked about him. 'Ask Mr Kidd to come back in, please.'

'Tell me now.' She felt an icy chill pass through her body.

'It's not tonsillitis. It's more worrying than that. I fear your little boy has diphtheria.'

Her hands went to her mouth. 'Diphtheria? Are you sure?'

'Sadly, yes, Mrs Kidd. His neck's swollen and there are signs of the infection in his throat. Quite visible.'

'Where? Let me see. You can't be right. It was just a bit red.' She leaned over the cot and looked into the child's mouth. There, at the back of his throat, was a white spider's web growing across his tonsils.

'Dear God! What's that? Can you get rid of it?'

'Unfortunately not, Mrs Kidd. The membrane is quite undeveloped and if I try to remove it, it will bleed heavily and he could choke, and anyway it will grow back again if it's cut. Better to wait until it gets tough and leathery and then we may be able to take it out – indeed it will drop off itself in the end if…'

She choked in despair. 'If he doesn't die first?'

The doctor didn't reply, and just shook his head gravely.

'What can you do?'

'Wait and see. And pray for him, Mrs Kidd. Pray for him. There's no apparent pattern in the outcome of this disease. Some come through it and others do not. I have to tell you though that the child's age does not help the prognosis.'

'There must be something?'

'If he were older I'd suggest gargling with a sulphur mix. But that would be tricky with a small child – he may not understand how to gargle and we can't have him swallowing it. Besides, he's barely conscious and could choke. You can burn sulphur in the room – that can help keep the infection from spreading, but there's nothing we can do but keep him as comfortable as possible and in complete quarantine and hope and pray it will pass over. There's no vaccine against diphtheria.' He shook his head and his lips set in a hard line.

'No one must be invited to the house; no one must leave and you need to keep the rest of the household away from him. That includes Mr Kidd. Under no circumstances let the baby near him. You're breast-feeding?'

Elizabeth nodded.

'You'll have to stop at once or risk infecting the baby too. Let me look in your throat.' He was wearing a mask and looked down Elizabeth's throat. 'So far, so good. But I want you to wear a mask too and I'll send someone from town to drop a tin of formula outside the house. If you intend to care for the lad yourself in here you'll have to leave young Mary to take care of the baby. On no account may she or your husband or the baby be in this room. I hope the baby isn't already infected. I'll take a look before I go. Remember, no one leaves until I'm able to declare that the quarantine period has passed.'

A few minutes later he returned, with a crying Susanna in his arms. His eyes above his facemask told Elizabeth all she needed to know. She gave a little gasp then reached out and took her baby into her arms. The doctor spoke quietly. 'I've examined Mr Kidd and Mary and neither show signs of the disease, but they must stay away from you and the children and they must have no contact with anyone else. It can take a week to incubate and it's highly contagious. You, Mrs Kidd, must wear a mask at all times. All we can do is wait and hope they pull through.'

The following days passed in a blur. Susanna cried incessantly at first, her tiny body incapable of communicating her suffering in words. After a while she became listless and unable to feed. She died in Elizabeth's arms. Elizabeth cradled her, unable to leave go. She had known Susanna such a brief time. Not long enough to discover her personality, to hear her speak, to watch her first steps. While Mikey was still battling for his life she could not give herself over to the grief she felt.

At first he seemed to rally and she almost dared to hope, but then his temperature rose and his body became limp, his eyes staring vacantly and his breath stentorian, as he struggled to breathe. She never left his side, holding the dead Susanna in her arms for hours, refusing to eat or drink while she kept watch. The little boy could barely breathe, his throat covered with a thick white rubbery growth where the delicate spider's web had been. His temperature remained high and Elizabeth tormented herself with thoughts that she had brought this upon him by wishing him to die before he was born. Now she would give anything to save the little chap who loved to play horsey, spot birds and filled her life with happiness.

When he died there was no drama. He just slipped away. His breathing was so slight and so laboured that it was like a slow drowning. Elizabeth felt his little hand turn cold, as the life drained out of him. She was blinded by her tears. Her body heaved and she wanted nothing more than to take his hand in hers and go with him to wherever he'd gone. To stay beside him. She gave a guttural cry then collapsed on the floor. Kidd found her there and carried her to their bed and laid her down, pulling the coverlet over her.

The funeral was the next day. The doctor insisted the bodies could not be placed in open coffins, because of the risk of infection. The ceremony passed in a haze to Elizabeth. She didn't even notice that the masked minister officiating was the same one who had married Michael and Harriet. The party at the graveside, all wearing masks, consisted only of herself and Kidd, Doctor Reilly, Will, Verity, the Oates and a tearful Mary.

She stood beside the open grave and watched the two tiny coffins lowered on ropes into the ground.

'Farewell, my darlings. I'll love you forever. I'll never forget you.' Her cheeks were dry. She had exhausted a lifetime's supply of tears.

With a flash of vibrant colour, a group of rainbow lorikeets burst through the trees just as the mourners threw their clods of earth on the coffins. She looked up at them, remembering how Mikey loved those birds. She watched them disappear behind a bank of tall gum trees. Maybe he and Susanna were with them, little lorikeets themselves, flying free above them all. As she thought it, she knew it was stupid. They were down there beneath their feet, already starting to dissolve into the soil, a feast for the worms. Her adored boy and her beautiful baby girl.

It had happened so quickly that it was hard to accept it was not a dream. Will was inconsolable. He had loved his little brother and had been devoted to his newborn sister. Now he too was bereft. He and Elizabeth walked from the grave arm in arm.

Kidd looked after them, and then stared down at the small coffins, as the gravediggers shovelled earth on top. He shook his head, recalling how many times he had stood in this place, burying stillborn children in miniature coffins, then watching as his wife's was lowered into her grave with the last of their dead children.

CHAPTER TWENTY

UNWELCOME GUEST

Michael was in Sydney. He'd been giving a lot of thought to his marital problems. Harriet was headstrong and immature. He took the marriage vows seriously and wanted to stand by the promise he'd made for better or for worse. His father's last letter was full of pleasure that he was married. He didn't want to hurt his parents again by telling them the marriage was already dead. He still wanted them to join him, but reading between the lines of his father's short letter, his mother was too ill for that to be a possibility yet.

He took a taxi from the railway station to the house that he'd reluctantly rented for Harriet in Potts Point. The place was an unnecessary extravagance, but he'd hoped if he went along with her wishes she might eventually grow tired of living in the city.

When he let himself in there was no sign of either Harriet or the housekeeper. He went upstairs to leave his bag in the bedroom. As he reached the door he thought he could hear a sound behind it. The low murmur of conversation. He hesitated then swung the door open.

Harriet was on the bed, propped against a pile of pillows, smoking a cigarette through a long mother-of-pearl holder with a glass of champagne in her other hand. She was wearing a nightgown and it looked from the state of the bed as though she'd only just got out of it. The curtains were still drawn at the windows and the room lit only by the light from a bedside lamp. Two empty champagne bottles lay on the carpet. At the other end of the bed, leaning against the velvet-upholstered footboard was a man, wearing evening dress without the jacket and with his shirt collar and white tie hanging loose from his neck. His highly polished shoes were still on his feet and he looked as though he'd just arrived from a party. Between them on the counterpane was a large book, in the centre of which was a small pile of white powder.

Harriet looked at Michael with narrowed eyes, then leaned forward and scooped some of the powder onto the back of her hand and snorted it up her nose. When she finished she looked defiantly at her husband.

The man turned round to look at Michael. His brilliantined hair was parted in the centre and his voice was arrogant and effeminate as he said with an exaggerated drawl, 'Hell-ohhh there! Who are you? Care to join us? Plenty here for all of us.' And he stretched out a hand to indicate the little heap of cocaine.

'I'm her husband. Who the hell are you?'

Harriet spoke. 'Tommie, meet Michael. He's a bit of a spoilsport, aren't you, darling?'

'Right, Tommie, lad. It's time you went home. Back to the rock you crawled out from.'

'He's going nowhere.' Harriet's voice was shrill. She put down her champagne flute and swung her legs off the bed. 'You're the uninvited guest here.'

Michael grabbed her arm and pulled her towards him, then pushed her in front of him towards the doorway. He looked over his shoulder. 'What are you waiting for? I told you. Time to go home. Or do you want me to throw you down the stairs?'

The man jumped off the bed quickly and gathered up his evening jacket from the chair. Harriet pulled away from Winterbourne and put her arm out to stop her friend.

'Ignore him, Tommie, darling. He's a big bully. Let's head over to your place and carry on the party.'

Michael reacted quickly and before she knew what had hit her, he swung her off her feet and over his shoulder like a sack of coal. She screamed in indignation and struggled to get down but he was too strong for her. He carried her across the room and dumped her in the middle of the bed, scattering the cocaine powder in a cloud.

The man was at the doorway, his face a mixture of fear and fascination. When he saw Michael move towards him he bolted from the room and clattered down the stairs, crashing the front door behind him.

Harriet's face contorted with rage. She spat her words at Michael. 'How dare you do that to me, you beast. This is my house and I'll do what I want in it with anyone I like. Go back to your filthy coalmine and leave me in peace.'

It wasn't going the way he'd envisaged when he set off that morning. Harriet pulled herself into a tight ball with her head on her knees and wouldn't look at him. He could hear her sobbing.

'Hat, we need to talk. We have to find a way to make this marriage work. I won't let you do this to yourself. Drugs are no good. You'll make yourself ill. You'll get into all sorts of trouble. I don't like you being around people like him. Wasters. Rich bastards with nowt better to do. You're a married woman, for God's sake. Act like one. Instead of a spoilt schoolgirl. Grow up!'

Through her sobs he heard her say quietly, 'I hate you. I wish you were dead. You've made a show of me. It's not fair! I'm married to an old wowser who wants to stop me having fun with my friends.'

He sat down on the bed beside her. 'Is he the one? The

chap as helped you get the abortion? Are you sleeping with him?'

She dropped her arms and brushed her hand across her face to wipe away the tears. 'Of course I'm not sleeping with him! Are you stupid? He doesn't like women. He likes men.'

Michael didn't know what to say.

Harriet rushed on. 'He's a good friend. We go to the theatre together. He knows all the right people. Now he'll never speak to me again and it's all your fault.' She began to wail.

He suddenly understood how some men could be provoked enough to hit a woman. It was tempting, but he'd never do it. He flung her silk dressing gown at her. 'Get dressed and come downstairs. We need to talk.'

He slept apart from her that night. She made it clear that she had no intention of sleeping with him again. She also made it clear that she didn't want to be married to him any more. They argued for hours until he acknowledged there was no hope of making her see reason about anything. He looked at her and wondered how he'd ever thought her attractive. Her expression had settled into a permanent sulkiness and her complexion was beginning to show the signs of her fondness for drugs and alcohol, with blotchy skin and puffy eyes. She clearly needed help. He was out of his depth. Nothing had prepared him for this. As he lay in bed, sleepless and exhausted after the rowing, he cursed his stupidity for agreeing to marry her in the first place. And for doing so for all the wrong reasons.

He needed to speak to Kidd to convince him that she must see a doctor. He'd failed to get through to her himself. The more he had tried, the more obdurate she became. He was exhausted. Spent. He could do now more. He no longer wanted to try.

Next morning he left while she was still sleeping. He had intended to look in on her before he left, but her bedroom door was locked. He booked himself into a small hotel and went to find a lawyer.

Elizabeth was losing weight. The sight of food made her stomach churn. It was as though she were sleepwalking, catatonic and barely conscious of her surroundings. Day ran into identical day. The nights were worse. She lay on her back in bed, gazing unseeing at the hammered tin ceiling.

She tortured herself with the accusation that she had somehow brought about Mikey's death herself. She knew it to be untrue – as well as her own children the disease had claimed several others, an elderly couple and a newly-wed bride – but she couldn't stop thinking it.

She was alone at Wilton's Creek. Kidd was at the mine.

Her spirits were lower than they'd ever been, even after the death of her father and her discovery of her pregnancy. It was too hard to accept that from one day to the next she had stopped being a mother. Motherhood had become the primary purpose in her life. It had been an unexpected joy and nothing could replace her children, even other children. She blamed herself for not protecting them better. But from what and how? She knew these thoughts were not rational.

Kidd seemed to understand what she was going through and her need to be apart from him and everyone else, including Will and Mary. Perhaps it was because his former wife had lost so many children? Whatever the reason, he raised no objection to her request to stay alone at the Creek.

She lay on the bed, listless, while her mind churned over the short illness that had caused the children's deaths. How was it possible they had ailed so rapidly, that a happy little boy could be stricken so fast and his end come so quickly? That a little baby could be taken before she had a chance to experience life? The letters of condolence lay unread in a pile on the small table beside the bed. What did these people know or care of Mikey and Susanna, or what she was going through now?

Her nerve endings jangled and her skin felt as though she'd been flayed. It was as if she inhabited a netherworld, strangely positioned inside the real one. The sun rising each morning and sinking each night was a mockery of her pain, as were the songs of the birds and the rain rattling onto the corrugated iron roof above her. How could life go on without the children? Why hadn't the world stopped too? She was trapped in an invisible cage, where all she could think about was her loss and the terrible brief suffering of her children.

Kidd stayed away, sensing his presence was neither needed nor wanted. After the funeral, he laid a hand on her sleeve and squeezed her arm in wordless sympathy, but she pulled away from him and stared silently out of the car window.

On the fifth day of her seclusion, she rolled off the bed and fetched some water. She could no longer bear lying there unkempt and unwashed.

Looking in the old spotted mirror above the kitchen sink, she was shocked at the person who looked back. Her face was gaunt with dark circles under her eyes, like bruises. Her normally lustrous hair was matted and dull and her lips were dry and cracked. She stripped off her clothes and put them in a basket ready for washing, filled the sink and began to wash herself. She stood naked on the rag-rug that had survived the improvements Kidd had effected over the past weeks, wincing as she splashed cold water over her face and neck – she could still feel after all. She scrubbed vigorously at her thin body with a washcloth and some lavender soap. The cold water and the aroma of lavender woke her from her torpor and she looked around the room. It was dusty and neglected.

Activity was what she needed to break out of her trance. It wouldn't deaden the pain, but it would distract her from thinking. She wrapped the towel around her and began to rub herself dry.

Her back was to the door so she didn't see him enter and nearly jumped out of her skin when he spoke.

'You're a beauty aren't you?'

She turned round, clutching the towel tightly. The man was short, dark-haired and the stubble on his chin signalled that he hadn't shaved for several days. His frame was wiry and his features like his father's. The resemblance was unmistakable. Elizabeth knew at once she was looking at Nathaniel Kidd.

He leaned against the doorpost, a cigarette dangling from his mouth. A long dull scar ran from the left corner of his top lip to his eyebrow, where it sliced a path through the brow, before petering out just above it.

'The old man did good!' He blew a pantomime wolf whistle. 'So where did he find you, Beauty?'

'Wait outside while I get dressed. I've been unwell and wasn't expecting visitors.' She moved behind the fabric screen that still divided the main sleeping area from the living area.

He called after her. 'Don't mind me. I'm not going anywhere, so don't hurry on my account.'

She grabbed the holdall that lay beside the bed, fumbling for clean underwear and a fresh blouse and skirt. She threw on the clothes and dragged a comb through her tangled and still unwashed hair and emerged again into the kitchen. Nat Kidd was sprawled in a chair, feet up on the gingham-covered orange-box that still served as a makeshift side table, a bottle of beer at his lips.

As she moved into the main area of the room, she was conscious of him appraising her. She went towards the kitchen sink and mumbled something about making tea.

'Not on my account, Beauty. I'm happy with a beer. Glad to see the old man has some in. He doesn't change. Care to join me?' He offered another bottle to her but she backed away, leaning against the kitchen sink.

'Your father didn't tell me he was expecting you.'

'I expect that's 'cause he isn't.'

'He's in town at the mine.'

'I know.'

'You've seen him then?'

He gave a dry laugh and took a swig of beer. 'Why would I want to see the old bastard?'

Elizabeth was feeling increasingly uncomfortable. There was a lot about the man not to like. After not eating for several days, her stomach was hollow and aching and she felt unsteady on her feet. She must have started to sway, as the next thing, he jumped up, caught her and helped her into an armchair.

'You look a bit crook. I'll get you some water.' He returned with a glass, which he held to her lips and steadied her as she drank it hungrily. 'What's wrong with you? You ill or something?'

'I lost…' she stopped, unwilling to tell him.

'You need to eat something.' He opened the tucker-bag he'd flung in the corner of the room and pulled out a loaf and a small oilskin parcel from which he produced a hunk of cheese. He broke off a portion of each and handed them to her.

'Eat it slowly. Looks like you haven't had a decent meal for days, Beauty.'

'Don't call me that.'

'Well I can't call you Mother can I? Although I suppose that's technically what you are?'

'My name is Elizabeth.'

'E-liz-a-beth' He repeated her name, slowly drawing out each of the syllables. 'The old man's certainly done all right for himself.'

She blushed. He looked at her as though still seeing her with just the towel round her. She shuddered at the thought that he might have been watching her through the window as she washed.

'You're Nathaniel?'

'The old dog actually mentioned me?'

'Will told me he had an older brother who left home years ago.'

'Ah little Willie. How is the lad? Still picking his nose and wetting his pants?'

Elizabeth frowned with distaste. There was a real animosity in his voice.

'I'm surprised the kid remembers me. He was just a wee lad when I *'left home'* as you put it.'

Elizabeth looked up, surprised.

'I'd have said *'kicked out on my arse'* was a more accurate description, if you'll pardon my French.'

'I'm sure that isn't true?'

'Can't imagine the old dog doing that?' He leaned back in his chair, nodding his head slowly. 'I hear he's quite the man about town these days. Owns the coal mine they tell me?'

'Yes. That's where he is now.'

'Leaving you here on your own? He doesn't appreciate you enough. An elegant woman like you shouldn't be stuck out here, shut away from folk.' He looked around him. 'Mind you, he's made some improvements to the old place. You could almost describe it as comfortable!' He laughed again with the same dry, hollow laugh. 'Not like it was when I lived here. Ma working day and night to keep food on the table and him off gambling the length and breadth of the county.'

She didn't reply but looked back at him, her curiosity piqued.

'Did little brother tell you the old man beat her?'

'She shook her head and felt her face reddening again, not wanting to believe this of Kidd, but remembering the night he had struck her across the face.

'He wasn't a regular wife beater if that's what you're worried about? Dare say he's never raised a fist to you has he? Well why would he? A looker like you. Or has he? You don't look too sure. Well he did hit my old lady. Only the once, but that was enough. He'd been gone for days. Ma was pregnant. She was pregnant all the time. The old goat wouldn't leave her alone.'

He looked her up and down smiling, then continued. 'He came back with empty pockets. She was angry and went for him like a mad thing. He was drunk. That's what made her flip. She hit him so hard he was reeling, then he whacked her back. He bashed her so bad he knocked her out. Then he was weeping and wailing and begging forgiveness. Of course the silly cow did forgive him.'

He spoke slowly, looking about the room, as though recalling the geography of the incident. Elizabeth felt sick, remembering how Kidd had begged her forgiveness too.

Nat Kidd went on, 'He put her to bed then took off to town again, promising to come back with food and money. That's when she got ill. Went down with the influenza. I went after him to try and find him and when I couldn't I kept on searching. I didn't come home for days and when I did Ma was dead and Hattie blamed me for not being here to fetch the doctor. The old man came back then and went into a frenzy. It was his fault she died. He should have been there for her. If he hadn't thrown his money away. If he hadn't bashed her. But he didn't see it that way. He just yelled at me and laid a punch on me that knocked me clean through the door. Told me never to come back. That's the last I've seen of him. Seven years ago. And to think the old bugger's now rolling in money. Too bloody late for poor Ma.'

'I didn't know.'

'He's hardly likely to tell you, is he? Will you marry me, Miss Elizabeth, if I promise not to beat the daylights out of you like I did my last wife?'

'What do you want, Nathaniel?'

'Name's Nat.'

'What do you want, Nat?'

'I want what's mine. When I heard he'd come into money and got himself a coal mine and a new wife I thought I'd have my share. You could call it my rightful inheritance. They tell me you and he have a couple of kiddies and I expect you'll have more if the old goat gets his way, so I want to make sure I get my share of the family fortunes before you and yours fritter it away.'

'My children are dead.'

'What?'

'Diphtheria. We buried them five days ago.'

'I'm sorry.' His voice was more respectful.

'I'm afraid I can't help you in any way. I want to be left alone to grieve for my children. As to money, you'll have to speak to my husband, not to me. I can't help you.'

'Oh but you can, Beauty.'

'How?'

'You can talk to him. Tell him to do the right thing. Insist on it.'

'Why should I do that?'

'Because it's the right thing. And because I'm going to be your shadow until you do.'

'I want you to leave now.'

'I'm minded to stay a while.'

'That's not possible.'

'I think it is. Don't worry, Beauty, I'll sleep out there.' He pointed to the hut where Will used to stay. 'In the meantime we can get better acquainted.' He leaned back in the chair, his feet scuffing up the red gingham cloth on the table, and pulled out his tobacco pouch. 'Why don't you fetch me another beer, there's a good girl.'

'All right. I'll speak to him. But only on condition you leave now. What do you want me to tell him?'

'Don't tell him you've seen me. Tell him you want him to give you five hundred pounds.'

She laughed bitterly. 'Why on earth would I do that?'

'So you can hand it over to me. And because if you don't, you'll be seeing a lot more of me. You and I could get very friendly all on our own out here.' He leaned forward and tucked a stray lock of her hair behind her ear. She jerked away.

'Get out! Get out and don't come back. If you want money ask your father yourself. I don't want you here.' As she spoke, the grief and despair welled up inside her again and she started to sob.

Nat Kidd took a last swig of his beer then ground his cigarette butt into the floor. 'You're upset, so I'll leave you for a while. Out of respect for your loss. But think on it, Beauty. A clever woman like you can find an excuse to get the money. I'm going to Sydney for a few days then I'll be back and I expect to find you've got the cash.'

He moved nearer so that she could smell the tobacco and beer on his breath as he pushed his face up close to hers. 'I'll be back Ee-Liz-A-Beth and you'd better be ready for me.'

Then he left as suddenly as he had arrived. She pulled back the curtain and saw him climb up onto a horse that was grazing untethered in front of the house. He kicked his heels into its flank and rode towards the blue glow of the distant hills.

The anger rose in her like a stimulant. She was no longer tired. She grabbed the remains of the bread and cheese and ate it hungrily. When her husband returned she'd tell him exactly what happened. It was as simple as that. He'd banished his son before, so he could do it again. She didn't care about the rights and wrongs of the situation. She only knew she disliked Nat Kidd intensely and never wanted to clap eyes on him again.

Elizabeth spent the next couple of days sewing and cleaning, as she re-established order in the little house. Kidd had extended the building by adding a large second bedroom. The main bedroom was now partioned off at the far end of the original large room that had previously served as a combined kitchen, bathroom, bedroom and living area. The second bedroom housed Mikey's cot, the cradle that had been Susanna's and a divan where Mary had slept.

The beds were a cold reminder of what might have been. She knew she had to carry on and try to rebuild her life and that meant moving away from the place where the children had died. But not yet. She couldn't tear herself away from them, in particular from Mikey. She fantasised he might return and she wouldn't be there for him. She stroked the coverlet smooth, then lifted the white cotton pillow and tried to smell the little boy. Only lavender and starch. Mary had seen to that. On the doctor's orders all the bedding and towels had been boiled to remove every trace of the disease. But she did sleep every night with his little blanket clutched in her arms. She'd saved that by hiding it in the trunk under the living room window. She was finding it hard to remember his little boy smell – the sweetness of his hair and the just-washed clean smell of his skin, let alone trace any scent of him in the blanket. It filled her with panic that soon she'd forget what he looked like. She cursed herself daily that she'd delayed arranging for Mr Wilson, the photographer, to capture the little boy on film. The only images she had were the plates taken at his christening, when he was a babe in arms. He was missing from the formal group photographs at Harriet and Michael's wedding as Mary had whisked him away before the photographer had arranged everyone to his satisfaction. As for Susanna, her life was so short she'd left no trace at all. Elizabeth's milk had dried up. There was nothing but the empty cot to mark that she'd ever existed.

Elizabeth picked up her violin from the cabinet where it lay gathering dust and put it under Mikey's bed. She couldn't bring herself to open the case and take it out, let alone play it. The sadness of its strings would bring the tears back and the memory of music was inextricably linked to her memories of Mikey, playing with his toys at her feet while she practised.

She went into the kitchen, boiled some water, filled the basin and set about washing her underwear and nightdress.

The door opened and she looked up. Jack Kidd stood there.

'Are you all right?' He came towards her and put his hand on her arm. This sudden solicitude was disconcerting. She sighed. 'I can't sleep any more. I've forgotten how.'

'I can't sleep either. It'll get better.' He leaned forward and pressed his lips against the back of her neck. She stiffened at the roughness of his whiskers on her skin. His behaviour was getting dangerously close to affection recently.

He reached around her and gathered the front of her cotton dress in his hands, then slipped one hand under it and stroked her bare thigh.

'Don't.'

Kidd moved his hand higher, pushing it between her legs and touching her through the thin silk of her knickers. She pushed his hands away, splashing him and scattering soapsuds. The sleeves of his shirt were soaked, but he didn't stop, continuing to work his fingers against her through the fabric. She gasped and leaned back against him, giving up resistance. She cried out. Maybe this was what she needed?

To lose herself for a while and let go of it all. To take comfort in the physical release that he offered.

Elizabeth was breathing quickly now as his fingers moved inside her. She arched her back against his chest and Kidd lifted her up, carrying her across to the bed. As he entered her he whispered. 'It'll be all right, girl, I promise you.'

As he thrust into her with increasing urgency, a single tear ran down her left cheek to soak into the pillow. She felt a terrible empty loneliness. When he finished, Kidd got up from the bed, rearranged his clothes and went to get a beer. Elizabeth tidied herself up then went back to the sink to finish washing her underclothes, before preparing a simple meal of boiled potatoes and ham.

When they sat down to eat she told him about Nat's visit. Kidd slammed his beer down, spilling some onto the clean tablecloth.

'I'm going into town to find that little runt and send him on his way. He'll not get a brass razoo from me.'

'He's not in town. He's gone to Sydney.'

'In that case you're coming to town with me tomorrow. I'll not have you on your own here.'

'He said he'll be there a few days. I want to stay here. Please. It's important to me. If you're worried about me maybe you could spare Will for a few days if you have to stay in town until Mr Winterbourne returns. Then you can be here yourself.'

'I'm worried Winterbourne won't come back. I've got a bad feeling he's going to bugger off. I don't hold out much hope of him patching things up with Hattie. We'll see. All right, I'll have Will come and stay with you on Friday. Will you be okay till then?'

'Of course I will. Nat won't be back till next week. I'll be alright.'

REUNITED

Kidd left early the next morning, before Elizabeth woke from her first uninterrupted sleep in days. When she opened the curtains, the sun was already high in the sky. She felt a surge of energy. The pain of the children was still raw and present, but she knew now she could go on and would go on. She finished her first cup of tea of the day and decided to throw herself into activity of some sort. The vegetable plot needed tackling – the neat ranks of vegetables she and Will had grown a few years back were gone and the area was an untidy mess of scrub and hard earth. She would ask Kidd to bring her seeds to plant. She dug over the impacted earth and hoed and tilled until the sweat poured off her and the soil was as fine as freshly sifted flour.

She leaned back and stretched, surveying her work, her foot resting on the top of the spade as she wiped her brow. There was a cough behind her and she froze, afraid it was Nat Kidd already back again to bully and threaten her. She was ready for him this time. She spun round yelling 'Get out!'

Standing there, his cap in his hand, was a startled look-ing Michael Winterbourne.

'I'm sorry' she said. 'I thought… my husband isn't here.'

'I know. I came to see you.'

'To see me?' She felt stupid as she echoed his words.

'I want to offer me condolences. I've been in Sydney so I only just heard about what happened to yer bairns.'

'Thank you, but there was no need for you to come all this way.'

'I were very fond of Mikey. And the wee bairn too. It's a terrible thing to happen. I'm sorry.'

'Thank you.' She looked down at the freshly tilled soil then up again at him as the words rushed out. 'You must know how I'm feeling…after losing your brother.'

She wiped the sweat off her brow with a dirty hand then realising, rubbed the soil residue off her hands and onto her apron. 'I'm a bit of a mess. I wasn't expecting anyone.' Then immediately regretting her words, she pulled off her apron and said, 'Come inside for something to drink.' It was still early spring, but the afternoon sun was warm. The digging and hoeing had made her hot and slightly dizzy and she was unsteady on her feet as she led him into the house.

Michael looked around him. 'It's quite a change from the big house.'

'Mr Kidd prefers it here. I don't think he's ever got used to being wealthy. He likes a simple life.'

'And you?'

'Right now it suits me.' She hesitated. 'The children spent their last days here and so … you know … it's quiet and I feel I'm still with them… or some echo of them. That sounds foolish, doesn't it?'

'No.' He looked straight into her eyes, in a way he had not done since that afternoon in Sydney. 'When you lose someone you love it's hard… being reminded of them everywhere you look. That's why I left England.' He looked at her directly again.

There was a long silence. Elizabeth walked over to the

window and with her back to him, said 'I was raped.'

She heard his sudden intake of breath behind her. 'I was raped by my brother-in-law. That's why I left England. I was running away too.'

She felt him moving towards her. 'Why didn't you tell me?'

She turned to face him as the words tumbled out, each one lifting a weight off her heart. 'I was too ashamed to tell you in Sydney. I thought you might think it was my fault it happened. I did nothing to encourage him but I kept thinking I must have been bad in some way for him to do that to me. For such a terrible thing to happen. Then I found out I was expecting his child. Mikey.'

Michael ran his hand through his hair, his expression bewildered.

Speaking rapidly, she told him how her father's debt to Kidd had compelled her to marry him.

'Why didn't you tell me about the baby?'

'I didn't find out I was pregnant until after you were gone. Marrying Kidd was the only way out. I had no money. I owed him thousands of pounds with no means of repaying it. And I didn't tell you about the rape as I was too ashamed.'

'Good God, Elizabeth, it weren't your fault.'

'I felt unclean, contaminated. I was …broken.' She slumped into a chair. Michael knelt at her feet and took her hands in his. 'Why, oh why didn't you say? It would have made no difference. I'd 've married you. If you'd 've had me that is.' He looked up at her then away again. 'Why didn't you turn up when we arranged to meet?'

'I tried. Oh God, how I tried! I was delayed after the funeral, trying to convince Kidd that I couldn't marry him. When he told me how much the debt was I didn't know what to do. I didn't know then about the baby. I just knew I had to see you. I thought you'd be able to make it all right. I thought you'd help me think how to get out of the obligation to Kidd. I thought we could go away somewhere he wouldn't be able to find me. But I couldn't get to you. I was too late.'

She paused, as though that day was just a moment ago. She felt again her rising panic and the push of the crowds, the anger of the people around her as she tried to force her way through.

'It was the Prince of Wales's visit. There was a huge a crowd. I couldn't get past. Thousands of people. It was hopeless. I couldn't even turn back – I was carried along in the crush. By the time I reached our meeting place it was dark and hours after we'd agreed to meet. You'd gone. I didn't know where to find you.'

His face was wretched. 'I saw the posters and the flags everywhere but I were that caught up with the thought of you I didn't even take in that the bloody prince were in Australia.' He shook his head. 'He ruined our lives.'

'I doubt that was the poor man's intention.' She smiled.

'I'm as patriotic as the next man. Dammit. I was prepared to give up me life for me country, but I tell you I'll never sing God save the King for him when his time comes, not after what he's done to us.' He put his head in his hands. 'I can't believe it. I thought you were dallying with me. That you'd realised you were too good for me. That I were just a passing fancy.'

'Michael, I went back again and again, every day, hoping to find you. I tramped the streets day after day, searching for you. Hoping and praying I'd find you. I was so alone. I was so frightened.'

He gave a long, low groan. 'I thought you'd had second thoughts. I told meself you didn't care for me, that I weren't good enough. I thought you'd come to your senses and realised that someone as cultured as you should want nowt to do with a miner. The lads as shared the cabin with me on the Historic were pulling me leg – they saw us saying goodbye when you left the ship and told me I'd no chance. I thought that once you'd had time to think about it you didn't want owt to do with me for killing our Danny. I were still feeling that bad about Dan and me Mam and all that, so I believed it were no more than I deserved. I drowned me sorrows in beer and met a chap in a bar who offered me the job at the mine. I came up to the Falls the day after. I'm a damn fool.' He put his head in his hands.

'What's done is done, Michael. We can't turn the clock back.'

'Why didn't you tell me when we met again?'

'When I saw you outside the school you looked at me as though you hated the sight of me. I was afraid. I was confused. I was already married and what was done was done. I'd no idea I'd see you again. No idea you worked for my husband. Then once Mikey was born everything was about protecting him. Jack Kidd gave him his name and I didn't want to do or say anything that might harm Mikey or run the risk of my husband disowning him. And you didn't exactly give me a chance to explain.'

'I'd never ever do anything to hurt you, and I'd never've done anything to harm that little boy. I wish you'd trusted me.'

'I couldn't. You were so cold and so different from before. You ran away from me. You wouldn't listen. I thought you hated me. I didn't know what to do.'

Her tears welled up again. Michael sat with his head in his hands. 'What a bloody mess we made we made of it.'

'I didn't want Mikey, you know. I prayed every night before he was born that he'd die. I didn't even want to hold him after he was born. I thought I'd see his father's face in him.' She almost choked over the words. 'But it wasn't like that. When they made me hold him I was lost. I fell hopelessly in love and I love him still. Oh God, I loved him so much.' Her sobbing swallowed up the words, which came out in starts, interspersed with coughing.

Michael fished in his pocket and pulled out a handkerchief and dried her eyes, then kneeling in front of her, he took her in his arms and stroked her hair. 'It's all right, my lovely. It's all right.'

'I can't help thinking that Mikey was taken from me before he could become like his father. If he'd lived, I might have come to hate him as much as I hated his father – but I couldn't have done that could I?'

'He were a good boy. He'd never 'ave turned into a bad person.'

'But as he grew up he might have started to look like him, or have his mannerisms or his voice. I might have come to loathe him. Perhaps I should be thankful that he died before he had the chance to find out his own mother was going to reject him?'

Michael put his hands on her shoulders and eased her away from him so he could look at her face.

'Listen to me, Elizabeth. It were a tragedy that Mikey and his sister were taken from you, but it weren't your fault. Innocent bairns die every day, many of 'em from the same horrible illness as took yours. It's not yer fault. He's gone and we'll all miss him and the wee lass, but you can't bring 'em back and it's not your fault. Life plays cruel tricks. Like keeping the two of us apart.'

She looked at him eagerly. 'Did you really like Mikey?'

'He were a grand little fellow. That's why I came to pay me respects, even though I thought yer wouldn't want to see me. I thought he were Jack Kidd's son, but now I know he wasn't, it makes no difference. I hate yer brother in law for what he did to you. I'd like to kill the bastard but I could never blame you or the child.'

'Thank you.'

He stroked her hair and then buried his face in it and

breathed deeply, drinking in the smell of her. She smelled of the fresh soil she'd been tilling, with an undercurrent of lavender. He pulled away and looked into her eyes. 'As God's me witness, Elizabeth Morton, I love you with every bone in me body. I wish you'd told me all this long ago, but what's done's done. There's something you need to know.'

She stiffened.

'I'm going to New Zealand.'

Elizabeth gave a little cry and pulled herself back into the chair. 'You're leaving? With Harriet?'

'She's staying in Sydney. You were right about us marrying. It were a terrible mistake. I only did it because I were angry with you. I wanted to punish you. And punish meself. I nearly backed out the night afore the wedding till Will told me at the buck's night you were having another bairn and I flipped. I wanted to hurt you as much as you'd hurt me and the best way to do that was marrying Hat. I thought it were also because you thought I weren't good enough for her, same as I weren't good enough for you.'

'Oh, Michael, how could you have thought that?'

'Once she got her hands on the money from her Da she didn't think about anything else. We never cared for each other. I were wrong to go through with it. I felt sorry for her after the races when her old man made a show of her. I thought I'd have to settle down at some point, so why not with her? I couldn't have the woman I loved, so why not Harriet? The gaffer wanted it and I thought mebbe with time we'd find a way to muddle along together. God knows I tried.'

'You still can! You can keep trying' she whispered, her head forcing out the words while her heart screamed in protest.

'No. It's pointless. I know now it can never work. She's shallow. She's cold. She despises me. I were just her means of getting away from the Falls and getting her hands on the cash. And I reckon she thought marrying me would get at you. She's not daft. She sensed there were summat between us.'

'I felt that she did too.'

'She's a mixed-up girl in lots of ways. She's never got over the death of her mam and there doesn't seem to be much feeling between her and her da. Or her and Will for that matter.'

'But Michael, ending a marriage when the ink's barely dry on the licence? It's only been eighteen months.'

'There's more to it. She's taken up with a bunch of people that are no good. Bone idle and filthy rich. The champagne set. Not that it's only champagne – there's cocaine as well.'

'That's dreadful. She's just a child.'

'A child who's quickly got used to the ways of the world. Look, I don't want us having any more secrets from each other, so I'm going to tell you everything. She were expecting a child and paid to have it aborted. She only thought it worth telling me after it were done and dusted. I'm not even sure it were mine anyway.'

He stared into the fire, avoiding her eyes. 'We didn't exactly have a lot of opportunity. I were up here and she were mostly in Sydney. She may have been sleeping with one of the sleazy characters she hung out with. I caught her taking cocaine with one of them – a rich bastard who thought the world owed him a living. She said she wasn't sleeping with him as he was a queer. But there may have been others. Some swine helped arrange for her to have the baby got rid of.'

'Does Jack know about this?'

'Not from me he doesn't, and I don't think it's me place to disillusion him further. He'll find out soon enough if she carries on the way she's going now.'

'But getting rid of an unwanted pregnancy is so dangerous. Do you have any idea how many women die in the process?'

'I know. She paid a small fortune for the best doctor willing to do it. No kitchen table job for her.'

'That's to be thankful for. I wouldn't wish that on anyone.' She hesitated. 'When I found out I was expecting Mikey, all I could think about was getting rid of him. I didn't think of him as human – just an 'it, a monster growing inside me. I went to a place in Sydney where a woman agreed to do an abortion. But it was vile - that's the only reason I went ahead with having him. It was literally going to happen on the kitchen table and a filthy one at that. She kept the instruments in a bag slung in the bottom of a cupboard and there were cats all over the place. I couldn't go through with it because I was disgusted and frightened. Frightened for me, not for Mikey. I thought of him as something to be expunged, expelled and flushed away. I can't bear to think about it. I feel ashamed.'

'Well you didn't do it. Though it were understandable that you thought about it, after what happened to you.'

'But Hattie? Going behind your back?'

'You see now why staying with her is out the question. A woman who doesn't tell me she's having me child, let alone that she's getting rid of it. A wife who runs around town, smoking and drinking, staying up all night taking drugs with some posh blackguard.'

'Are you sure about the drugs?'

'Aye, she made no secret of it. Snorted it up her nose in front of me. There's a lot of talk of that going on in Sydney.'

'It's sad. She had every opportunity – education, brought up by a loving mother and then by lovely Verity, money, good looks, intelligence. Why, oh why, has she thrown it all away? Michael, I'm so sorry.'

'I don't like the idea of divorce, and I don't know what I'll tell me folks. I wish now I'd never told 'em I were married in the first place. But I've made enough mistakes in me life and staying with Harriet would make this one worse. If we were to keep up the charade it'd ruin both our lives. It were wrong to marry 'er in the first place. I'll not make it worse by sticking around. The more I've tried to help her, to encourage her to get help, the worse she is. If I'm not there for her to kick against, mebbe she'll grow up. Anyways, now I know the truth about you, I couldn't be with her again. Never.' He reached out as though he was going to kiss her but Elizabeth held him away, her hands planted on his chest, her eyes fixed on his.

'Does Mr Kidd know you plan to divorce?' She felt the need for formality in describing her husband, given the sudden shift in her relationship with Michael.

'He's known for a while but thought we'd not go through with it, but I told him this morning it were for definite and that I were giving in me notice.'

'And?'

'He were angry. He shouted. He swore. He told me I were sacked and to go at once.'

Elizabeth smiled. 'I can picture that.'

'He wants to bring Harriet home to the Falls and take 'er settlement back, but she's seen a lawyer in Sydney and there's nowt he can do. The money's hers. I can leave with a clear conscience that she can support herself. I don't want a penny of it.'

'If you divorce won't there be a scandal?'

'She'll not care a hoot. Her society friends will think she had a lucky escape. And I won't be around to care for me own account. The lawyer says if I leave her she'll get a divorce on grounds of desertion after three years. She'll still only be twenty-two. The divorce laws in New South Wales are the easiest in the whole Empire.'

'Why New Zealand?'

'There's work there – the kind I want to do. Rearing sheep. I hate the mine. I hated it back in England. I hated being underground during the war and I hate it even more here watching other poor buggers blast the coal out. I only did it for money for me folks. I think Kidd plans to sell up anyways. If he can get out now he'll have a pot of money to do what he wants to do. I mean to do the same. I've bought me ticket. I came back to collect me things and break the news to 'im, and then I heard what had happened to yer bairns.' He reached for her, pinning her arms against her sides as he wrapped his arms around her, crushing her to him. 'Elizabeth, come with me. I love you and I don't want to lose you again.'

'I can't,' she whispered.

'Why not? You don't care for Kidd, do you?'

'He's a decent man. He's done me no wrong. I can't just abandon him.'

'He's a miserable bastard and yes you can. For God's sake, he hit you. Remember? I was there!'

'He lost his temper. He didn't mean it. He was upset about you and Hattie. He apologised abjectly afterwards.'

'He didn't mean it? That's what every beaten-up woman says – right up until the next time he clobbers her.'

'It won't happen again. He was angry. And in his way...'

'In his way what? You're not going to tell me you love him? Oh God, no!' He paced up and down running his hands through his hair, a look of anguish on his face.

'No, I don't love him. Of course I don't. But I'm grateful to him and he needs me. I can't just walk away and leave him. It would be wrong. When I was destitute he took me in. He gave a name and a home to my son. We had a child together. We've lost that child. He's grieving too. I made promises. I have to honour them.'

'You think because I were foolish enough to marry Harriet I should do the same?'

'I don't know what Harriet's motives are. Clearly she's on a path to self-destruction, especially if she's taking drugs. But Jack Kidd has been kind to me in his own odd way. He may have little to say, but he cares about me. I can't abandon him, especially now I know what's happening with Harriet and now that Susanna has gone. She was our daughter after all. He may not show his grief to the world but I know he's grieving.'

'But we love each other… don't we?'

'I love you, Michael Winterbourne, with my heart and my soul and with every breath in my body. I've loved you all this time. Even when I believed you hated me. I'll love you till the day I die. There's not a night has passed that I haven't gone to sleep thinking of you and not an hour in every day that I haven't thought of you, wondered what you were doing, imagined what things would have been like if we'd been together. Everything that's happened to me since we parted I've told you about in my head. Everything I've seen or heard I've imagined seeing or hearing with you. All the time. The pain of losing you was the worst pain I've ever felt. As bad as I feel now about my children. Worse than losing my parents. Never doubt me again, Michael. Never ever doubt me.' She looked into his eyes and gripped his arms so hard he felt the blood stopping.

'Then come away with me. We'll start a new life and put all this mess behind us. We've both made mistakes. We've both lost people we love. We can make a future together and put it right.' He looked at her and then, deciding enough had been said, he planted tiny kisses all over her face. She gasped and leaned back into her chair, afraid of her own emotions. His kisses were light, teasing and gentle, but there was a growing urgency in them.

'Oh God, Michael. What are we doing?'

'What's right and what we want. It's what I've dreamt of every night these past years.'

'Me too.'

He found her mouth and with a small cry she kissed him back, hungrily tasting him, drinking him in. Any thoughts of duty or responsibility towards Jack Kidd fled as she kissed him. It felt right. She gave herself up to the kiss, knowing that all the suffering she had endured, the loneliness, the loss, were somehow redeemed in this moment. How could it be wrong?

She pulled away slightly as they emerged from the kiss, so she could look at him. She felt cherished, loved. The pain and loss of Mikey and Susanna was still present, but was somehow poignant and sweet instead of empty and bitter. She felt what she had only experienced when holding her children. Unconditional love.

He leaned down and kissed her again. 'Can you ever forgive me, my darling? I've been such a stupid fool.'

'It's all right. I know how it must have seemed.'

'But I shouldn't have doubted you and thought you capable of behaving like that. Please forgive me. I felt so bad about meself that I couldn't believe that you could care for me. I didn't think I were worthy of yer.'

'Hush' she breathed. She stroked her fingers down his cheek. 'Enough. I want to show you how much I love you. I've waited so long.' She undid the buttons on the front of her dress and let it slip to the floor, then stepped into his arms.

After they made love, as they lay entwined on the rag rug, they were oblivious to Nat Kidd watching them through a gap in the green gingham curtains.

Michael rose naked from the tumble of cushions and bedding they had flung on the floor in front of the woodstove and went to pour them each a glass of water. Elizabeth had piled logs on the fire and dragged the eiderdown onto the floor in front of it. Not that they were aware of the cold or the hardness of the floor, lost as they were in their discovery of each other. She watched him as he poured the water, taking in the height of him, the muscles across his back, the long legs and the narrowness of his hips. His body was so different from the small wiry frame of her husband. Not that she was thinking of Jack Kidd now. Michael saw her appraising him as he moved back to her and he smiled. 'Now will you come to New Zealand?'

'I want nothing more in the world, but to leave my babies in that cemetery? To be so far away from them, unable to visit their graves.'

He couldn't help but think of Minnie wanting to stay close to the war memorial that bore her father and brother's names. He held her tightly, stroking her hair.

She spoke again. 'I keep thinking about the poor little mites alone under the ground.'

'Don't do this to yourself, Elizabeth. Please.'

'I can't help it. I dream of them being eaten up by worms. Their little legs turning into skeletons. Mikey was always afraid of the dark.'

'Stop it! Don't do this! Stop torturing yourself. Think of them turning into new life, into trees or birds. Flying away. Free.'

She thought for a moment. 'I like that. A pair of little birds. Maybe kookaburras? Or Noisy Miners? No – lorikeets. That's it! Lorikeets were Mikey's favourites. He called them lollykeets. It's strange – a group of rainbow lorikeets flew past at the funeral as if they'd come to say goodbye.'

'Well then, think of the bairns' spirits flying away with them. Mebbe they can fly over the sea to New Zealand.' He smiled.

They fell into silence, then Elizabeth spoke. 'I'm not the kind of person who walks away from responsibility. We're doing this now and I know that it should be wrong... but somehow it isn't wrong. I know the right thing is to do my duty and stand by the man I married, for better or worse, but I don't think I can. Not now, Michael. Not after this. Not after us.'

He gasped and pulled her into his arms.

As he held her, a fleeting memory of Stephen crossed her mind – on the sands at Birkdale, talking of "doing the right thing". 'I can't help thinking about what duty did for my fiancé – how it cost him his life. I'm sick of putting others first – apart from you. Nothing can bring my children back and I want to grab a chance of happiness and that can only be with you.'

He looked at her eagerly. 'You'll come with me?'

'Michael, I don't know. I feel bad about Jack. If I leave him I don't know what he'll do. In his own cockeyed way I think he loves me and I don't want to hurt him.'

'But you'll hurt me?' His voice was a low moan. 'The man forced you to marry him, Elizabeth. You owe him nowt. He took advantage of you.'

'I know you can't understand, but it's who I am. It's how I was brought up to behave.'

'I can't stand it. I can't bear to think of that old goat touching you, making love to you. Doing this.' He cupped his hand over her breast.

'It's not like that. It's not the same. With you it's love, it's passion; with him it's more like comfort or consolation. He's a lonely, unhappy man and I brought him some solace. It's hard not to take account of that, to feel some responsibility…'

'It's wrong. You and I are meant to be together. We've at last got a chance to make it right. Kidd's had his time with you. It's more than he deserved and I won't let him have you any longer.'

Elizabeth couldn't bear to see the hurt in his eyes, knowing that she could so easily remedy it. 'I know it's unfair. But how can I let that turn me into a person I'd feel ashamed of. And I would. You must understand that? We have this brief time together to treasure and look back on for the rest of our lives. Whenever I feel sad or alone I'll think of us here tonight. Now I'm strong enough to face anything. You've given me that strength.'

She hesitated. 'Perhaps you could try and seek a reconciliation with Harriet. I know you feel betrayed that she didn't tell you about the baby, but you don't know what it feels like to carry a child you don't want to have. She's very young. She wasn't ready. She was frightened. She'll think differently in the future.'

'I'll never go back to her. I'd rather be alone if I can't be with you. I'm leaving in the morning and I want you with me. If you won't come, then I'm going anyway. I meant to go months ago – after that bloody awful dinner when I found out you were married to Kidd. Something made me stay and I'm glad I did, so this could happen. But now I'm starting a new life. I want you in it. I can't live up here and not be with you. If you won't come I have to go anyway. It'll tear the heart out of me – but me heart's already yours anyway.'

'I know.' She turned her face to his and drew him into a kiss, then said 'Let's make the most of tonight, then. I don't want to talk about Kidd. And I don't want you to ask me again. If this is all we've got, let's not waste any more time, my love.'

The next morning the fire had gone out and there was a chill in the spring morning air and a slight touch of frost lacing the earth that Elizabeth had tilled so assiduously the day before. She sat beside Michael, as they drank tea on the veranda steps. She looked around her and asked herself if she could face living here for the rest of her life? With no Michael, no Mikey, no Susanna, and before long Will would doubtless marry and leave. There was only the faithful Verity and her days were occupied with the school. Why should she feel loyalty to Kidd when she had not married him of her free will?

Sitting next to Michael, her hand in his as they sipped their tea, the warmth of his body against hers, she knew with absolute certainty that she was meant to be with him.

She was about to speak when he put down his empty mug. He fished in his pocket and handed her a small stone. She rolled it over in her palm, seeing the hole in the middle of what was otherwise an unexceptional large pebble.

'It were our Danny's. He never let it out of his sight. Drove Mam and me Da crazy. He'd play with it at table. Rolled it around in his hands. Slept with it under the pillow. God knows why. He picked it up when he were just a wee thing and never let it go. We called the dog Stone after it. Danny had it in his hand when he died. It's me most precious thing and I want you to have it.'

She frowned. 'I can't take that from you.'

'I want you to keep it. So I can tell meself that you have something of me.' He pressed her fingers around the stone. 'Keep it safe, lovely, along with me heart.'

'It will be with me always. I still have your handkerchief.' She reached into the pocket of her apron and pulled it out. 'It's grubby as I couldn't bear to wash it. I cried into it so many times thinking of you.'

She jumped up 'Wait! There's something I want you to have – as important to me as this stone is to you.'

She ran into the house and returned with a gold ring which she pressed into his hand. 'Mother's wedding ring.'

'I can't take that.'

'You can. Just as I'll take care of this stone.'

He looked down at the small gold wedding band then closed his palm over it and stood up, looking away from Elizabeth.

'I'd best be heading off then. I've things to do before I go. I need to clear me stuff out of the house in Sydney and tell Harriet she'll get her divorce in three years.'

He pulled her roughly to him and held her against his chest. She could hear the beating of his heart. They stood motionless and suddenly she knew she couldn't stay here without him. It was like a dam breaking and all the pent up emotions and fears of the past few years broke through and she held onto him as though he were a rock in a stormy sea.

'I'll come with you. I can't live without you. Not any more. Not after this. I couldn't bear it.'

'You mean it? You'll come? I'll never let you regret it for a moment. You've made me so happy.' His eyes shone and she fancied she could see the beginnings of tears in them. 'My dearest darling. Thank you.'

'But you need to give me a few days. I have to tell Jack. I owe him that much.'

'We'll tell him together.'

'No. You have to let me do this. If you're there he'll be angry and who knows what he'll do. You have to trust me to deal with it myself. And I want to say goodbye to Verity and Will. You go on to Sydney and sort the tickets and I'll join you. When does the ship sail?'

'Noon on Thursday from Circular Quay.'

'I'll see you there then. On the quayside.'

'I should stay here with you and face Kidd together.'

'Trust me to do this myself. I know how to handle Jack. It's better I do it on my own. He'll be back here tomorrow. I'll tell him then. Now go, my darling.'

He slung his bag over his shoulder and pulled on his hat and they walked hand in hand along the worn dirt track to where he had left the small truck he had driven out in. He gathered her into his arms for the last time, kissed her slowly and tenderly then climbed into the cabin and drove away. She watched, with a longing for him that was like a physical pain, until the truck had disappeared in a cloud of dust.

CHAPTER TWENTY-ONE

THE KILLING

She was hanging out the washing. Absorbed in the mundane task she didn't hear his approach until his hands were over her eyes.

'Jack?' she cried, surprised at the unusual show of affection. Her stomach flipped knowing she must break the news of her leaving him.

She felt the roughness of his skin and smelled the alcohol on his breath, then when he dropped his hands she saw it was the son, not the father.

'Get out of here!'

'Not so fast, Mother dear. We have a lot to talk about.'

'I want you to leave immediately. My husband will be home any minute and he'll be angry if he finds you.'

'I dare say he will, Beauty. Especially when he hears how his lovely wife has been entertaining her fancy man while he's safely out of the way.' He put his hand on her breast and she jumped away as if his touch were poisonous.

'Get out of here – now.'

'Come on, Beauty. Don't play the shy one. The old man's not enough for you? Can't say I'm surprised. A woman like you must take a lot of satisfying.'

She wrenched her arm back and swung her open palm across his face in a stinging blow. At once his manner changed and he snarled at her.

'Think you're too good for me, do you, bitch? You didn't look so high and mighty doing the dirty with your son-in-law. Yes, I know who he is. I ran into my little sister and she told me her new husband has run off and left her. I looked at her wedding photographs while she was chucking them on the fire. When I saw you and him through the window I thought he looked familiar. You're the reason he's dumped her I suppose?'

'Leave now.'

'I'm going nowhere. I took rather a fancy to those breasts of yours when you had them out on display for him. It looked like he had his hands full. Let's have another look.' He grabbed the neck of her blouse and tore it open, sending little ivory buttons flying across the bare ground. She backed away, but tripped over the basket of laundry. Nat reached out and steadied her from falling, then jerked her towards him.

'Let me go.' She screamed at him.

'Have you talked to the old man yet? Have you got the money?'

'Not yet.' She was trembling with fear, but didn't want him to see she was afraid. 'I haven't seen him yet.'

'Liar. You've had your chance to play it the easy way and now we'll play it my way. You can give me a bit of what Pa and your fancy man have been getting and then you'll do exactly what I asked and get him to pay me what's due to me. If you don't, I'll have to tell him all about you and his son-in-law – as well as what you and me are going to do now.' He snarled out the words, spraying her face with spittle. She wiped her cheek with her hand and was overcome with a visceral anger that took over her whole body. *No one's ever going to rape me again.*

She struck out at his face with a blow he wasn't expecting. As he lurched backwards she grabbed the rake and held it up, using it to hold him at bay.

'Your father owes you nothing. You're bad to the core and I'll never intercede on your behalf.'

'Shut it! You can't talk to me like that! I'm an Anzac. A fucking war hero! Show some respect.' He grabbed the wooden shaft at the end of the rake and pulled her towards him with a jerk. She lost her balance and her hold on the rake. He yanked her upright, but before he could take hold of her, a familiar voice rang out.

'Leave her alone! Let her go.'

Will charged at Nat, pushing him to the ground and the brothers wrestled on the dirt path. Elizabeth dragged herself onto the steps. Will was in a frenzy, pummelling his brother with uncharacteristic savagery. He had the advantage of surprise and his rush upon Nat had taken the older man's breath away.

'Will, stop! Please stop! You'll kill him.' Will was kicking his brother's prone body and shouting.

'You bastard! How does that feel? That's what Ma felt when you kicked the lights out of her, you drunken bum.'

Nat kicked out violently with his right foot, making contact with Will's shin and throwing him off balance, then took advantage to scramble to his feet. Elizabeth saw a flash of metal in the sunlight.

'Will! Look out!' she screamed. Too late.

A shot rang out and Nat dropped, landing on top of Elizabeth like a felled tree, the knife clattering from his hand onto the steps of the homestead. She lay unmoving under the weight of him, as the sticky warmth of his blood pooled over her torn blouse onto her hair and face.

Then the weight was lifted off her and Jack Kidd was standing over her. A rifle lay on the ground where Kidd had let it fall.

'He's stabbed Will.' She crawled on her knees to where Will lay. He was still breathing.

'Will! Can you hear me?'

Kidd knelt beside her and cradled his son in his arms. He lifted Will by the armpits and Elizabeth took hold of the boy's feet and they carried him inside and laid him on their bed. She filled a basin with water while Kidd opened the boy's shirt to reveal a gaping wound in his side. She doused some cloths in water and set a kettle to boil, as Kidd tried to soak up and stem the blood that was pouring from him. Will was conscious, but weak.

Kidd spoke at last. 'It looks worse than it is.'

'He needs a doctor. You fetch him and I'll try and stop the bleeding,' she said.

'I don't think it's penetrated any organs. But he's losing a lot of blood and he could be bleeding inside.'

Will's face was white as milk and the blood was flowing freely onto the bed sheets. She gathered up the counter-pane and pressed it gently over the wound. 'Go and get the doctor, Jack. Hurry!'

'I don't want to leave him.' Kidd leaned over his son and took the boy's hand.

Will's breathing was faint and Elizabeth held a damp cloth to his parched lips. 'Go and get the doctor. Hurry – he could go into shock.'

He looked at her torn blouse, her breasts half exposed and the remains of her blouse drenched in blood.

'Did he hurt you? Did he do anything to you before we got here?'

'No.'

'He tore your blouse?'

'Will arrived before he could do anything else'

'He's dead, isn't he? I killed him?'

Elizabeth nodded.

'May he burn in hell.' Kidd's eyes hardened. 'Clean

yourself up, you're covered in blood and your shirt's in tatters.' He looked at her sadly. 'I should never have left you here alone.'

He went onto the porch and pushed his foot against the body of his oldest child so it rolled off the step and lay, eyes wide open, on his back. Kidd went back into the house and grabbed his oilskin jacket and threw it over the corpse.

'Take care of my boy. I'll be back as soon as I can.'

When he returned with Doctor Reilly in tow, the doctor stopped beside Nat's body, still lying in front of the veranda steps, but seeing Elizabeth in distress on the threshold, he stepped over the body and went to attend to Will, after telling Elizabeth and Kidd to wait outside.

Kidd paced up and down, while Elizabeth sat on the step-top, head in hands praying for Will's life and trying not to look at the large oilskin-covered lump in front of her.

Eventually the doctor reappeared in the doorway.

'He's lost a lot of blood but he's a strong lad. He'll live. You did a good job at staunching the bleeding, Mrs Kidd. I've cleaned the wound and stitched him up. He needs complete rest for a few days. I'll send the ambulance as I'd like to keep an eye on him in the hospital to make sure he doesn't get an infection. The stitches can come out in a couple of weeks. He'll be chopping logs and snaring rabbits again in no time.'

He turned to Kidd. 'I presume whoever's under that oilskin is no longer in need of a doctor's help?'

Kidd nodded.

'Maybe you'd better tell me what happened and let me take a look. I'll have to issue a death certificate.'

'He's carked it. I shot him.'

The doctor frowned. 'Let's have a look.' He pulled the oilskin off the body. 'This is your lad, Jack, isn't it?' The doctor's face was grim.

'Yup. It is.'

313

'Good God, man! What happened?'

'He got what's been coming to him for a long time.'

He reached for Elizabeth's hand and spoke quietly. 'I should have done for him years ago. He may have been my flesh and blood but he was evil to the core. Even as a small lad he was bad. Bane of his mother's life. I wore out shoe leather trying to knock sense into him, but it was never any good. The missus tried to see the good in him and always took his part, but he did for her in the end.'

His voice broke and he brushed the tears away from his eyes.

'He was only fourteen. His mother found him drinking a bottle of my whisky and took him to task. He was blind drunk and hit her so hard her eyes were black as two pieces of coal and she'd bruises all down her face.'

Elizabeth decided not to share the fact that Nat had twisted the tale to accuse him of hitting his wife. 'So you threw him out?'

'I wish I had. If I'd been around I'd have kicked him to back o' Bourke. I was in Sydney. He and the other two were here with their mother. She was eight months gone with another baby and weak with the influenza. She was tired and defenceless and he bashed the daylights out of her. Then he buggered off and left her with Hattie and Will. The bashing brought the labour on.' He turned to the doctor, 'You know this as well as I do, man.'

The doctor took up the story. 'Will ran all the way into town to fetch me but by the time we got here it was too late. She'd died just after the child was born. The baby died soon after – his skull was fractured from the kicking his mother received. Nat was gone. The police were on the lookout for him and some of the men got up a search party but there was no trace. Most people thought he was lying dead at the bottom of the canyon. If the police had caught him he'd have been arrested.'

314

'Prison would have been too good for him.' Kidd's voice was barely a whisper.

'I'm sorry.' She laid a hand on his arm.

The doctor coughed. 'He was a bad egg, Jack, and you've trouble enough, losing your children just a few days ago, but to shoot your own son in the back, man? The law should have dealt with him.'

'He had it coming and I'm ready to face the consequences. I'm glad I killed him before he could harm her or my boy. I'm glad I was here in time.'

'What will we tell the constable?'

'The truth.'

Elizabeth started to speak. 'You can't...'

'The police aren't fools, are they, Doc?'

'But they'll...' Elizabeth could barely speak.

'They'll charge me with murder? They probably will and if they do, it's no more than I deserve. I should have killed him years ago.'

'Get yourself back to town, doc and tell the constable I'm waiting for him.'

CHAPTER TWENTY-TWO

ARRESTED

Elizabeth stood on the steps as the constable led Jack Kidd away to the police truck. Nat's body had already been taken to the mortuary for the post mortem examinations. As McDonald Falls had no police cell, Kidd would be taken into the next town and held until a magistrate determined whether to charge him or not. She had little doubt of the likelihood of that.

She went back into the house and took up her place again beside Will's bed, waiting for the ambulance. The boy drifted in and out of consciousness and was clearly very weak. She held a cup of water to his parched lips to help him drink whenever he was able to accept it.

Here she was again, keeping a bedside vigil beside a sick child. This time, although the doctor's prognosis was good, her anxiety was acute. Her stepson, while not of her own blood, had come to feel like her own. Will had been her first real friend in this place and a true and faithful one. She had rejoiced in his growing confidence and the way he'd taken care of her own little boy and from the moment of his birth treated him as his brother.

He called out Elizabeth's name in his sleep. As she sat

beside him, holding his unresponsive hand in hers, she realised he had been nursing a crush on her. It explained his attacks of blushing and the increasingly frequent tongue-tied silences in her presence. She smiled and whispered, 'Whoever wins your heart, Will Kidd, will be a very lucky woman.' He showed no signs of hearing and continued his restless sleep.

His brow was clammy so she wiped it with a damp cloth and reached again for his hand. It was harder to believe that Will and Nat had been brothers than that he and Mikey were. She shivered to think how close they had been to losing Will. But at what price? She was afraid now for Jack Kidd. She'd seen another aspect of him recently and tonight's revelations had intensified that. The loss of his first wife and the estrangement from his son had conspired to harden him. A rough and ready countryman from the start, any softer sides to his character had been brushed aside when he'd built a hard shell to present to the world. Not so different from herself? Underneath the brusque and cold exterior, was an unhappy and disappointed man, whose early struggles to keep his family fed and clothed and whose losses of successive children and then his wife, had killed any joy and capacity for happiness.

She knew she must stand by him and help him face what lay ahead. He'd killed Nat to save her life. Standing by him was the least she could do. She'd postpone joining Michael in New Zealand – she couldn't add to Kidd's suffering by abandoning him for another man, his son in law and trusted foreman to boot. Her heart ached for Michael, but Kidd needed her. Michael would understand and they could be together soon. Once this mess was sorted and Kidd out of custody, she'd find a way to break the news to him and follow Michael.

Will stirred, opened his eyes and tried to pull himself up. She put her hand on his shoulder. 'Steady on, Will. You need to rest.'

'Elizabeth!' he looked both shocked and overjoyed to see her sitting at his bedside. 'What's happened? Where am I?'

'You're safe with me at Wilton's Creek. Can you manage a bit of clear beef broth, my darling?'

A look of alarm crossed his face as the memory of the fight rushed back. 'Where's Nat? What happened?'

'Nat's gone. We'll talk about it later. You need to rest and get well.'

His eyes darted round the room and he realised he was in his father's bed. At the same moment he became aware of the pain and with a groan, sank back and closed his eyes, just as the ambulance pulled onto the hard standing outside the house.

Once she had seen Will safely installed in the small hospital at McDonald Falls, her thoughts turned to Michael. She went to the post office to send a telegram.

TERRIBLE ACCIDENT WILL INJURED AND BROTHER NAT SHOT DEAD - STOP - KIDD ARRESTED - STOP - GO WITHOUT ME - STOP - SEND ADDRESS I WILL FOLLOW WHEN ABLE - STOP - E.

At the same time she sent a second telegram, addressed to Harriet.

WILL IN HOSPITAL - STOP - NOT SERIOUS BUT NATHANIAL DEAD AND JACK ARRESTED COME QUICKLY STOP E KIDD

Over the next few days, Will gained strength. Elizabeth helped him walk a few steps across the ward and sit upright in a chair. When she felt he was strong enough to bear it, she broke the news of his brother's death and his father's arrest. He bit his lip and gripped her hand. As she looked at his face to read his reaction, she saw something in him had changed. The wide-eyed enthusiastic teenager had gone, and there was a world-weariness in his face.

Doctor Reilly visited daily and showed his approval of Will's progress. When Will was fit enough to return to home, Verity was waiting at Kinross House for them, standing beside Mrs Oates and Mary in a welcoming line-up. As they embraced, Elizabeth saw that Verity was crying.

Once Will was dispatched to his bed, they sat down in the drawing room.

Verity said, 'I can't believe it, Elizabeth. I don't know why the good Lord has sent you so many troubles. It's not right. It's not fair.'

Elizabeth was silent, but inside her, despite all this, the thought that drowned out all others but could never be expressed, was that she had to go through all this without Michael. She pulled herself up to her full height and took a deep breath. 'I have to be strong. My husband needs that. I have to be there for him.'

'I'm sure they won't hold him long. They can't possibly. He did what any man would do in the circumstances. He protected his family from an intruder. The police will realise there's no case to answer and he'll come home soon.'

'It's not so straightforward. The intruder was his own son, Verity.'

Verity gasped. 'Nathaniel?' Her hand was clasped to her mouth.

Elizabeth nodded.

'Everyone thought he was dead,' said Verity. 'He hasn't been seen in years. Mr Kidd thought he was an intruder?'

'I don't think so. I think he knew exactly who he was.'

'Dear goodness! Tell me what happened.'

'Nat turned up out of the blue at Wilton's Creek. He surprised me and made advances to me. Very aggressively. Will arrived and came to my rescue. Nat pulled a knife on him and my husband shot Nat to save Will.'

'Goodness gracious!'

'I gave the police a statement and told them that Jack was acting to defend both Will and me. Nat was a nasty piece of work.'

'I hope and pray Mr Kidd will be released soon. What on earth made Nat attack you?'

'He wanted money and was trying to force me to help him get it from his father. I refused. Maybe I should have said I'd help him. He said he'd been in the war. Perhaps he was shell-shocked? But I didn't like him, Verity. There was something frightening about him. I didn't trust him. But look what's happened now...'

'Don't blame yourself. And don't worry about Mr Kidd. The police will understand. The whole town knows Nat Kidd was no good. Hattie said he kicked and hit their mother, God rest her soul. They're bound to let Mr Kidd come home soon.'

'That's unlikely. The New South Wales Police take a pretty dim view when someone is shot in the back, regardless of the circumstances. They've told us they intend to charge him with murder.'

Verity clasped her hand to her mouth with a little strangled cry.

Miranda passed the telegram back to Harriet.

'Hell's bells, Hat, what a terrible thing. What exactly happened?'

'You can read as well as I can. Pa's in jail, Will's in hospital and Nat's dead.'

'I thought Nat died years ago? Where's he been all this time?'

'In the army. He was in Gallipoli and since the war ended he's been living in Perth. He turned up here last week. I was so shocked to see him I let him in but it turned out he just wanted money. I wish he had died years ago. After what he did to Ma. I hate him. I'm glad he's dead.'

'Are you going to go to the Falls? It sounds like your step mother needs you.'

Harriet raised her eyes. 'She can go to hell. I called Kinross House and Mrs Oates says Will's going to be all right and is already out of hospital. There's nothing I can do and I'm not dancing to that woman's tune. Besides I need your help.'

'Me? What can I do?'

'I need you to run a little errand tomorrow. Read this.' She handed another brown telegram form to her friend.

Miranda read it quickly and looked up. 'My God! They were having an affair and she's running away with him! You were right about him after all. What a bastard. You're well rid of him. But this is addressed to him. What if he finds out you've read it?'

'He won't. He was out when it came, presumably buying their tickets to New Zealand. I'm not going to let him see it as if he reads it, he won't get on that boat without her and I want him gone as soon as possible. The sooner he's off the sooner I get my divorce. And I can't stand the sight of him any more.'

'But when she doesn't turn up to get the boat he's unlikely to go without her. He's bound to go back to the Falls to find her and then you'll be really in the soup as he'll discover you took the telegram.'

'That's where you come in, my dear Randa. Let me explain.'

It was almost time for sailing and there was still no sign of her. Michael paced up and down the deck, growing more anxious. He stationed himself near the top of the gangplank where he had a good view over the quayside. A few last stragglers made their way on board and he watched the crew make the final preparations for departure.

He looked at his watch and decided that if she didn't turn up in the next five minutes he would disembark and find out why she was delayed. They could take another ship later in the week. There was still time to grab his baggage and get off. Just then he heard a couple of crew members talking. One held a clipboard in his hands and was consulting the list.

The other man spoke. 'How many we got then, Jim?'

'All here. We can cast off when you're ready, sir. Three no shows. A couple missed their train and wired to switch to the Friday crossing. Then there's a woman who died. Purser's looking for her travelling companion to break the news. Otherwise it's a full house, sir.'

'Righto.' He called out to the men at the top of the gangplank. 'Raise it up, boys. Cast her off!'

Michael grabbed the arm of the man with the clipboard, his chest pounding in fear. 'The woman who died? What was her name?'

The man looked at him, and then frowned. 'Your name is, sir?'

'Winterbourne.'

The man nodded. 'I'm very sorry, sir. We had a message this morning from a Miss Verity Radley to say that Mrs Elizabeth Kidd was killed in a car accident yesterday on her way to the railway station. Miss Radley asked for you to be informed. Mrs Kidd was killed instantly.'

The world stopped. The words made no sense.

'It can't be true? She can't be dead.'

'I'm sorry, sir.' The man laid a hand on Michael's arm and patted it. Then with a shrug towards his crewmate, made his way along the deck, leaving Michael slumped against the railings, his head in his hands, as the ship pulled away from the quay and into the harbour, churning the blue water into a milky soup.

Miranda waited on the quayside until she could no longer see the vessel, then made her way up the hill to the cocktail bar of a hotel where Harriet was waiting, her habitual champagne flute in her hand.

'Well?'

'He's gone. It's done,' said Miranda and sat down beside her.

'Then we must celebrate.' Harriet started to fill another glass from the bottle standing in its bucket next to the table.

'No thank you. I don't feel like celebrating.'

'Why ever not? We did it! He's gone for good. I'm free at last. If that's not worth a celebration I don't know what is?'

'I feel ashamed. It was a cruel thing to do. It wasn't even necessary. Why couldn't you have let him have the telegram and let them be together? I thought you wanted to be rid of her too? I can't understand why you should be so selfish.'

Harriet's face contorted with irritation. 'You know I hate her. And anyway I have plans for her too. The evil conniving, money-grabbing, lying bitch is going to get her just deserts.'

'You didn't see him, Hat. He crumpled like a house of cards when the man passed the message on. He was a fair way away but I could tell he was devastated. Broken hearted. I felt awful. It was so unnecessary. He did nothing wrong to you. How can you take pleasure in destroying his life like that?'

'How can you even ask me that, Randa, after what he's done? Marrying me when he was in love with her. Cheating my Pa out of his money. And her cheating me and Will out of what's ours. It's her fault my brother's dead. It's her fault Pa's in gaol. Why the hell should I give a damn that he's broken hearted? He'll get over it. At least he's free. At least he's alive. It's more than he deserves.'

'I'm sorry, Harriet. I want no more to do with this and with you. I feel ashamed and I wish I could undo what I've done. Don't call me again. You're no longer my friend. You're no longer welcome in my home.'

She walked out of the bar. Harriet stared after her, stunned at the outburst, then shrugged and called to the waiter. 'Bring me another bottle of this.'

Elizabeth longed to be with Michael. If she had agreed to run away with him immediately, Will would not be wounded, Nat would still be alive and Jack Kidd would not be locked in a prison cell.

She wanted to confide in Verity, but feared the older woman would disapprove of her liaison with Michael and she didn't want to risk the only friendship and source of support she had.

The days became weeks and she heard nothing from Michael. He must be in Auckland by now so why he had not written? She had no idea of his final destination there and no means of finding out.

The silence from Michael was matched by silence from Harriet. Neither of them had acknowledged their telegrams. Elizabeth fretted that they had not been delivered but after checking with the post office was assured that they had. She tried to reach Harriet on the telephone but the housekeeper told her the girl was out every time she called.

She prevailed upon Verity to speak to Hattie. When Verity put down the telephone receiver, there were tears on her cheeks. The schoolmistress reported back that as far as Harriet was concerned, her father was dead to her.

Verity said, 'I don't understand. She was such a nice little girl, but as she grew up I let myself become blind to what she was becoming. I can't believe it – to be so cruel about her father.'

'I'm sorry you had to hear her speak that way – but I can't say I'm surprised.'

'She said Mr Winterbourne has gone overseas. Probably back to England. She sounded pleased. What can have happened between them?'

Elizabeth felt herself blushing but Verity didn't notice.

Elizabeth asked, 'Is she in contact with him?'

'No. They quarrelled before he left. She doesn't seem to care that he's gone. She kept saying she's happy to be free of him. I hope her poor father doesn't find out - as if he doesn't have enough to worry about. And the mine? What's to become of the coal mine? With both Mr Kidd and Mr Winterbourne gone and Will sick.' She dabbed at her eyes with her handkerchief.

'The mine! I'd forgotten about that. I must find out what his wishes are.'

'There are so many men in this town whose livelihoods depend on it,' said Verity.

'Right. They need to be paid, at least until alternative arrangements can be made.' As she spoke, she felt a surge of energy. She could not prevent her husband's incarceration. She could not bring her children back. She would be separated from Michael until he wrote to her and until the trial was over. But meanwhile she could do something about the colliery and about Will and she could try to protect the livelihoods of the miners and their families.

'I'll go there and find out what needs to be done. I don't want Jack worrying about that on top of everything else.'

'Elizabeth! Really! What do you know about running a coal mine!' Verity's face was a picture of disbelief. 'You can't possibly be serious?'

'Oh but I can! And I am!'

'But what...how?'

'I don't know. I'll find a way though!' She jumped up and rang the bell. Mrs Oates appeared in the doorway.

'Ma'am?'

'Mrs Oates, I need to talk to someone about the colliery. Does Mr Kidd have a lawyer, or an accountant – someone who knows the business and can help me understand what's going on? The workmen need to be paid so I'll have to make arrangements on Mr Kidd's behalf to keep things going in his absence.'

'Mr Oates can tell you, Ma'am. He's in the garage - I'll send him in.'

Oates raised his eyebrows when Elizabeth explained what she wanted. 'Mr Robinson the accountant might be able to give you the information you require. But…'

'I need to review the books so the employees can be paid. Oates, take me to this Mr Robinson now, please.'

'But Elizabeth, don't you think you should speak to Mr Kidd first?' Verity was looking nervous.

'No time like the present, Verity! He has more than enough on his plate.' She hugged her friend, then with a brisk 'Come on, Mr Oates, let's get a move on!' she left the room.

CHAPTER TWENTY-THREE

THE COLLIERY

The late afternoon sun burst through the clouds and lit up the escarpment. The ground dipped away in front, giving a view of the tall trees and the sandstone cliffs on the opposite side of the gorge. The treetops were densely packed and looked like a crumpled green counterpane. The top of the escarpment was flat and wooded above the hard edges of the exposed cliffs below, bathed in yellow sunlight with ridges and gullies carving their way down the surface, so the rock stood out in sharp contrast to the green of the trees, like a giant hunk of blue-veined cheese. It was all so wild, so vast and so empty that Elizabeth caught her breath. No matter how often she looked at these mountains, the changing light made them look fresh and different and she never tired of their savage beauty.

The car swept down the hill into a section of road that was new to her and she regretted how little she had explored the area beyond the town and Wilton's Creek in the time she had lived here. The trees crowded close to the sides of the road and obscured the view. The air was chilly and she drew her coat closer around her. Mr Oates nodded his head at the road ahead. 'We're approaching the mine, Madam.'

They passed under a wooden archway bearing the roughly painted words *Black Water Colliery*. It didn't inspire confidence in the scale and professionalism of the operation. The road ahead was a rough dirt track, bordered on both sides by dense ferns and bushes but as they rounded the corner, the site opened out to reveal a collection of buildings: a tall brick chimney, a pair of large wooden towers with wheels and pulleys and a collection of single storey buildings and sheds. In front of it all were heaps of coal and a number of wooden trucks, filled with yet more coal, ready to make their way down the hill on a single-track railway that disappeared into the trees at the edge of the site. In the distance there was a collection of huts, some with canvas stretched across tree bark frames, others made of galvanised tin. Small children played in the dirt in front of the huts – or humpies as she knew they were called: the humble dwellings of many of the mineworkers and their families.

Oates pulled up beside one of the brick buildings and a short fat man with a bow tie and a resemblance to Fatty Arbuckle waddled over.

'It's Mrs Kidd, isn't it?' He held out his hand to her. 'I'm Henry Robinson, Chief Accountant at Black Water.'

Elizabeth resisted the temptation to dislike him at first sight. Everyone deserves a chance she told herself, while shuddering as his limp, sweaty palm held hers.

'Mr Robinson, as you know, my husband is in some trouble at the moment.'

The man nodded.

She hesitated, and then decided to say as little as possible. 'I need to understand the financial situation. Following my husband's absence and the departure of Mr Winterbourne, I've decided to find out how things are and see how I can help.'

The man barely tried to conceal his derision, letting a

little snort escape and then half heartedly attempting to cover this up by pretending to cough. 'You don't need to worry, Mrs Kidd. I have those matters under control.'

'Who's in charge?'

'I am. I do the books and pay the wages. The men turn up for their shifts or they don't get paid. The shift foremen make sure the work gets done and the chief engineer checks everything's working as it should. Nothing for you to be concerned about, Ma'am. I've been here twenty years, since Mr McDonald was the owner and I run a tight ship.' His face was smug and she had a sudden desire to slap it.

'I'd like to see the books.'

'I don't think that's either necessary or appropriate, Mrs Kidd.' He folded his arms and puffed out his chest, over the top of his large sloping stomach. His brown suit was so tight that the waistcoat gaped between the buttons to reveal little splashes of white fabric from the shirt underneath. It must have been a long time since he'd seen his feet.

'Well, Mr Robinson, I do. So shall we get on with it?' Before he could answer, she swept past him into the building. Three men were sitting with their heads bent over ledgers and plans. All of them looked up in surprise as she wished them a good afternoon. She looked around the room. The walls were furnished with a blackboard, a map of the surrounding area and a series of charts showing geological cross-sections and technical drawings of the coal seams and the mine workings.

Mr Robinson was looking alarmed. 'I don't know what Mr Kidd would have to say about this? It's most irregular.'

'Let me worry about Mr Kidd, you just show me the books and explain what's going on. I want to understand everything. Where the money's coming from, how much is going on wages, expenses, everything.'

Robinson was about to answer when she continued 'We can do this the easy way and you can talk to me like a grown-up person and tell me everything I need to know and then I'll be gone. Or we can do it the hard way, in which case I'll be spending a lot of time with you until I have the answer to every one of my questions – no matter how long that takes.'

He sighed pointedly, then said, 'Where do you want to start?'

Two hours later, with the help of a couple of large ledgers and a lot of scribbled figures which he made on the black-board, Mr Robinson had given Elizabeth a comprehensive overview of the Black Water Colliery's finances.

Elizabeth inhaled slowly. 'So, if I've understood you correctly, the mine is in a perilous position? The main seam is getting too thin to work economically; opening a new seam involves significant risk and investment; on top of that, the price of coal is dropping as many newer, more automated mines are entering the market? As a result my husband had already begun to look for a way out, but has so far been unable to identify an interested buyer? The current work-force consists of 120 men and in the absence of an alternative plan, you believe we'll need to consider layoffs before the end of the year?'

The three men at their desks all looked up at her then swiveled in their seats to see Robinson's reaction. He looked as though she'd asked him to swallow a slug.

'Yes. That's it in a nutshell, Mrs Kidd. You've grasped the situation perfectly for, for …a person new to the mining industry.'

'Thank you. For a moment there I thought you were about to say 'for a woman'. I'm so glad you didn't. Now we need a plan.'

'We do… but that's not something that you…'

'I will be back on Thursday afternoon. By then I'd like you to work up some alternatives for the business – what it would cost to develop a new seam? what possible new markets can be identified? are there any potential local buyers for the coal? – we could sell at a lower price if the transportation costs were less. I'd like the Chief Engineer to join us and anyone else you think should be present. It may be some time before Mr Kidd can attend to these matters and I don't want him to worry about this at all. Is that clear?'

'Perfectly, Mrs Kidd.' His oleaginous features were beaded with sweat and glowing red. He took a large, spotted, silk handkerchief from the pocket of his waistcoat and wiped his face.

Elizabeth left the room with a nod to the other men. Little work had been done that afternoon, so avidly had each of them listened to the exchanges between the fat accountant and the boss's wife.

As she drove away, she felt exhilarated. For the first time since being in Australia, apart from being a mother, she had a sense of purpose.

'Michael's gone away, Lizbeth.' Will was sitting in a chair in the garden, the rug that she had draped over his knees abandoned on the grass beside him. He walked slightly further around the garden each day and the colour was coming back to his face.

Elizabeth's head shot up and the expression on her face was eager. 'Have you heard from him? Where is he?'

'Nah. Not from him. I spoke to Hat last night. He's gone abroad. England or maybe New Zealand! They've split up and they're going to get divorced.'

'Yes, I did know that.'

'Why didn't you tell me, Lizbeth? I can't say as I'm surprised he's left her. But New Zealand? Why would he go there. It rains all the bloody time. Nothing but sheep and rain. Hat wouldn't have put up with that for a second! Not with her fancy clothes.' He looked at Elizabeth for

331

corroboration but she avoided his eyes. He carried on. 'More likely he's gone back to England – he told me a while back his mum was ill. I'm sorry he's gone. He was the only person I liked at the mine. My life will be worse for him going, that's for sure.' He looked glum.

'Does Harriet know his address?' her voice was hesitant.

'No. She's going to divorce him for desertion so she doesn't want to know where he is.'

She pretended to be absorbed in her embroidery, but was stabbing the needle into the fabric, blind to the stitches.

William, unaware of the effect of his words, carried on. 'It's strange isn't it? Just a few weeks ago I'd three brothers and now I've none. Mikey's dead. Nat's dead. Michael's buggered off and when the divorce comes through he'll not be my brother any more.' The boy looked crestfallen.

'Sorry, Will. It's been very distressing for you.'

'I'm bothered more for you. Having to look after me. And all the worry of Pa's trial coming up. And the mine and everything. All this and losing little Mikey and the bub.'

She smiled at him. 'As the philosopher said, "That which does not kill us makes us stronger".'

'You're a very strong woman, Lizbeth. And you've looked after me so well.'

'Looking after you, Will, is an absolute pleasure.'

'Do you think they'll hang Pa?'

'Will! What on earth makes you say that?' She felt a stab of fear.

'Because it's the law. If you kill someone it's murder and the law says you get the drop. If they do hang him it'll be my fault.'

'What on earth are you talking about?'

'He was trying to save me.'

'And you were trying to save *me*. Once the court hears what happened, your father won't be found guilty. Certainly not of murder.'

'But he could get manslaughter and still go to prison for years.'

'If he does we'll face it together. But once the jury hear the circumstances he'll get off. I'm sure of that.'

'If he does stay in prison I can still live with you, can't I?'

'This is your home, Will. You've as much right to live here as I have. But before too long you'll be getting a home of your own. When you marry, I mean.'

'I won't be marrying.'

'Don't be silly. Of course you will. When you meet the right girl.'

'No I won't.' He looked down at his hands.

'Why ever not?'

'Because the only person I want to marry is already taken.'

Elizabeth looked up from her sewing nervously.

'And who might that be?'

'You know who I mean. Don't make me say it.'

She raised her eyebrows. 'I've no idea.' She shrugged, 'I'm sure you'll eventually meet someone else much prettier and much nicer then her, whoever she is. All good things come to those who wait! You have so much time. You're still so young!' She laughed.

To her surprise William got up and went into the house, calling back angrily over his shoulder.

'Why do you want to make fun of me?'

He slammed the french door to the dining room behind him.

The remand wing of the Willagong Prison was over-crowded. The population had outgrown the original planner's expectations in terms of serious crime, and Kidd found himself in close quarters with many undesirables and unfortunates. Not that he was afraid of roughing it: he felt more comfortable in the company of these men than he ever had mixing with the wealthier citizens of McDonald Falls. Being accused of murder, he was denied bail and it was expected to be several weeks before his trial.

The prison had been built more than a hundred years earlier by convict labour and was a stern and grim place. The days there were tedious and the routine unvarying: an endless repetitive round of being locked in the cells, let out of the cells, queuing for food and walking in the small exercise yard. Kidd hated the confinement. It was worse than being down the pit – at least there he could emerge from the depths and breathe the clear mountain air and he had decisions to make and people to marshal. Here it all boiled down to doing what the wardens told you to do, staying on the right side of the tougher long-termers, doing the odd deal for a bit of baccie and generally trying to keep your nose clean.

Unlike the sentenced men, who were allotted only twenty minutes visiting time each month, as a remand prisoner Kidd was allowed regular meetings with his lawyer and a weekly half hour meeting with Elizabeth. The sentenced men were all herded into a large area and expected to shout through a wire mesh barrier, at their assembled nearest and dearest several feet away whereas those on remand were afforded the privilege of an interview room, with only a single prison guard to look on and listen in to the conversation.

Elizabeth brought her husband fruit and some of Mrs Oates' homemade biscuits, but the guards who checked her in took them from her. There'd be smiles on the faces of their wives that evening. Still in mourning for the children, her black silk coat put her in sharp relief against the grey-painted walls of the gaol.

Kidd was thinner than the last time she'd seen him.

'How are they treating you?'

He grunted. 'No worse than I can take.'

'Have you seen the lawyer? Any news on the trial date?'

'He reckons it'll be a couple of weeks minimum. More like a month.'

Elizabeth gasped. 'That's terrible. We must do what we can to bring it forward. We should ask again for bail. Surely they can't possibly believe you're a danger to the public? For heaven's sake, you killed a man who was attacking your son and your wife.'

'Murder's murder. Round here they think a man who'd shoot his own son in the back is a good candidate for the gallows.'

Elizabeth shuddered. 'Don't talk like that, Jack Kidd! Once Will and I testify, no jury will ever convict you. You'll be out of here soon. I'm sure of it.'

'You won't be testifying.'

'What do you mean?'

'The law won't allow it. 'Spousal incompetence' they call it. Can't testify for or against, on the grounds that the law considers a husband and wife to be one and the same person.' He smiled.

'That's ridiculous.'

'Maybe, but you can't change the law.'

'What about Will then?'

'Lad's been through enough. I don't want him dragged into court.'

'Surely he'll be called as a witness?'

'Like as not the Prosecution will want him to testify.'

'Why not the Defence? He can tell them what Nat did. He stabbed him, for heaven's sake!'

'Yes he can tell them that. But it won't make any difference. He's alive and his brother's dead and nothing will take away the fact that I shot him.'

'If that's what the lawyer is saying, then we need to find a new lawyer.'

'There's nothing wrong with Cody. He's got as good a record as you'll find anywhere in New South Wales. I'll take my chance.'

'But if they find you guilty?'

'I am guilty.'

'But you aren't going to plead guilty?' The alarm in her voice was evident.

'I'm not that daft. I'm not signing my own death warrant.'

'My God. Don't say that.'

'Well that's what I'll get for sure if I plead Guilty. That's what the law says. It's no different here from in England.'

'So what does Mr Cody say?'

'Has it in his head to try to get me off on the grounds of temporary insanity.'

'And?'

'He spouted a lot of Latin stuff at me, but I think he reckons I was acting without thinking in killing Nat to stop him killing you and Will. Said something about provocation and something else. Hang on – I wrote it down – automatism.'

'What?'

'I know. It's a load of old gibberish to me.'

'I will go and talk to Mr Cody.'

'Keep out of it, woman. I mean it. I don't want you messing about with all that. Leave it to the lawyer. I'm paying the man enough. Now talk to me about something else in the few minutes we've got left.'

'We could talk about the mine.'

'What about it?'

'It's in trouble.'

'Says who?'

'I've been there and looked at the books and talked to that very supercilious accountant of yours, Mr Robinson.'

Kidd laughed. 'What the hell do you know about mining or about anything to do with business?'

'I know enough. My father used to talk about his business. My sister and I often spent time in the office with him. I picked up enough to know how to read a balance sheet.'

Kidd whistled. 'Well, well. You never cease to surprise me, girl. So what do you reckon?'

'That the mine isn't viable without significant investment. The seam you've been working is narrowing and it's becoming uneconomical to extract the coal.'

Kidd raised his eyebrows but she continued. 'On top of that, the market's becoming more competitive and you're being undercut by competitors that are more highly automated than you are. It looks to me that, without some significant investment to open up a new seam and buy more modern machinery, or developing an ancillary business such as iron smelting, or finding some local outlets for the coal you can produce who are willing to pay the prices you need, or finding a buyer who is prepared to do some or all of this, the mine's going to have shut before the year's out.' She was breathless by the time she finished.

Kidd whistled. 'I'm impressed. There's a lot going on under that pretty little hat of yours.'

'Please don't patronise me, Jack Kidd.'

'I wouldn't dream of doing that.' He laughed.

'So?'

'So what?'

'What do you think? Do you agree with me?'

'I think you've hit the nail on the head.'

'Good. I've called a meeting with Robinson and the Chief Engineer and the Surveyor chappie and I've asked them all to come prepared with some options. I can then review all the alternatives so we can make a decision on the future of the mine as soon as possible.'

'Have you now?' Kidd was frowning.

'You don't look very pleased. But we can't just let things

ride. There are 120 men and their families depending on the Black Water Colliery to keep bread on their tables.'

'Do you think I don't know that?' Kidd's voice rose and she could see the anger in his eyes.

'I'm sorry. You know I wouldn't dream of interfering, but Will's still sick, Winterbourne's gone. You're in here. Someone has to keep things moving. Obviously I won't take any decisions without consulting you first.'

'You know Winterbourne's gone?' he looked up at her sharply.

She hesitated and then said quickly. 'Yes. When you were arrested, Verity and I made a trunk call to Sydney to tell Harriet. She told us they'd parted. I thought you knew.'

'Of course I knew. Winterbourne told me. We had an argument. I know the girl's a handful but I thought he was man enough to handle her. Seems I was wrong.'

'Do you know where he's gone? Since we don't know how long you'll be stuck in here maybe we should try to get him to come back – just till you're able to take control again? Has he been in contact with you since he left?' She struggled to keep the note of hope out of her voice.

'I'll not have him back after what's happened with Harriet and anyway I don't know where he's gone. Took the pay that was owed him and went on his way. Shame, as I actually liked the fella. Should have handled Hattie better though. For God's sake, she's his wife. And now she's running round Sydney like a bloody flapper girl. God knows what she's up to. If you'd put your time against convincing that girl to come back to the Falls instead of worrying about my mine…'

'She won't listen to reason. Verity's tried. She won't even speak to me. She's determined to stay in Sydney. Jack… I think you need to know… I'm afraid she's cut herself off from the family.'

Kidd looked down at the floor then lifted heavy eyes

to look at her. 'Can't say that I'm surprised. Having a gaol bird for a father doesn't sit well with her society friends in Sydney, I suppose?'

Elizabeth was about to reply when there was a rap on the door and the guard, who had been chain-smoking in the corner of the room, jumped to attention and called to them. 'Time's up. You need to leave now, Missus.'

Kidd leaned across the table and took her hands between his. His eyes seemed to fill with tears, but afterwards Elizabeth convinced herself it was just the smoke in the room.

'I know I haven't been the best of husbands.'

She looked towards the door, eager to get out as quickly as she could now. She was unused to tenderness from him.

'Hurry up, lady,' the prison guard said.

'I'll see you again next week. Everything's going to be all right. I promise you, Jack.'

As she reached the door and looked back at him, he spoke again. 'Don't make promises you can't keep, Elizabeth.' Then the door of the interview room swung shut behind her and the heavy metal clank resonated hollowly through the empty corridor.

Over the following weeks, Elizabeth spent most of her days inside the scruffy office building at the Black Water mine, going over pages of numbers with Robinson and talking at length with the engineers and surveyors. She held meetings with the bosses of the McDonald Falls Electric Light Company, the iron foundry in the next town, and the bank manager.

It became clear to her that, as well as the uneconomic nature of the coal seams, the mine was subject to other negative forces. The whole country over the past five years had witnessed the return of men from the battlefields of the Great War, putting pressure on employment. Mining in particular was suffering, with flat demand for production causing employers to cut wages and their workforce. Elizabeth discovered that Kidd had not moved in line with most of the other pit owners. He had held wages, then reduced working hours to avoid making layoffs. As revenue declined, the payroll was becoming unsustainable. On top of that she was beginning to harbour the suspicion that Robinson had been creaming off money, probably for a number of years.

She asked Robinson about the wages bill, surprised that Kidd had not done as most of his peers had, and forced wages down and hours worked up, as unemployment in the region rose.

'Mr Kidd wouldn't budge on the wages. I told him we were out of line and he insisted that the men have families to feed. We've been paying nine pounds a week here. The minimum wage is about half that and most of the other mines are paying around six quid a week.'

'I see.'

'Mrs Kidd, we can't sustain this. The cash flow is negative and I can only meet the payroll for another month or so.'

She asked to see the wages book again and went through it once more to check that the numbers tallied with what Robinson had told her. She looked up from the pages and said, 'Don't the men have to sign for their wages?'

'No, ma'am. I make the packets up and they're given out at the end of the Friday shift.'

'I see. Who decides what each man is paid?'

'It's a fixed rate for the job. Nine pounds underground and five pounds ten to the surface workers. Hourly rate equivalent to five quid a week for the casuals.'

That evening she spoke to Will and asked him what were the pay rates.

'I got same as the other fellas. Eight quid a week. Michael obviously got more.'

'And the men who work on the surface?'

'A fiver a week. Why do you want to know?'

'I believe Robinson has been skimming a cut from the wage packets. According to the ledgers, it's a pound more for underground and ten shillings more for the surface. I think he was probably taking a cut from the casuals too.'

Will whistled. 'Slimy bugger. I never liked him. He had it in for Michael too. I think Michael suspected he was up to something. Are you going to tell Pa?'

'Not yet. I don't want him worrying about that too. I'm going to give Mr Robinson the sack.'

Will grinned at her, his moodiness after their recent conversation about his marriage intentions forgotten.

The following morning she arrived unannounced at the mine.

'Mrs Kidd, are you going to work a miracle on the fortunes of the Black Water Colliery, or are you now ready to acknowledge that what I've told you is correct and there's no long term future for the place.' He tilted his head on one side and gave her a smug look. There was a dusting of sugar grains stuck to his upper lip and she glanced at his desk where there was a plate with a half eaten doughnut.

'You're quite right there may be no long term future for the place, but what is absolutely clear is that there is no future whatsoever for you. You are dismissed. Clear your desk. Hand over the keys and get out of here. I don't want to see you again anywhere near this mine. And consider yourself lucky I've decided not to call the police.'

'I don't understand.'

'Oh I think you understand perfectly.' She held up an empty wage packet. 'I don't know how long you've been robbing my husband blind. But it's over now. Get out of here and don't come back.'

Even allowing for the cessation of Robinson's embezzlement, Elizabeth reached the reluctant conclusion that the only option was to close the mine down. Her talks with local businessmen and other mine owners secured jobs for about half the men; the rest were going to have to try their own luck outside the area. Times were hard and all the signs were they were going to get harder.

Elizabeth understood now that, despite the amount of time her husband had spent at the mine, he'd never really grasped its economics. It was not surprising really, she reflected: he was a smallholder who'd got lucky with his gambling habit. He was not a seasoned businessman and the mining business was alien to him. What did surprise her was that he'd shown a stubbornness and compassion to his employees, refusing to behave as the other employers did, instead holding on and hoping that things would improve. She felt a new affection for him, for his naivety and his stubbornness. He may have become for a while a wealthy man, but she realised his heart had always been that of a working man.

Meanwhile the legal costs were running up and her conversation with the bank manager left her with the unequivocal conclusion that Jack Kidd's fortune was all but exhausted. He'd made generous settlements on Harriet and Will, spent significant sums purchasing land adjacent to Wilton's Creek and the declining fortunes of the colliery meant there was little left. Perhaps he'd known this? Perhaps he hadn't really cared? She decided to act now and worry about Kidd's reaction later. She accepted a good offer for Kinross House and the best she could get for Wilton's Creek and in their place rented a modest 4-room single storey house in the town. The buyer of Kinross House, a retired doctor from Sydney, was happy to take on Mr and Mrs Oates and the cook, so Elizabeth was able to walk away with a clear conscience and a much-reduced list of monthly outgoings. Mary agreed to accompany her and would be the only servant, helping prepare simple meals, and doing general housekeeping.

All the while, she worried about the looming trial. Her efforts to engage Kidd in discussion of his case were rebuffed. Finally Cody, the lawyer, sent a request for her to attend his chambers.

It was with a mixture of relief and trepidation that she mounted the steps to the large brick building a few yards from the Court House. It smelled of old books, leather and pipe tobacco. The reception room where the clerk told her to wait was sombre: the walls were painted in a deep forest green, broken up by heavy gilt-framed, badly executed portraits of old men in wigs and court robes and the floor was covered in a dark, burgundy, patterned carpet that seemed to suck in what little light there was in the room. A line of stiff backed, upright, wooden chairs with leather upholstered seats, were lined up against one wall, so that sitting there she felt under the scrutiny of the stern portraits on all the others.

After keeping her waiting half an hour, the elderly clerk returned and asked her to follow him. He led her through an anteroom into the large but equally gloomy office of Mr Herbert Cody KC. He rose from behind the piles of briefs stacked on the desktop and reached out to shake her hand, then motioned her brusquely to the chair in front of his desk.

'I'll try not to make this too protracted, Mrs Kidd.' His voice was arrogant and patrician in nature and she could detect a slight curl of the lip as he spoke.

'As you are doubtless aware, if your husband is found guilty of capital murder, there is an automatic death sentence which the judge will apply.'

She was about to speak, but he ignored her and continued, addressing his words to a point just above the top of her hat.

'I intend to make the case that Mr Kidd whilst in *actus reus* was not in *mens rea*. Which, to put in words that you will, I hope, understand, means that while he may have performed the act of killing Nathaniel Kidd he did not do so with criminal intent. I will draw the jury's attention to the fact that the victim was in the process of attacking your stepson with a knife and indeed occasioned serious bodily harm to the young man, hence your husband acted in an involuntary manner due to severe provocation and an instinctive desire to protect you both.'

'And how will the jury respond to that?'

'That, Mrs Kidd, is an unanswerable question. Every jury is different. How a member of a jury responds may depend on whether he ate a hearty breakfast, or likes the look of the defendant. It also depends on how the judge directs them. He will be guided by the law – but again if his toast was burnt or he has indigestion…' He chuckled and looked rather pleased with himself.

'You've made your point, Mr Cody. Please don't labour it. We're talking about my husband's life.'

The lawyer looked irritated and leaned back in his chair, directing his gaze at the ceiling.

'Your husband has indicated he does not wish you to be called as a witness.'

'He told me I couldn't be called. Something about spousal incompetence. Are you saying now that I could and my testimony might help him?'

'You can and it might, although juries tend to assume that a spouse will support her husband and may ignore what you say. On the other hand, if you don't testify, they could place a negative interpretation on it. If we do not call you to the stand, the prosecution cannot do so. That is what is meant by spousal incompetence. You can't be forced to testify against your spouse – but you can testify in favour. I imagine Mr Kidd was trying to save you from an ordeal when he told you that you would not be allowed to speak.'

'Then I will testify.'

'You realise that if you do, the prosecution will be permitted to cross examine you.'

'Let them. I have nothing to hide.'

CHAPTER TWENTY-FOUR

IN COURT

Elizabeth couldn't help herself: she didn't want to tempt fate but she couldn't stop feeling a growing sense that everything was going the right way. The court had been sitting for two days. The prosecutor, an elderly man who kept fiddling with his small moustache, seemed to have a great deal of difficulty finding what he was looking for in his papers. He appeared distracted, even bored by the proceedings and had not built a convincing case that Jack Kidd was a cold-blooded murderer. He kept pushing his ill-fitting wig higher up his brow, only for it to find its way back down again a few minutes later. It was clear from their expressions that the jury were unimpressed by his performance.

For the defence, Cody produced a procession of witnesses, some testifying to the good moral character of Jack Kidd and others to the thoroughly bad character of his eldest son. She had to hand it to Cody, pompous as he may have been, he was doing a good job. Nat Kidd was convincingly shown to have been a drunkard, a womaniser and a troublemaker. The general sentiment among the crowds packing the public gallery was that if he had been on fire, they would not have bothered to throw a bucket of water over him.

The latest witness was a woman who had been Nat's landlady for a few weeks, until she had thrown his bags onto the street after one drunken episode too many. Elizabeth studied the faces of the jury. The twelve men were listening intently and frowned in disapproval when the woman spoke of Nat Kidd's behaviour. It was definitely going well.

A pale and subdued William Kidd was called to the witness stand and answered everything put to him in a straightforward and polite manner that also appeared to be playing well with the jury. He described how he had ridden out to Wilton's Creek on his pony from McDonald Falls, in order to stay with his stepmother, who was mourning the death of her children. He told the court that when his father had found out Nat had returned to the area he didn't want to leave Mrs Kidd unprotected. On arriving at the smallholding, he found Nat physically attacking Mrs Kidd.

In response to Cody's questioning he said, 'He was holding her very roughly. She was struggling to get away and her blouse was torn open. I tried to drag him off her and that's all I remember until I woke up and found myself all bandaged up in bed.'

'Prior to this, when was the last occasion you saw your brother Nathaniel?'

'When Ma died. Seven years ago.'

'How was your relationship with your brother?'

'Same as everyone's. Bad. He was no good. Always picking fights and getting drunk. I used to look up to him when I was little but when he hit Ma I never wanted to see him again. Everyone thought he was dead; he's been gone all these years. Now he's brought trouble on my Pa.'

'Did you know your father was going to Wilton's Creek that day?'

'No, sir. He said he had to stay in town to sort things out at the mine.'

'You knew your brother was in the area? Did you expect to see him when you rode out to the house that day?'

'No, sir, but Pa told me he'd been sniffing round the place and had frightened Lizbeth, I mean Mrs Kidd, so he wanted me there just in case he showed up.'

'And were you armed when you went to Wilton's Creek?'

'No, sir.'

'But you told the court your father wanted you there to protect your step-mother from what sounds like a thoroughly unpleasant character.'

'He was my brother. I didn't expect he'd be coming at me with a knife. I thought if he turned up I'd just tell him to sling his hook. To be honest I didn't think he'd come back.'

'No further questions.'

The judge banged his gavel and adjourned the proceedings for lunch. Cody approached Elizabeth as they left the courtroom.

'I venture to say, Mrs Kidd, that matters are proceeding quite well. I will put you on the stand this afternoon. The questions will be exactly as we discussed and I want you to stick to the answers we have prepared. I don't imagine the prosecution will have a lot to ask you, based on their performance so far."

'I'm ready.'

'Very good. Very good.' He left the court, walking briskly, his clerk scuttling along in his wake.

Elizabeth stood tall in the witness box as she took her oath. Cody began by thanking her for agreeing to testify when she had so recently been bereaved of two children. The jury members looked at her with sympathy and there was a murmur around the courtroom from the public gallery.

'I will try to make this as brief as possible, Mrs Kidd, and I trust my learned friend will do the same if he has any questions.'

The Prosecution counsel, uncomfortable with making

an objection that could turn the jury against him, instead coughed loudly and pointedly and the judge reprimanded Cody. 'Mr Cody. I will be the one to advise Mr Wilson if I believe he is overtaxing the witness. Get on with it.' There was a susurrus of disapproval in the room and the members of the jury looked with a mixture of sympathy and curiosity at Elizabeth.

She told the court what had happened that day. When she described a raging Nat Kidd drawing a knife and stabbing his own brother, the jurors were transfixed.

Herbert Cody approached her and asked 'The victim had his back to the defendant when the shot was fired?'

'Yes.'

'Can you describe exactly what happened?'

'I saw a flash of metal in Nat Kidd's hand and realised it was a knife. William stumbled and fell and there was blood all over his shirt. I think I cried out and then heard a shot and Nat Kidd fell forward and landed on top of me. My husband pulled him off me and I realised he was dead. I saw the gun on the ground. I went to Will who was unconscious. My husband and I carried him into the house, then he checked that Nat was dead and went to fetch the doctor while I tried to stop the bleeding from Will's wound.'

'Mr Kidd made no attempt to escape?'

'Certainly not. He went to fetch the doctor. He'd saved my life and he was now concerned with saving William's. There was nothing to be done for Nat.'

Another murmur went around the courtroom and the judge banged his gavel angrily.

'Continue, Mrs Kidd.'

'The doctor arrived and treated William and my husband asked him if he would return to town to summon the constable, while we waited at Wilton's Creek with William. When the police arrived my husband went with them willingly.'

'He suggested to the doctor that the constable be called?'

'Yes, he did.'

'Thank you. No further questions.'

The prosecutor took Cody's place. As he began to cross-examine her, Elizabeth for the first time felt nervous. The rather ineffectual lawyer seemed to be finding his stride and his manner was more aggressive than it had been with any of the other witnesses.

'How long have you been married to Mr Kidd?'

'Objection!'

Immediately the judge responded. 'Overruled. It's a matter of fact. Let her answer.'

'Almost four years.'

'I can't help but notice, Mrs Kidd, that you are a very attractive woman and much younger than your husband.'

'Objection!' This time the judge reprimanded the prosecution and directed the jury to ignore the comment.

'Were you happily married?'

The judge held his hand up, anticipating Cody as he rose again to his feet. 'Mr Wilson I am struggling to see the pertinence of this line of questioning.'

'Your Lordship, I am trying to establish motive. I intend to demonstrate that Mr Kidd killed his son in a fit of jealousy because the victim was having a relationship with Mrs Kidd.'

There were gasps around the packed courtroom.

'That's absurd! How dare you!' Elizabeth cried out.

The judge banged his gavel and called for order.

At that moment, the door at the back of the court swung open and a woman entered. Harriet was dressed in black, wearing an elegant wool dress with a matching coat and a fur stole slung nonchalantly over the collar. She stopped in the middle of the aisle and, pointing towards Elizabeth, called out, 'That woman should be on trial not my father. She's an adulteress and she's responsible for my brother's death. My father is trying to protect her – but she is the guilty one. She destroyed my marriage and now she's destroying my father's life.'

The judge and the two lawyers looked at Harriet Kidd in astonishment, before the judge sprang to attention and began to bang his gavel angrily. At this point the court ushers, who had been as stunned as the rest of the assembled audience, jumped into action and began to drag her from the court.

The judge banged the gavel again and signalled to the ushers to wait. 'Young woman, if I hear another outburst like that from you, you'll be thrown into the cells for contempt of this court. Now wait outside, until I'm ready for you.'

Turning to the prosecuting counsel, he said, 'Mr Wilson, in the light of what has just been said, inappropriate as the young lady's interruption has been, I suppose you will want some time to consider potential new evidence?'

The man nodded. 'Yes, your Honour.'

'In which case the court will adjourn until 2 o'clock tomorrow afternoon.'

'Your honour, I was unaware of this lady until just now. I've never met her before. May I request a little more time than that?' Wilson said.

'2 o'clock tomorrow. And if I hear any more from you it will be 9 o'clock tomorrow morning.'

'Yes, your Honour.'

Cody was on his feet, his face flushed with anger.

'Your Honour. This is not acceptable! This woman has not been declared as a prosecution witness. The defence has had no opportunity to prepare for her testimony.'

'Don't blame me for your own inefficiency, Mr Cody. I'm surprised at you. You usually have all the ground covered. The prosecution has a right to explore every avenue to prove its case. One man has died and another is on trial. I think we owe it to both of them to ensure all the evidence is examined.'

Harriet sat down in the witness box after taking the oath and lowered her eyes, looking fragile and wistful. She fumbled in her velvet clutch bag for a handkerchief, which, from then on, she squeezed between her hands and used very convincingly to dab at her dry eyes, punctuating these actions with the occasional little sigh.

After giving her name, she turned to the judge and said 'Please, your honour, I would like to apologise for what happened yesterday. I didn't wish to show contempt for the court, but I was very distressed by what's been happening to my family and in particular to my dear father.'

The judge nodded and waved his hand at the prosecutor to move on.

'Mrs Winterbourne. Please tell the court what you know about the relationship between your brother Nathaniel and Mrs Kidd.'

Cody was on his feet immediately.

The judge waved him aside impatiently, and then turned to the prosecuting counsel. 'Mr Wilson, I will indulge you for a moment but unless you demonstrate quickly that this line of questioning is more than hearsay I will ask for it to be stricken from the record and I will be seeing you afterwards in my chambers. Mrs Winterbourne, you may answer.'

'My stepmother was having sexual relations with my husband. When I found out I told my brother, Nathaniel, and he confronted her with it.'

There were gasps in the courtroom.

'She was the cause of the breakdown of my own marriage. My husband showed no interest in me and walked out on me soon after we were married.' She let out a strangled sob and gazed misty-eyed at the jury.

'I didn't know what to do or whom to turn to. I was at a loss to understand why he didn't love me and I was all alone in Sydney, where he left me on our honeymoon.' Again she feigned sobbing into her silk handkerchief and the disapproval of Elizabeth from the people in the public gallery was now apparent.

'I hadn't seen my older brother in many years. We met by chance in Sydney and we were both so happy to be reunited. He had run away to join the army when he was still a boy and we thought he was dead. He was a brave man and was decorated for his bravery at Gallipoli.' A buzz of voices went round the room and the judge hammered his gavel again. 'I was desolate after my husband left me and too embarrassed and ashamed to go back to McDonald Falls and tell my father. I told Nat that our father had married a woman I believed to be a fortune hunter and she was the reason my husband left me. I'd always suspected there was a relationship between them. I believe they knew each other before either came to McDonald Falls and they plotted to get their hands on my father's money.'

The murmuring in the gallery reached a crescendo, forcing the judge to bang his gavel again impatiently. 'Any more noise and I'll throw the lot of you out of court. Carry on, Mrs Winterbourne.'

'My brother was very distressed at what I told him and decided to go to McDonald Falls to investigate. The day before he was killed, he telephoned me to say he had come upon that woman and my husband together. He told me terrible things. He had seen them together...' Her voice broke.

'Objection. Hearsay!' Cody was on his feet.

'The evidence is admissible where the relevant witness is dead. I will allow it' said the judge. Cody sat down, his face etched with anger.

Harriet sobbed again and started to cough. The judge signalled for the usher to bring her a glass of water.

'Mrs Winterbourne, please don't distress yourself. We can take a break now and reconvene later.'

'Please, Your Honour, I'd rather get this over. It's painful and I don't think I'll have the strength to do this again.'

She squeezed the handkerchief and turned to face the judge, lip trembling. 'He saw them together at the house at Wilton's Creek. They didn't know he was there. He saw them through the window. They were naked. They were having … sexual inter...' Again her voice broke and the judge nodded sympathetically to her.

'Go on, my dear. What happened next?'

'Nat told my father what they were up to but he refused to believe it.' Her voice rose. 'That woman has always had a terrible hold on Pa. He's been hoodwinked. He believed her rather than his own son.'

The judge appeared to be as moved by Harriet's testimony as the men of the jury evidently were. He called to the usher, 'Bring the witness more water.'

After further judicious patting of the eyes with her handkerchief and a few sips of water, Harriet continued. 'Nat was going to Wilton's Creek to try to persuade her to go away and leave our family alone. He was going to appeal to her better judgement and good nature … he didn't realise she doesn't have any. She just wants my father's money.'

She buried her face in her hands.

From that point on, Elizabeth observed the proceedings in a daze. She sensed the hostility in the eyes of the jury. The people around her in the courtroom were whispering and nudging each other. Many were local townspeople, who only a few months ago had written letters of condolence at the loss of the children and now looked at her as though she were the reincarnation of Jezebel. She looked over at Jack Kidd in the dock. He was expressionless, staring ahead as though blind to all the emotion in the room.

Cody was frowning. He approached the bench and said something to the judge, who summoned the prosecution counsel to join them. After a few moments, the judge adjourned the proceedings for the day.

As the crowd spilled out of the room, noisily discussing what had unfolded, Cody pulled Elizabeth aside.

'This is not good at all. Not good at all. Now, before you protest your innocence, Mrs Kidd, I don't want to know. There's no way we can prove it either way, but the inference of your alleged infidelity is enough to swing the jury against you.'

Elizabeth did not know what to say. She felt her cheeks burning and knew she would be unable to deny the truth about her liaison with Winterbourne if asked.

'I am about to meet the judge and Wilson in chambers. I will be arguing that the last witness's testimony should be struck from the record. Convincing that old fool is unlikely. One never knows what Justice Hargold will do. He rejoices in being unpredictable and is the personification of the expression 'a law unto himself'. Even if we succeed and he directs the jury to ignore Mrs Winterbourne's testimony, I doubt they will. Every last man of them now believes your husband has a motive for pre-meditatively killing his son.'

'What motive? He was protecting William and me. You know what Nat Kidd was capable of!'

'I agree with you, Mrs Kidd, but I fear the gentlemen of the jury won't. As far as they are concerned, Jack Kidd killed his own son, a war veteran and hero, in a fit of anger because he maligned your good name. As so many witnesses have already testified, there was no love lost between father and son. I have very carefully built up our testimony to demonstrate that Nat Kidd was a thoroughly bad character, who merited no familial love or concern, but that very strategy has made it all too easy for them to believe that years of pent-up anger and frustration have culminated in the son impugning the honour and reputation of the stepmother. The prosecution has sown the seeds that Jack Kidd set out for Wilton's Creek with the intent of killing his son.'

'But that's wrong!' Elizabeth gave a plaintive wail.

The following morning one last witness was called. Doctor Reilly made his way to the stand, shaking his head sadly as he passed Kidd in the dock.

Cody ran through his questioning quickly. The doctor confirmed the general good character of Jack and the thoroughly bad one of Nat. He confirmed what Elizabeth had said about Kidd willingly waiting for the doctor to return with the constable. Cody thanked him and sat down.

Elizabeth had started to hope that things might swing their way again, with this final testimony fresh in the jurors' minds, until Wilson began to question the witness. 'Doctor Reilly, when you attended the scene of the crime on September 2nd last, what was the purpose of your visit?'

'I was asked by Jack Kidd to treat his son William Kidd for a knife wound.'

'When you arrived at Wilton's Creek, what did you see?'

'There was what appeared to be a body under an oil skin outside the house but whoever it was, he was clearly beyond my care so I went inside to treat William Kidd. Mrs Kidd had done a good job cleaning the wound already, so I made sure he was comfortable, treated the wound with antiseptics and gave him something to manage his pain.'

'What happened then?'

'Mr Kidd showed me the body outside the house in front of the veranda steps and I confirmed that the man was dead.'

'Did you recognise the victim?'

'It was Nathaniel Kidd, Mr Kidd's eldest son. I hadn't seen him in several years, but I've known the family for years and I knew at once it was he.'

'Did the defendant tell you how his son came to be lying dead there?'

'He said he'd shot him.'

'And you sir? What did you say to that?'

'I expressed surprise. I examined the body and ascertained he had been shot in the back. It was obvious that Mr Kidd had mistaken his son for an intruder.'

'Did you put that assumption to the defendant?'

The doctor hesitated, then replied. 'I think I might have done.'

'How did he reply?'

The doctor hesitated again and looked around the court as though seeking deliverance from the need to answer the question.

'I've known Jack Kidd for twenty-three years and he's a good man.'

'Answer the question, please, Dr Reilly.'

'He told me he knew it was his son.'

'Did you ask why he had come to shoot his own son dead?'

'Yes.'

The judge looked impatient and spoke tetchily to the doctor 'Please answer the question, Doctor. And Mr Wilson, please take more trouble in crafting your questions. I don't appreciate having my time wasted.' He waved his hand at Dr Reilly.

'He said he should have killed Nat years ago; that he was a bad person and had it coming to him.'

There were gasps throughout the packed courtroom.

Wilson smelt blood and moved close to the witness box, 'Let me be sure I've understood this, Dr Reilly. The defendant said to you *"I should have killed him years ago"*?'

The doctor looked down then brushed his hand across his brow. 'Yes.'

'Did the defendant appear to be distressed by what had happened?'

The judge looked annoyed. 'Mr Wilson, you are leading

the witness. This is the last time I'll ask you to choose your words more carefully.'

The prosecution counsel tugged at his moustache and rephrased his enquiry. 'Can you tell the jury how Mr Kidd reacted to what had happened?'

'He was distressed. Very concerned about the lad. Yes, worried for the boy.'

'That is not what I meant, Doctor. Let me make myself clearer. How did the defendant react to the fact that he had shot dead his elder son? In the back. Did he show any signs of anguish, remorse or contrition?'

The doctor paused before answering and looked apologetically towards Elizabeth. 'No, he did not.'

'No further questions.'

As each barrister made his concluding arguments, Elizabeth listened with a growing sense of alarm. Harriet's intervention had blown a hole through all Cody's carefully constructed arguments and Elizabeth's good name with the jury. The doctor's testimony had made it worse.

Inside her coat pocket she found the little stone talisman Michael had given her and squeezed it tightly in her palm. She closed her eyes and tried to shut out the sound of Wilson's voice. The rather bored drone, with which he had started the proceedings, was replaced by a dramatic rise and fall in timbre, as he strove to deliver an oratorical perfomance.

He concluded with the words 'I put it to you, gentlemen of the jury, that the defendant on the afternoon of September 2nd 1924, with malice aforethought, set out for his smallholding at Wilton's Creek, knowing his elder son to be there and with the clear intent to take his life, harbouring a long felt grudge against his son and disbelieving his story, in favour of that of his young, attractive and wayward wife...'

'I must object' Cody said. 'Mrs Kidd and her reputation are not on trial today.'

The judge turned to the jury. 'Ignore what Counsel has just said about Mrs Kidd being wayward.'

The corrective words served instead to reinforce the message.

The prosecution counsel continued. 'Fearful of the scandal that his son might unleash on the reputation of his wife, he cold-bloodedly shot him in the back. Yes, I am sure the fact that Nathaniel Kidd had drawn a knife upon his brother was cause in itself for the father to seek to protect the younger, well-loved son, from the older, estranged one, but I put it to you that the defendant's prompt arrival with a shotgun at the ready is a clear indication of malice aforethought.'

He paused in front of the jurors and leaned his arms on the front of their bench and cast his eyes around them all in turn, before pulling himself up to his not very substantial full height and puffing his narrow chest out as far as it would go. 'Gentlemen, you may feel that the defence has painted a picture of the character of the deceased as a less than attractive person. That may be true. But I remind you that it is not the deceased who is on trial here. Whether he had a tendency to walk a little too often on the wilder side of life is not the point. He was twenty-two years old, fit and healthy and with his whole life ahead of him. A man who, whatever his faults, had risked his life for King and country. Who knows, once those wild oats were all sown, he may have become a man of honour and character? Perhaps a man of the law, a man of the cloth, or maybe just an honest and humble smallholder? We will never know. I repeat, we will never know. And we will never know because his own father was blinded by anger and fear that a scandal might not only cost him his own reputation but possibly also cost him his pretty young wife.

'My esteemed colleague will try to convince you that this was a spontaneous act to defend his younger son and his wife, but I say again, gentlemen, why then did he arrive on the scene with his gun at the ready? Why did he not call out to the deceased and ask him to back off and drop the knife? Doctor Reilly, a long-standing friend and advisor of the Kidd family, has testified that the defendant was without remorse or contrition when he realised he had shot his own son. Indeed the defendant was so unrepentant that he declared – *"I should have done it years ago."* Think about that, gentlemen: what clearer admission of full, unambiguous guilt can you have than his own words *"I should have done it years ago"*.

'Nat Kidd was outnumbered. The defendant could easily have pulled the victim away from ...that woman... instead of executing him in cold blood – shooting him down. To murder his own son, his first-born child and to do it when his back was turned. He shot him in the back, straight through the heart. Had he intended just to stop the attack he could have shot him in a leg or an arm. No, gentlemen, this was no spontaneous act of a man defending his family, it was the cruel and despicable, premeditated murder of a young man in the prime of his life.'

With that, he sat down with a thump of his fist on the desk. Clapping started in the back of the court, but was immediately silenced by the judge.

She knew there was no hope for Kidd now. Cody, with all his Latin legal jargon, was no match for the rhetoric of the prosecution counsel with his flagrant use of emotion. The judge looked bored and ready to send the jury away. Elizabeth felt he too had been swayed by the tide of emotion in the court. She knew the hope was forlorn of him directing the jury to focus on the facts, rather than what her untrained mind felt was circumstantial evidence. While there had never been any doubt that Kidd had pulled the trigger, she was sure that until Harriet's intervention, he would have been seen as acting in defence of his family and would have been exonerated. Now she knew that even the lesser offence of manslaughter, which the judge had asked the jury to consider alongside murder, was looking like a very long shot.

Her fears were grounded. The foreman, a burly man with a full beard, stood to attention when the jury returned after barely an hour's deliberation, and delivered the verdict in stentorian tones. 'Guilty!'

There was no time to take it in before the judge reached beneath his bench and pulled out the black cap and placed it at what was almost a jaunty angle atop his wig.

'John Vernon Kidd, having been found guilty by a jury of your peers to the crime of murder of Nathaniel John Kidd on September 2nd nineteen hundred and twenty-four, the sentence of the court is that you will be taken from this place to a lawful prison, where you will be hanged by the neck until you are dead and thereafter your body buried within the precincts of the prison; and may the Lord have mercy upon your soul.'

CHAPTER TWENTY-FIVE

SACRIFICE

Lying in bed that night, unable to believe the import of the judge's words, she allowed herself some self-pity. Didn't she deserve to feel sorry for herself? As she faced the prospect of Kidd going to the gallows, she realised she did care for him in a strange, unfathomable way. Yes, surely she had the right to shed some tears into her pillow and rail against the unfairness of it all.

The night was long and sleep eluded her. As she tossed and turned in the big empty bed, she had never felt so alone. Everyone she'd ever cared for had been taken from her except for William and Verity. Was she cursed? Bringing disaster upon all those fool enough to get close to her? Her nerve endings felt exposed, painful, raw.

She missed Kidd. His gruffness and monosyllabic responses. His rough unromantic caresses. The long periods of silence and the barked orders. She had felt wanted and, recently, needed. He had a strange way of showing it – or rather he actively tried to cover it up, but she knew he'd become reliant on her and there was no mistaking the physical need he had for her. Eventually, she reflected, it was probably inevitable that such a dependency would give rise to some reciprocal feeling. It was not love and never could be, but there was a very real fondness on her part for him.

The icy chill she'd experienced when the judge pronounced his terrible sentence passed through her again whenever she thought about what awaited Kidd. The words "Hanged by the neck until you are dead" conjured up terrifying images. She tried to put them out of her head and to banish the thought of that thin, wiry man dangling from a rope. Would it be a fast death? She knew enough to know it depended on the calibre of the executioner and how carefully he made his calculations.

'Stop it!' she cried aloud to herself. Until he stepped onto the gallows, she would not give up hope or stop fighting. After the sentencing, everything had happened very quickly, but Mr Cody said he would be reviewing the grounds for appeal. The case for the prosecution had been won by Harriet Kidd and the testimony of Doctor Reilly had been damning. The poor man appeared devastated when he left the court, unable to look Elizabeth in the eye. She could not blame him. He had spoken the truth under oath. What choice had he?

As these thoughts went through her mind, Elizabeth felt a new sense of purpose. There was work to be done. She would meet with Cody – haunt his chambers until he had explored every avenue for an appeal and prepared a case that would at least succeed in commutation of the sentence to manslaughter.

As the sun rose, she sprang out of bed, impatient and filled with new energy. She would go to Sydney and find a way to do her own research in the legal library at Sydney Law School. She would leave no stone unturned. What else could she do? There was still no word from Michael and she started to realise there never would be. It was three months since he'd gone. She refused to doubt his love for her, but she started to suspect an accident had befallen him. A bleak feeling of loss haunted her. She had held his love in her grasp and let it slip away. There was nothing she could do about it and rather than confront the prospect of a future without him, she threw all her energy, anger and disappointment into getting a retrial and reprieve for Kidd.

It was too early to call on Cody yet. The sun was barely up. She decided to take a leisurely bath before forcing down some breakfast. The little house where she and Will now lived lacked the scale and splendour of Kinross House, but, unlike Wilton's Creek, it boasted a rather temperamental water heater. She lay back in the bath, watching the steam rise as she soaped herself. She ran the washcloth over her body, then with a shock of realisation, sat bolt upright.

How could she have failed to notice? She'd been pre-occupied with the trial. Her thoughts raced ahead, as she realised all the signs were there. Her stomach was slightly swollen. Since Kidd's arrest, she'd lost her appetite and her clothes had felt quite loose – but then the styles of the moment were loose around the middle anyway. She ran her hand over her breasts. Her nipples felt tender. It must be weeks since her last period. Grabbing a towel she scrambled out of the bath and dripped her way into the bedroom and to the small escritoire where she kept her diary.

'Rack your brains woman! When was the last time?' she asked herself.

She had not menstruated since some time before the children's deaths. She had failed to register the changes in her own body. Her heart skipped a beat at the prospect of another child. She could not wait to tell Kidd. He had looked so defeated in the brief moments she was allowed to share with him after his sentencing. He had barely spoken, just squeezed her hand as he stared into the middle distance. But now another new life coming would give him hope and the will to fight on. She was all the more determined that he would not die.

The meeting with Mr Cody did not go well. The barrister had taken the loss of the case to heart and his annoyance about being bested by the Crown seemed to bother him more than the fate of his client. He kept Elizabeth waiting for almost an hour before granting her a brief interview.

'Mrs Kidd, I regret that the trial did not go our way. The Crown started off making a very poor fist of it and I was hopeful that we had won the jury over. I am disappointed you failed to alert me to the potential for damaging testimony that your stepdaughter represented.'

'I had no idea myself. She had refused all contact with the family and indicated to a friend of the family that she would not testify on her father's behalf.'

'It's unfortunate she did not stick to that conviction, as she proved to be, even unwittingly, a hostile witness. Had I the opportunity to meet with her beforehand, we could have called her as a defence witness and tutored her in the importance of keeping her feelings about you to herself if she wished to avoid the eventuality of her father's conviction. Her accusations about you were a critical factor in turning the jury against your husband. Whilst her evidence was circumstantial, added to that of the doctor and our case was lost.'

'Can we appeal?'

'Yes. I can argue again that her testimony should have been ruled out as hearsay, but that of Doctor Reilly was damning in its own right.'

'What my husband said to the doctor was spoken in the heat of the moment. He was distraught. He was in shock. He thought Will might be mortally wounded. He would never have killed him had Nat not attacked William. It was a moment of fear and desperation to save William and me. Didn't you say there was a difference between the act and the intent?'

'Indeed, but the evidence from the doctor that your husband long harboured a wish to kill his son....'

'It was the heat of the moment. He was anxious for William and in shock at what happened. It wasn't a statement of intent.'

'Possibly.'

'If there is any possibility we must take it.'

'Then there's the matter of the shotgun. Your husband came to Wilton's Creek prepared.'

'For heaven's sake! He keeps a gun in the truck or the cart all the time. He spends half his time in the bush. If possession of a shotgun is evidence of intent to kill, they'd have to arrest most of the men in this town.'

Cody scowled. 'Is there anything else we might use?'

Elizabeth swallowed then spoke. 'Harriet Winterbourne uses drugs and is a heavy drinker.'

Cody raised an eyebrow. 'What kind of drugs?'

'Cocaine.'

'That could help discredit her as a witness. I'll have someone look into it and see what we can gather. Otherwise I intend to discuss the matter with my colleagues. It may be appropriate to assign someone else to conduct the appeal.'

'I thought you would do it?'

'I plan to pass the case to Mr Somerton, a promising young fellow, keen to cut his teeth on a challenging case.'

'Cut his teeth? Are you telling me he's some kind of trainee lawyer?'

'I would not use the word trainee, Mrs Kidd. Mr Somerton did extremely well in the bar examinations and is a competent and intelligent junior barrister. All of us at Bracket, Fincham & Cody have high expectations of him.'

'Mr Cody, I am expecting a child. My husband doesn't know yet, but I intend to tell him when I see him and make him understand that he has everything to live for and that you and your firm will stop at nothing to prove he is innocent of premeditated murder. Even if he has to serve a long prison sentence for manslaughter, I want him to know that at the end of it his child will be there beside me, waiting to welcome him home. Do you honestly expect me to tell him his barrister believes there's so little hope that he's going to assign a trainee to plead his case and he'll probably never live to see his child born, let alone have a chance of getting to know him or her? And what am I to tell my child? – "You're the orphan of an executed murderer, whose own lawyer didn't believe his case was worth fighting for"?'

Cody leaned back in his chair and raised his eyebrows at the tirade.

'First of all, Mrs Kidd, may I offer my congratulations for your forthcoming happiness.'

'My forthcoming happiness? How can I even think of happiness when my husband is condemned to die for saving the lives of his wife and son?'

'Very well. I will discuss this with my partners.'

'If it's about money?'

The lawyer's lip curled, as if money was a word too coarse to be uttered in these hallowed chambers.

'You've made your points well, Mrs Kidd. We will make the appeal and I will lead the case. Mr Somerton can assist me.'

'I intend to assist you myself too. Rest assured I will be studying every point of law in the book until I find a way to prove my husband has been wronged. I will be assiduous in sharing my findings with you.'

'Mrs Kidd, that will not be necessary.' Again the lip curled. 'We will as always, be rigorous in our endeavours.'

367

'We shall see.'

She rose and stretched her hand to him. 'Good day, Mr Cody.'

Will arrived home soon after she returned from the lawyer's chambers. He had been avoiding her since his outburst in the garden. During the court proceedings he'd sat apart, reluctant to talk. Elizabeth was puzzled at this out of character behaviour, but concluded he was distressed about his father.

He walked into the small drawing room, wearing his oilskin jacket and holding a woollen cap in his hands. He stood in front of the fireplace.

'Lizbeth, I'm going away.'

'What?' she tried to hide the rising panic in her voice.

'I'm going to sea.'

'What? Why? What about your father?'

'I can't do anything for him now. I can't stand to see him die when he did nothing wrong but save my life. It isn't fair.'

'We're going to help him, Will! You and I. I've just seen Mr Cody. There are grounds for appeal. We'll get the sentence commuted! He won't die, Will!'

'You and the lawyer can get him off. There's nothing I can do. I'm just a simple lad with no book learning. I've wasted enough of my life and I've made my mind up now. I'm going to go to sea. It's what I've always wanted. I have to get away from here. I want...' he hesitated.

'What, Will? What do you want?'

He stared down at his feet and she saw the blush rising up his neck to his cheeks.

'Tell me, Will.'

He raised his eyes to hers and spoke in what was little more than a whisper, 'I want to get away from you.'

'From me? I thought we were friends.'

The young man snorted. 'Oh yes, we're friends.'

'So what do you mean? I don't understand.'

'It's all we'll ever be.'

'I know I'm not your real mother, but I'm as fond of you as if you were my own son. And right now we've only got each other and I need you to help me get through this terrible time.'

'I don't want to be your son, damn it.'

'Will. Please!'

'Was Hat lying about you and Michael then? Tell me the truth.'

'Will...'

'You don't have to. I can see it in your face.'

'Will. You need to understand...'

'Understand? Yes I understand perfectly. I can't even blame you, Lizbeth. Pa's an old man. Michael would be much more your cup of tea. But I can't stand that you and he have both been lying to me. I trusted you both. He was my friend. And there you were sneaking behind my back and the old man's. Not to mention Hattie's.'

'It wasn't like that, Will. We never lied to you. Hattie had it all wrong. Michael and I did discover we had feelings for each other, and that's why he went away. I'm here for your father. And your father needs you too.'

'I love you, Lizbeth. There I've said it now. I can't keep it bottled up any longer. I know you don't think of me that way. And I can't bear to think of my old man having you. And if I stay here I'll just be wishing for him to be dead and I don't want to wish that 'cause he's my Pa and he saved my life and I don't want him to go to the gallows. But sometimes I can't stop myself from hating him. And if he does die I know now you'll never love me anyway because of Michael. So I've made my mind up. I'm going away. Maybe I'll come back one day and you'll see me differently. Maybe then you'll look at me as a man not as a young lad like you do now.'

369

'Oh, Will!'

'Don't feel sorry for me. I couldn't bear that.'

'You believe you love me, but I promise you it's just a crush. Once you get out in the world and meet some young women you'll realise that I'm right. I'm years older than you, Will. You can do better than an old girl like me!'

'Don't mock me.'

'I'm sorry, Will. I don't intend to.'

'You think I'm just a snot-nosed boy who'll grow out of it. But I'm not and I won't.'

'I know you're not, Will. You're a wonderful person and one of the people I care most for in the world, but you will grow out of it. I love you as a mother or a big sister even, but I can never love you as a wife. And anyway, you deserve better. I know you'll find happiness because you're such a good and loveable person – not to mention a good-looking fellow. Your time will come.'

'Maybe it will. Maybe it won't. I'm not staying here waiting to find out. I've had enough of these mountains. There's no future for me here. There'll be only bad memories of all the bad things that happened. Mikey's dead. Su's dead. Hat's dead to me now after what she's done. Michael's gone. Nat's dead and Pa's sentenced to death. Then there's you and Michael. I've had enough. I want a new life. You're right, I'm young and my future's ahead, so I'm going to go and find it. I'm going to sea and I'll sail across the world. I want to look at those stars in the North skies that you told me about. Maybe I'll go to England or America. Who knows?'

'Oh, Will.'

'Don't try to change my mind, Lizbeth. I've had plenty of time to think about it and it's what I want.'

Elizabeth wondered whether to tell him about the baby she was carrying. A new brother or sister might change things for Will. But she concluded that it would be rubbing salt in his wounds. She'd wait and see if he changed his mind in a few days.

He spoke again. 'You'll say goodbye to Pa for me? I don't want to see him in gaol. I want to remember him as a free man. I've written a letter to him. It'll be full of mistakes I know – never was much good at reading and writing – but he'll understand. Give it to him for me, will you?'

She took the letter.

'If anyone can get him out, you can, Lizbeth. You don't need me for that. Tell him I said thank you. Tell him I'll try my best to make him proud of me. Then maybe one day...'

'When do you leave?'

'Now. I'll take the pony and ride her slowly down to Sydney, then I can sell her to help me get by, till I find a ship to take me. There's the money Pa gave me when Hat got wed. I can't touch it till I come of age, but I'll get by on my rabbit skin money till then. I told you that's what I was saving it for.'

'But you know nothing of the sea.'

'And you knew nothing of the bush, but you managed to get by. I'll cope. If my Pa taught me anything he taught me to look after myself.'

Elizabeth had to wait days before she was granted permission to visit Kidd. She was shocked at the change in him in the short time since the trial. He'd shrunk in on himself, like an old and infirm man. His eyes were empty, showing no flicker of emotion. His skin had a greyish hue and he had the beginnings of a scraggy beard, flecked with white.

She tried to hide her shock and instinctively reached out for his hand, only for the guard to snap at her: 'No contact!'

She and Kidd sat down on opposite sides of the small table. The guard rolled a cigarette and slouched against the wall. It was so hard to have a private conversation with a stranger watching, ready to pounce if she gave any sign of so much as grazing her hand over her husband's.

'Don't come any more, Elizabeth. You've done your duty by me. I don't want you coming here any more.'

'Of course I'll come. I'm sorry it's taken me so long – this was the earliest they'd let me visit. Your appeal is lodged so they've told me I can see you once a fortnight, but Mr Cody will keep me informed of how you're doing, as he can see you whenever he needs.'

'I don't want you to come. I don't like seeing you in this place.'

'I like even less to see *you* in this place, but, God willing, Mr Cody will succeed with the appeal and get the verdict revoked and you'll be free again.'

Kidd looked at her sadly. 'I'm not going to be free again. And I don't want the appeal. I killed my son and now I'll take the punishment given me. You'll be a free woman again, Elizabeth. I'm sorry there won't be much money left for you. I don't want the appeal to go ahead. You've thrown enough money at lawyers. William will be all right when his trust comes through. What's left is for you.'

'Don't talk like that.'

'I know I've not been a good husband. I know I'm not good at talking. And I know I'm not in the same class as you with your fancy education. You're a lovely woman, Elizabeth, and you've been a good wife. When they give me the drop you'll be free to do what you want.'

She started to speak but he held his hand up.

'Let me have my say, woman. I did wrong to force you to wed me. I took advantage of your father and then I took advantage of you. But I fell for you as soon as your father showed me your photograph. I'd never seen anyone like you. I wanted you, but I wanted to punish him too. It felt as though he was looking down his nose at me and I wanted to show him and the world that I was as good as he was.

I've had plenty of time to think about what I've done and I want to say I'm sorry.'

'You don't...'

'Damn it, woman, let me finish! I've said bad things to you and I'm sorry. I had no right to call you the names I called you. My first wife was a good woman and a good mother but she wasn't like you. When you... you know... in bed...when you seemed to take pleasure... you know what I'm saying... it was different. She acted like it was one of the household chores like hanging the washing out or scrubbing the floor. It was different with you and I'm sorry that I didn't show you more kindness. But you need to know you made me happy. I'm sorry I didn't have the guts to show you at the time. I know you don't love me. And don't try to lie to me that you do, Elizabeth. But I like to think there's a connection between us. An understanding. You've been good to me and I'm thankful, but now I want you to go and get on with your life. Find some happiness. You deserve it.'

'Oh, Jack.'

'My daughter wrote me a letter. Said she was sorry that what she said had made things worse for me. She asked to visit me, but I've told her I don't want to see her again. I can't forgive her for the lies she told about you and Mick and the shame she brought on us all. I should never have pushed Winterbourne into marrying her. I knew she was a basket of trouble and I can't say I'm surprised he walked out on her. She's had all she'll get from me. There's not much left but it goes to you and Will.'

Elizabeth began to sob.

'I'm not worth your tears, girl. You've done enough crying for our baby girl and the little lad and your father. Don't waste your tears on me. I don't deserve them.'

'Jack, we're having another baby. I found out the day after the trial. I've seen Doctor Reilly and it's due in five months. I'd been so preoccupied I hadn't even noticed.'

Kidd looked away.

'Did you hear what I said? We're having a baby! You have everything to live for. A new life. New hope! We"ll fight to get you free. This baby is a sign. You mustn't despair. One day you'll walk out of here a free man and I'll be waiting with our child to take you home.'

He looked at her, his eyes filled with tears.

'You've made me happy, Elizabeth. I'll treasure the thought of the baby in the time I have left. But it's all the more reason why I don't want to appeal. I want you to bring the child up somewhere no one will know its father was a murderer. Don't let the child know either. Say I died of a heart attack. Do that for me, Elizabeth?'

He took her hand and this time the guard looked the other way.

'I'm ready. Just let me get it over with. I told Cody this morning to drop the appeal. He said you'd never agree, but I want you to accept my decision. I feel old. I'm tired. If it happened again I'd do the same thing. That boy had the devil in him. He was responsible for his mother's death and I wasn't going to let him do for you too. I'm ready to take my punishment. I'll die happy now, knowing you'll have a child to love; a kid who'll grow up clever and smart and speak well like you. I'll have fathered at least one child with a chance of leading a life that's better than its old man's.'

Elizabeth swallowed and fought back her tears.

'Will you do that for me, Elizabeth? Please?'

'I can't let you give in like this.'

'Do this for me. I've had my innings. Say goodbye today and don't come again, especially not for the end. I don't want you here for that.'

He squeezed her hands and bent to kiss them.

'Go now. Be happy. Live long. Bring up my child and tell it that its Pa would have loved it. Loved it almost as much as he loved its mother. Will you do that for me, Elizabeth? I beg you.'

CHAPTER TWENTY-SIX

GLEBE HARBOUR

She was drunk. That wasn't unusual, but there had been a kind of desperation in her drinking tonight. The money had run out. So had her so-called friends, even Tommie. She'd expected him to stand by her. After all hadn't she kept him in champagne and cocaine for the last twelve months? When the others dumped her after her father was executed, he had been a constant presence. He chivvied her, tried to cheer her, and reassured her that she was not to blame for what happened. He coaxed her into leaving the house and accompanied her on visits to drinking dives. But now that the money had all gone he too disappeared into the ether and no longer answered her calls. The only person who had any time for her these days was Verity, telephoning faithfully each week. She had offered to take her in, but Harriet couldn't face the prospect of returning to McDonald Falls, where everyone knew her as Jack Kidd's daughter. So she had stayed in Sydney but now the bailiffs had called and she had to quit the house before the end of the week or somehow find the rent.

How had it come to this? Maybe she should try and find her husband? The divorce wasn't through yet so she could try to search for him. But she couldn't even drum up the cash to buy a ticket. Besides, she didn't know where to start looking and even if she found him Michael wouldn't want anything to do with her. Not after the things she'd said to him. And being broke didn't change how she felt about him.

Today she had intended to find new lodgings. Unable to afford to stay in Potts Point she pawned what was left of her jewellery and was looking for a room in Glebe Harbour. The area was very run down and depressing, the houses small and squalid-looking and the people out of work and down at heel and Harriet found the prospect of living among them a dismal one. She sought consolation in a bar and now she could barely stand on her feet.

The night was hot and sultry, with barely any breeze and she felt lethargic. As she stumbled along the edge of Blackwattle Bay, she noticed the full moon. Its light spread out over the surface of the harbour like molten ore against the dark night waters. She sat down at the water's edge, kicking off her shoes and pulling off her stockings to dangle her legs in the cool water. She remembered how she used to do this as a small child on hot days in the billabong near Wilton's Creek with Will and her mother.

She began to cry, big, silent tears that flowed unstoppably, almost blinding her, so that all she could see was the blurry, yellow brightness of the moon on top of the dark water. It danced on the surface and she stared at it through her tears as though hypnotised. She still had the remains of a bottle of gin and took a swig, feeling the burning warmth of the liquor as it went down her throat. She hurled the empty bottle into the water and watched the ripples break up the orb of the moon's reflection, until it settled back into a calm circle again.

Then she saw her. Reflected in the water, the familiar remembered outlines of her mother's face shining out from the moon's in the large pool of yellow light on the inky water. Harriet fancied her mother was calling out to her, beckoning her, summoning her home. She leaned forward, her arms outstretched towards the light and lost her balance and toppled into the harbour. The cool, calm waters wrapped around her like a soothing balm and her limbs felt weightless. She gave herself up to the water like a bride to her lover. It was so easy. So very easy. She felt euphoric: everything was all right now. She moved down through the depths into the darkness, looking up above her towards the light of the moon as it played across the surface. She felt a perfect calm, a deep sense of tranquillity, as though she were sinking into a long and restful sleep. She opened her mouth and called to her mother and felt her arms around her as her troubles dissolved into the dark water and she moved into the light.

CHAPTER TWENTY-SEVEN

SYDNEY HARBOUR

December 1938

The wool brokerage was packed. Michael moved through the crowd, checking the prices and noting the quality of the different fleeces. He was happy with the business he'd done today. The prices he'd achieved were better than last season's and he was selling his wool at the top end of the scale.

It had not been easy. He'd worked hard since leaving the Blue Mountains. During the years in New Zealand he'd scrimped and saved every penny until he was able to come back to Australia and buy a sheep station and slowly expand his stock. He had done well in New Zealand but the climate there was too like England and he found himself longing to be back in Australia with its sunshine and huge empty landscapes.

For the first two years he sent money home to his parents. When his mother died he paid for his father's passage. The old man enjoyed helping him work the station, but since the move to Australia, his age had become more evident and he was mostly content to sit on the porch, smoking his pipe, watching the sun rise and set each day and calling out advice or encouragement to the stockmen, whether they wanted it or not. The loss of his wife had hit him hard and some of the spirit had gone from him. Two months back, Michael found him asleep in his chair on the porch and realised he would never wake up again.

He missed the old man. Life on the station could get lonely, but all things considered, he was satisfied with his lot. He made a decent living, despite these hard times and loved working in the open. The dankness and darkness of the mine was a distant memory, along with the filth of the coal that was never completely washed away at the end of the shift and the grumbling and unrest from the men, who were not paid as much as they deserved for the risks they took each day. Instead, he revelled in the immensity of the outback: its big skies and red soil and the land that stretched as far as the eye could see and further. He enjoyed the company of the stockmen, with their easy camaraderie and competitive spirit, each striving to outdo the other, blow for blow, as they sheared.

His isolation was not unusual. He didn't stand out: the shearers came and went from season to season, working their way from station to station. The nearest town was miles away and not much of a one at that, just a bar for a beer and a shop for essentials and collecting any mail.

Reluctant to leave his father alone, he had not made this trip into the city for a long time, leaving it to his head stockman to come to the brokerage and do the deals. The much-improved prices he'd achieved this time, indicated that perhaps Joe was not the best of negotiators. He walked between the men in the crowded building, exchanging the odd g'day with other graziers, then decided to call it a day and head for the nearest bar and a welcome cold beer. He left the big, red-brick, wool brokerage and walked along Darling Harbour.

After a quick beer in the Pyrmont Bridge Hotel, he was

about to return to his lodgings, nearby. Instead he stepped onto the bridge and walked across into the city. The late afternoon sun was still blazing but there was a gentle breeze over the Harbour. He put his hands in his pockets as he walked and felt the outline of the ring where it was tied up inside his handkerchief. No matter how much time passed, he knew he would never stop thinking of her. He'd almost married again in New Zealand, a few years after his divorce came through, but somehow the relationship just petered out. He couldn't summon up enough enthusiasm. Catherine was a good woman, but she was not Elizabeth and having made such a mistake with Harriet, he was reluctant to try again. He'd thought of returning to McDonald Falls and a few years back he had written to William to tell him he was back in Australia. The letter was returned marked "Gone Away".

As he strode along, he felt himself drawn towards the Domain and the Botanic Gardens. The idea of sitting under the trees, watching the sleeping bats, seemed irresistible. You sentimental old fool he told himself, but found his pace picking up as he headed past Circular Quay and onto the grassy sward beside the Harbour. He felt again the pain of those moments before his ship sailed away when they told him she was dead. A hole had been ripped in his heart that had never healed and he knew never would.

He looked up at the trees, searching in vain for the enormous bats. He asked a man sweeping the pathways where they'd gone.

'The flying foxes? The camp went years ago.'

'What happened?'

'Culled, mate. Bloody menaces. They're still around, though. Feed here occasionally but they don't roost any more, thank goodness.'

'Everything changes I s'pose.'

'You're right about that, mate. Looks like there's a war

coming and all. Thought we'd seen the end of all that with the last one. Just hope we can stay out of it this time around.'

Fearing the man was set for a lengthy discourse on world politics, Michael nodded and walked away quickly. The seat in the rock was there waiting for him and he sat down and rolled a cigarette and looked out at the boats criss-crossing the harbour. Maybe he was ready now. Ready to make the trip back to the Falls. Ready to stand in front of her grave. Ready to say goodbye properly and get on with the rest of his life. He could drive up there tomorrow en route back to the station. It would add a few hours to the journey but he was in no hurry to get home.

He glanced back along the pathway and saw a boy walking towards him. The lad was barely in his teens and for a moment Michael thought he was seeing a ghost. It could have been Danny. He had the same lolloping swagger and his hair was the same dappled brown flopping over his brow, from where he swept it back impatiently, exactly the way his brother used to do. The boy gave him a friendly smile that lit up his face.

'G'day!'

Even the tone of his voice was like Danny's, though the accent was Australian. Michael couldn't speak for a moment, then he returned the boy's greeting.

'Mind if I sit here? It's my favourite spot.' The lad slumped into the seat beside Michael.

'It's my favourite too,' said Michael.

'I come every day. Sometimes on my own and sometimes with my Ma. She likes it here too. I've not seen you here before?' The boy looked up at him.

'I've not been back here in years.'

'Why not, if it's your favourite place?'

'I don't live in Sydney. Been living in New Zealand and now up north. But I had to come into the city today, so I thought I'd see if this spot's the same as I remembered it.'

'Is it?'

'Yes, except there used to be loads of big bats hanging from the trees. They killed them all off.'

'Bats give me the creeps but I like them more than snakes. I like cats. But I really wish I had a dog. Ma says I can't because we live in the city.'

Michael was convinced he was looking at his brother's ghost. The absent-minded air about him, as though he were miles away in his own little world, and the restless way he swung his legs back and forth in front of him' letting his heels crash back into the rock. It was years since Danny had died. He would have been thirty-two. Probably would have been married with a big brood of bairns. While not a day had passed in all those years when Michael hadn't thought of his brother, the pain had lessened with each passing season in a way that the loss of Elizabeth had not. He'd heard of reincarnation - something the Hindus believed in, apparently. He'd never met an Indian and he'd never given the concept much thought, but now he would have staked his life that this was his brother born again.

'Is smoking nice?'

'No, it's a filthy habit. Don't ever try it.'

'Well, I might try it just once. Just so I know what it's like. But not till I'm older or Ma would kill me. Didn't you like it in New Zealand then?'

Michael was slightly nonplussed by the boy's unconnected thought patterns. Again, it was just like Danny. As he studied him closer he realised his eyes were brown while Danny's had been green. And he was not as tall as Danny had been and not so skinny.

'It were all right. I like it better here though.'

'Do you want some apple?' The boy took a few bites and passed the apple to Michael. 'Go on. Have the rest. I can't eat it all.'

Michael bit into the apple. It was firm and slightly tart, just as he liked them.

The boy spoke again. 'I don't really like apples but Ma says they're good for you.'

'Sounds like yer Mam talks a lot of sense.'

The boy pulled a face. 'You talk funny.'

'That's cause I'm from England. In all these years I've never managed to lose the accent.'

'My Ma's from England but she doesn't talk like you.'

'Aye well there's all sorts in England.'

'Better go now. It's nearly time for my tea. G'day mister. See you again some time.' He jumped up and without a backward glance, set off back along the pathway.

Michael waited a few moments then fell into step behind him, not knowing why, but feeling compelled to follow. The boy walked with a lolloping gait that was almost skipping. He had taken something from his pocket and was throwing it in the air and catching it as he went along. Michael suddenly knew what it was and felt a pounding in his chest as the realisation of whom he was following finally dawned on him. But it wasn't possible. He must be a ghost. Unless...

The lad headed towards the Rocks to a large house with a well-polished door knocker and freshly painted woodwork so that it stood out in the rather shabby street. A cat was curled up on the doorstep. The boy stopped to stroke the cat quickly, before going inside. He saw the sign then. The Morton School of Music.

Michael sat on a wall opposite, took out his tobacco and rolled another cigarette. He didn't smoke often, but he needed another one badly now. His hand was shaking so much that he could hardly light the cigarette. As he sat there in the fading light, trying to get a grip on his emotions and wondering what to do next, the door opened and she stood on the threshold. She was still beautiful, her hair escaping from the chignon she continued to wear, despite the changes in hair fashions over the years. She was still slender. Her face was slightly tanned and there were now small but characterful lines around her eyes and her mouth.

'You'd better come inside, Michael Winterbourne. I've been waiting to hear from you for a long time. You have some explaining to do. And there's someone you need to meet.' Her voice was unchanged. Michael gave a guttural cry.

He ran towards her and gathered her into his arms, lifting her off the ground. 'They said you were dead. They said you were killed in a car crash. But you're not. Oh my darling, you're alive. You're here.'

'Very much so. What on earth made you think I were dead? Is that why you never wrote to me? I thought *you* had died when I didn't hear from you.'

'It were a message sent to the ship. From Verity Radley.'

'Verity? That's not possible.'

Then they both said the name at once, 'Harriet!'

He crushed her against his chest and held her tightly, overwhelmed by his emotions, almost suffocating, drinking in the smell of her, holding onto her as though if he let go she would drift away like smoke. His heart hammered in his chest and he could hear the blood pounding in his ears. 'I'll never let you out of me sight again, Elizabeth.'

'I couldn't believe it when I saw you through the window just now, Michael. I still can't believe it's really you. How did you find out where I lived?'

'I didn't.' The boy emerged from the house and stood on the doorway and Michael nodded in his direction. 'I met the lad. And then I knew.' He bent down and kissed her again on the top of her head.

'Ma? What's going on? You all right?'

'Harry, come here - I want you to meet your father.'

The road to New Hunter's Down was a long one. They drove squashed together in the cab of Michael's truck, with the back piled high with luggage on top of the empty woolsacks and bits of machinery he had picked up in the city. Elizabeth and Harry took turns to sit in the middle, and Michael rejoiced in the feeling of each of their bodies close to his in the small cramped cabin.

What a difference a few days could make. Until now, he reflected, change had usually seemed to be for the worse. A single moment dividing the innocent happiness of his youth on that other Hunter's Down, from years of loss, grief, pain and guilt. Just a few short days ago he had driven in the opposite direction, the seat beside him empty, the back piled high with wool, his heart lonely and his expectations low.

He looked past the boy with the floppy hair and the big smile, to the woman who was at last going to be his wife. She smiled back at him and stretched her hand out across the back of the seat to touch his hair as if reassuring herself that he was really there.

THE END

ACKNOWLEDGMENTS

Jo Ryan, always there at the end of a phone or email to pick me up when I was down. Lis Long who did a great job proofing the first edition. Annabel Sutton for wise counsel, encouragement and much advice about publishing. Jenn Brown who waded through the first truly dreadful draft back in 2007 and made me laugh when I was miserable. Chris Girling, who fed and watered me while I worked on my editing in Sydney, lent me his sat-nav for my fact-checking mission to the Blue Mountains and gave very helpful feedback when I finally let him read it. Peter Laing for insights into life on board the great steam liners and background on SS Ceramic. The SS Historic is based on the Ceramic but the latter didn't actually come into use as a passenger ship, after its use as a troop ship, until six months after my characters sailed. Joel Donovan QC for invaluable advice about matters legal – any errors in legal procedure are wilfully mine not his. Tom Flynn for cracking a thorny plotting issue. My early readers, Michele Elliot, Beric Davis, Michelle Van Vlijmen, Robert Lundy, Dee McLean, Mary Grundy, Eileen Riddiford, Anne-Marie Flynn and John Brook - thanks for all your encouragement and very helpful feedback. Anne Tattersall for her generosity of spirit and encouragement to keep writing (and her gorgeous flowers!). Tina Betts of Andrew Mann Literary Agency, for professional feedback and working hard to find me a publisher. Barbara and Barry Anderson for making my fact-checking trip to Sydney comfortable and affordable.

And finally thanks to the nasty burglar who stole my laptops and forced me to start again. I think it came out better second time round.

ABOUT THE AUTHOR

Clare Flynn is a graduate of Manchester University where she read English Language and Literature.

After a career in international marketing, working on brands from nappies to tinned tuna and living in Paris, Milan, Brussels and Sydney, she ran her own consulting business for 15 years and now lives in Eastbourne.

When not writing and reading, Clare loves to paint in water-colours and grabs any available opportunity to travel - sometimes under the guise of research.

Get in touch with Clare
    Website http://www.clareflynn.co.uk
    Twitter - https://twitter.com/clarefly
    Facebook - https://www.facebook.com/authorclareflynn

ALSO BY CLARE FLYNN

Kurinji Flowers

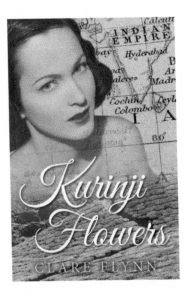

1936. Ginny Dunbar, an 18 year old reluctant debutante, has been exploited for years by a charismatic older man. The fallout from this abusive relationship jeopardises her prospects for marriage. When a nude painting of her is exhibited in a west end art gallery Ginny is forced to flee London and her royal presentation.

Exiled to Yorkshire, she gets a second chance with a new start in India. Alone to cope with the repercussions of her past, she battles her inner demons, the expectations of the people around her and her own prejudices about India and its people.

Set mainly in South India during the years of the second world war and the struggle for independence, Kurinji Flowers traces a young woman's journey through loss, hope and betrayal to love and self-discovery.

"A sweeping, lush story – the depiction of India in all its colours, smells and vibrancy is pitch-perfect in its depiction. You will be grabbed from the first chapter" *The Historical Novel Society*

"You would enjoy Kurinji Flowers if you are drawn – as I am – to stories of individual human relationships." *The Review Group*

ALSO BY CLARE FLYNN

Letters from a Patchwork Quilt

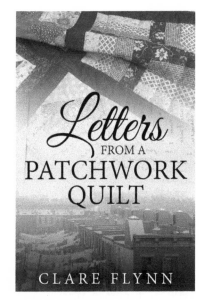

Jack Brennan runs away from home in Derby to avoid being forced into the priesthood like his older brothers, and heads to Bristol to follow his dream of becoming a teacher.

When Jack falls in love with Eliza Hewlett, and she agrees to marry him, his future looks rosy – until Mary Ellen MacBride, the slow-witted and petulant daughter of Jack's landlord, names Jack as the father of her unborn child.

Mr MacBride and the parish priest refuse to accept Jack's innocence and want to force him to marry the girl.

Just as Jack and Eliza think they have escaped they are torn apart. Jack is arrested and Eliza trapped on board ship en route for America. How will she survive, alone and penniless in a strange country? Will Jack marry Mary Ellen? Will the lovers ever see each other again?

"A story of love, loss and tragedy - a heart-breaking and moving tale". (Readers' Favorite).

ALSO BY CLARE FLYNN

The Green Ribbons

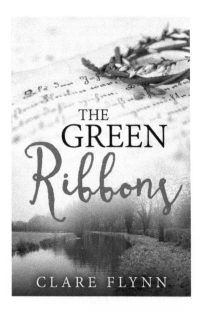

How far would she go to save her marriage? How far would he go to keep a promise?

1900. Eighteen-year old Hephzibah Wildman, homeless and destitute after the tragic death of her parents, becomes a governess at Ingleton Hall. Befriending Merritt Nightingale, the local parson and drawn to the handsome Thomas Egdon, she starts to rebuild her life. When she attracts the unwanted advances of her employer, the country squire Sir Richard Egdon, she makes the first of two desperate decisions that will change not only her own life but the lives of those around her.

Get a FREE short story

Get an exclusive short story from Clare Flynn, set in Victorian London during the Great Exhibition of 1851.

Not available elsewhere.

To get your FREE short story go to Clare's website, www.clareflynn.co.uk or use the QR code below. You will be the first to know about new book releases, special offers and freebies.